Coming Back

Also by Jessi Zabarsky
Witchlight

Coming Back

Jessi Zabarsky

RH
GRAPHIC

NEW YORK

Coming Back was drawn on smooth Bristol board, with a 3H pencil and Kuretake disposable brush pens.
It was lettered in Procreate and colored in Photoshop.

Text, cover art, and interior illustrations copyright © 2021 by Jessi Zabarsky

All rights reserved. Published in the United States by RH Graphic, an imprint of Random House Children's Books, a division of Penguin Random House LLC, New York.

RH Graphic with the book design is a trademark of Penguin Random House LLC.

Visit us on the web! RHKidsGraphic.com • @RHKidsGraphic

Educators and librarians, for a variety of teaching tools, visit us at RHTeachersLibrarians.com

Library of Congress Cataloging-in-Publication Data is available upon request.
ISBN 978-0-593-12543-4 (hardcover) — ISBN 978-0-593-12002-6 (paperback)
ISBN 978-0-593-12004-0 (ebook)

Designed by Patrick Crotty

MANUFACTURED IN CHINA
10 9 8 7 6 5 4 3 2 1
First Edition

A comic on every bookshelf.

To everyone who has had to find a
truer story to tell about themselves

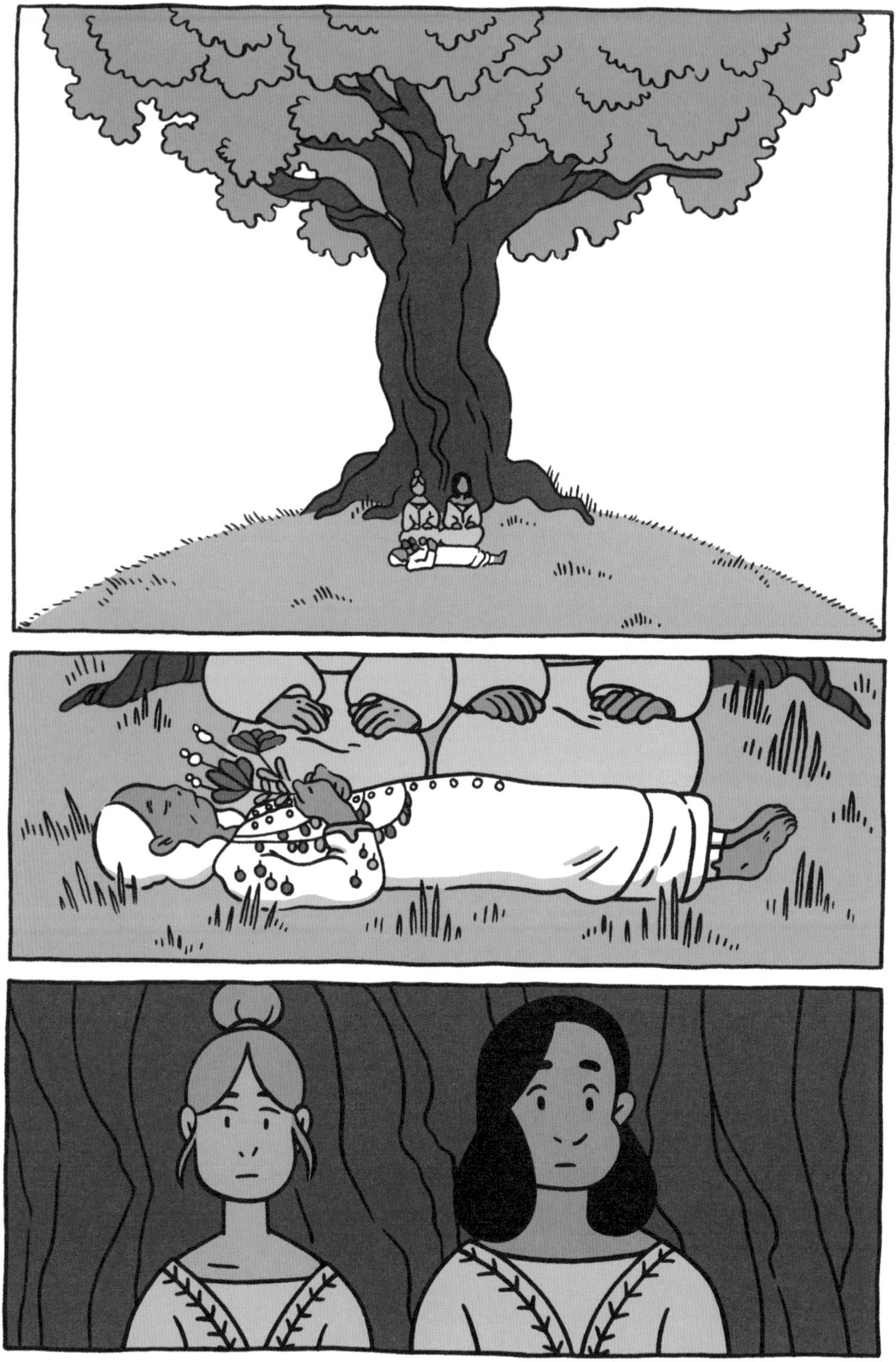

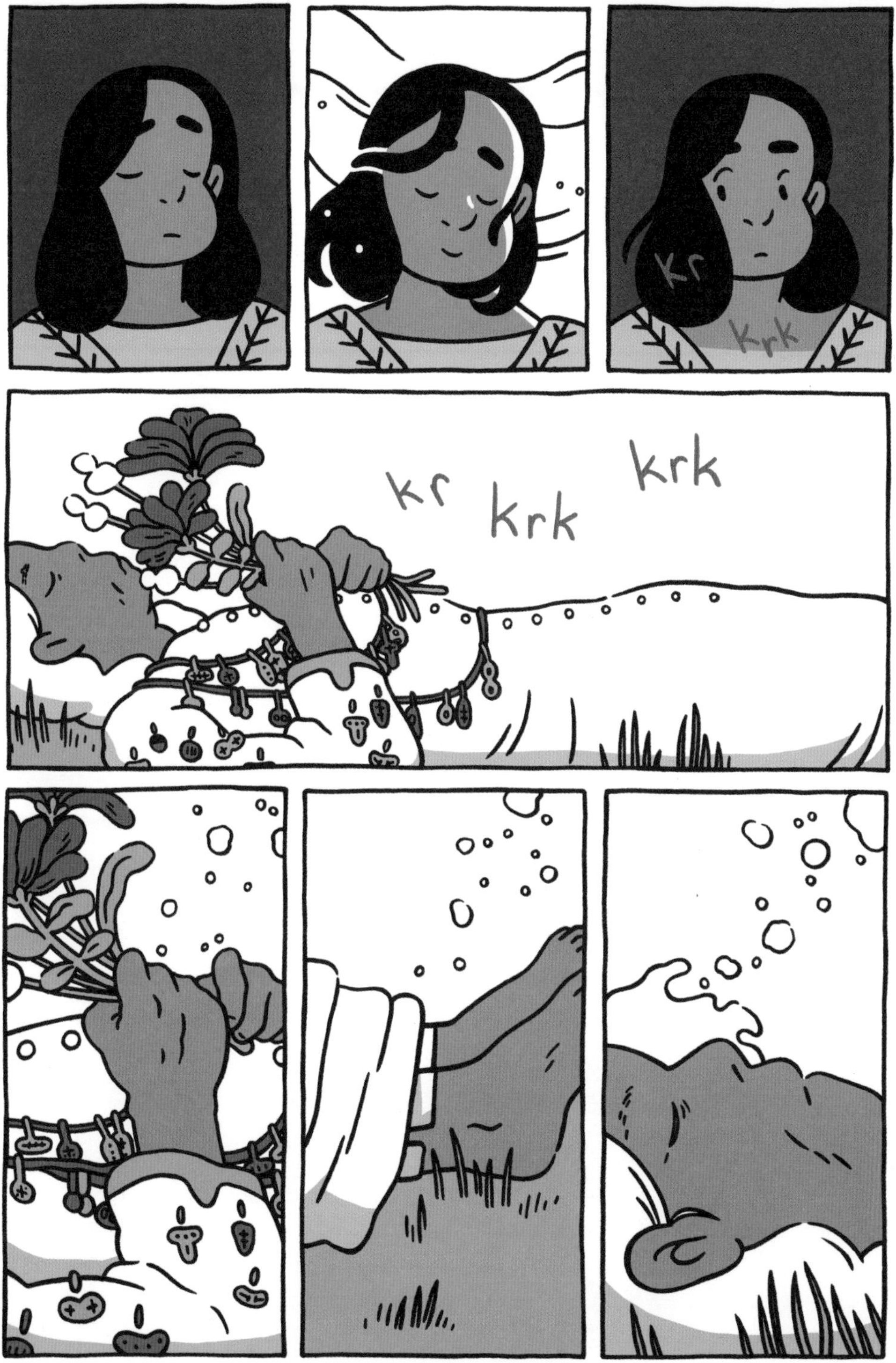
kr
krk
kr
krk
krk

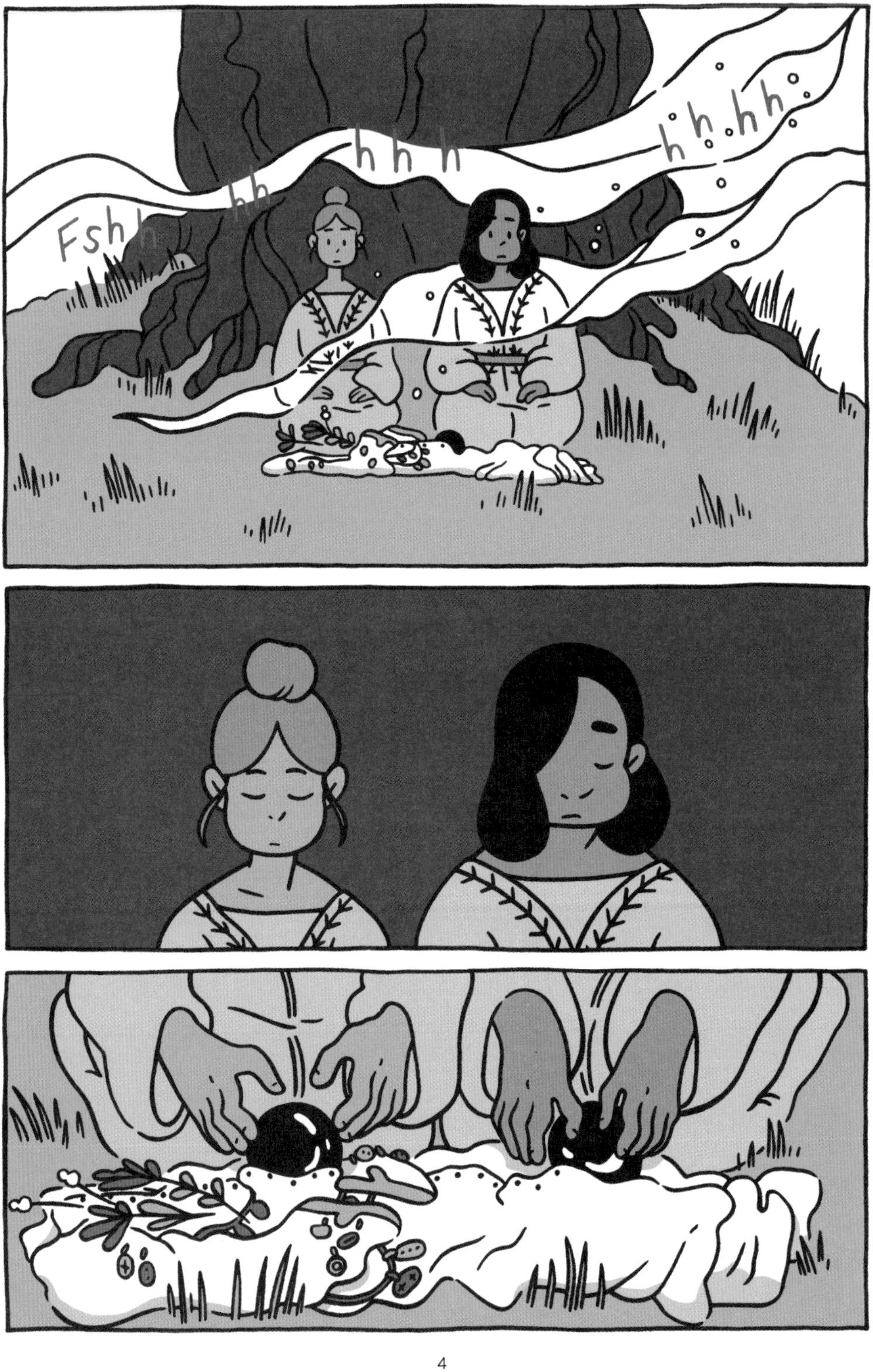
Fshhhhhhhhhhhh

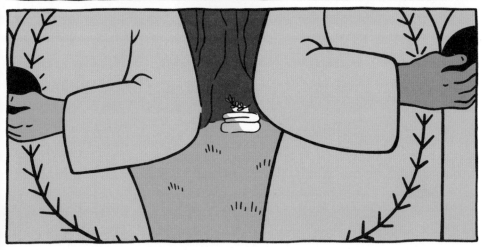

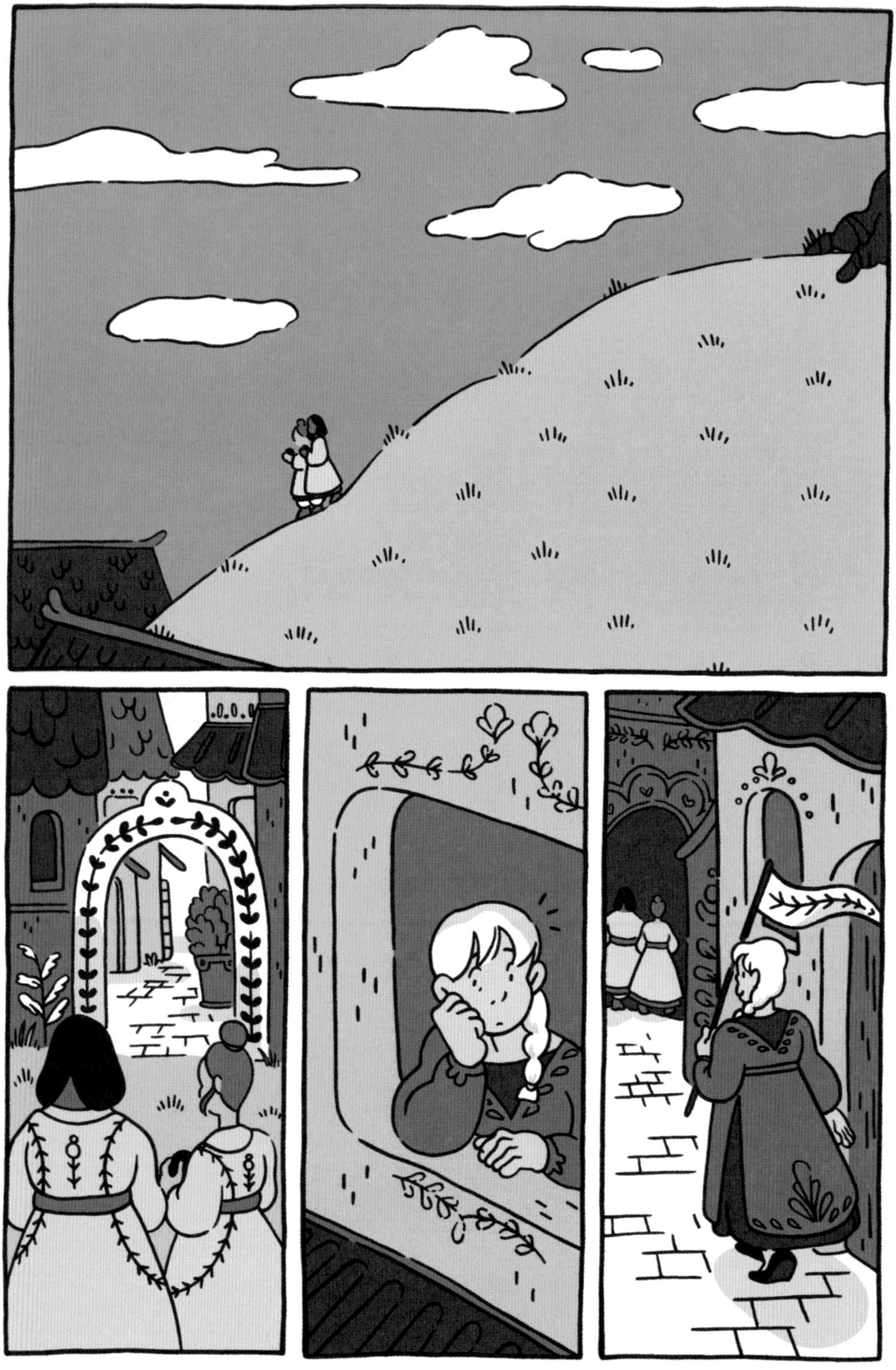

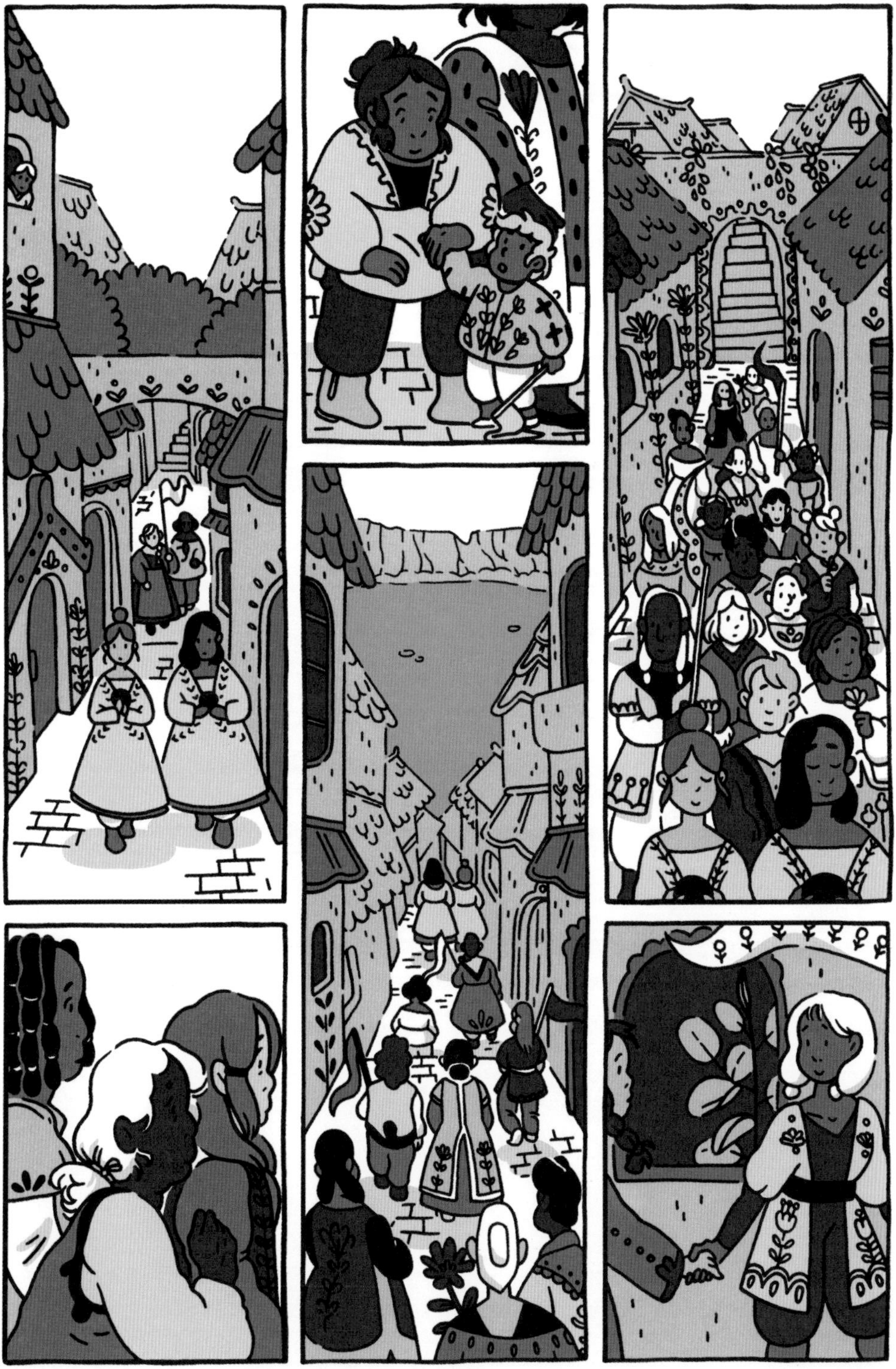

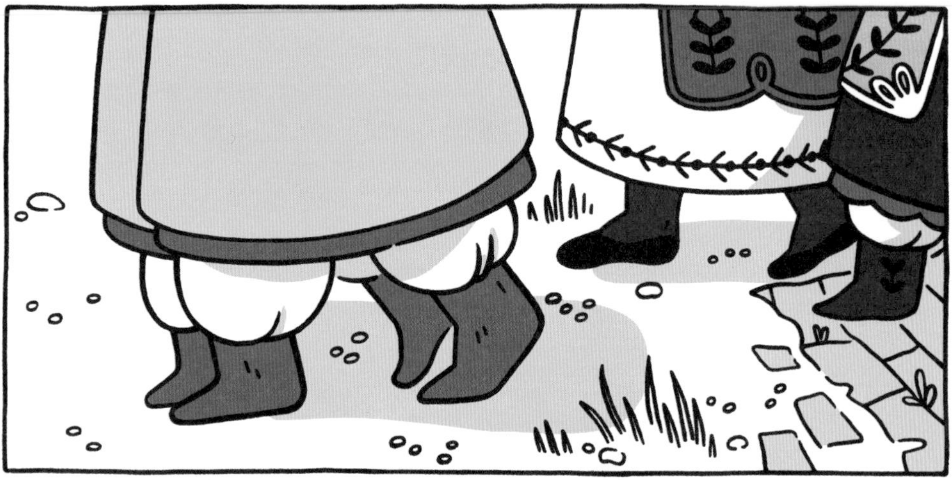
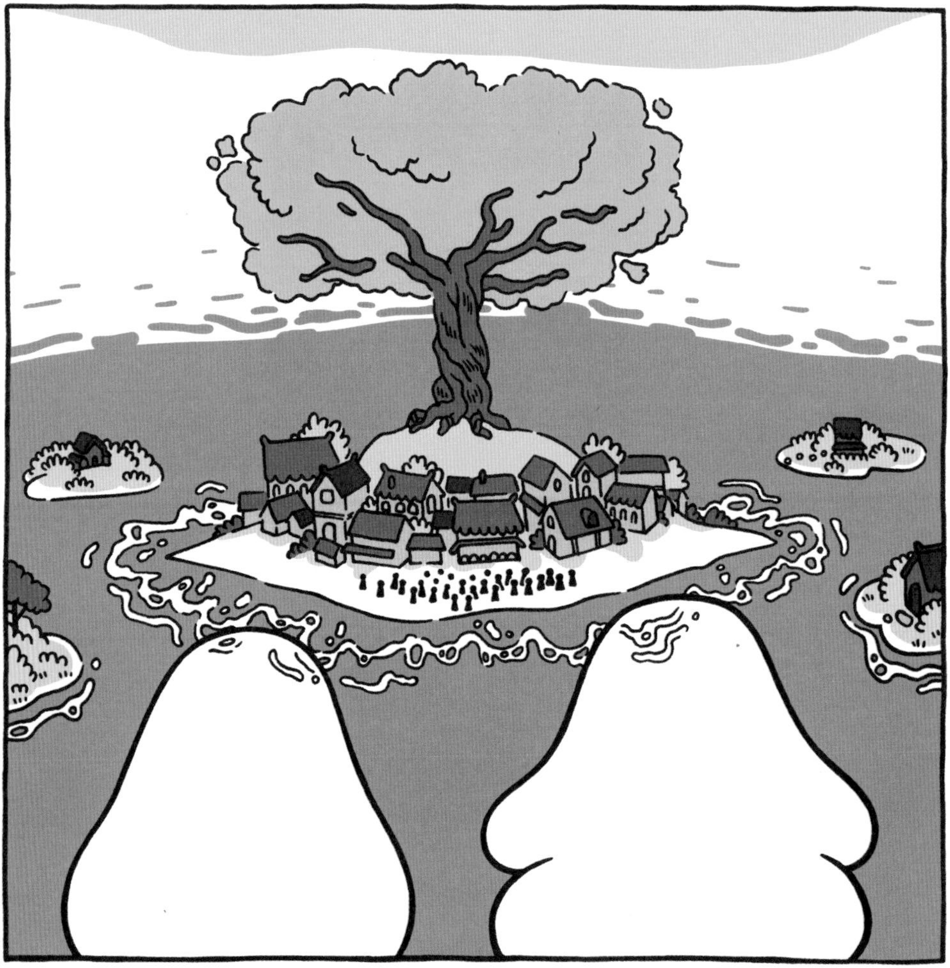

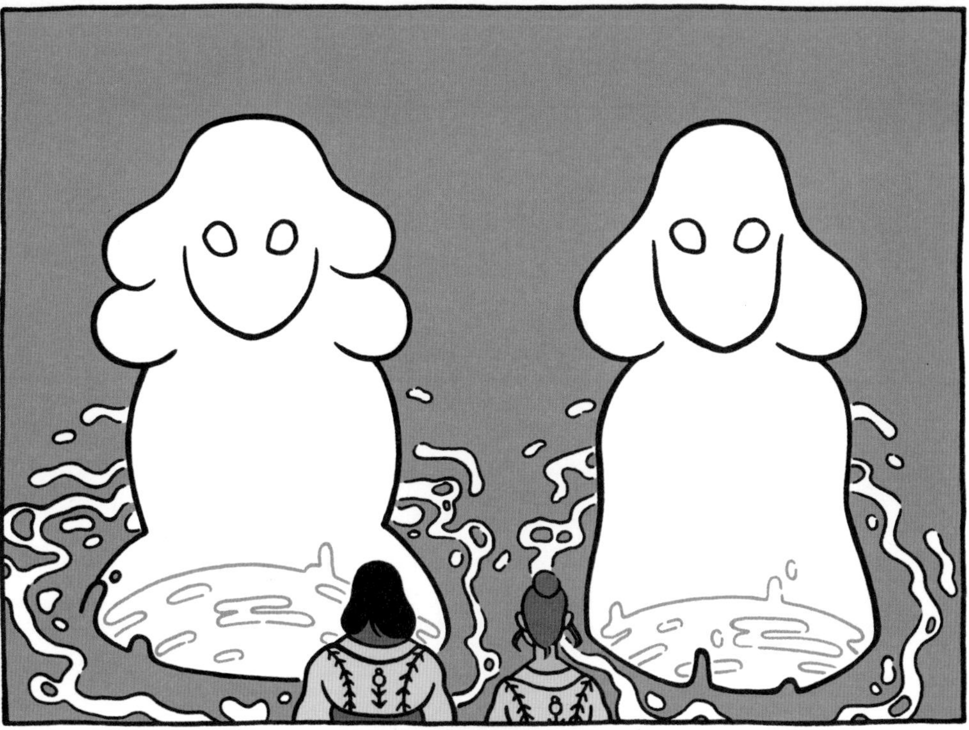
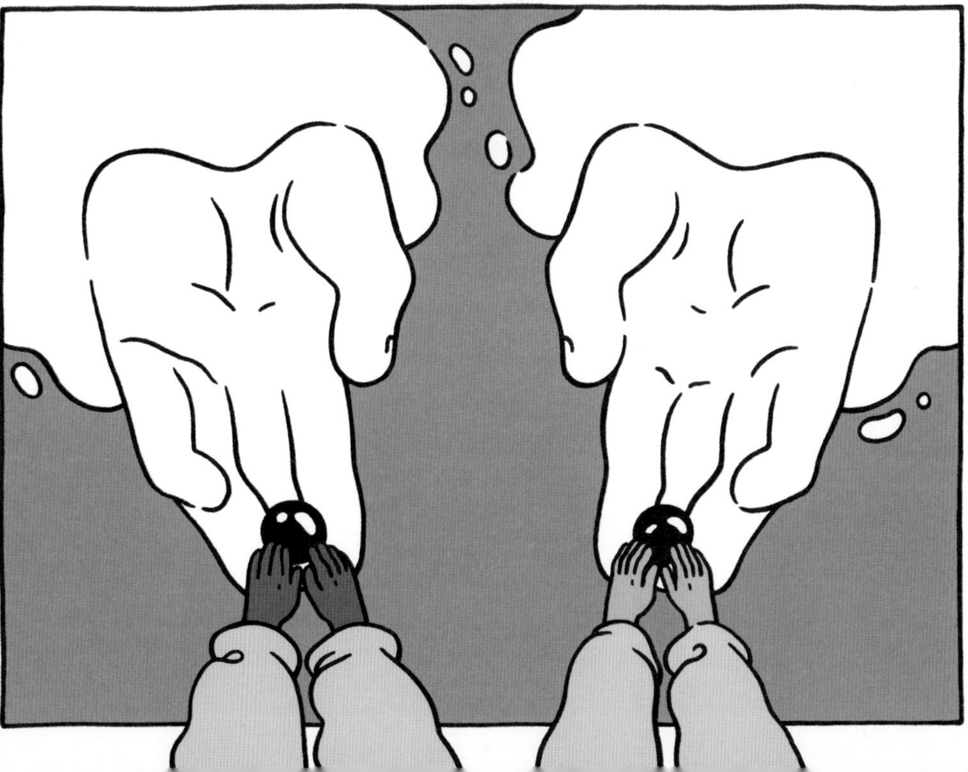

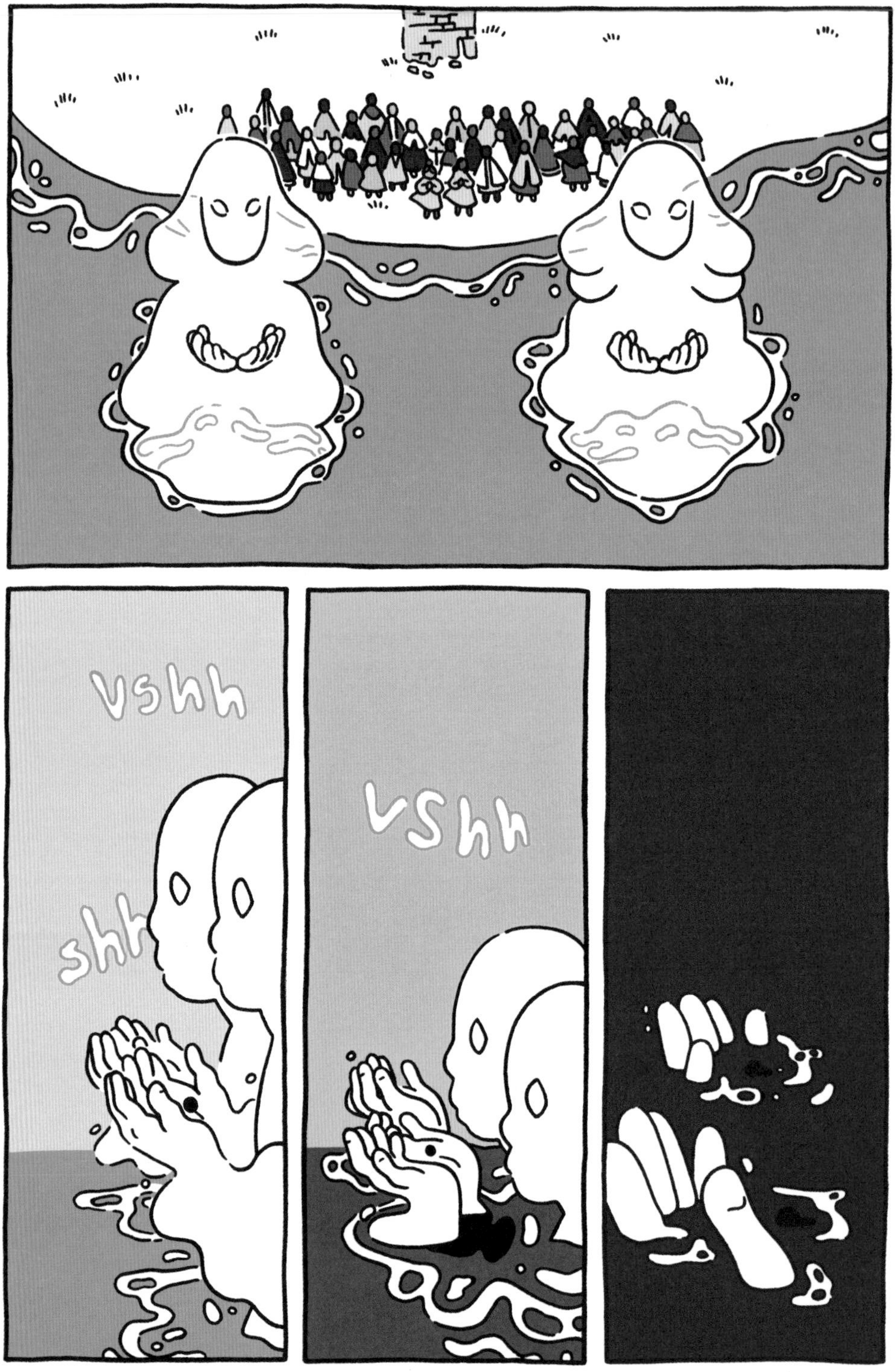
vshh
shh
vshh

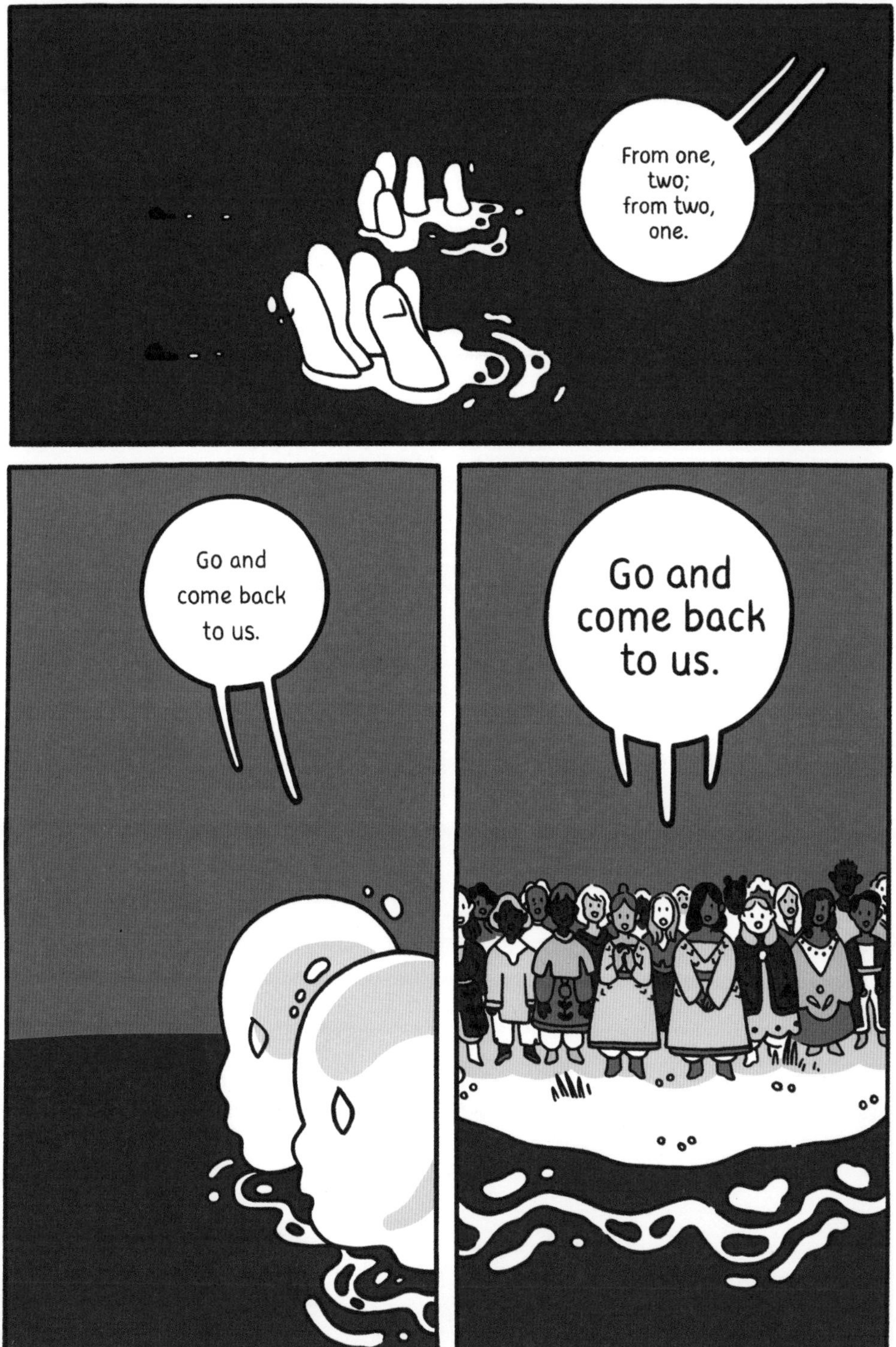
From one, two; from two, one.
Go and come back to us.
Go and come back to us.

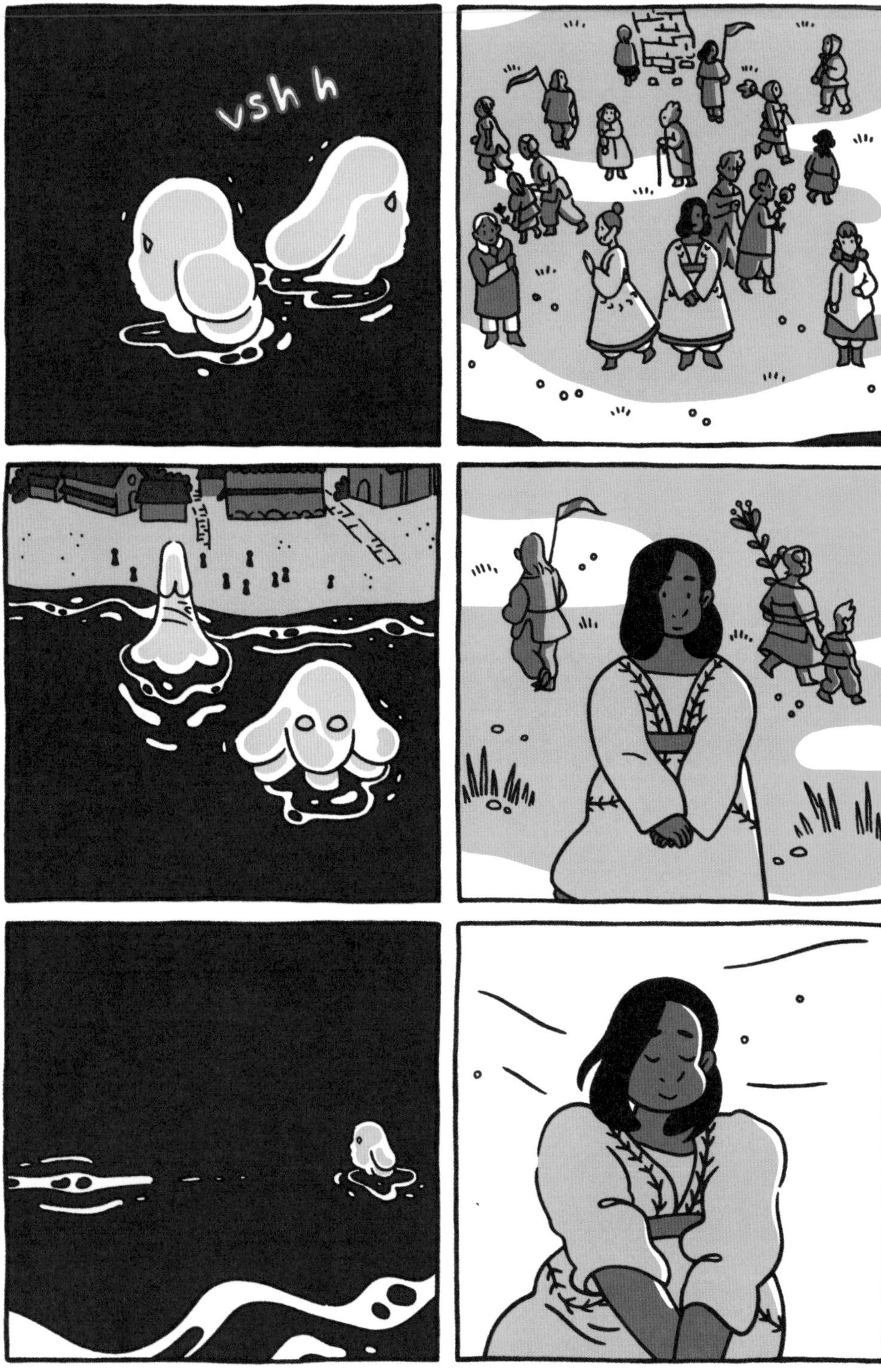
vsh h

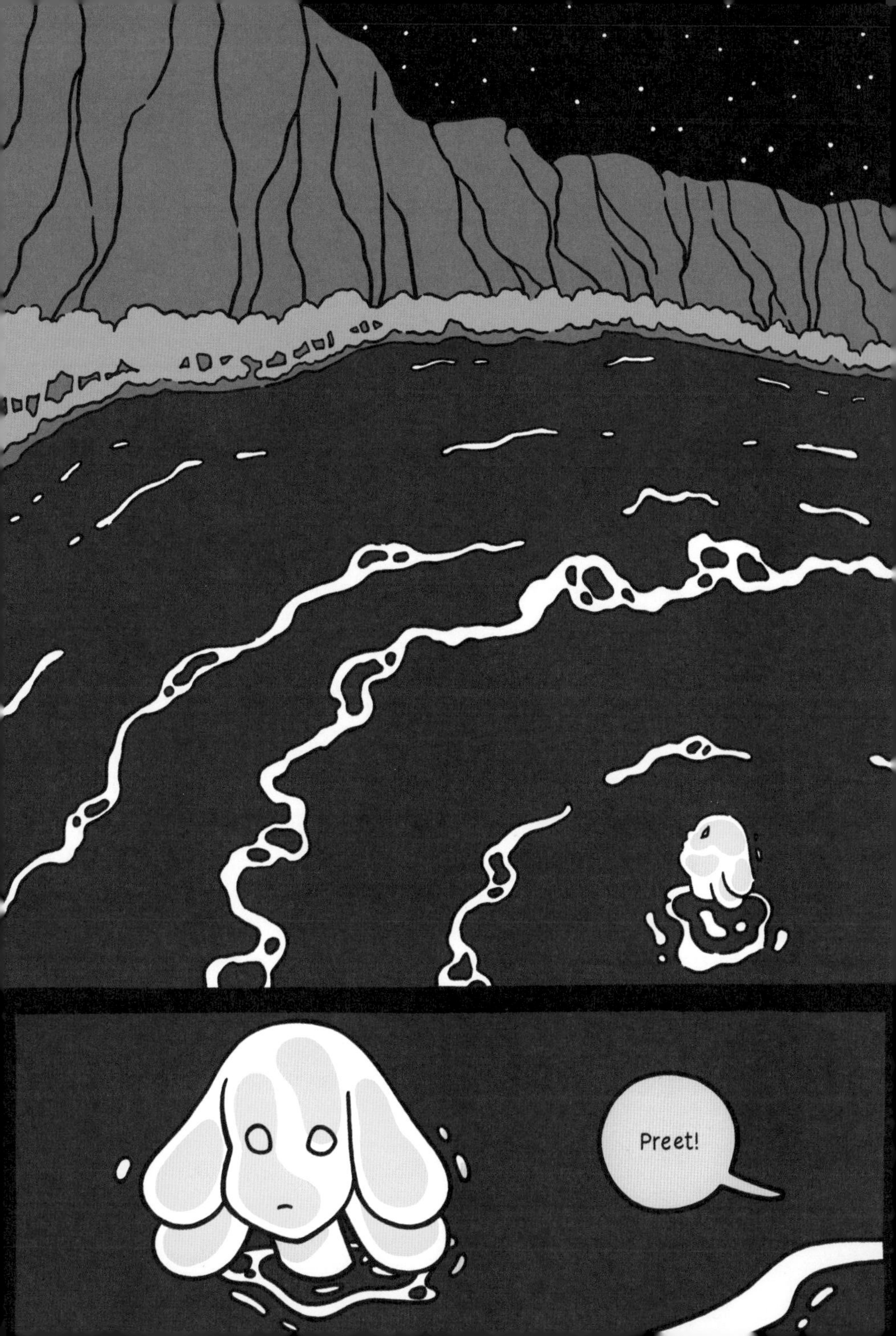
Preet!

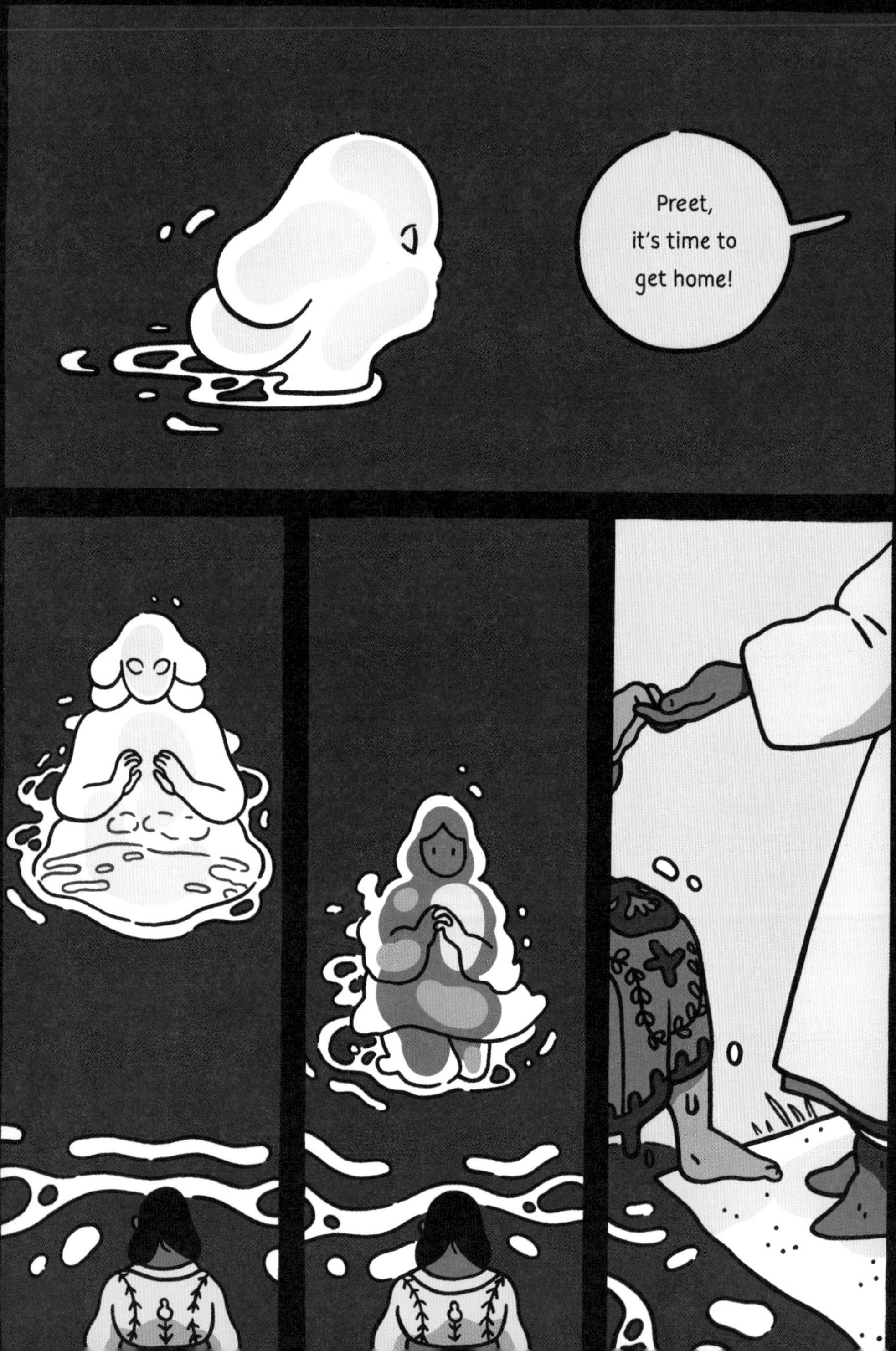
Preet, it's time to get home!

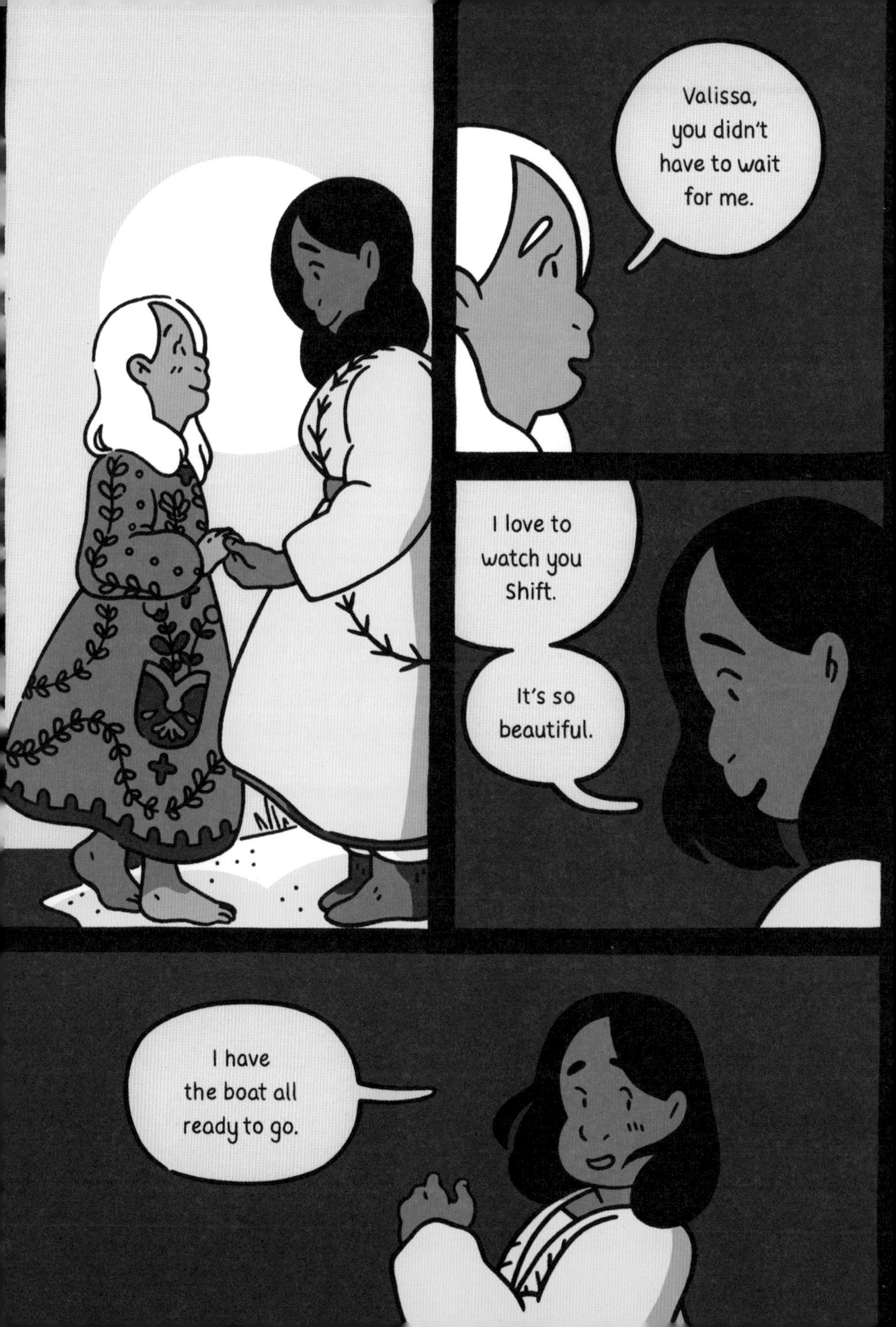
Valissa, you didn't have to wait for me.
I love to watch you Shift.
It's so beautiful.
I have the boat all ready to go.

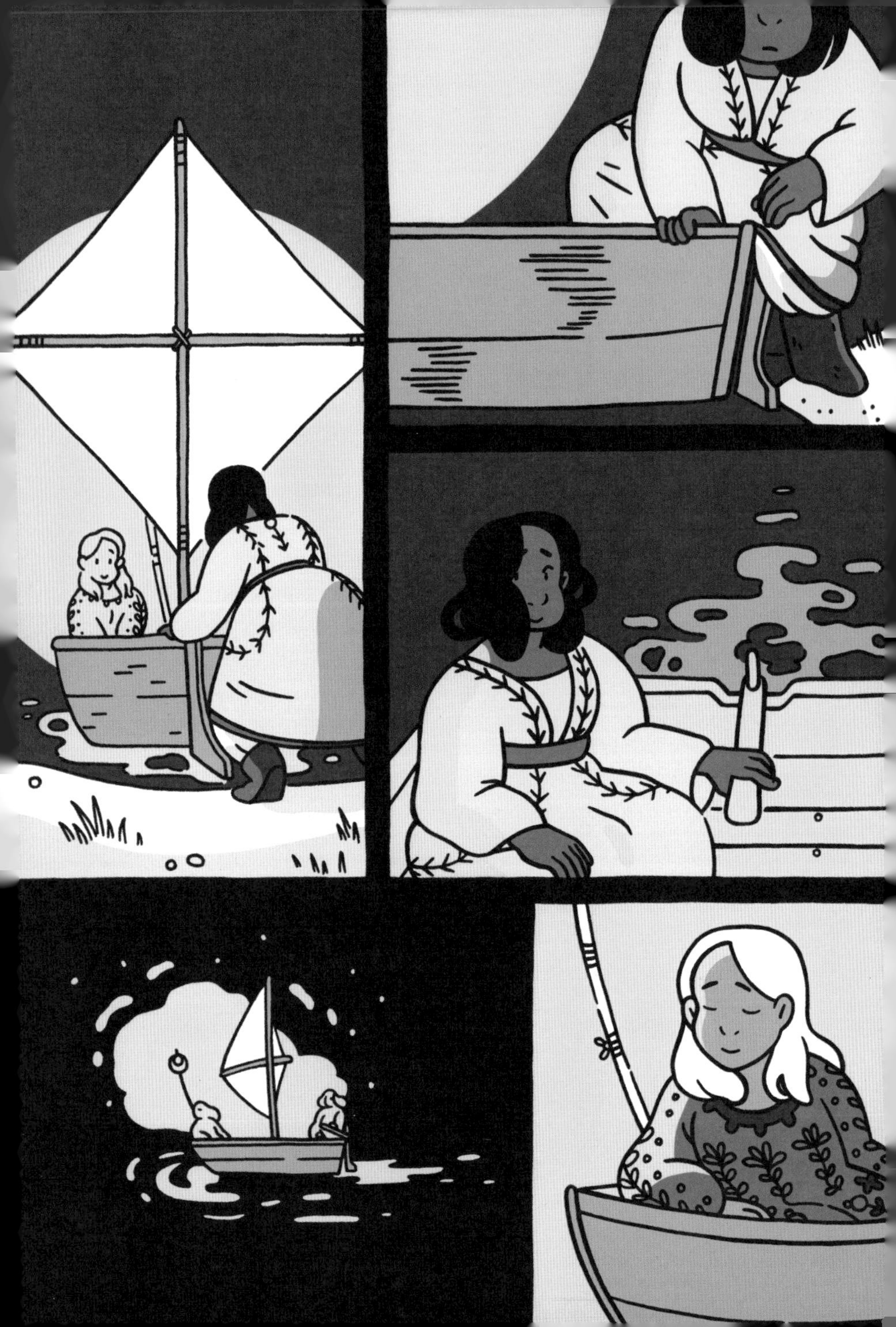

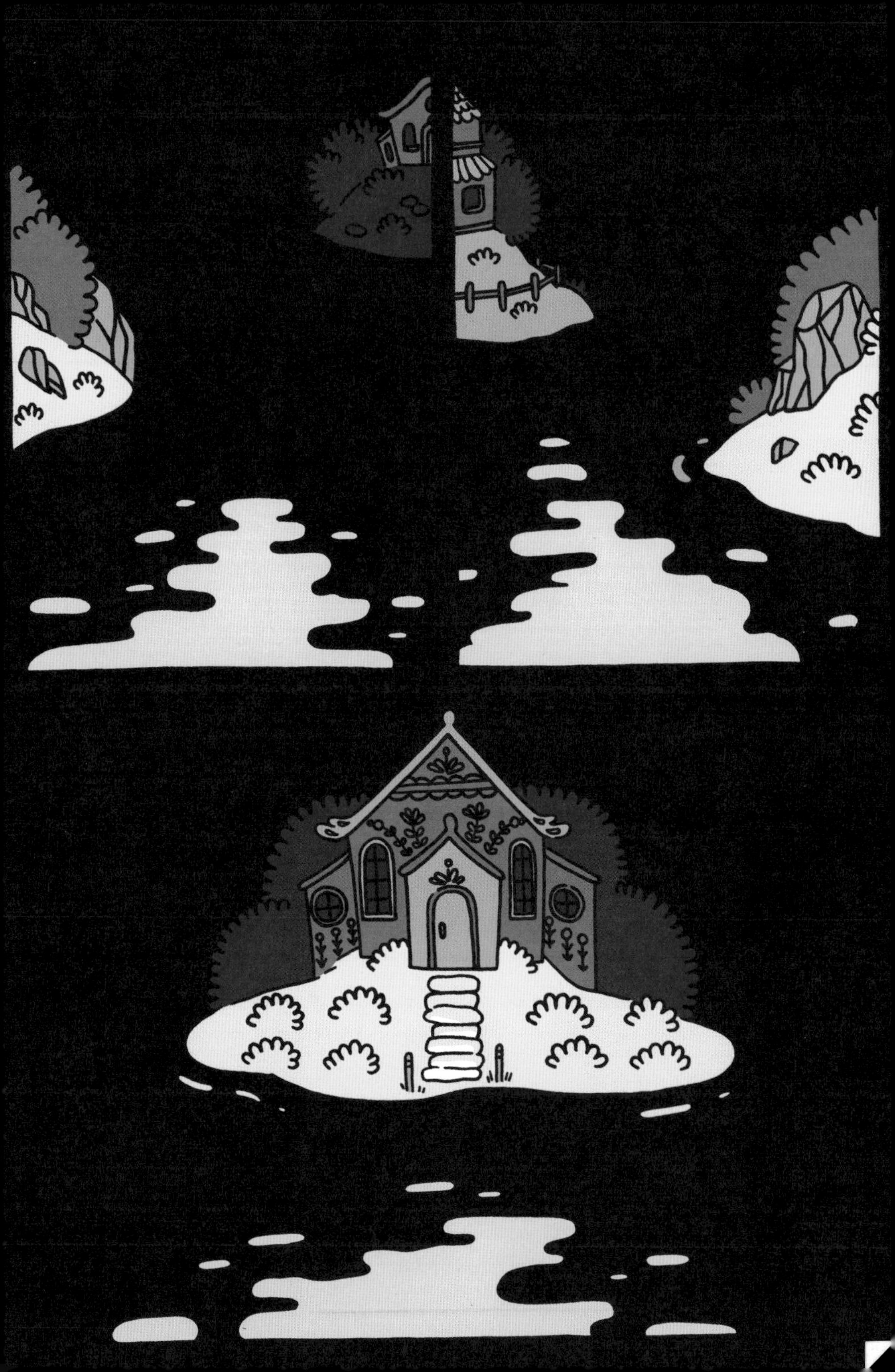

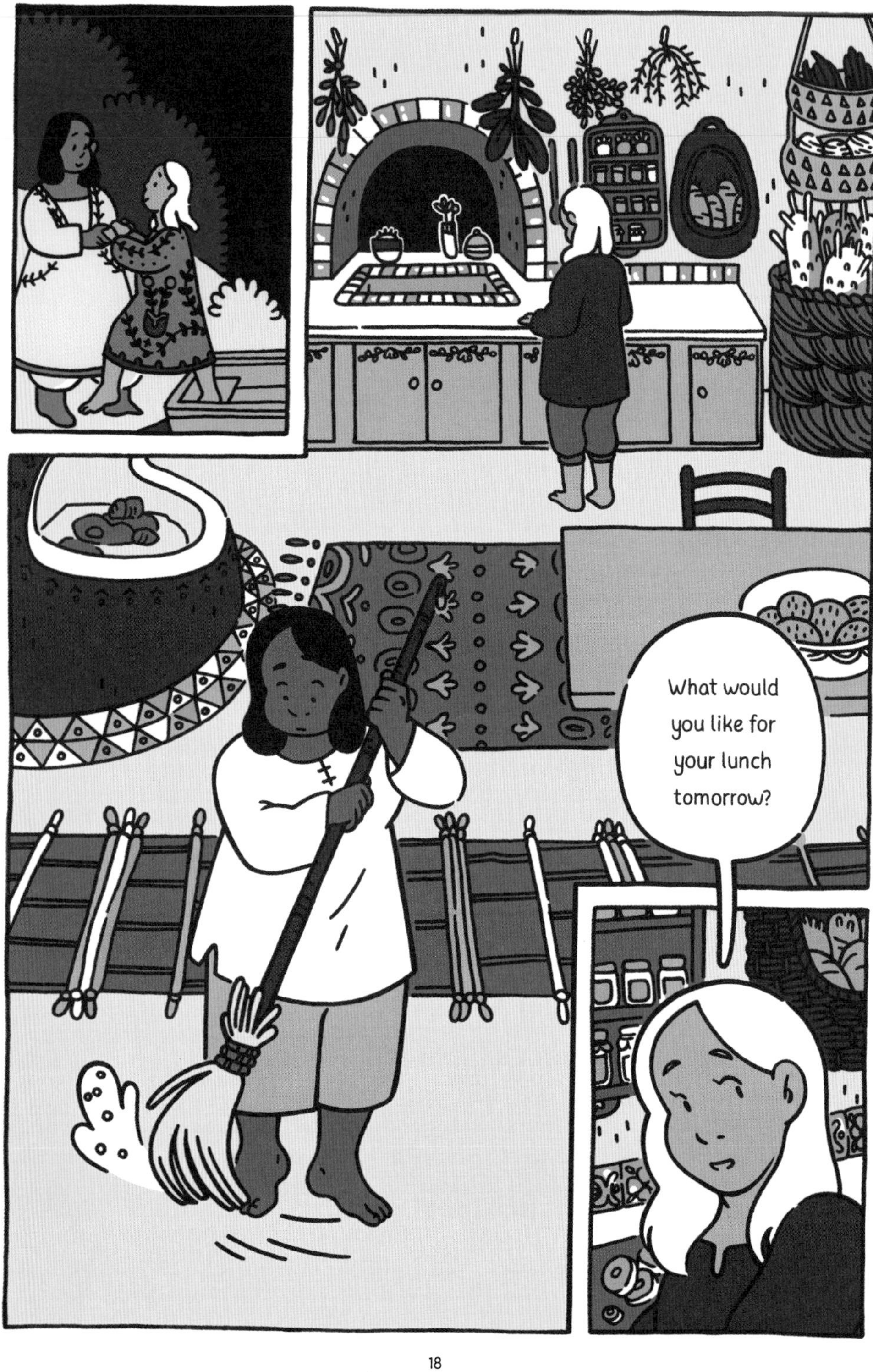
What would you like for your lunch tomorrow?

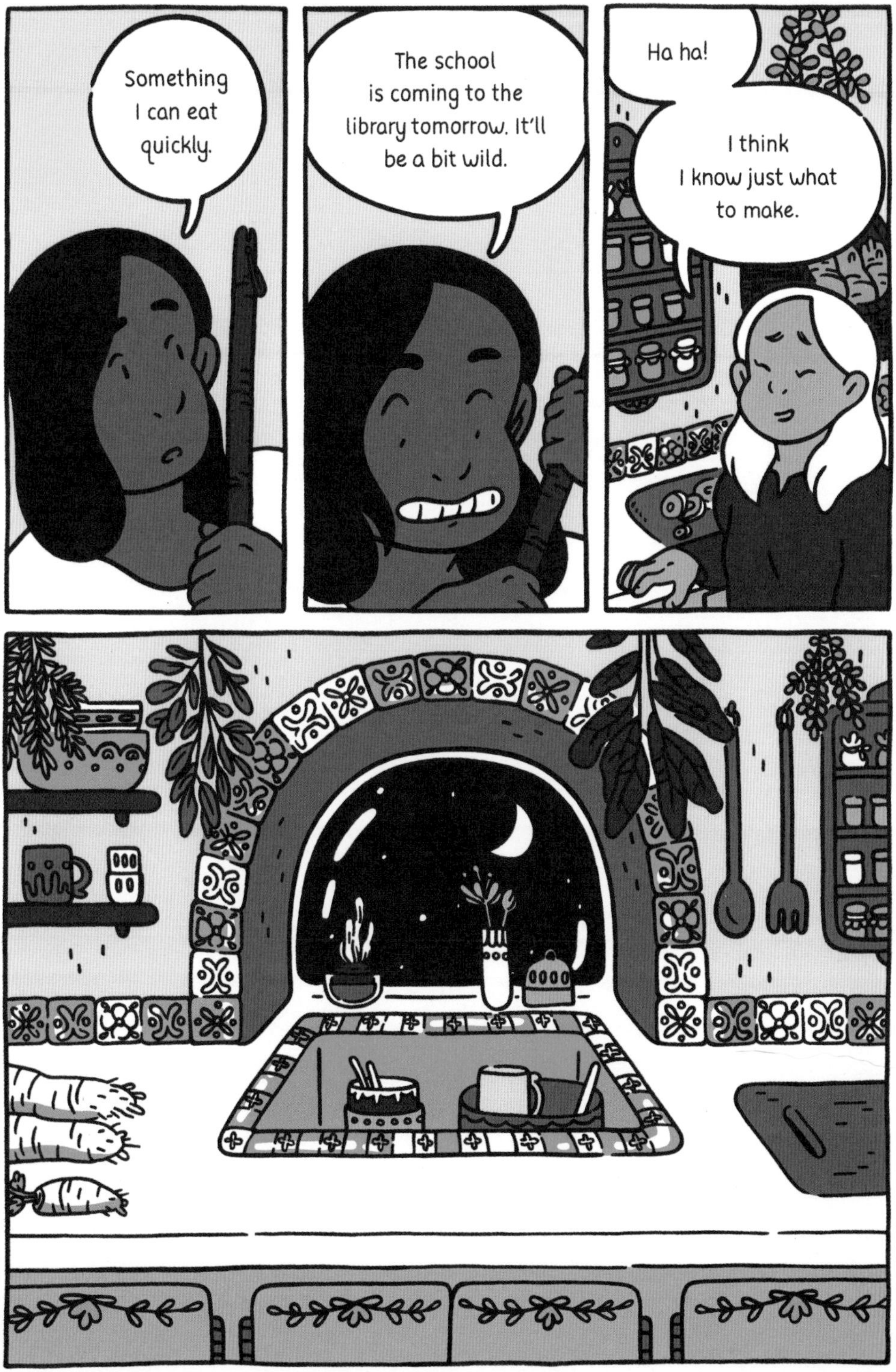
Something I can eat quickly.
The school is coming to the library tomorrow. It'll be a bit wild.
Ha ha!
I think I know just what to make.

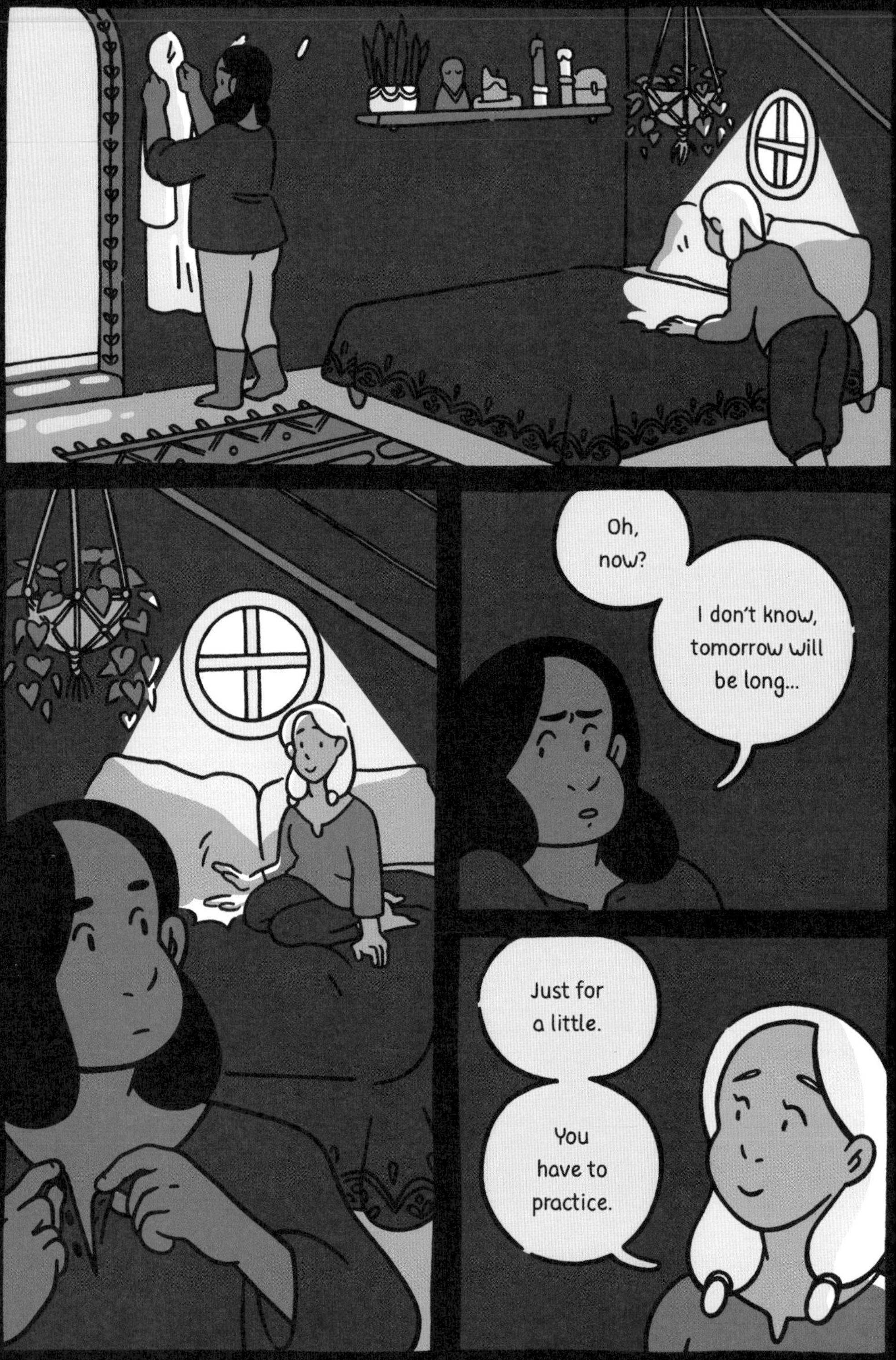
Oh, now?
I don't know, tomorrow will be long...
Just for a little.
You have to practice.

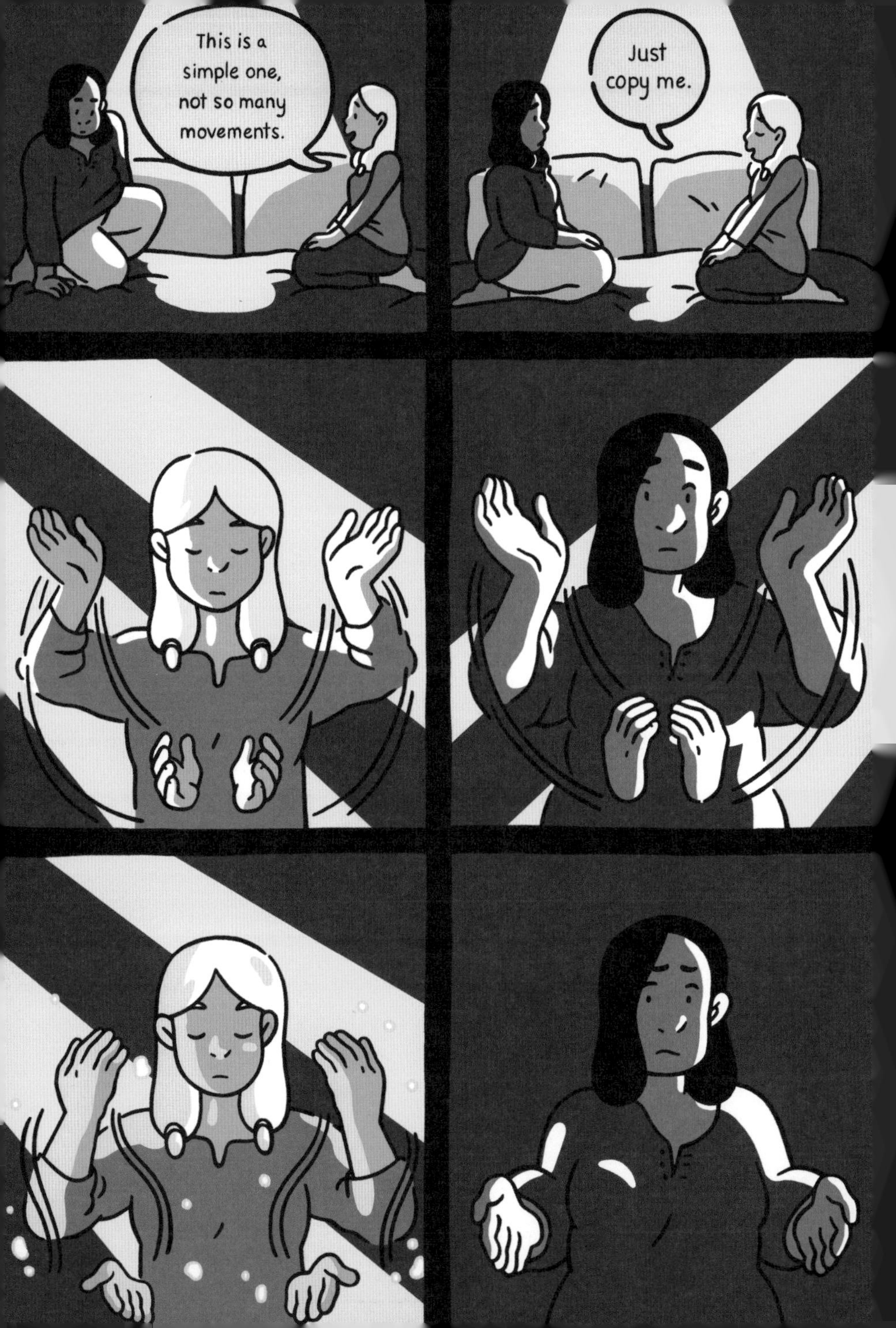
This is a simple one, not so many movements.
Just copy me.

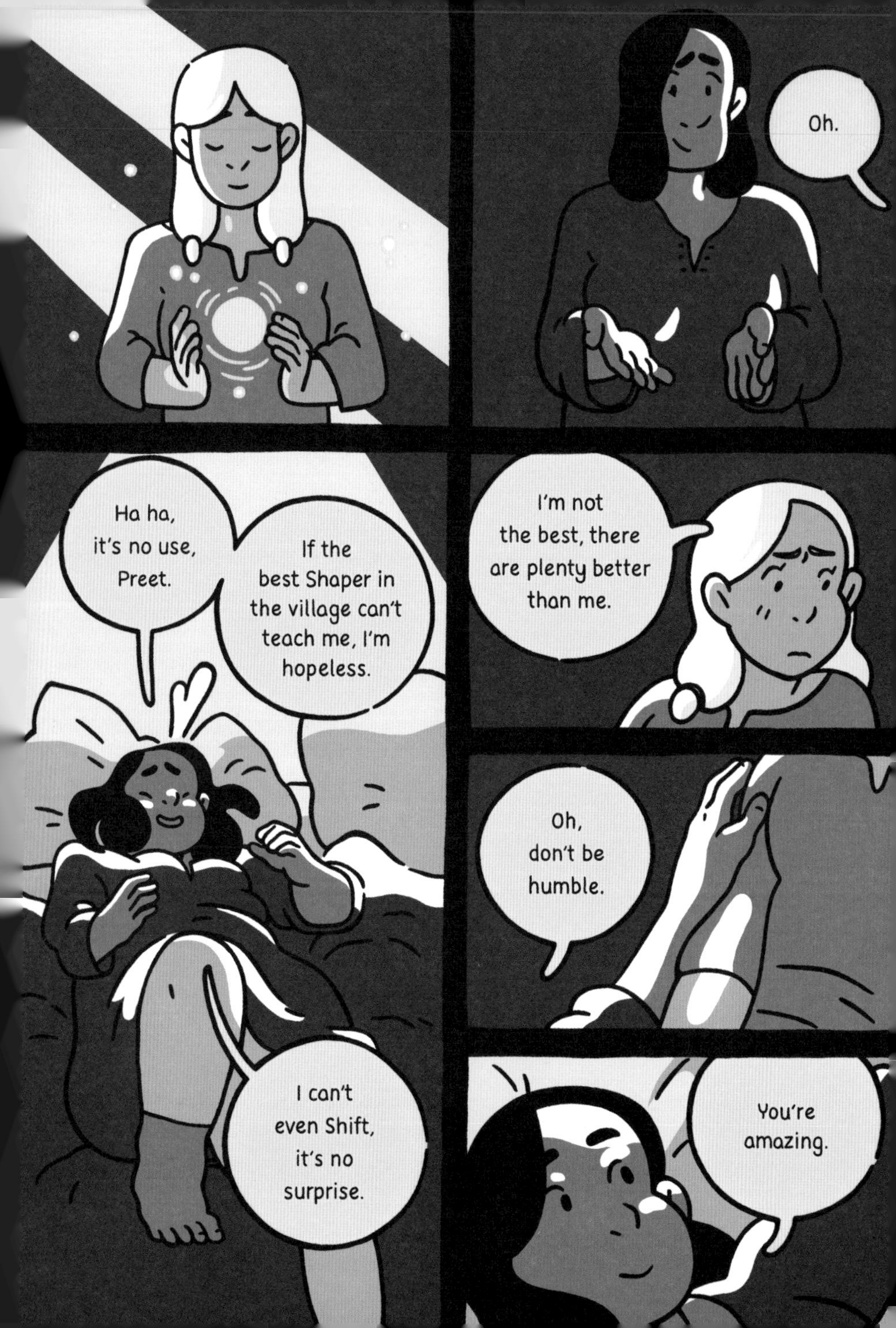
Oh.
Ha ha, it's no use, Preet.
If the best Shaper in the village can't teach me, I'm hopeless.
I'm not the best, there are plenty better than me.
I can't even Shift, it's no surprise.
Oh, don't be humble.
You're amazing.

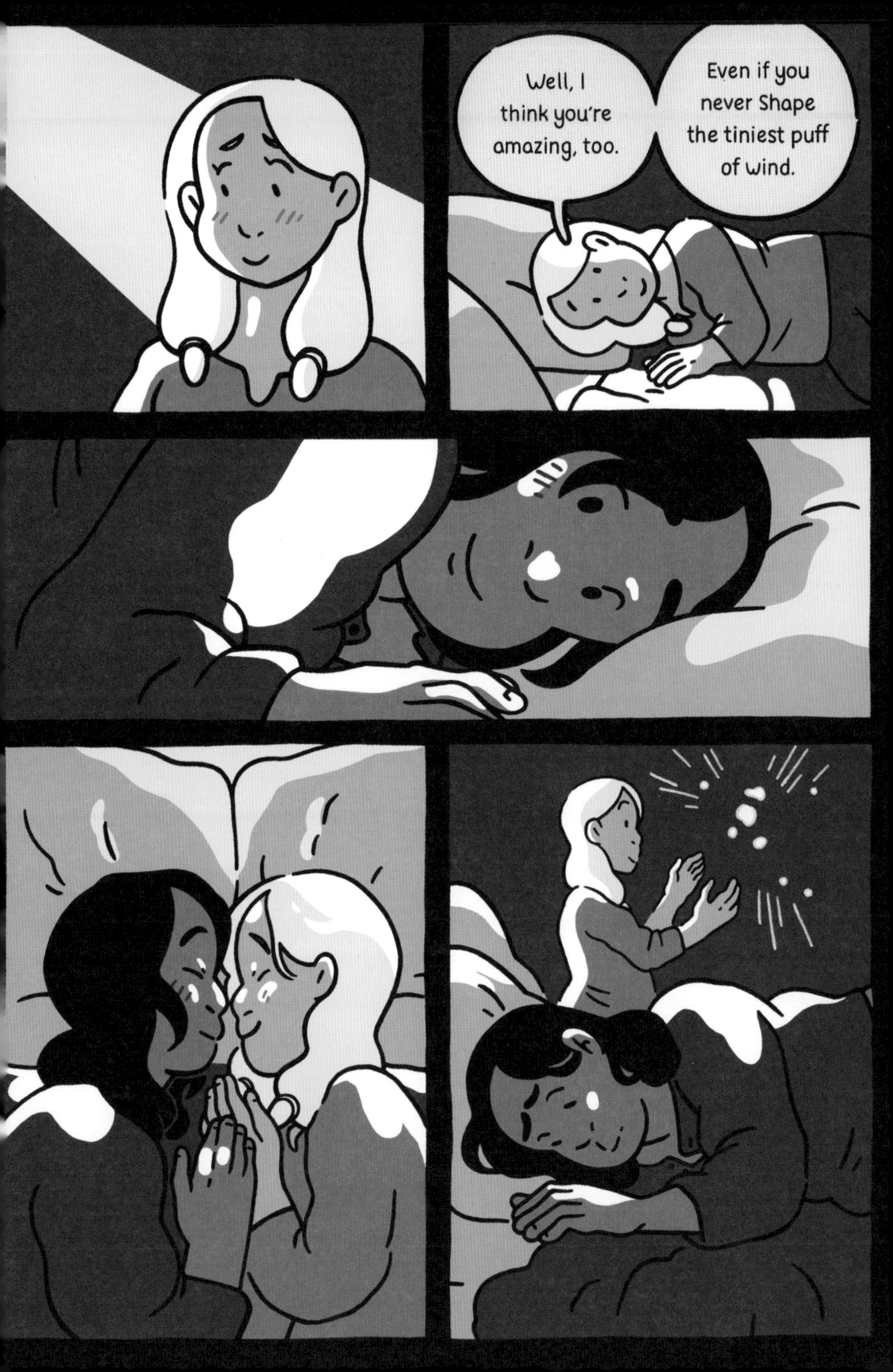
Well, I think you're amazing, too.
Even if you never Shape the tiniest puff of wind.

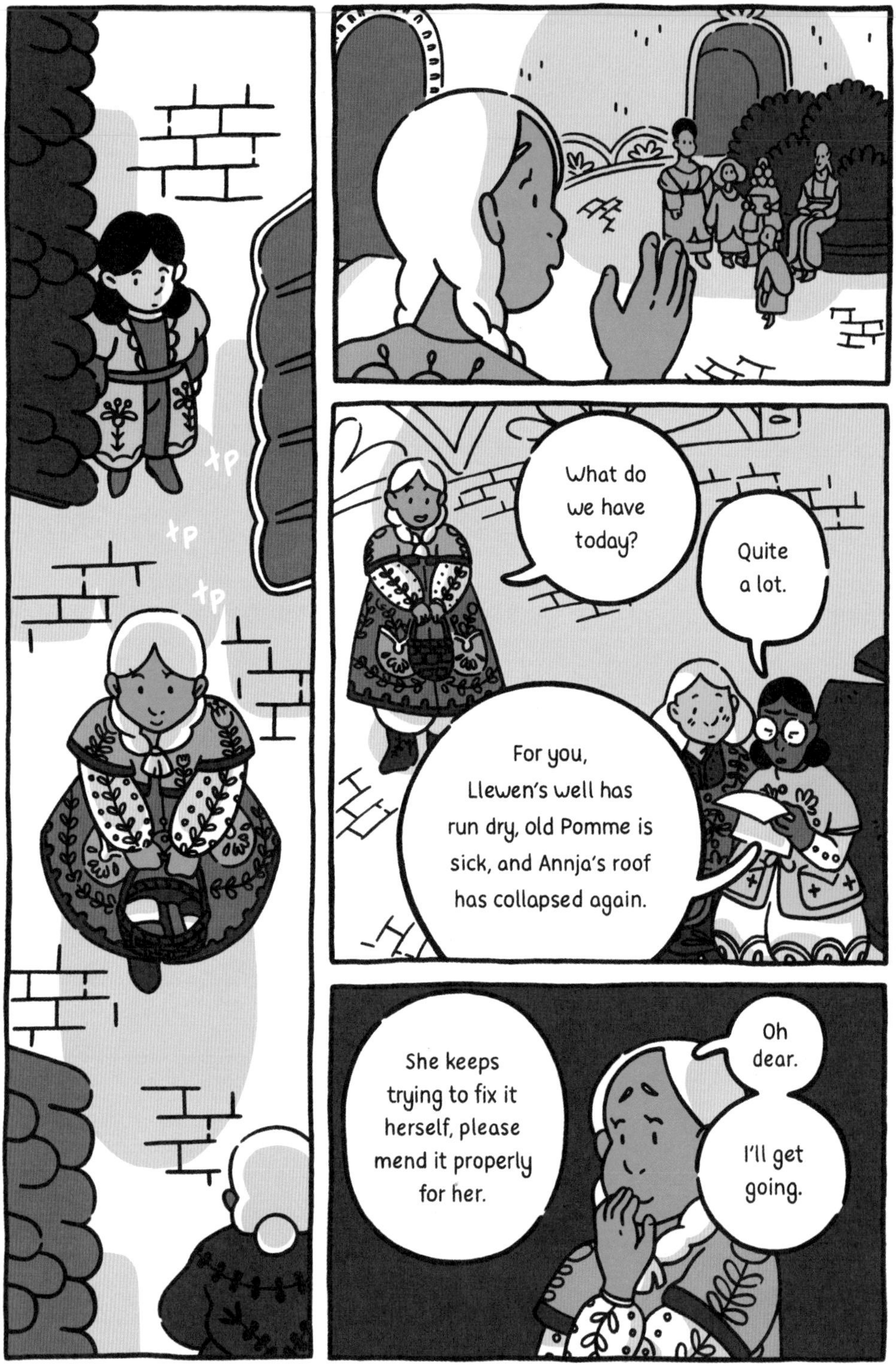
tp
tp
tp
What do we have today?
Quite a lot.
For you, Llewen's well has run dry, old Pomme is sick, and Annja's roof has collapsed again.
She keeps trying to fix it herself, please mend it properly for her.
Oh dear.
I'll get going.

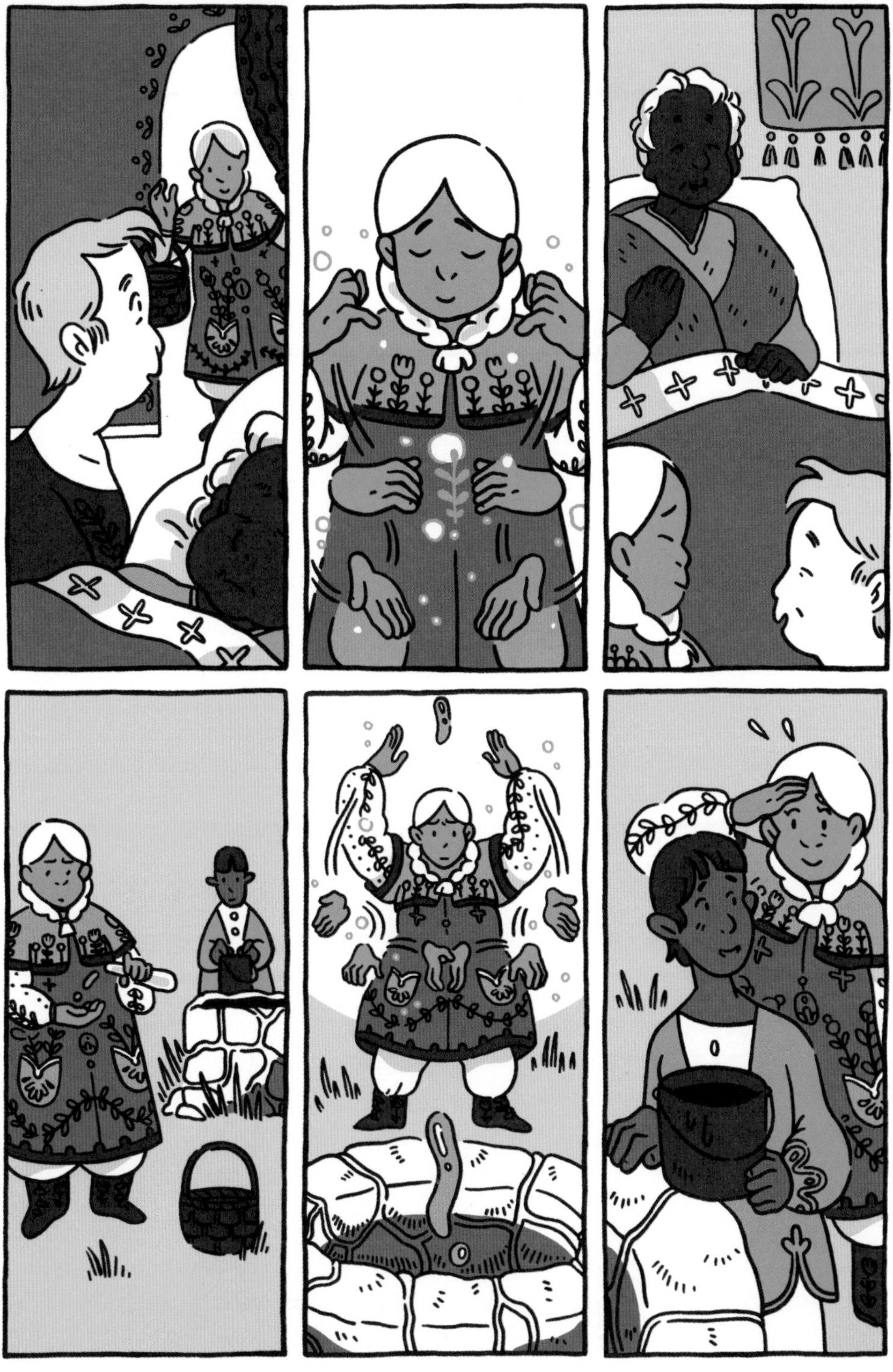

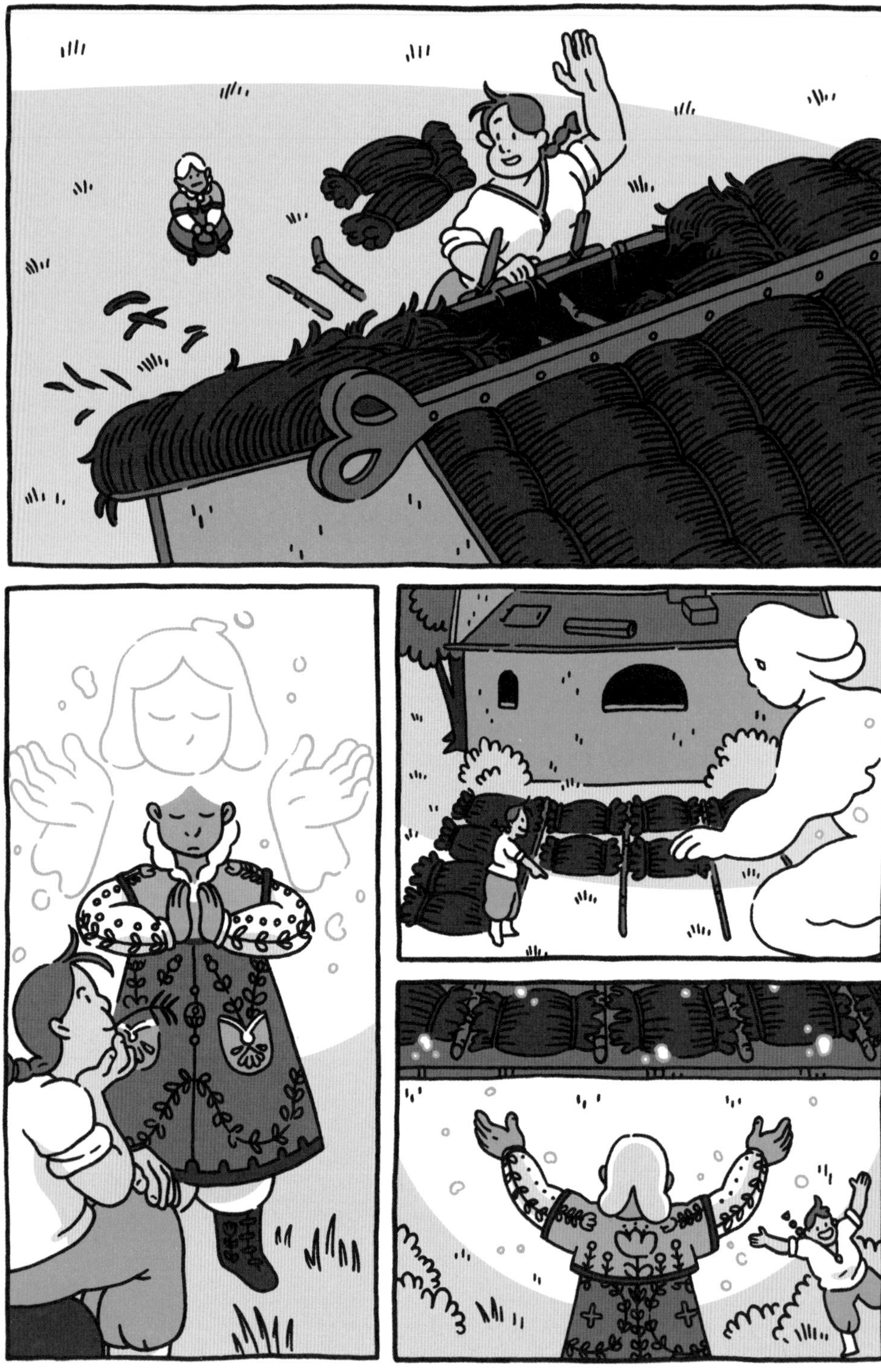

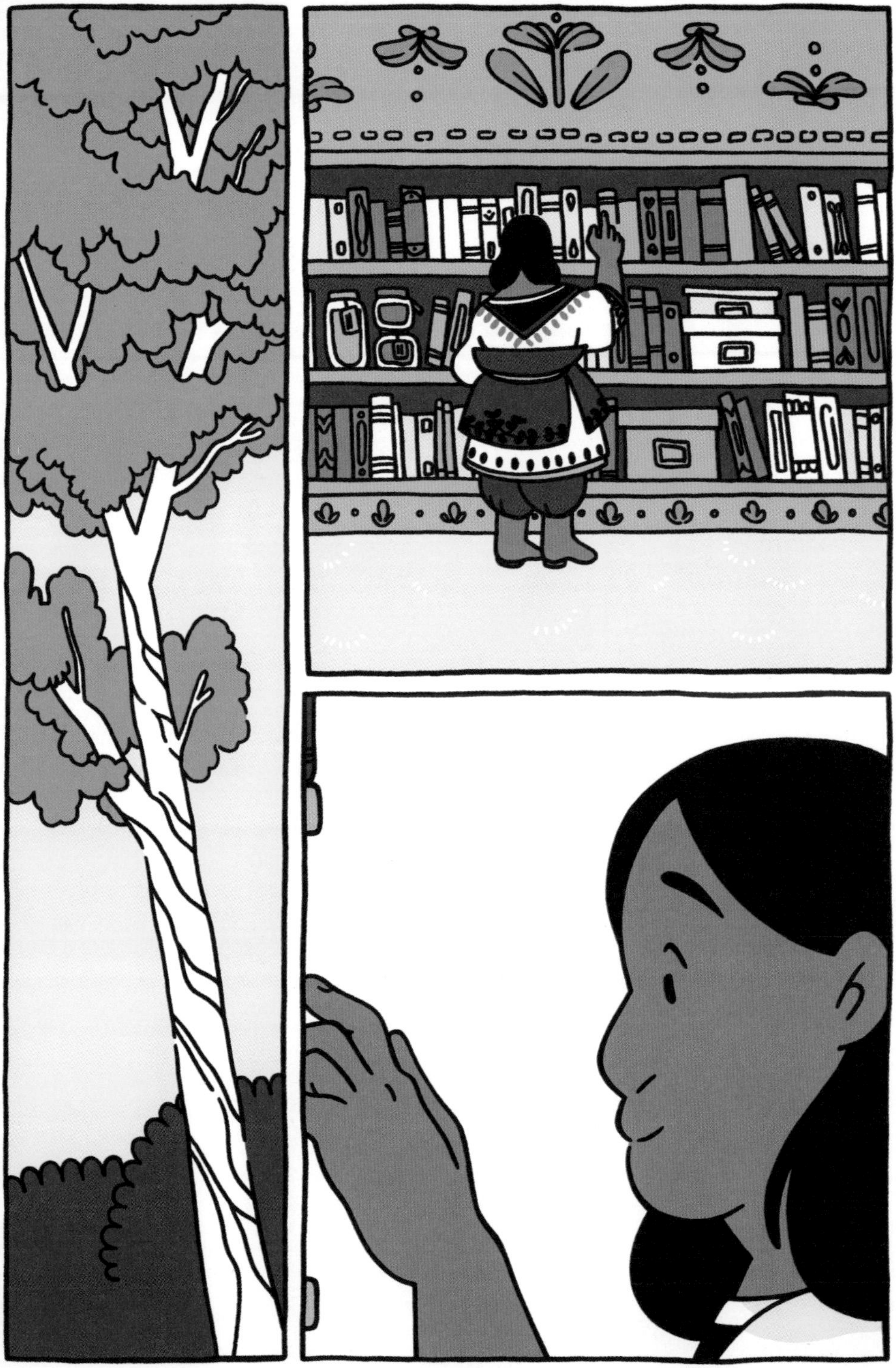

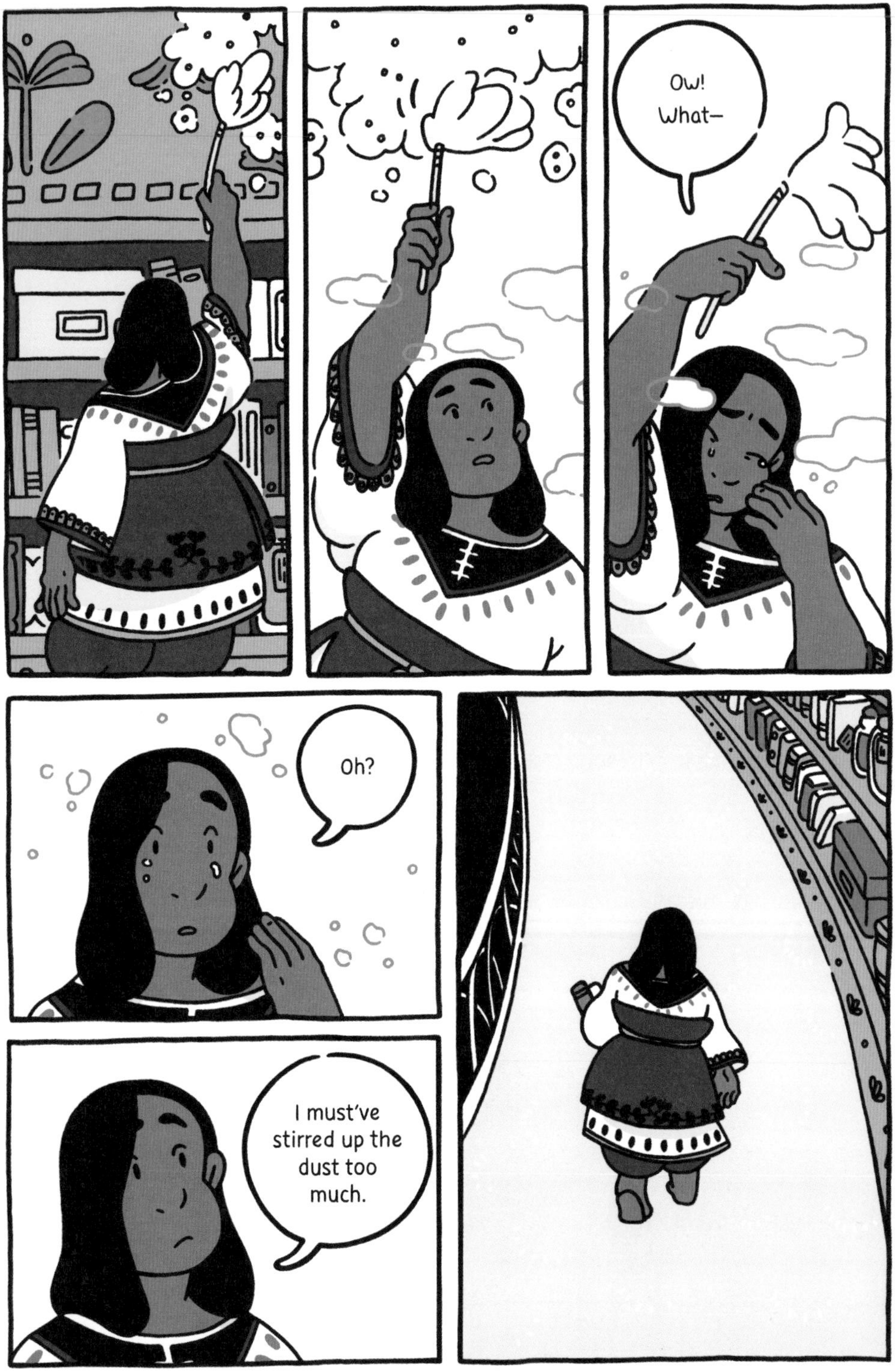
Ow!
What–
Oh?
I must've stirred up the dust too much.

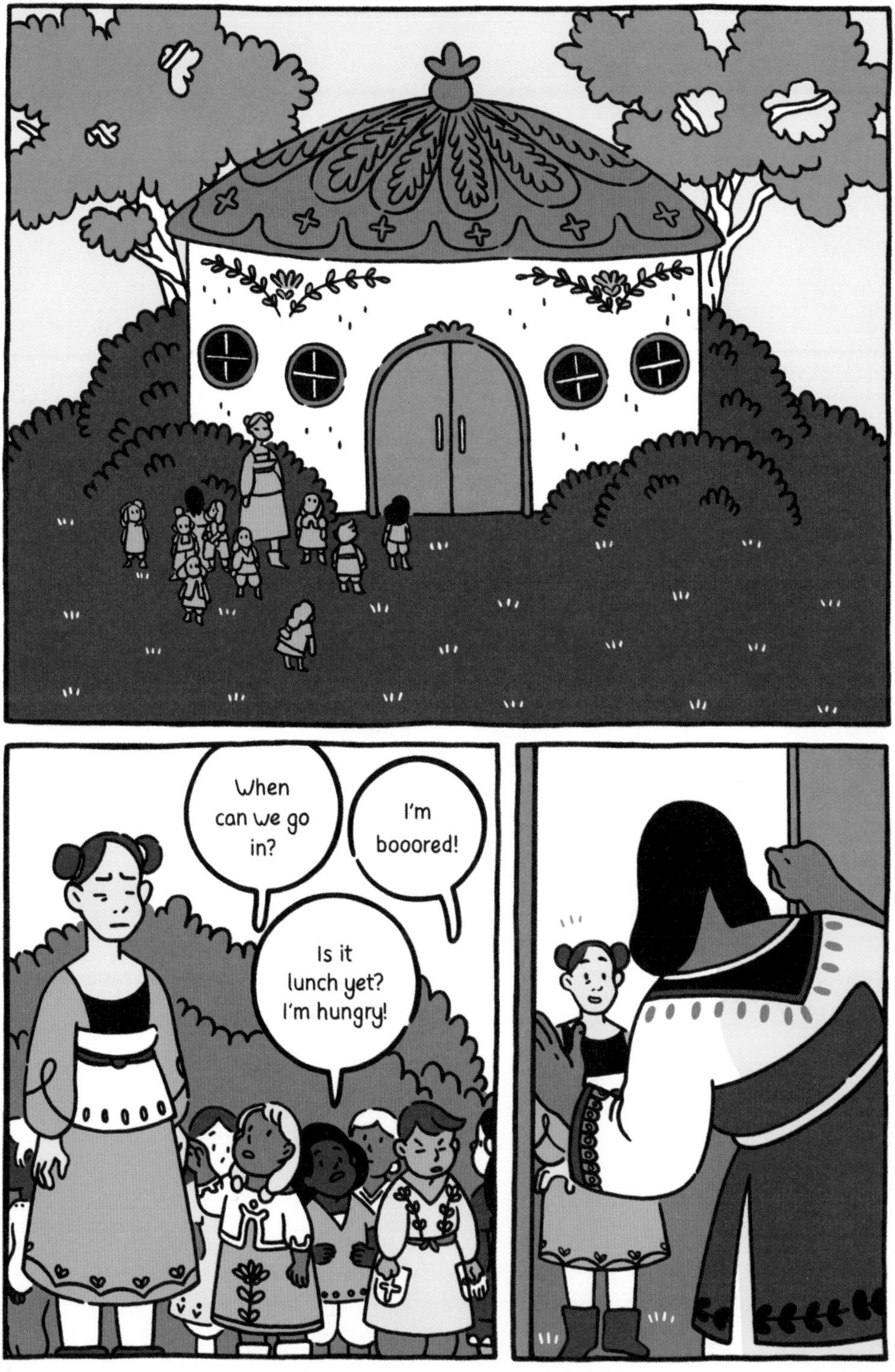
When can we go in?
I'm booored!
Is it lunch yet? I'm hungry!

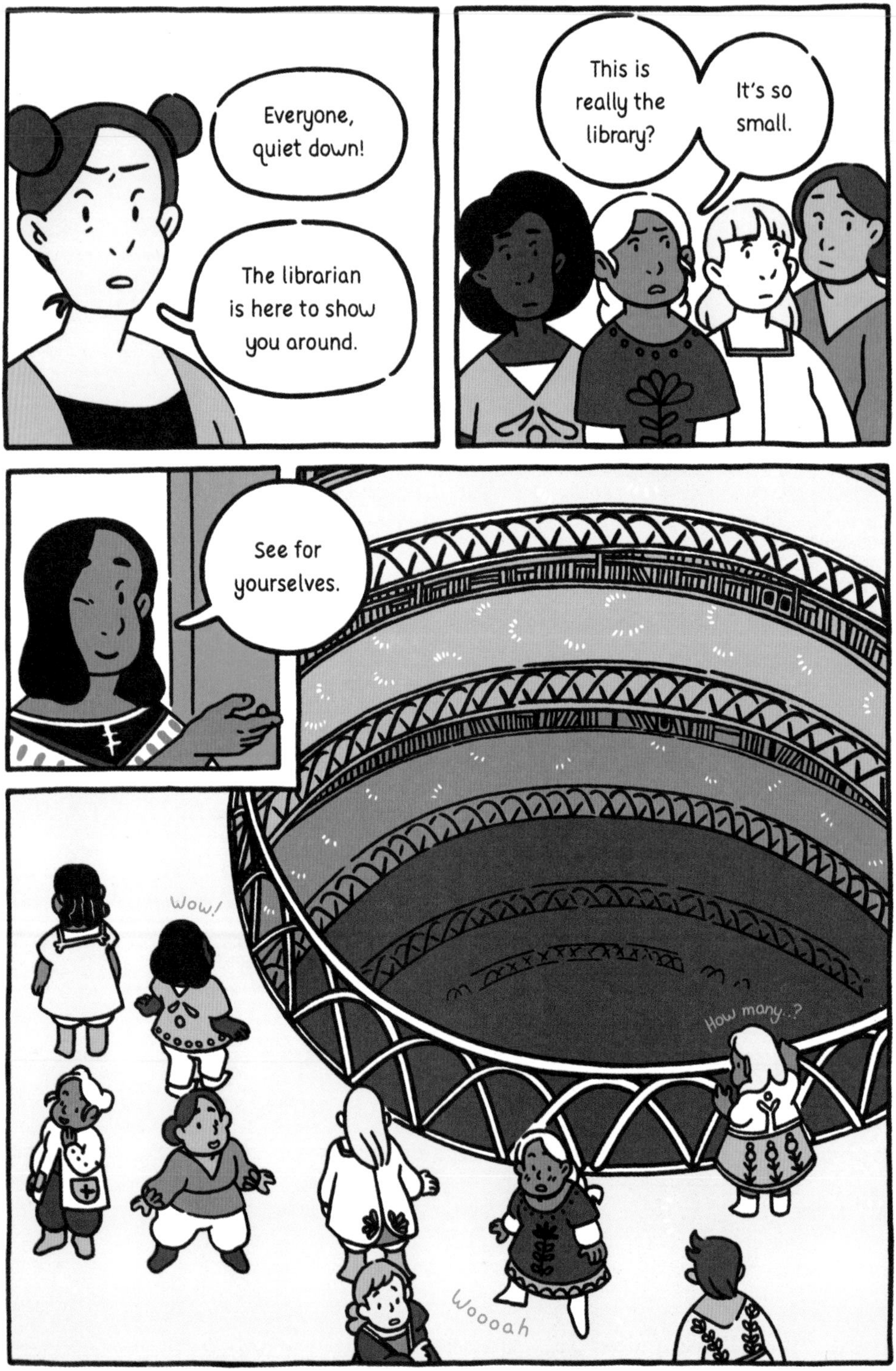
Everyone, quiet down!
The librarian is here to show you around.
This is really the library?
It's so small.
See for yourselves.
Wow!
How many..?
Woooah

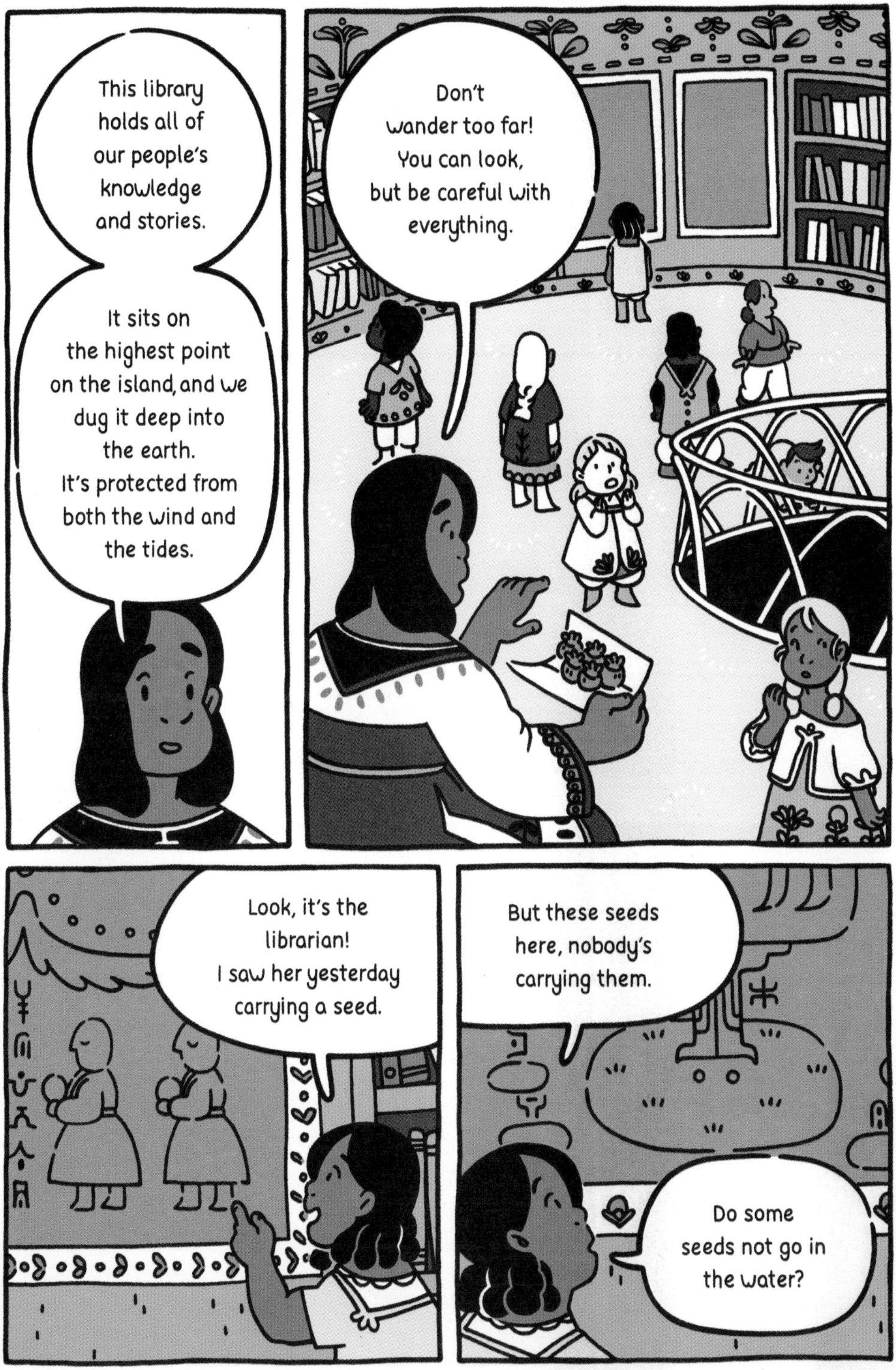
This library holds all of our people's knowledge and stories.
It sits on the highest point on the island, and we dug it deep into the earth. It's protected from both the wind and the tides.
Don't wander too far! You can look, but be careful with everything.
Look, it's the librarian! I saw her yesterday carrying a seed.
But these seeds here, nobody's carrying them.
Do some seeds not go in the water?

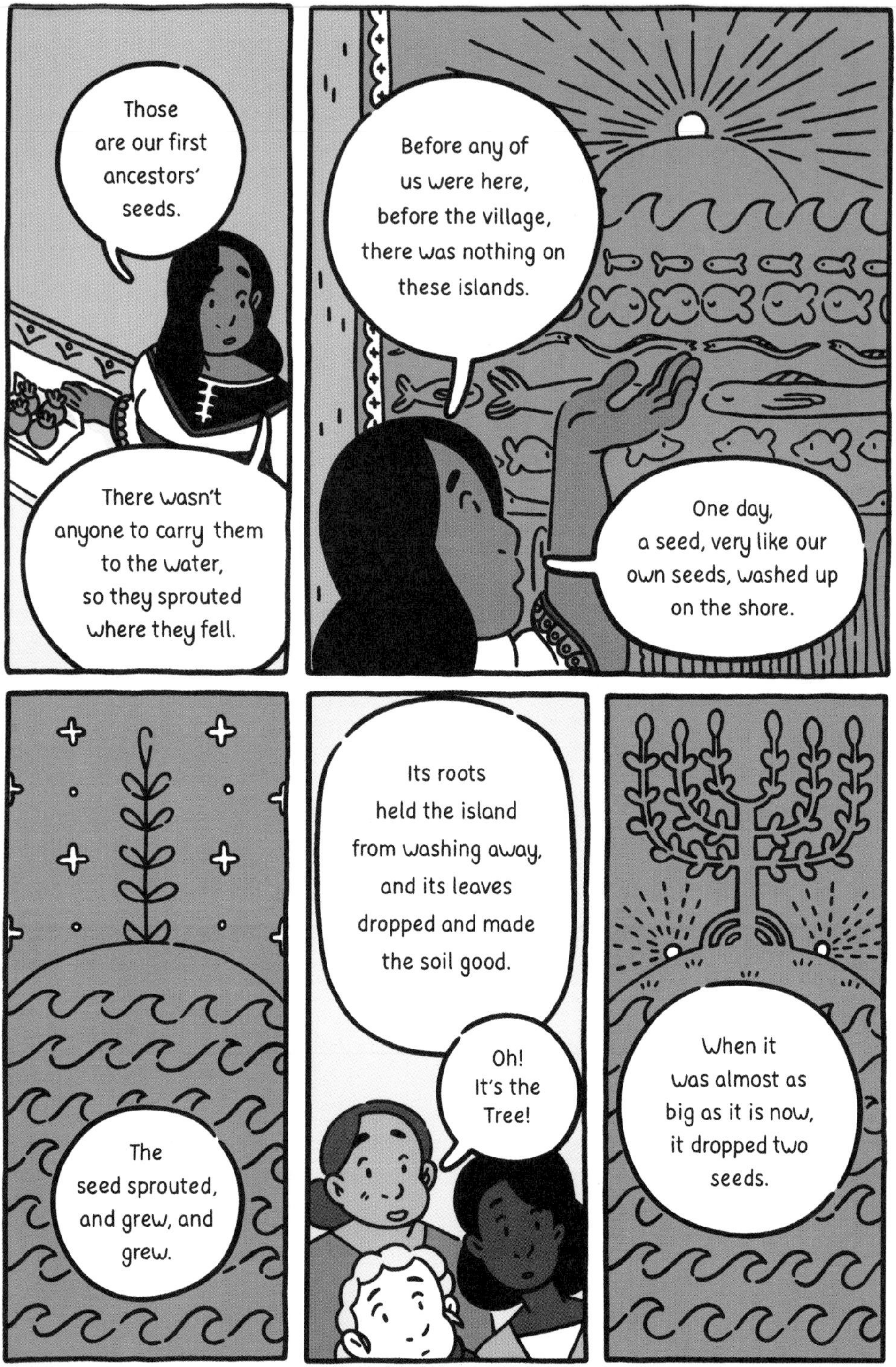
Those are our first ancestors' seeds.
There wasn't anyone to carry them to the water, so they sprouted where they fell.
Before any of us were here, before the village, there was nothing on these islands.
One day, a seed, very like our own seeds, washed up on the shore.
The seed sprouted, and grew, and grew.
Its roots held the island from washing away, and its leaves dropped and made the soil good.
Oh! It's the Tree!
When it was almost as big as it is now, it dropped two seeds.

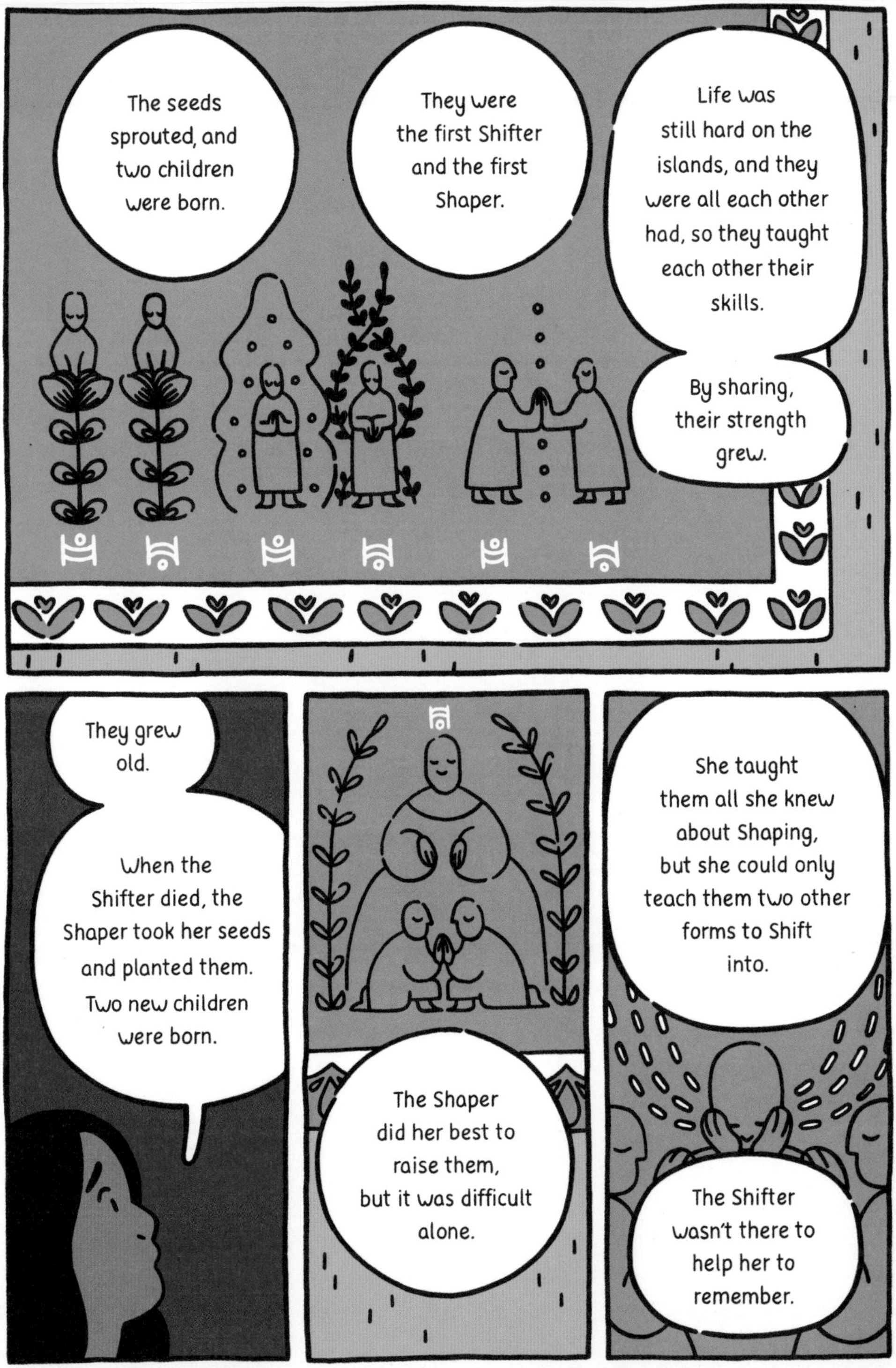
The seeds sprouted, and two children were born.
They were the first Shifter and the first Shaper.
Life was still hard on the islands, and they were all each other had, so they taught each other their skills.
By sharing, their strength grew.
They grew old.
When the Shifter died, the Shaper took her seeds and planted them. Two new children were born.
The Shaper did her best to raise them, but it was difficult alone.
She taught them all she knew about Shaping, but she could only teach them two other forms to Shift into.
The Shifter wasn't there to help her to remember.

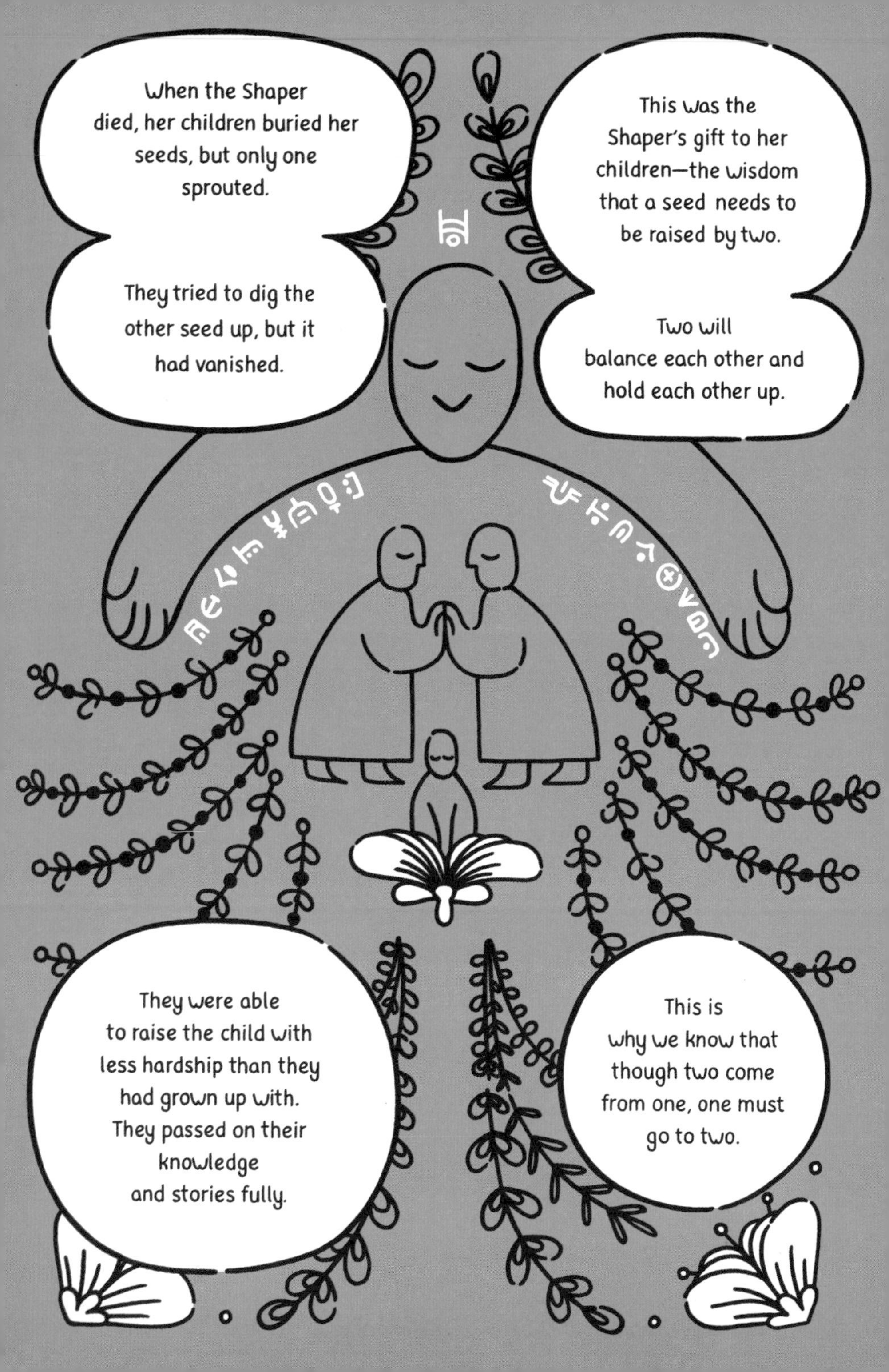
When the Shaper died, her children buried her seeds, but only one sprouted.
They tried to dig the other seed up, but it had vanished.
This was the Shaper's gift to her children—the wisdom that a seed needs to be raised by two.
Two will balance each other and hold each other up.
They were able to raise the child with less hardship than they had grown up with. They passed on their knowledge and stories fully.
This is why we know that though two come from one, one must go to two.

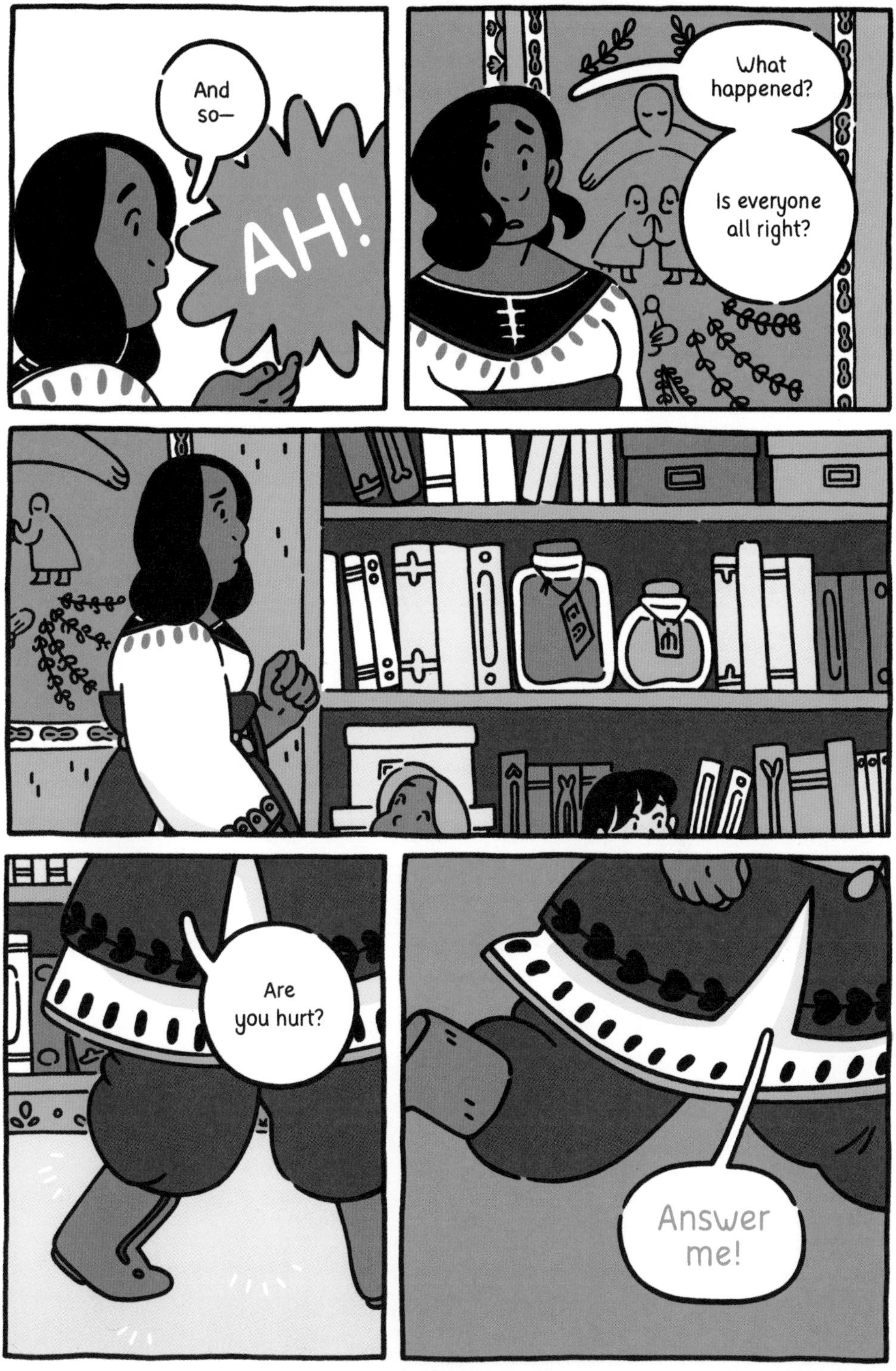
And so—
AH!
What happened?
Is everyone all right?
Are you hurt?
Answer me!

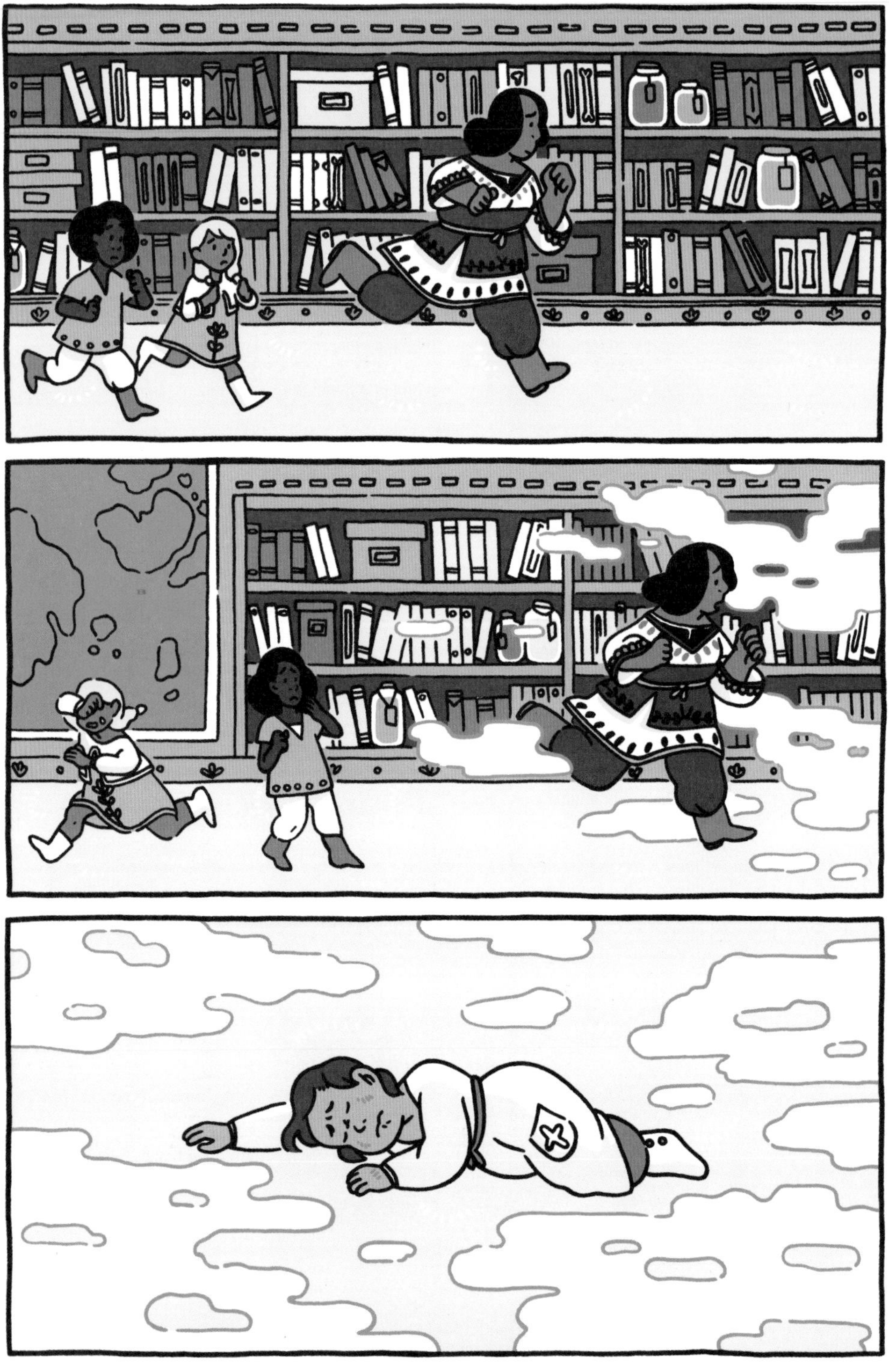

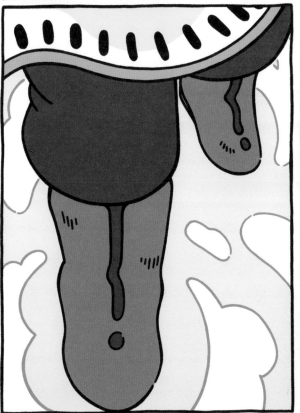

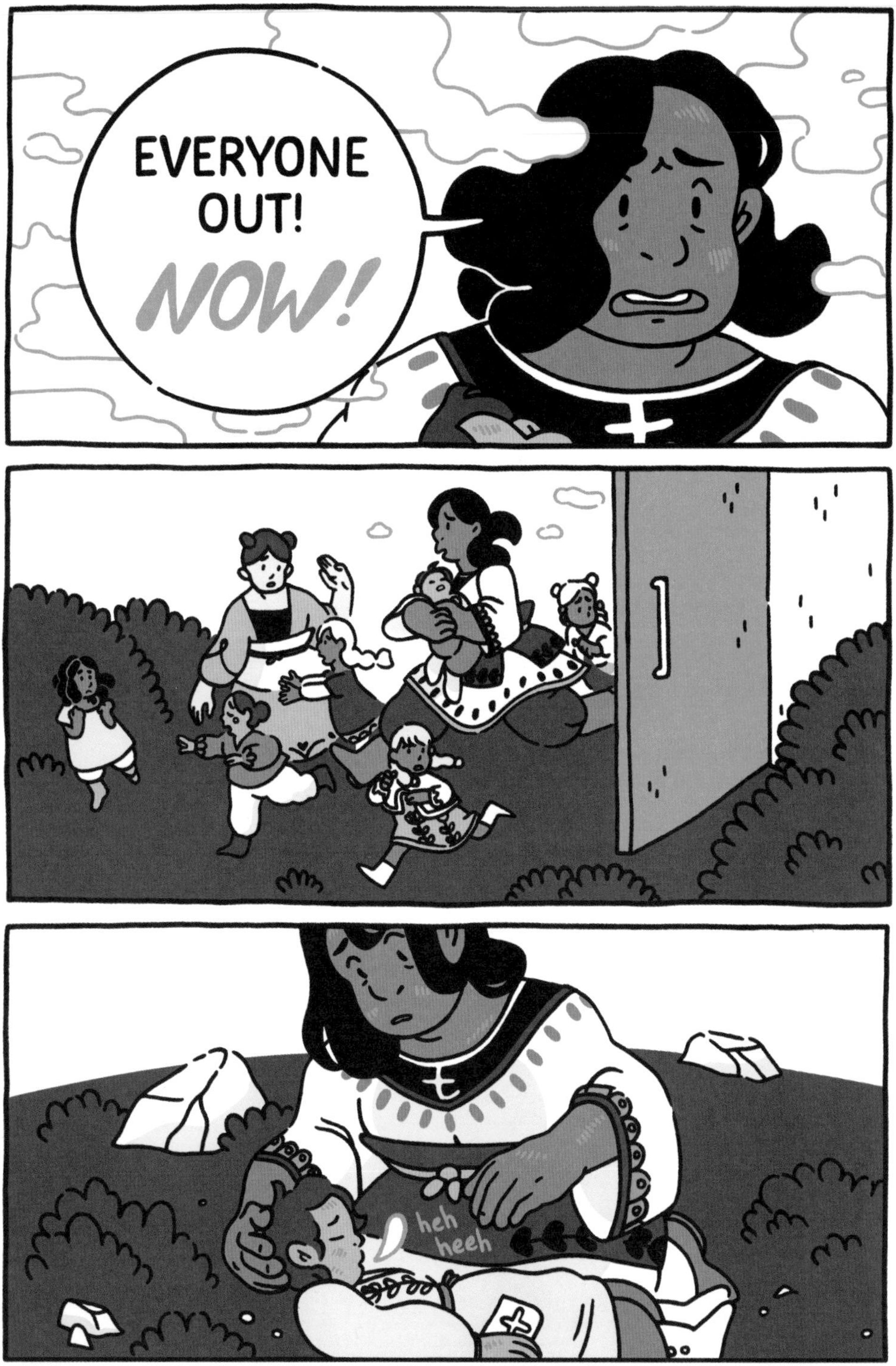
EVERYONE OUT! NOW!
heh heeh

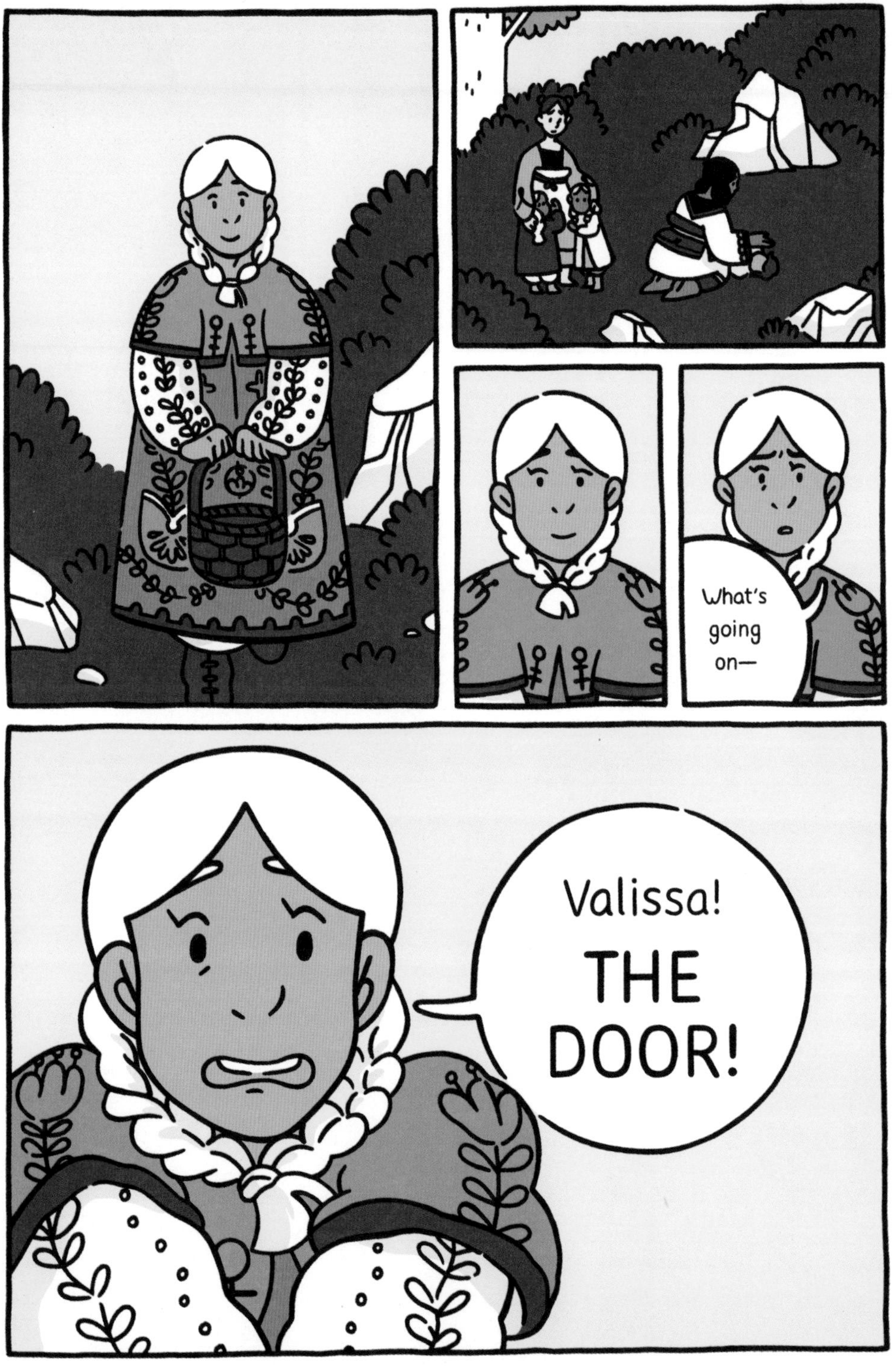
What's going on—
Valissa!
THE DOOR!

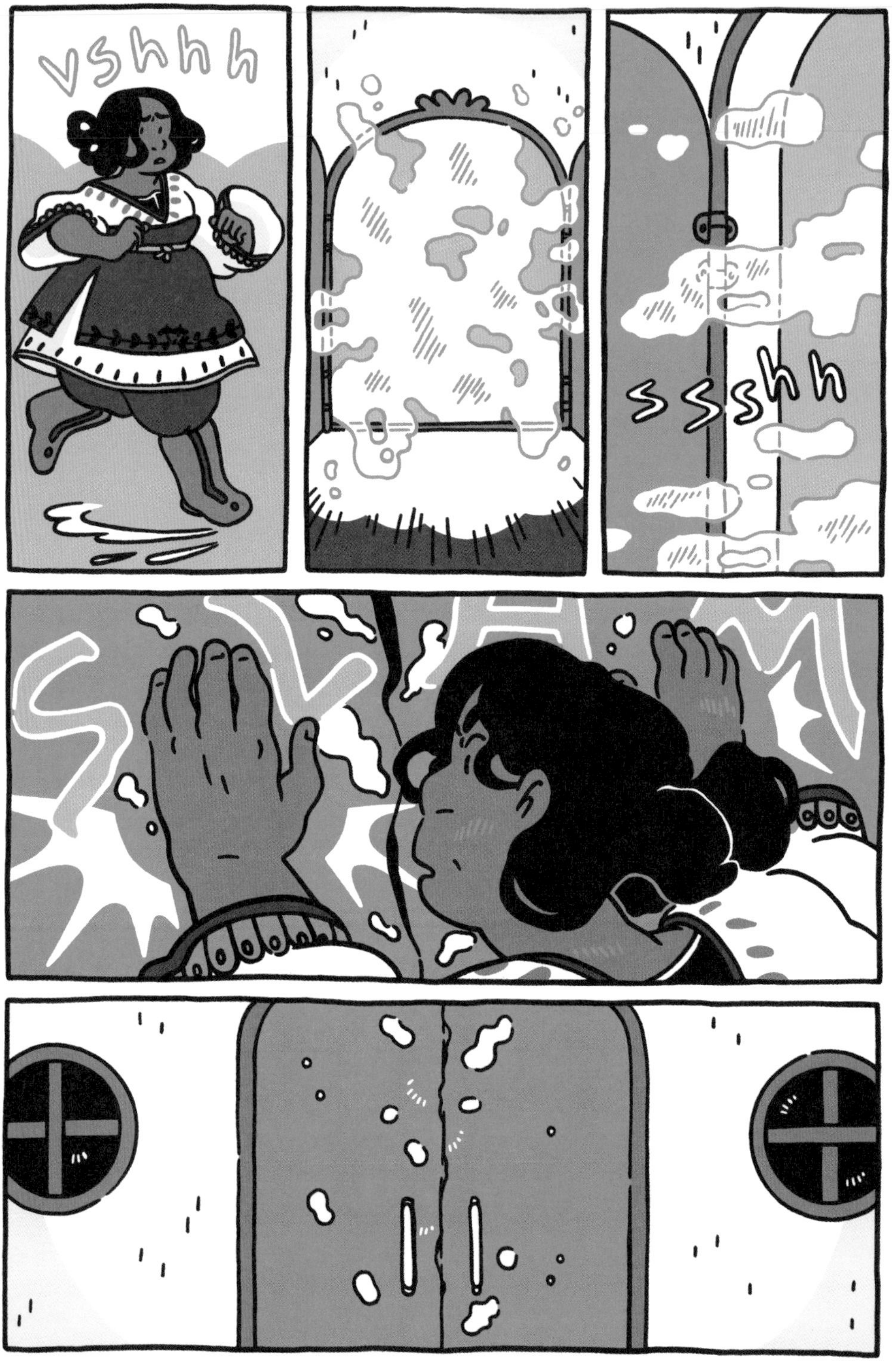
vshhh
ssshh
SLAM

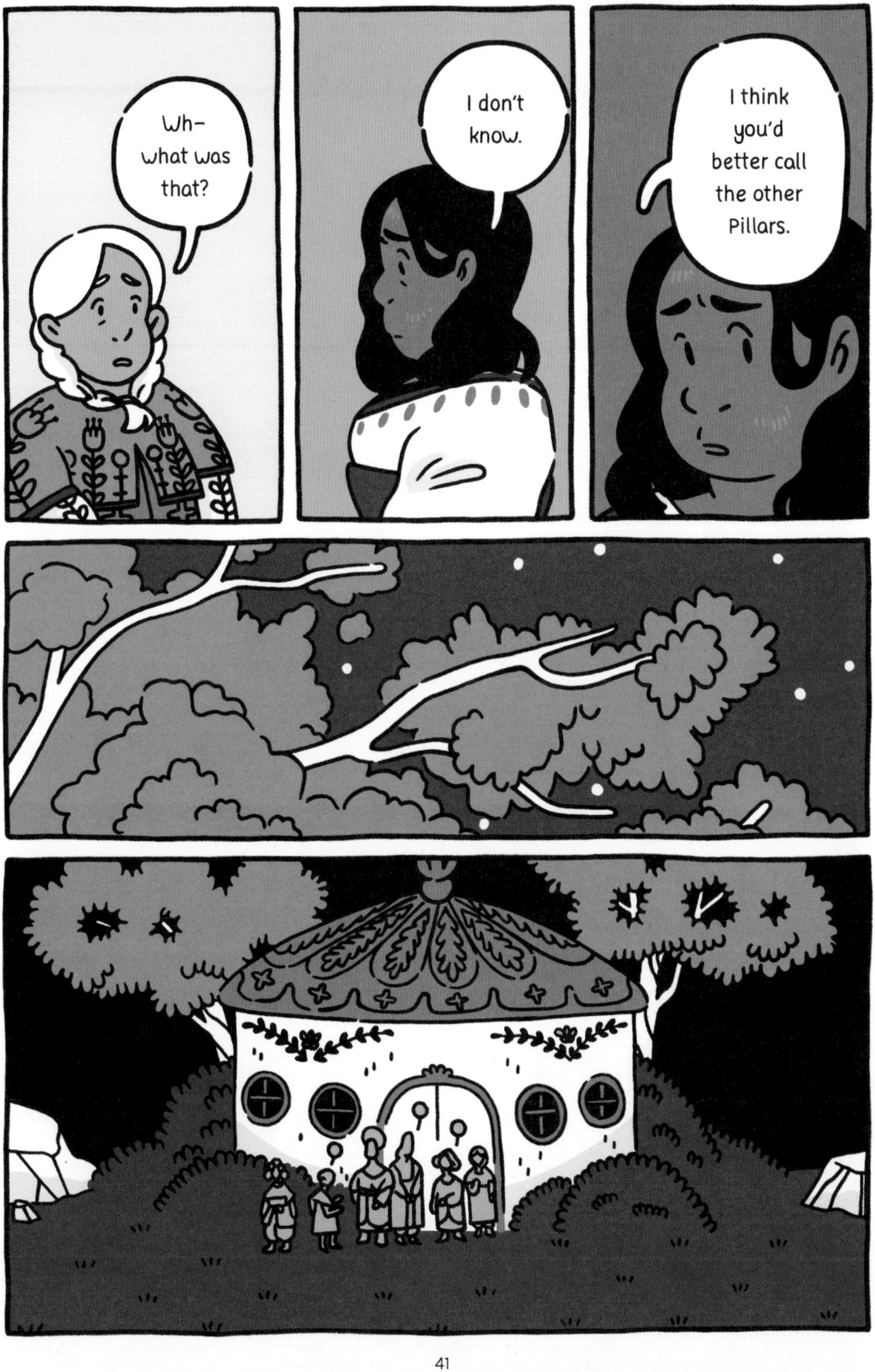
Wh- what was that?
I don't know.
I think you'd better call the other Pillars.

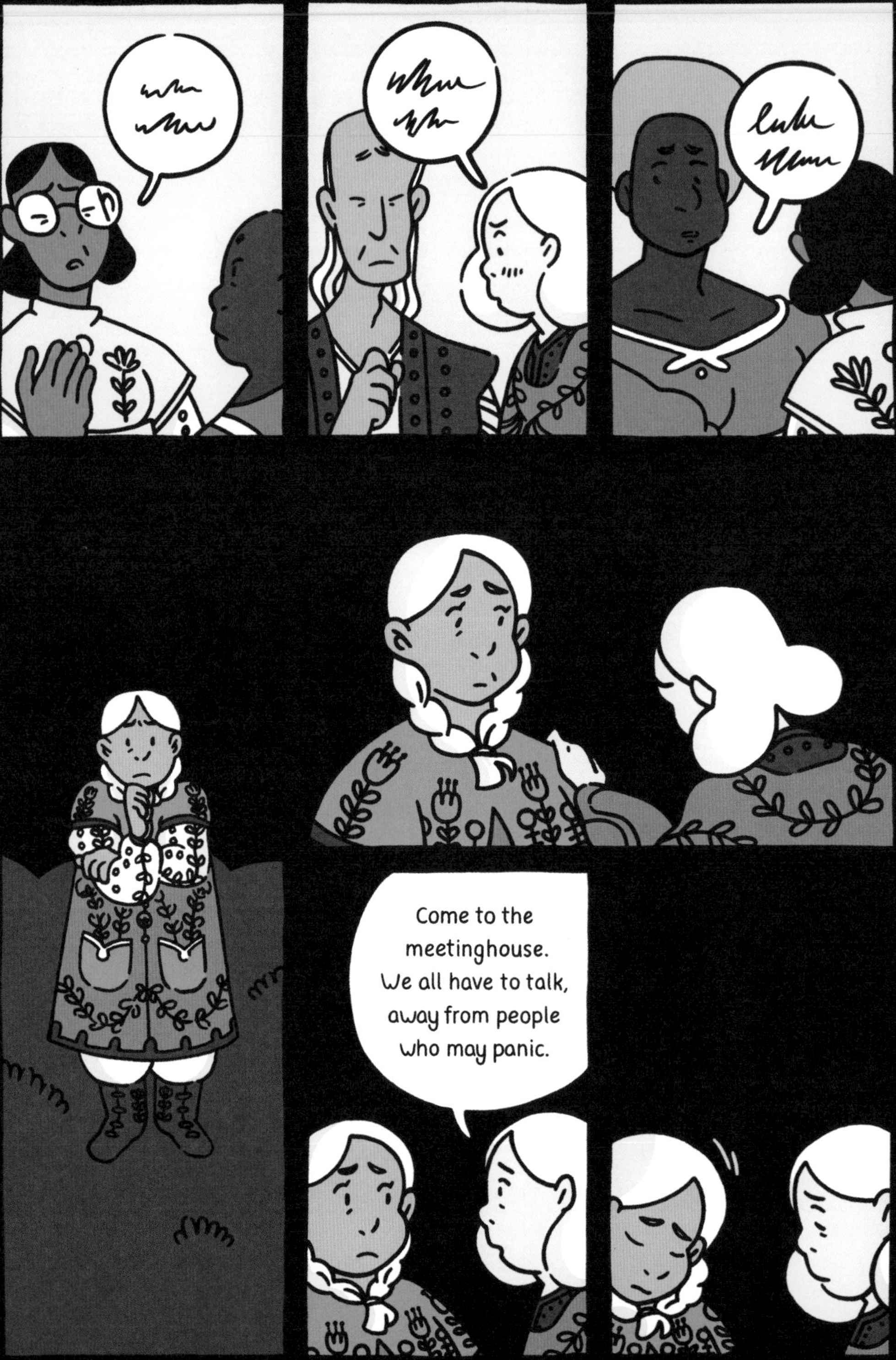
Come to the meetinghouse. We all have to talk, away from people who may panic.

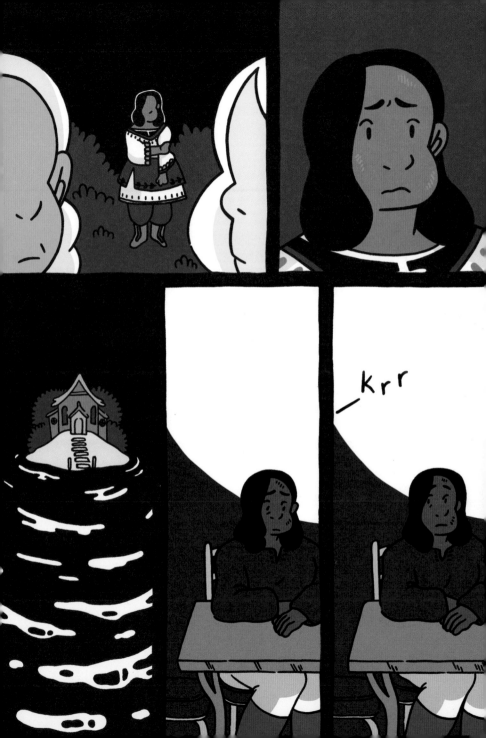

krr

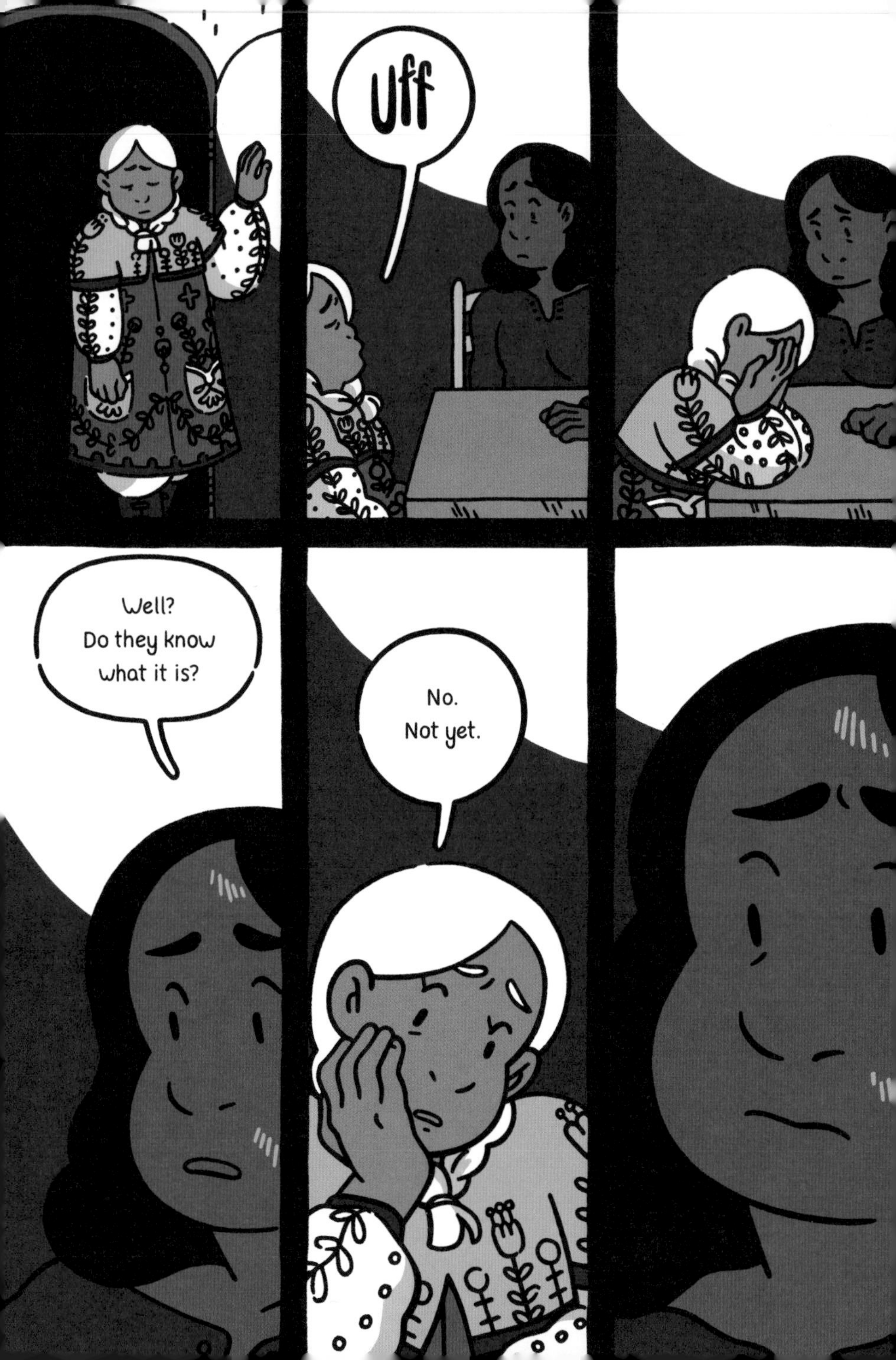
Uff
Well? Do they know what it is?
No. Not yet.

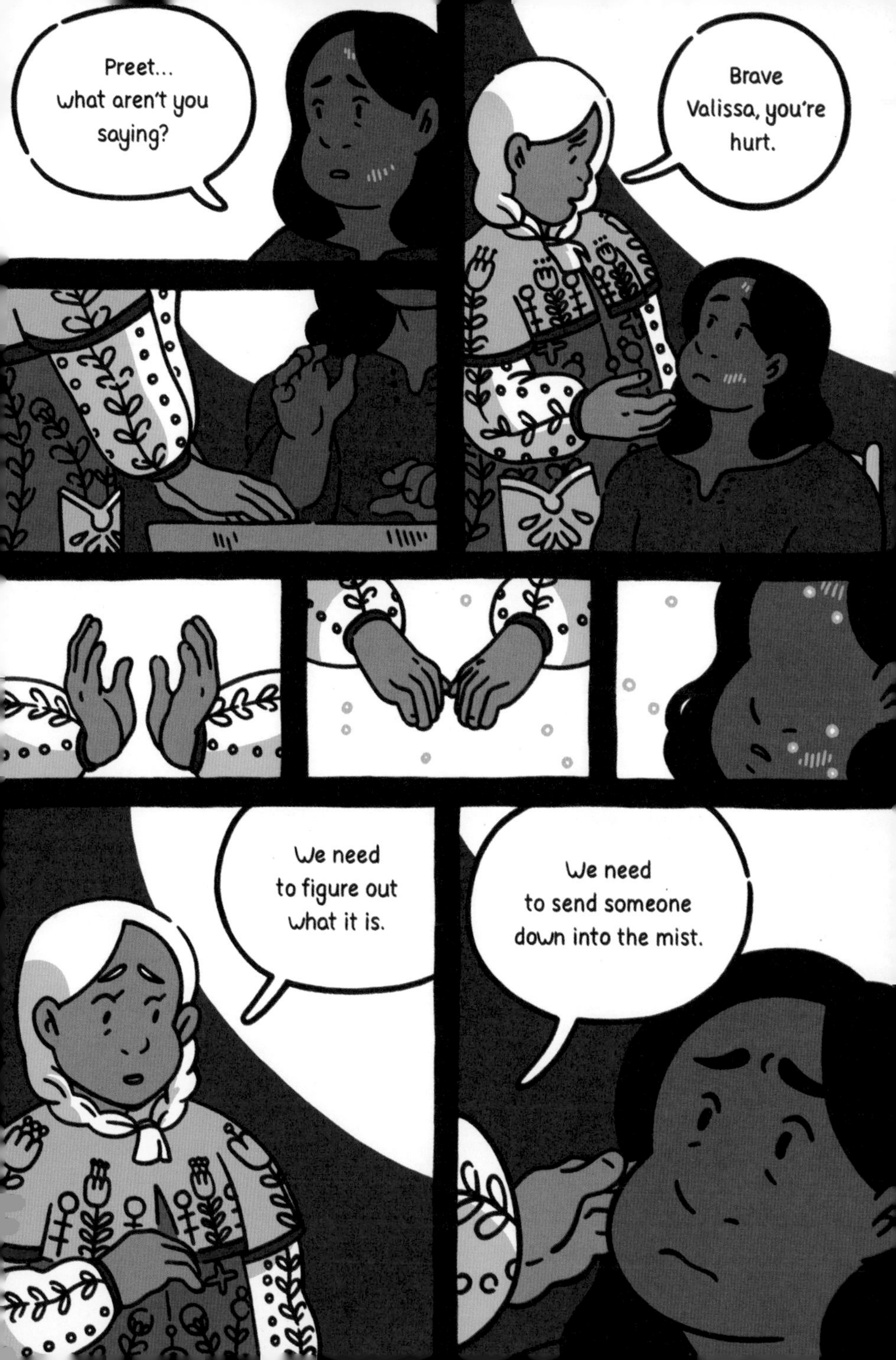
Preet...
what aren't you
saying?
Brave
Valissa, you're
hurt.
We need
to figure out
what it is.
We need
to send someone
down into the mist.

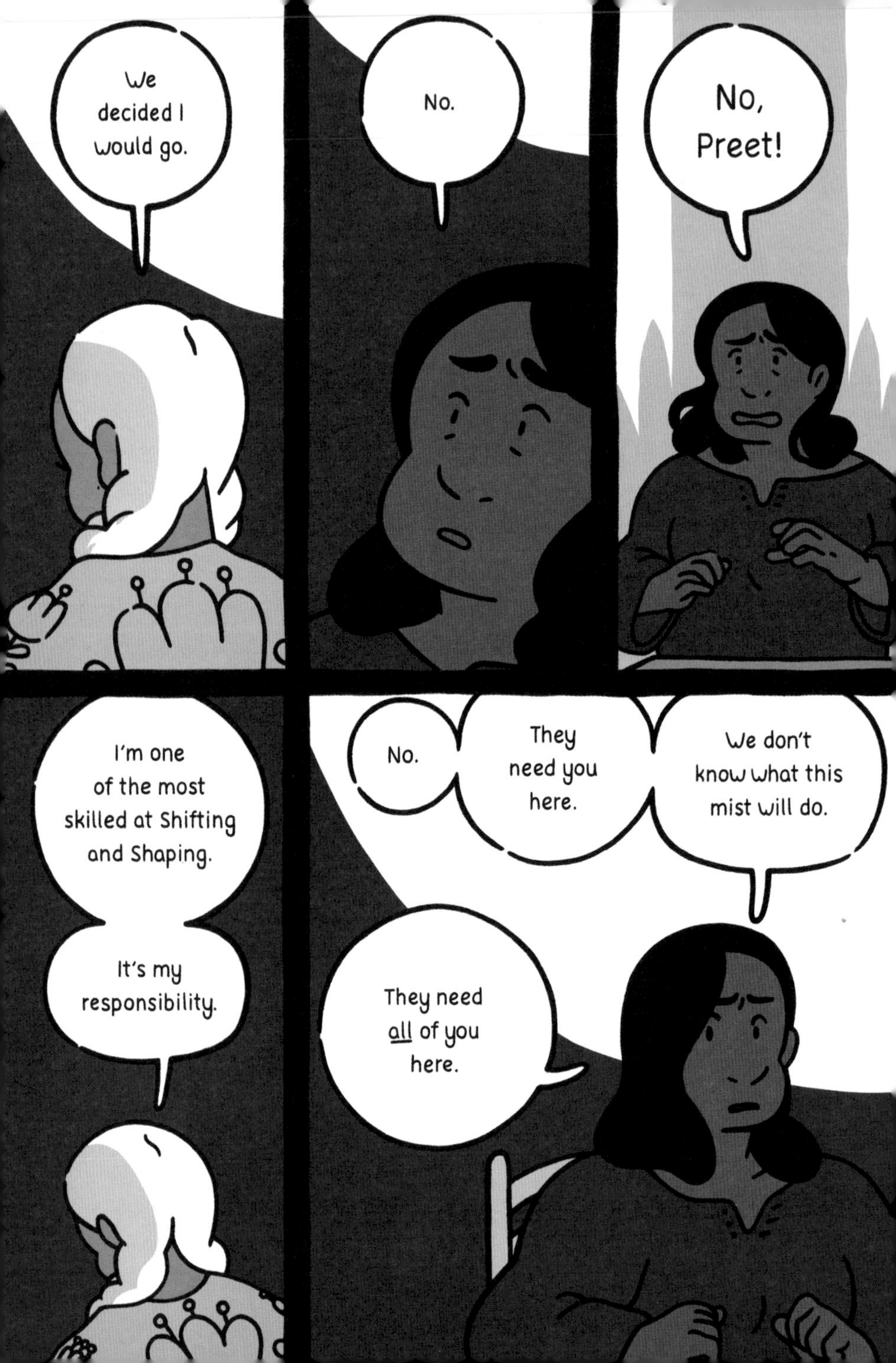
We decided I would go.
No.
No, Preet!
I'm one of the most skilled at Shifting and Shaping.
It's my responsibility.
No.
They need you here.
We don't know what this mist will do.
They need all of you here.

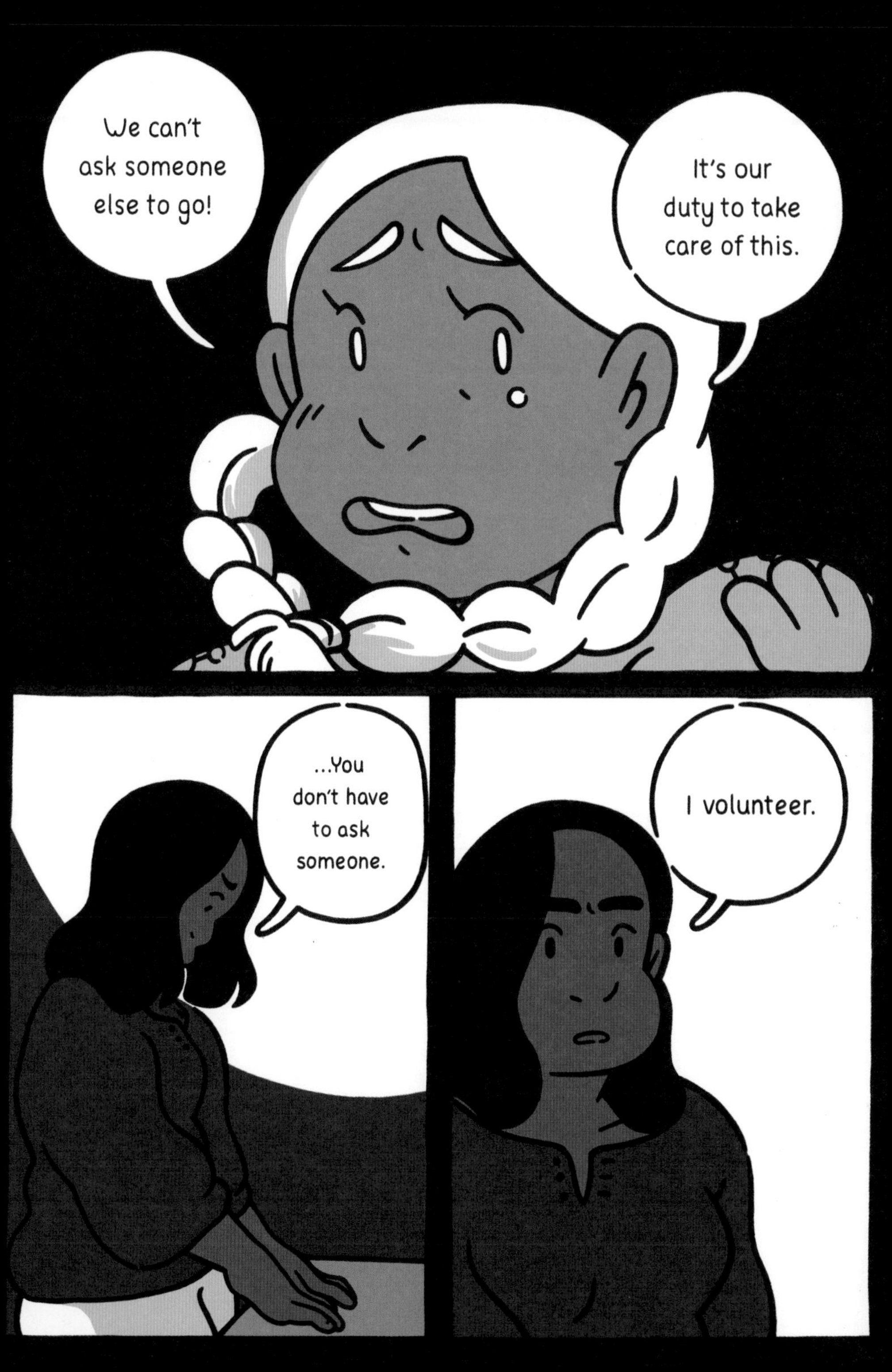
We can't ask someone else to go!
It's our duty to take care of this.
...You don't have to ask someone.
I volunteer.

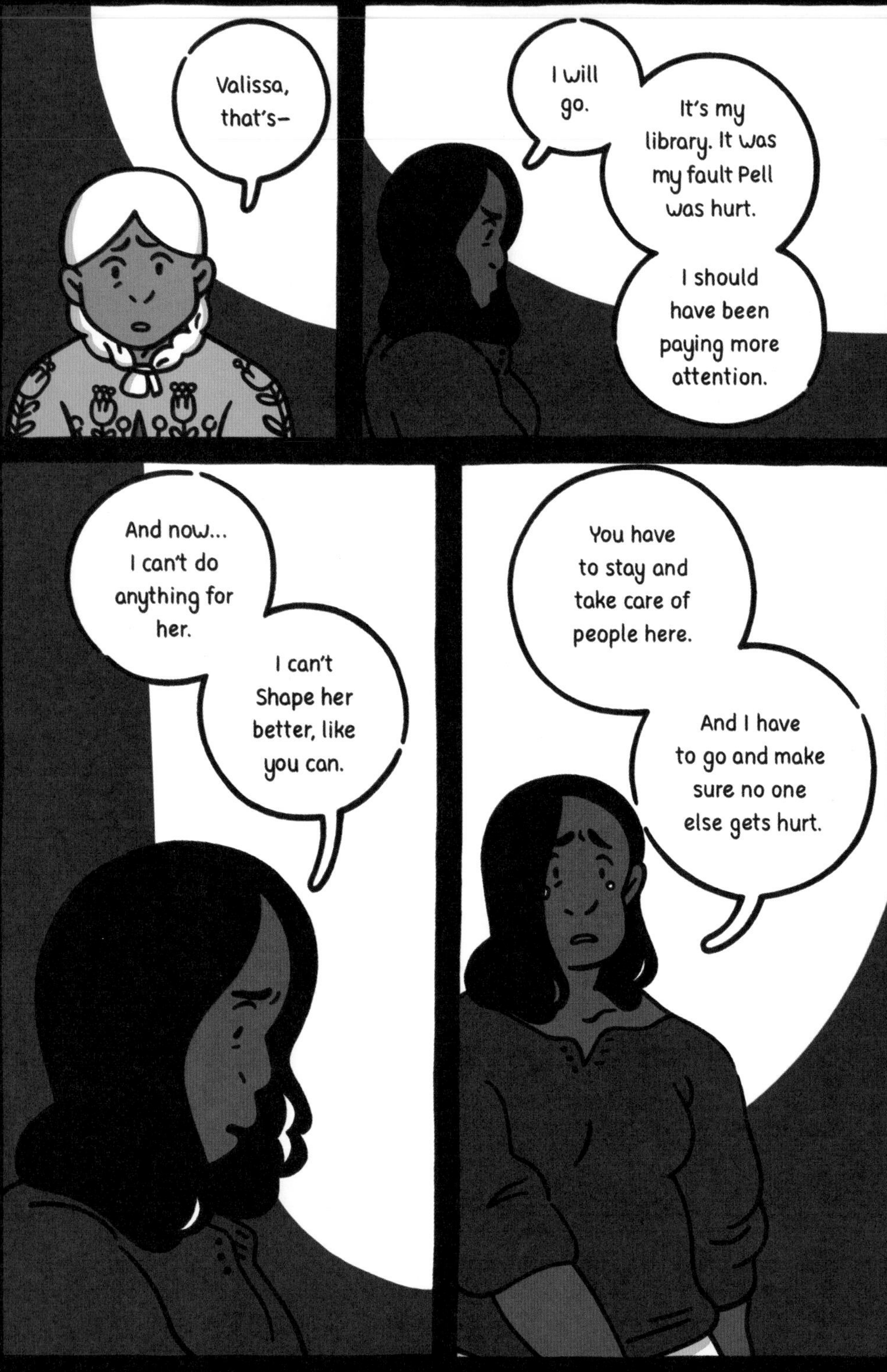
Valissa, that's–
I will go.
It's my library. It was my fault Pell was hurt.
I should have been paying more attention.
And now... I can't do anything for her.
I can't Shape her better, like you can.
You have to stay and take care of people here.
And I have to go and make sure no one else gets hurt.

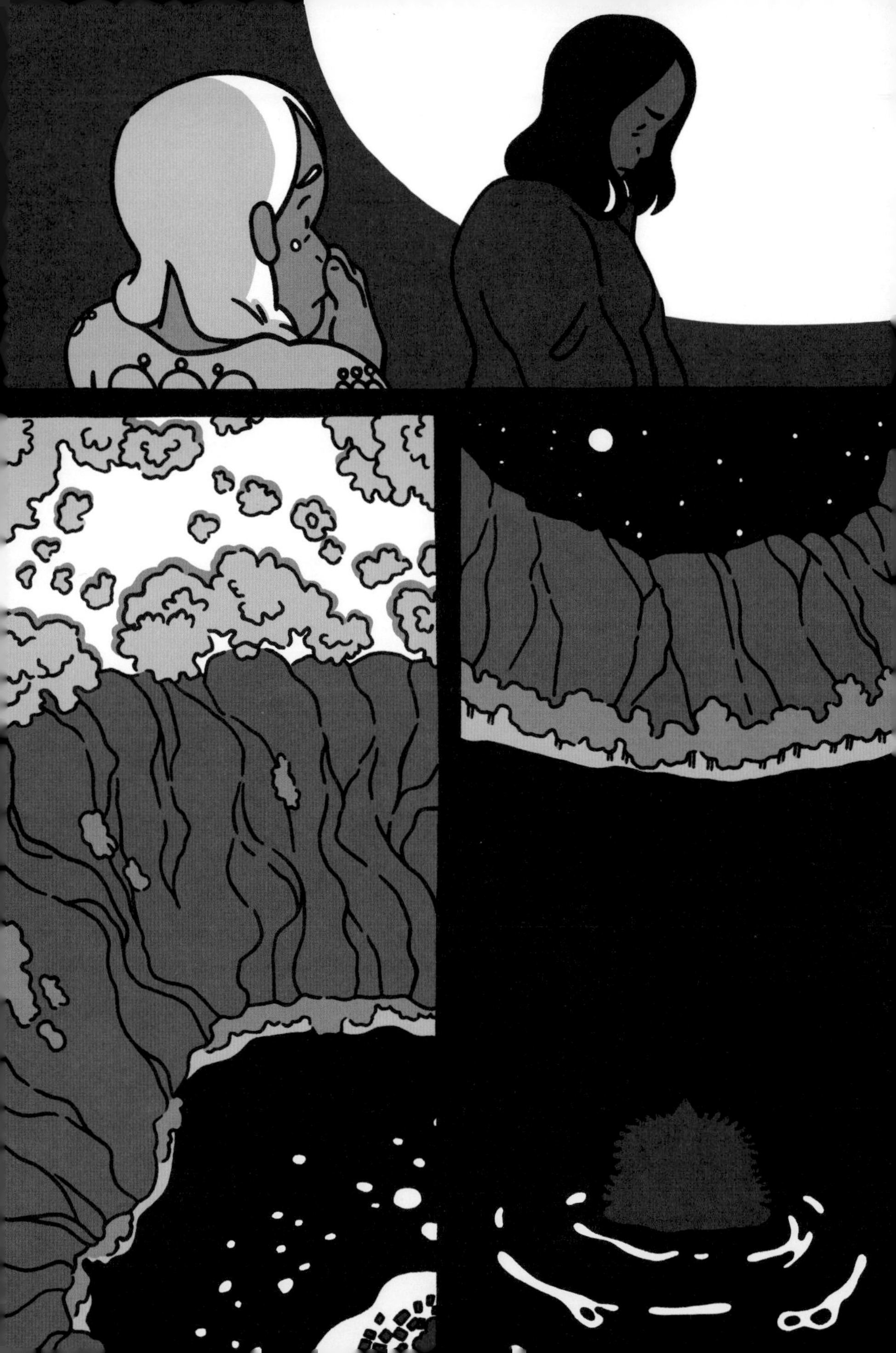

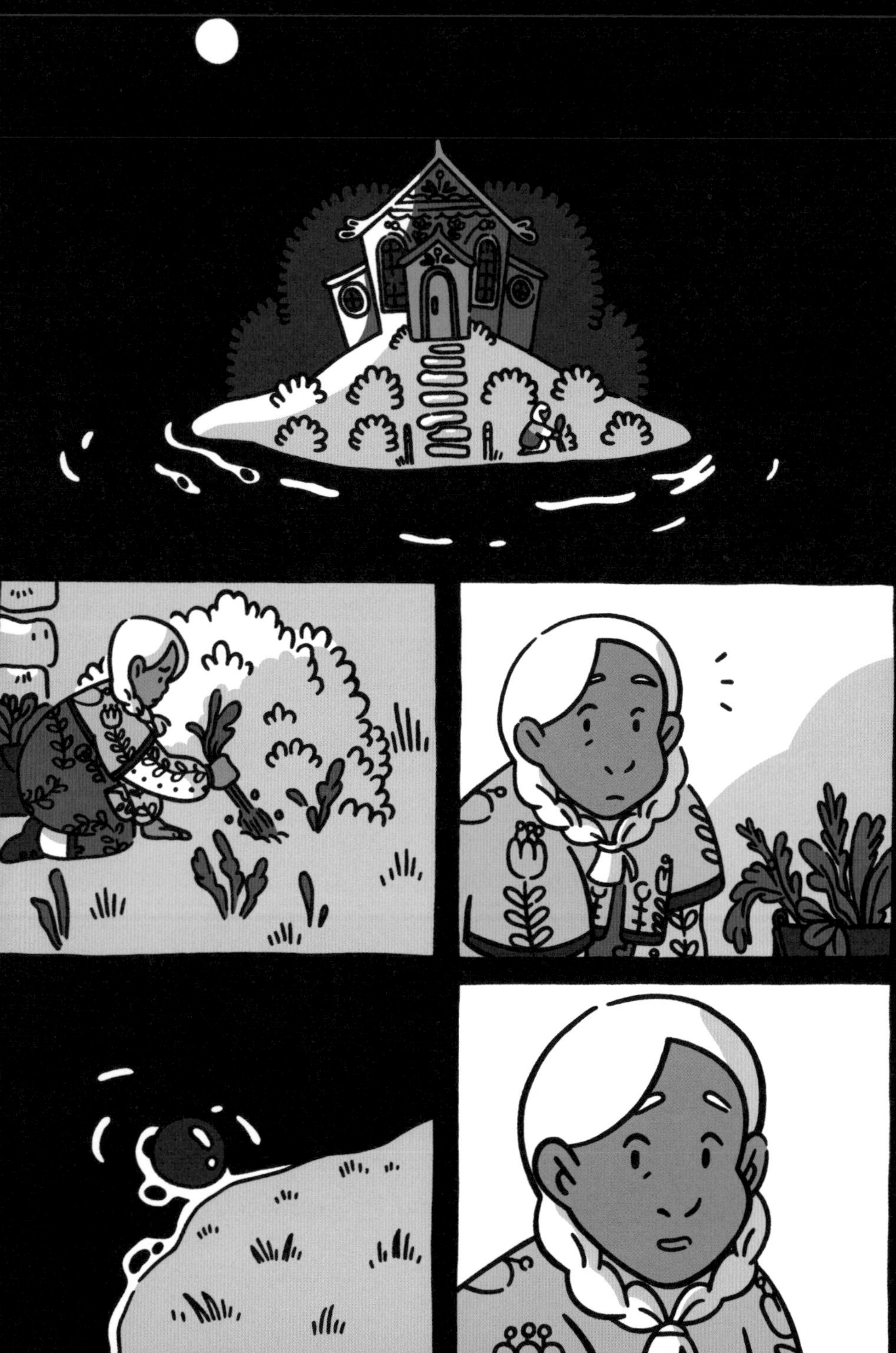

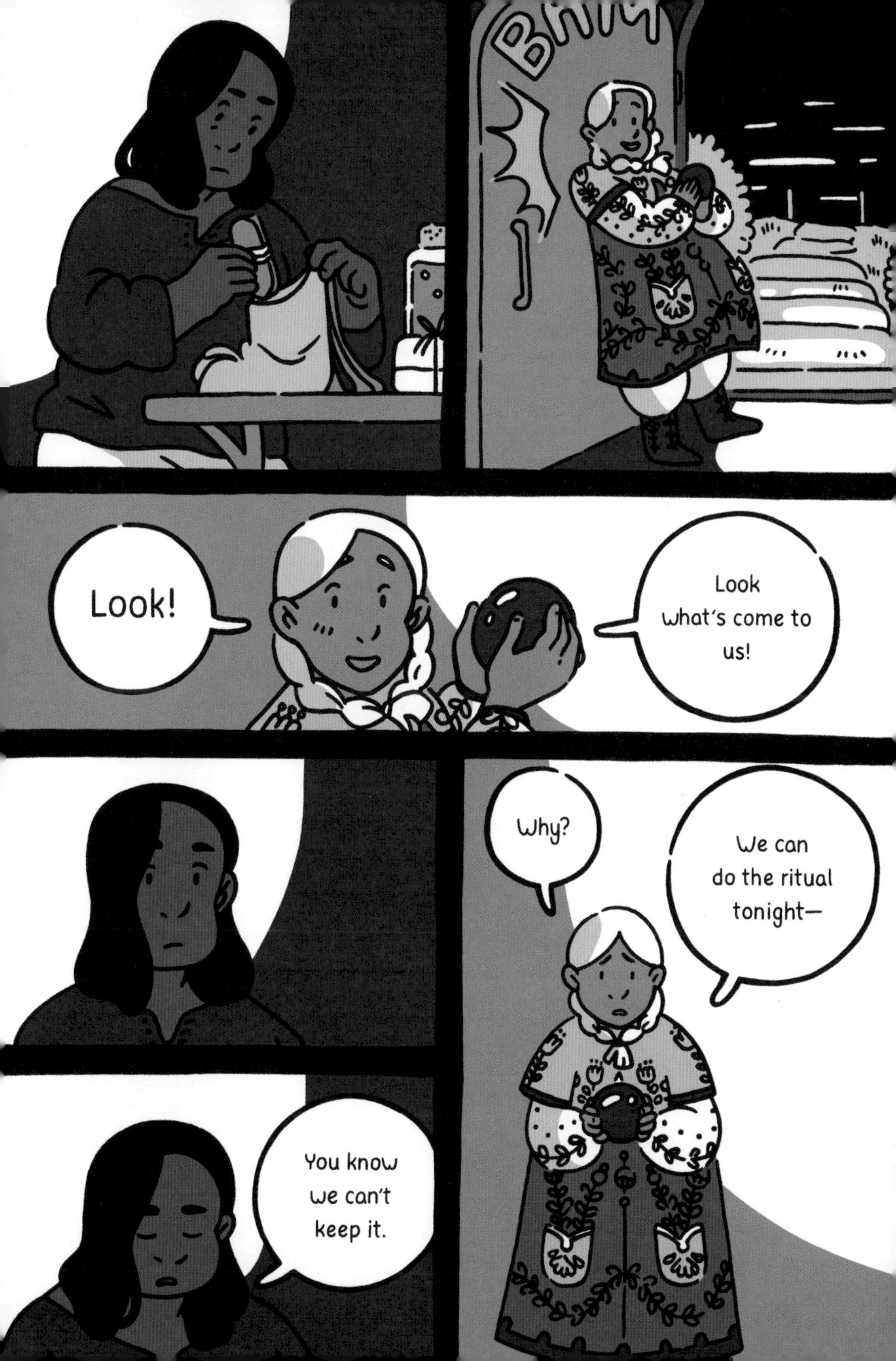
Look!
Look what's come to us!
Why?
We can do the ritual tonight—
You know we can't keep it.

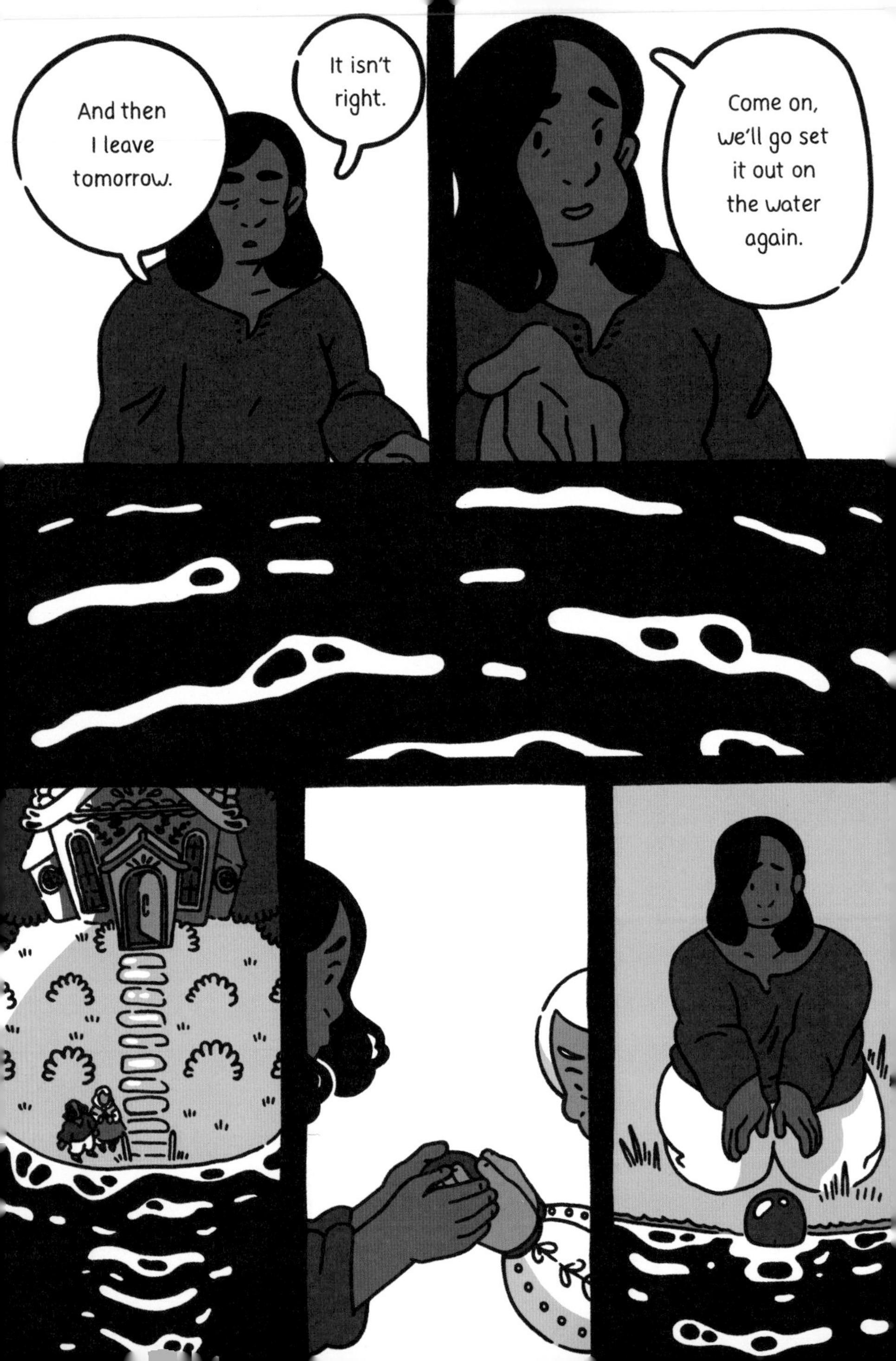
And then I leave tomorrow.
It isn't right.
Come on, we'll go set it out on the water again.

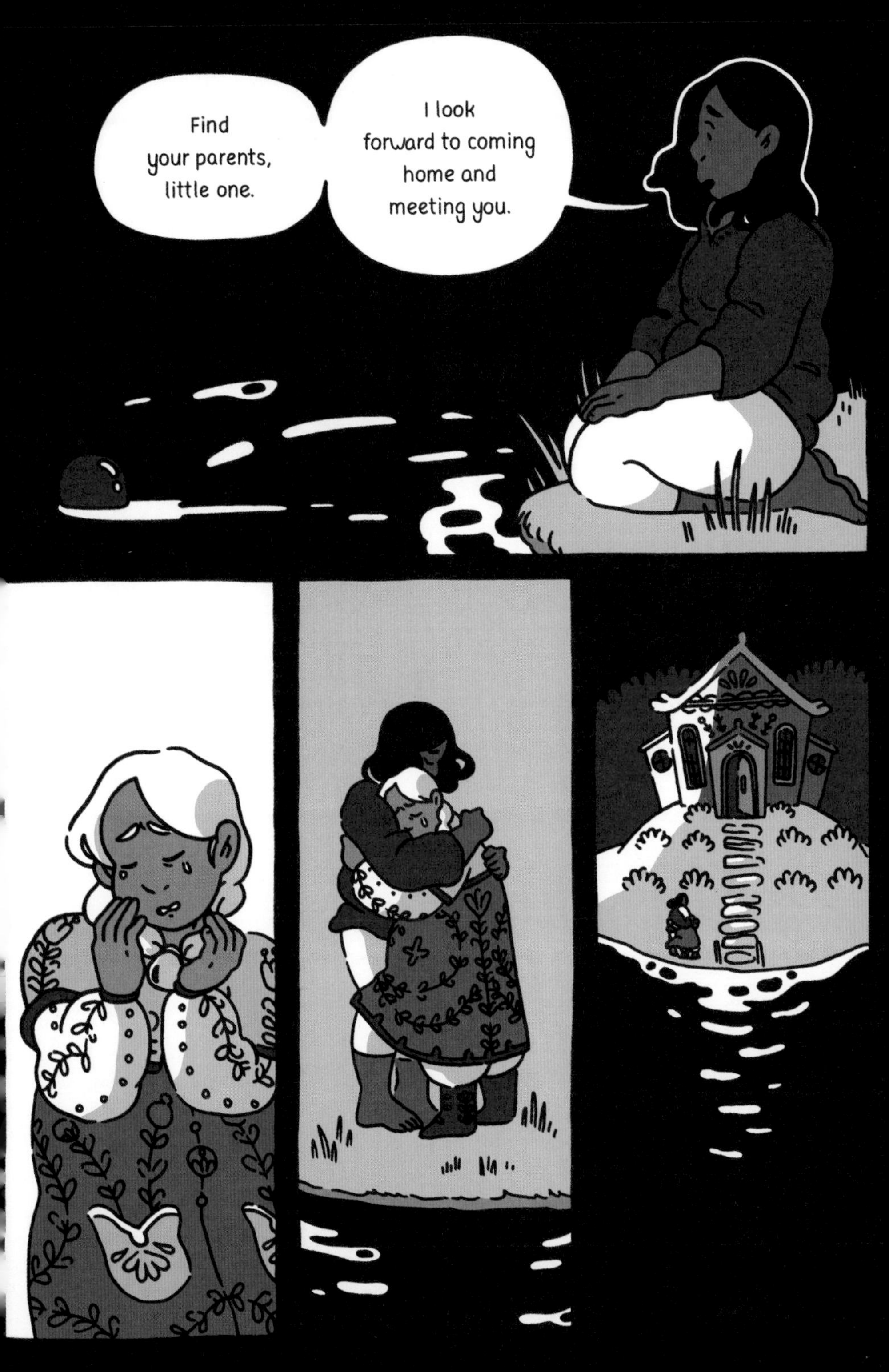
Find your parents, little one.
I look forward to coming home and meeting you.

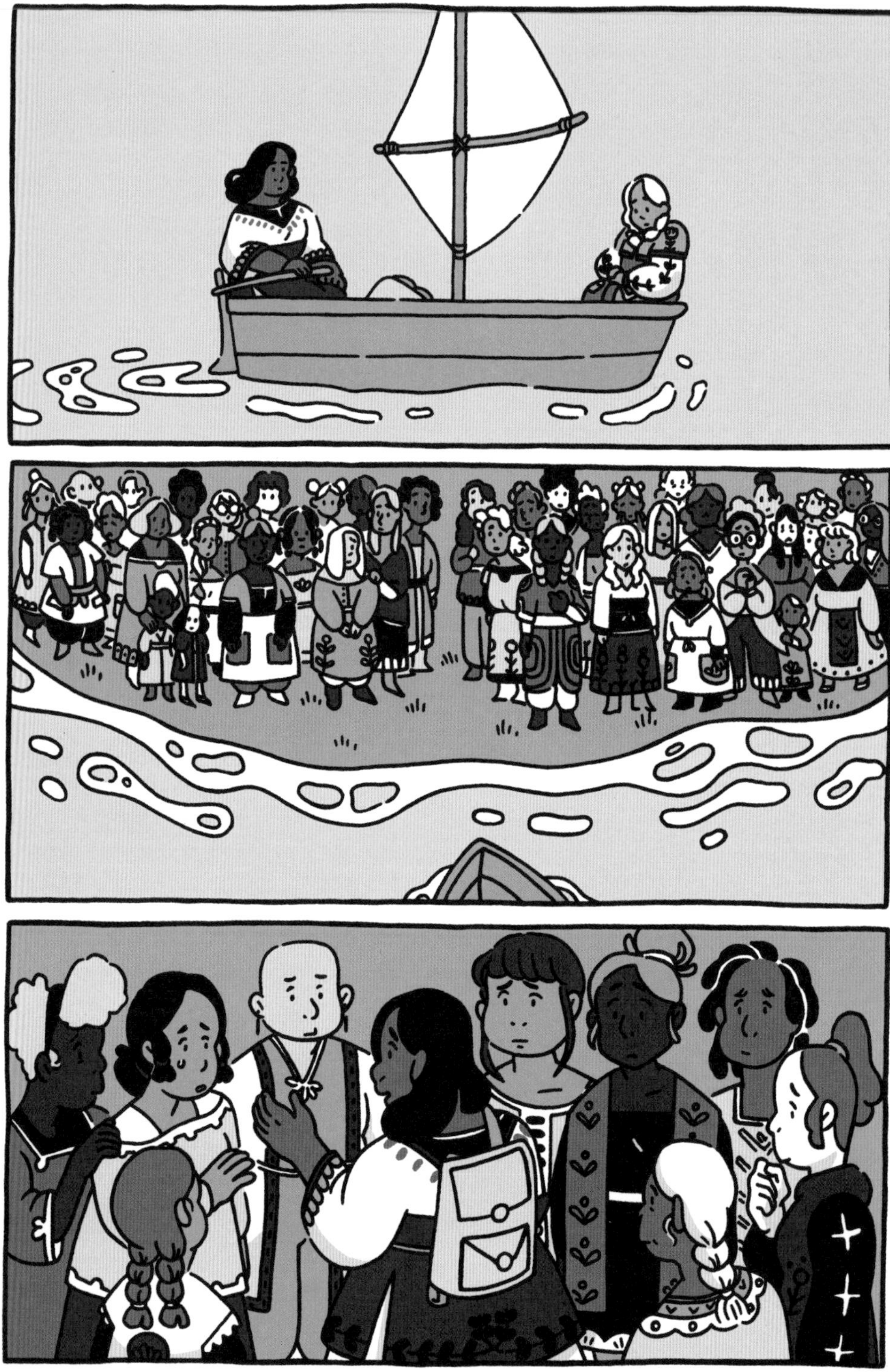

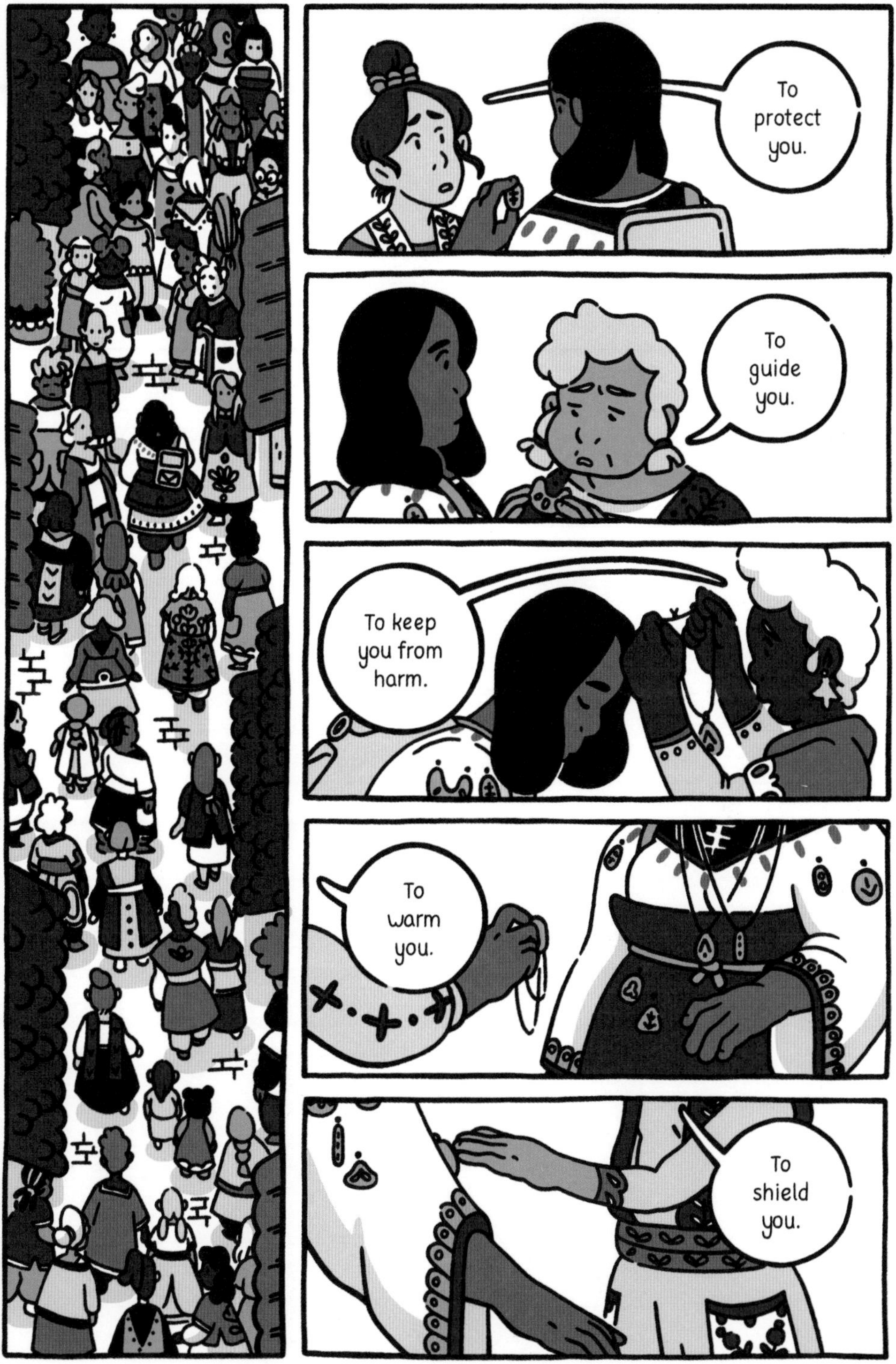
To protect you.
To guide you.
To keep you from harm.
To warm you.
To shield you.

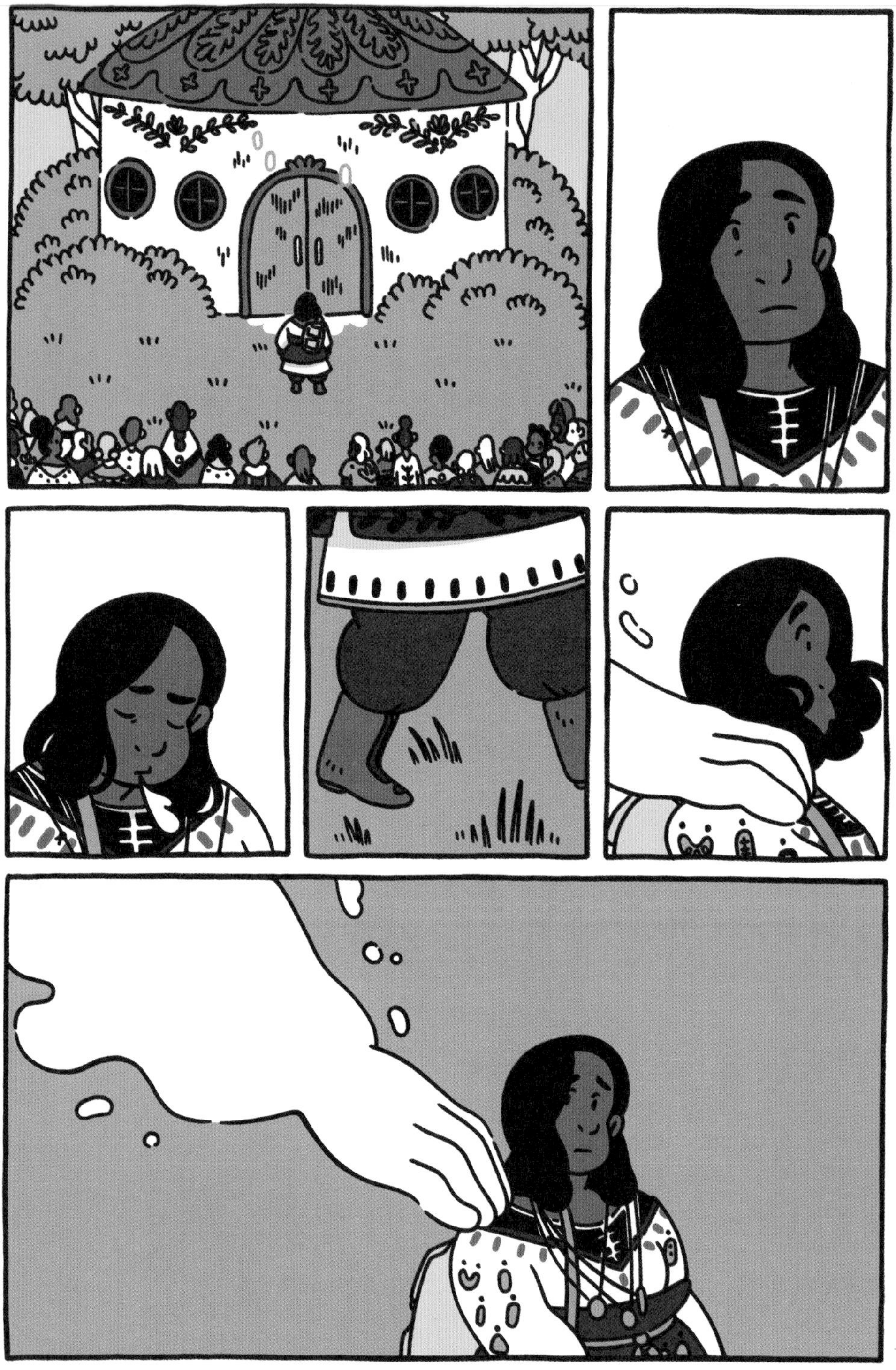

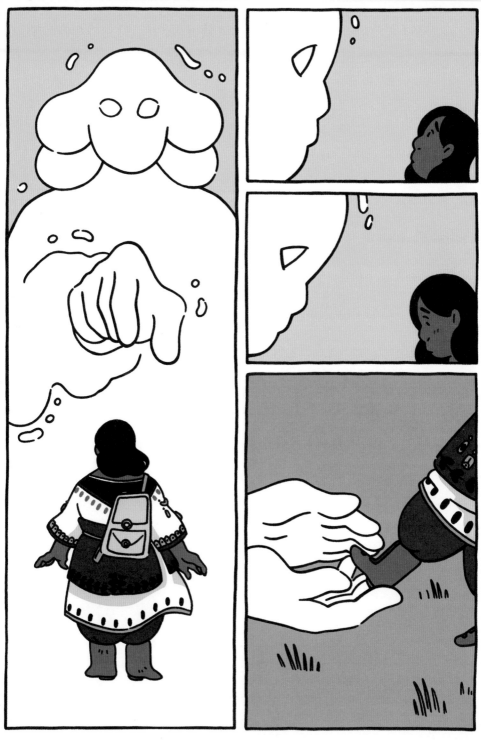

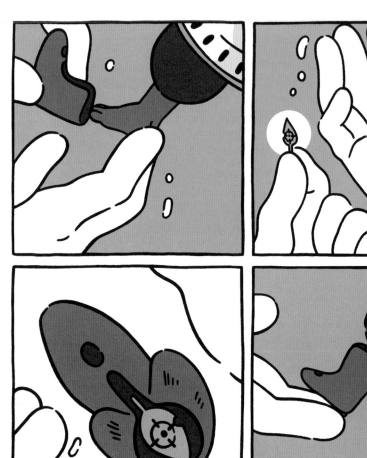
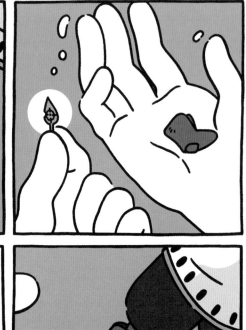

Preet—

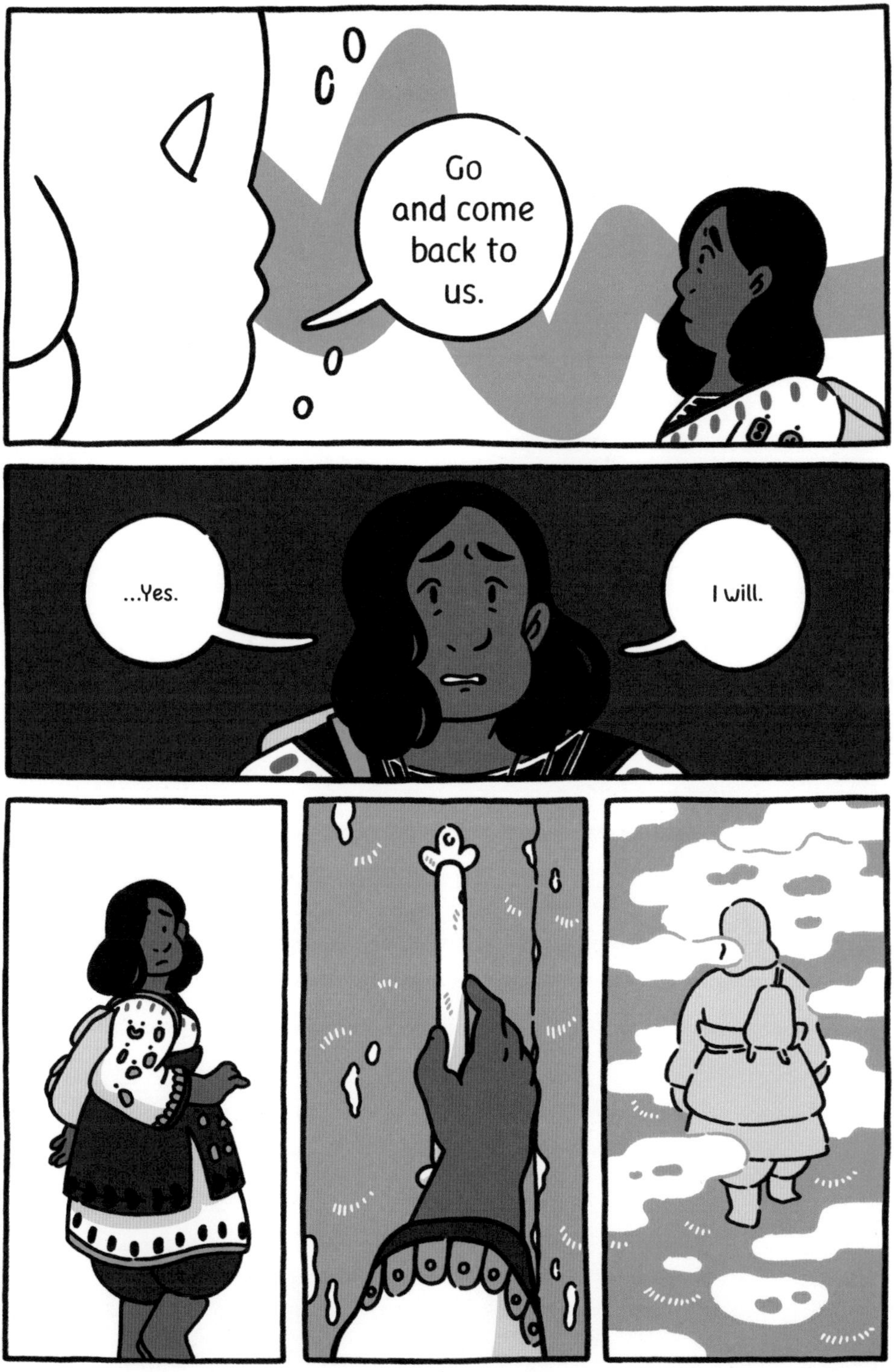
Go and come back to us.
...Yes.
I will.

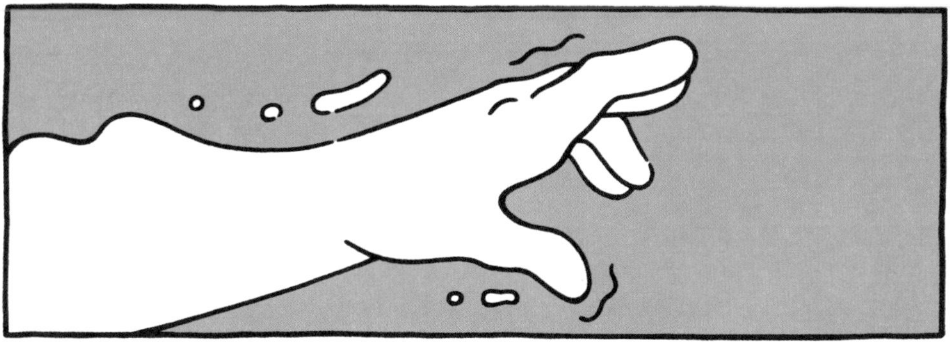

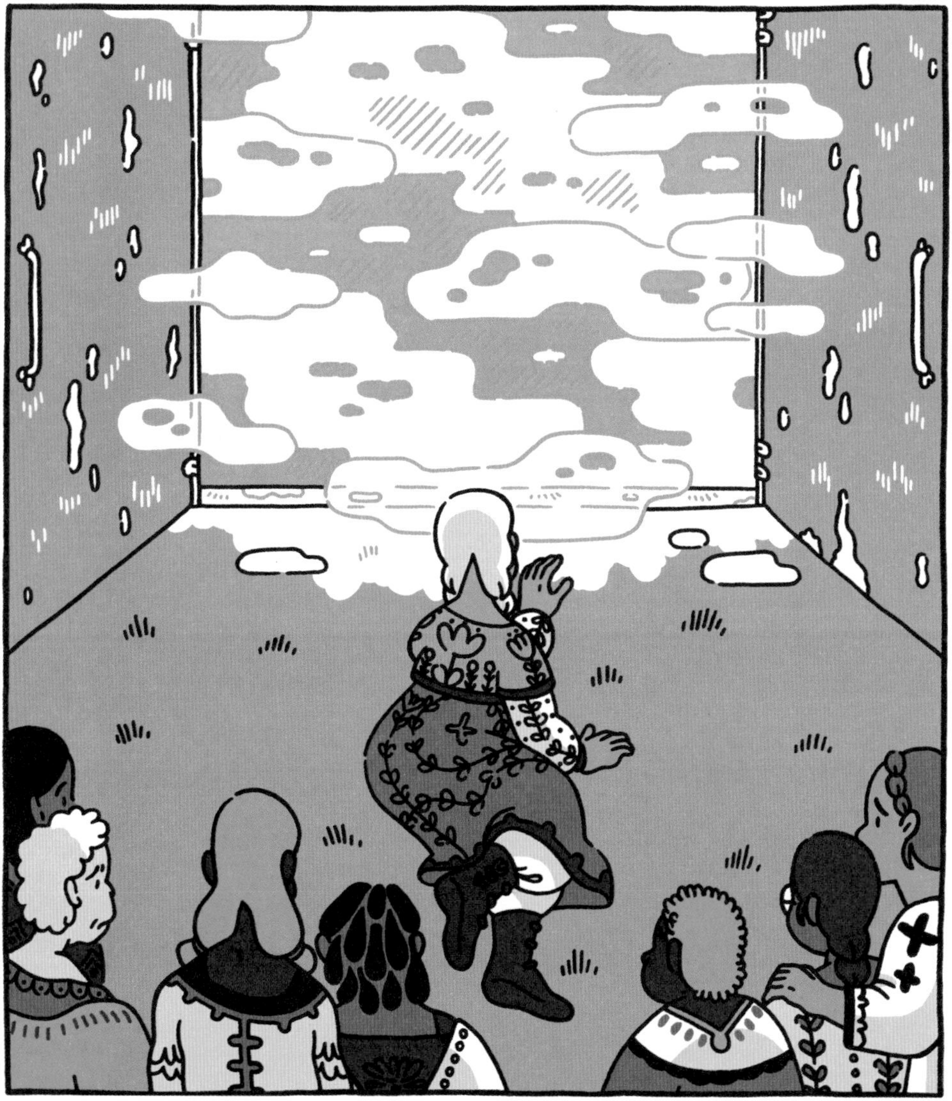

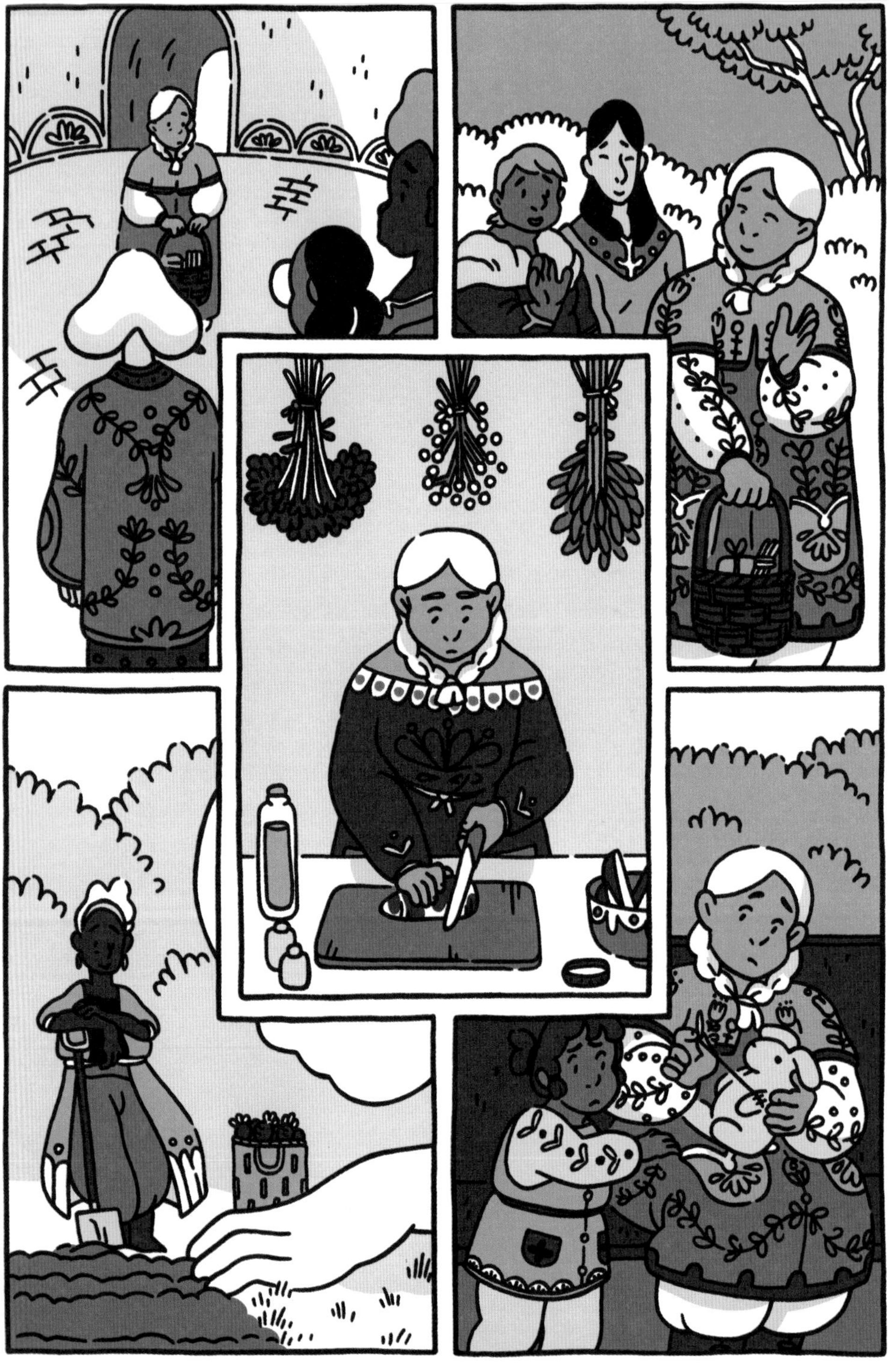

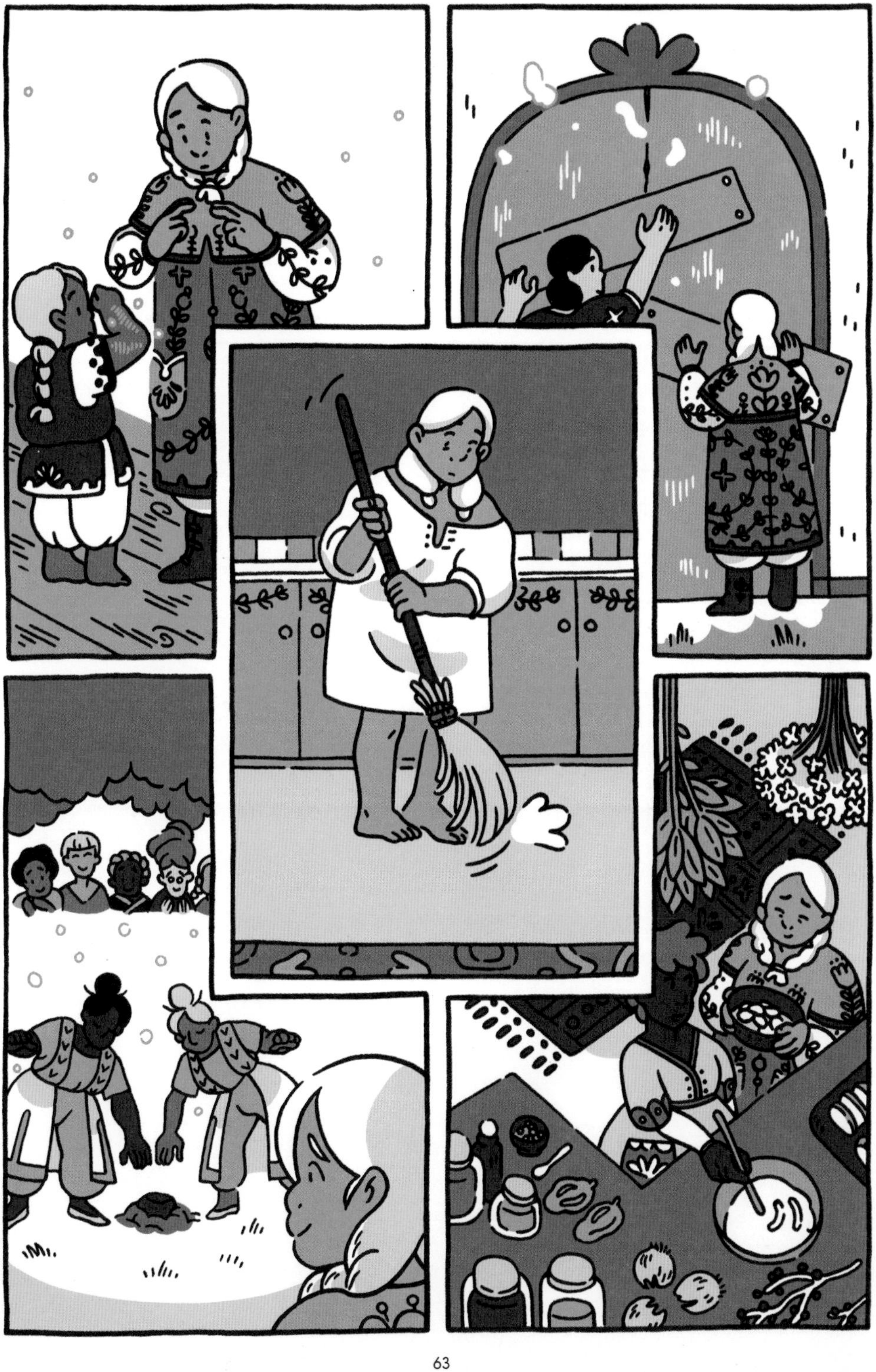

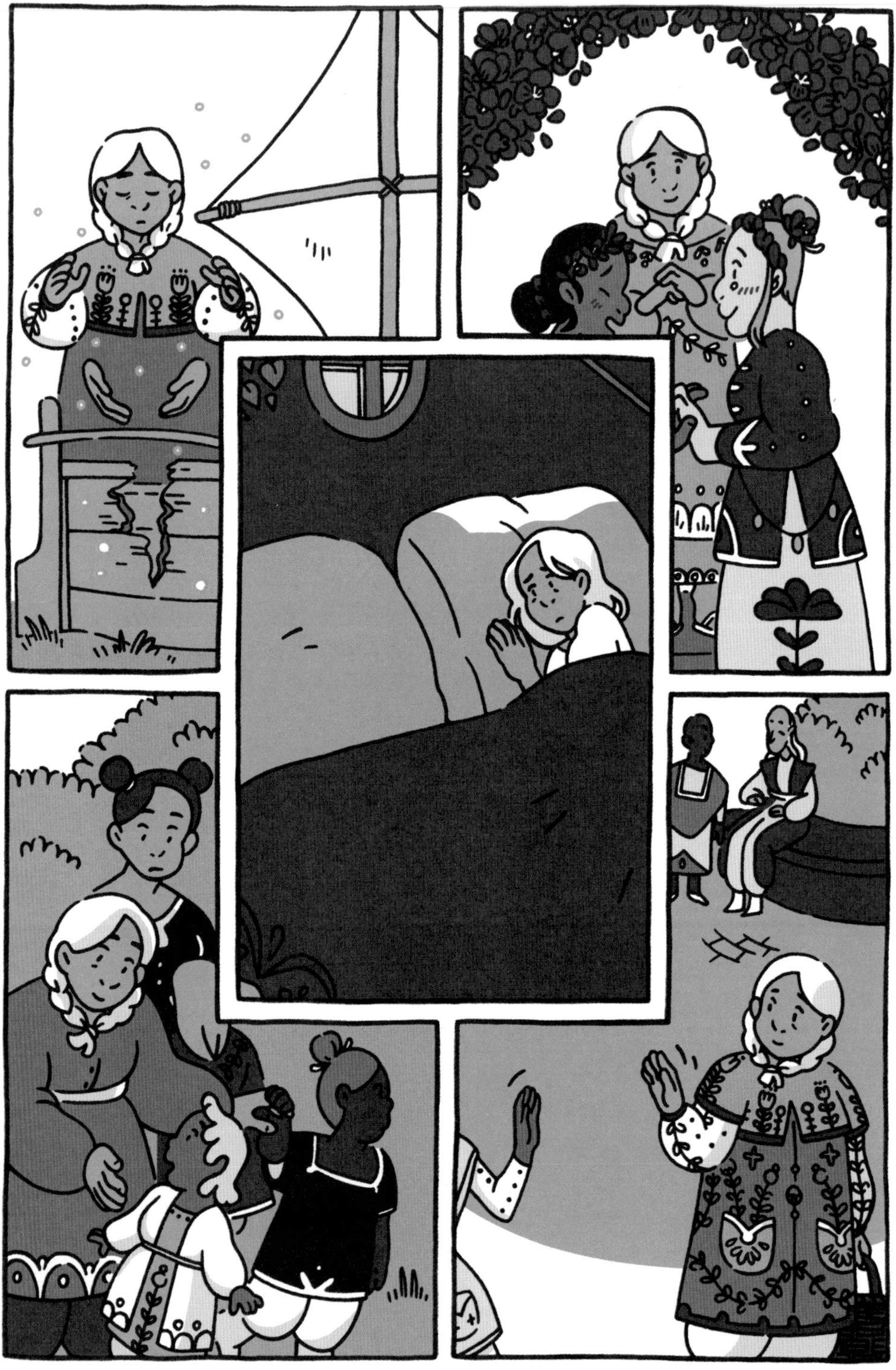

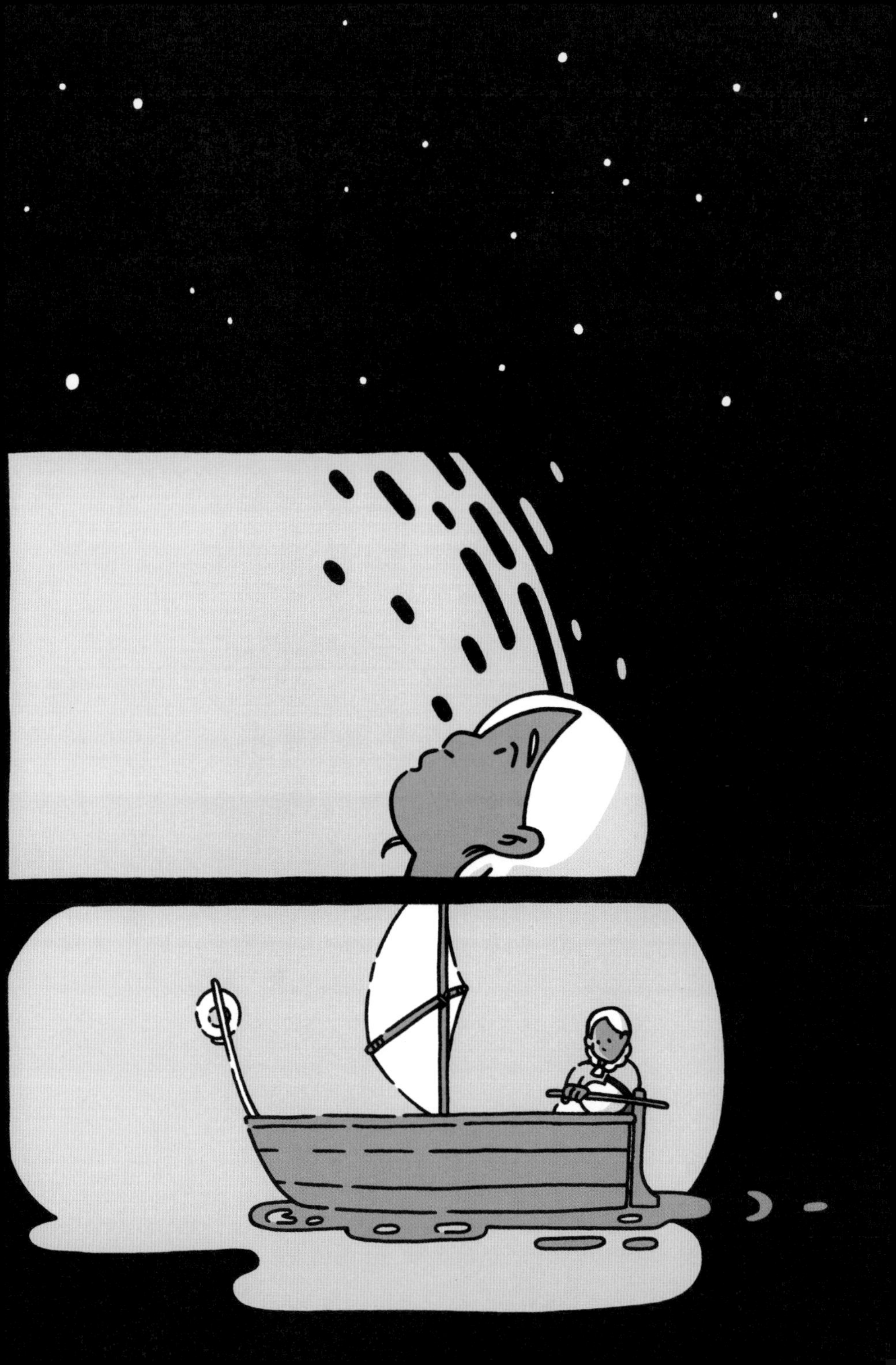

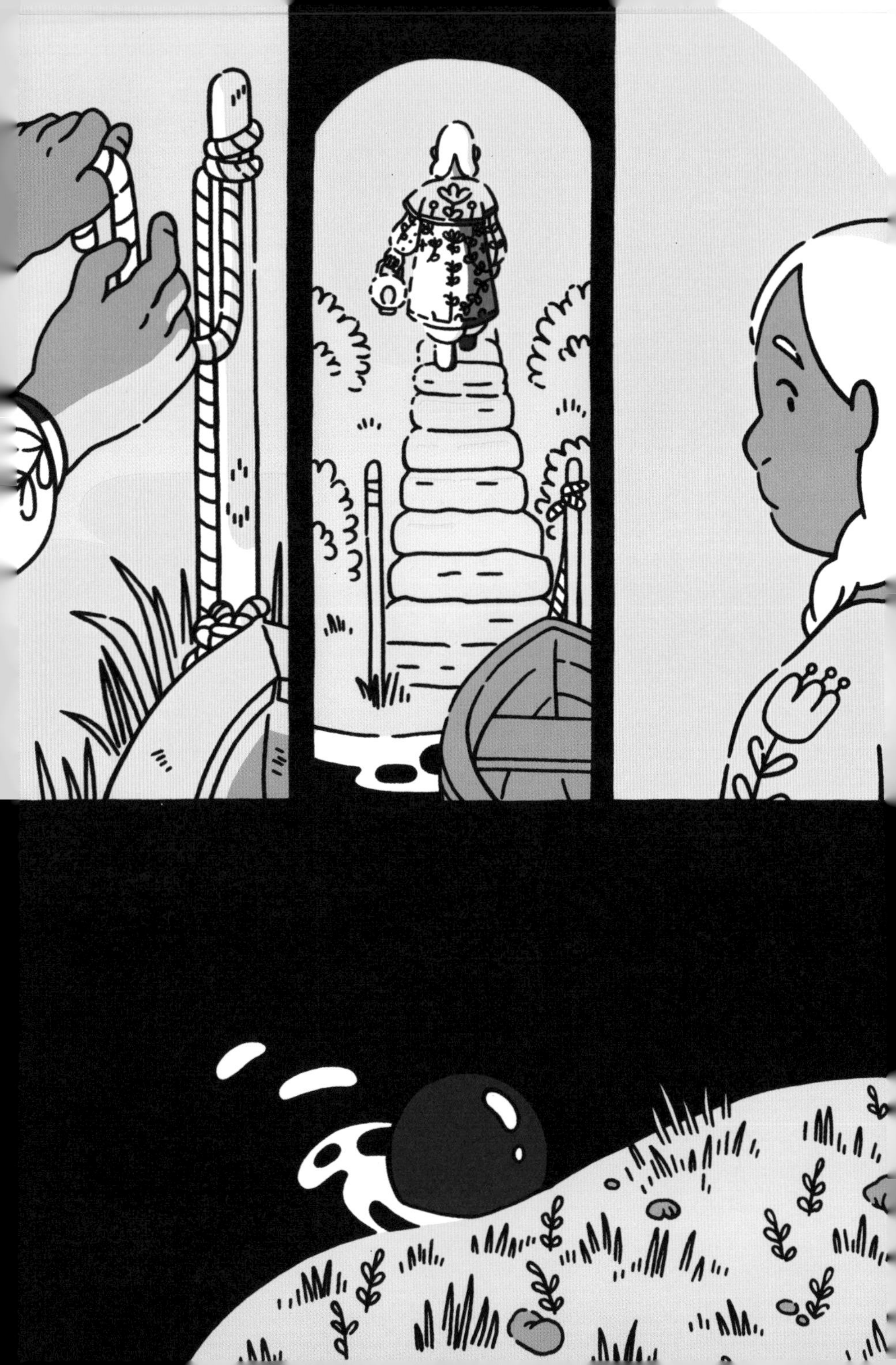

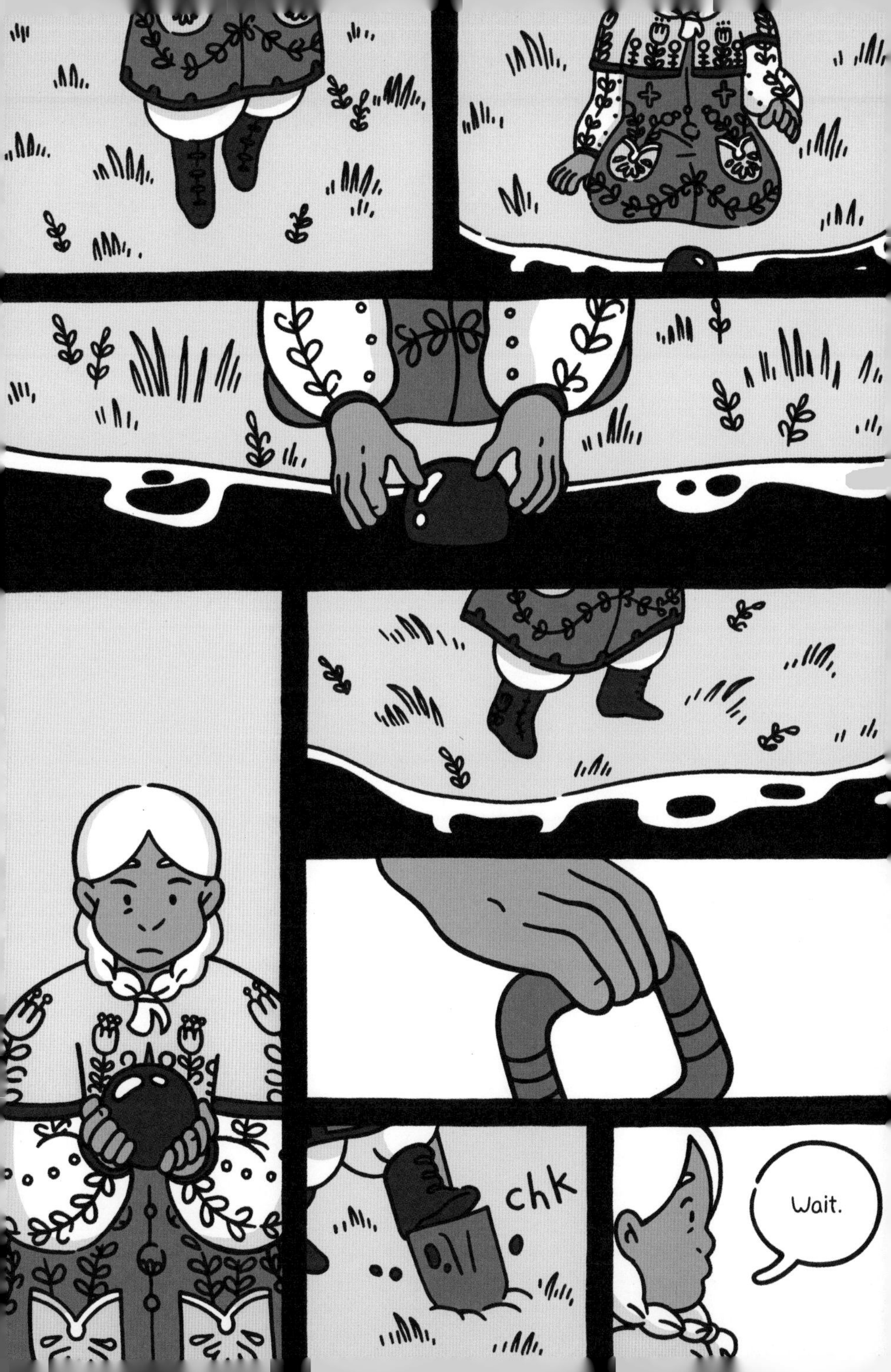
chk
Wait.

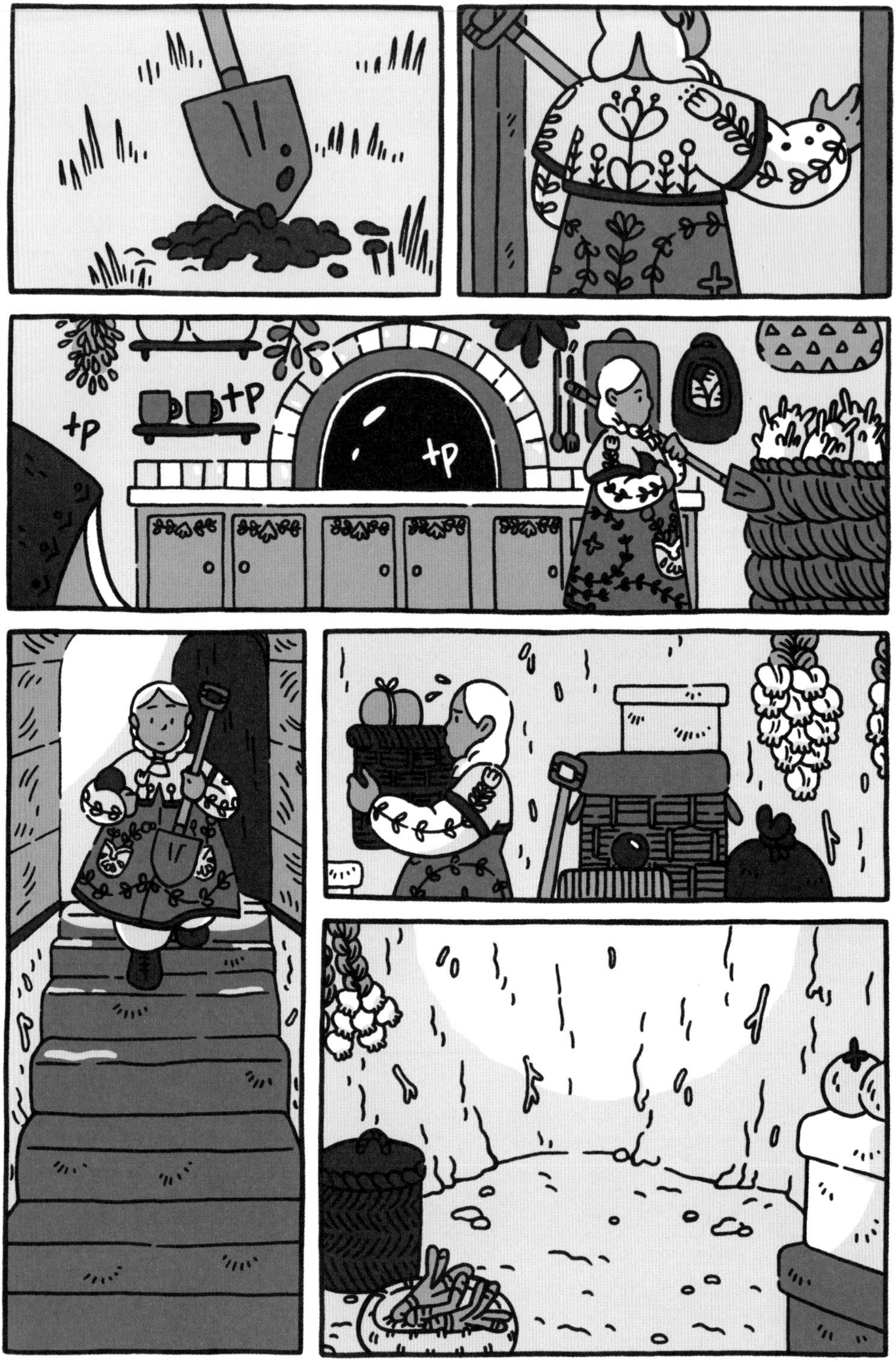
tp
tp
tp

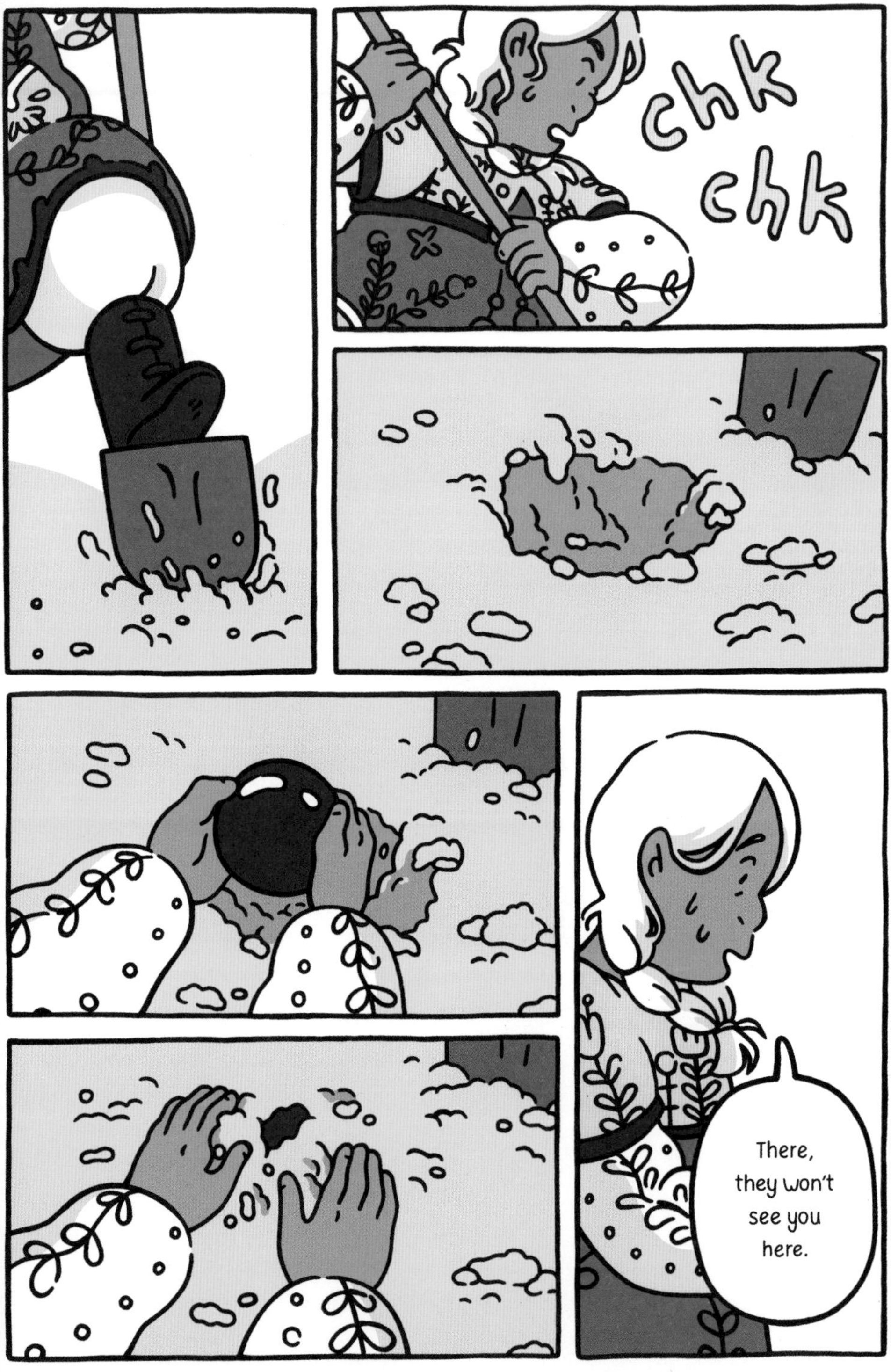
chk
chk
There, they won't see you here.

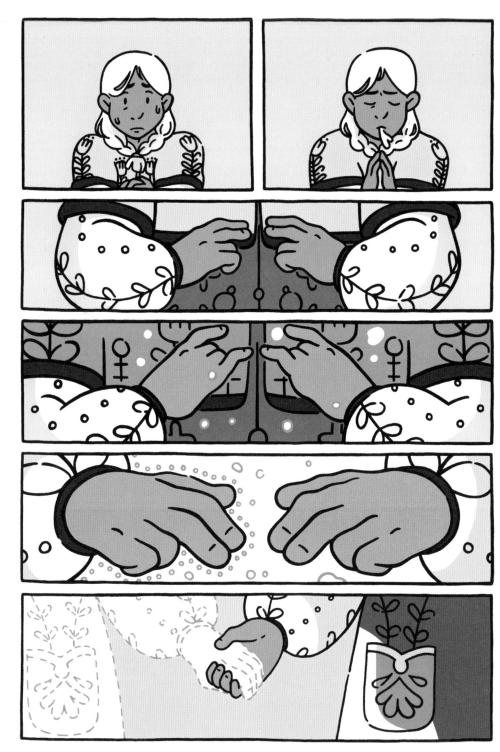

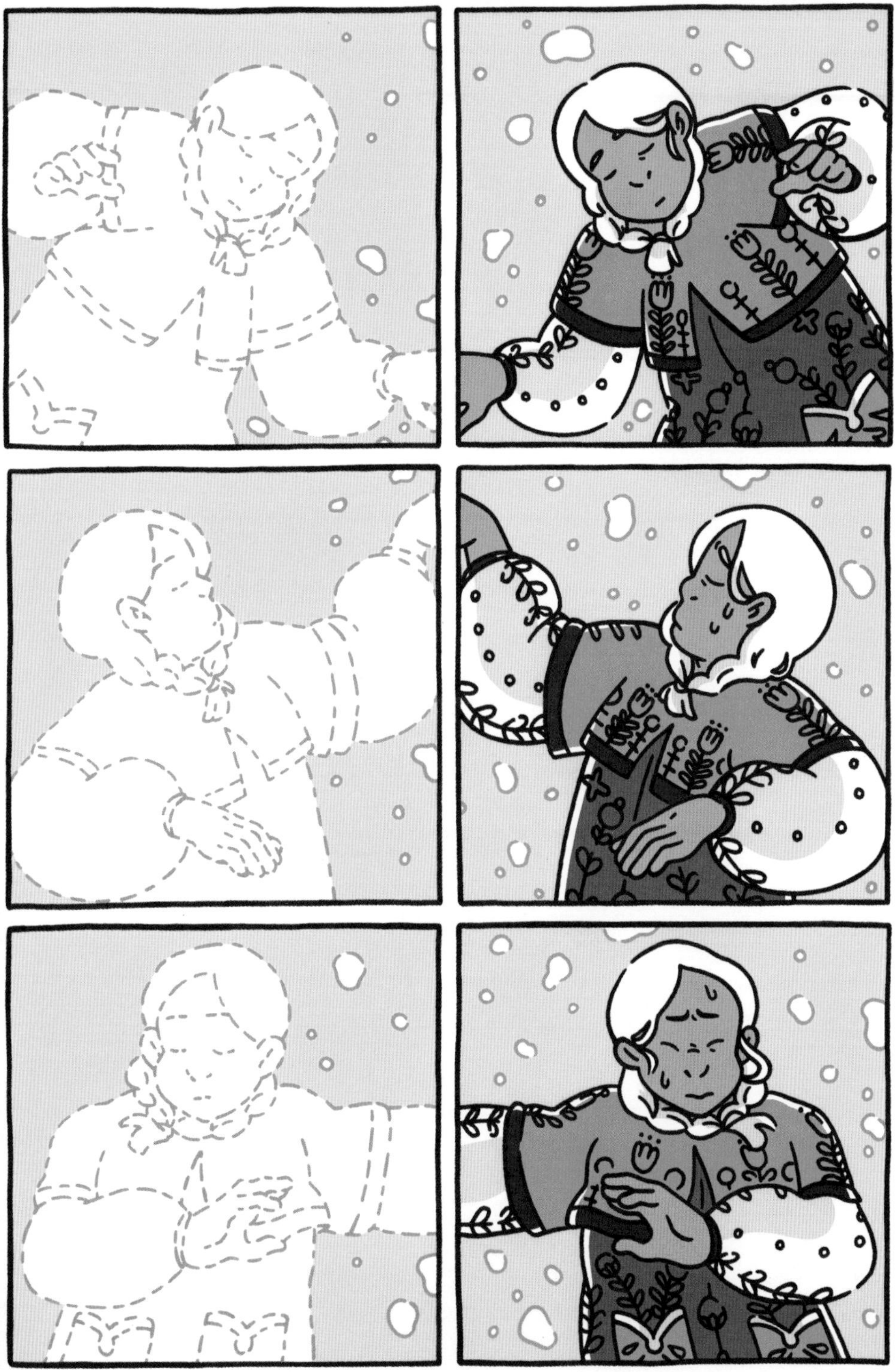

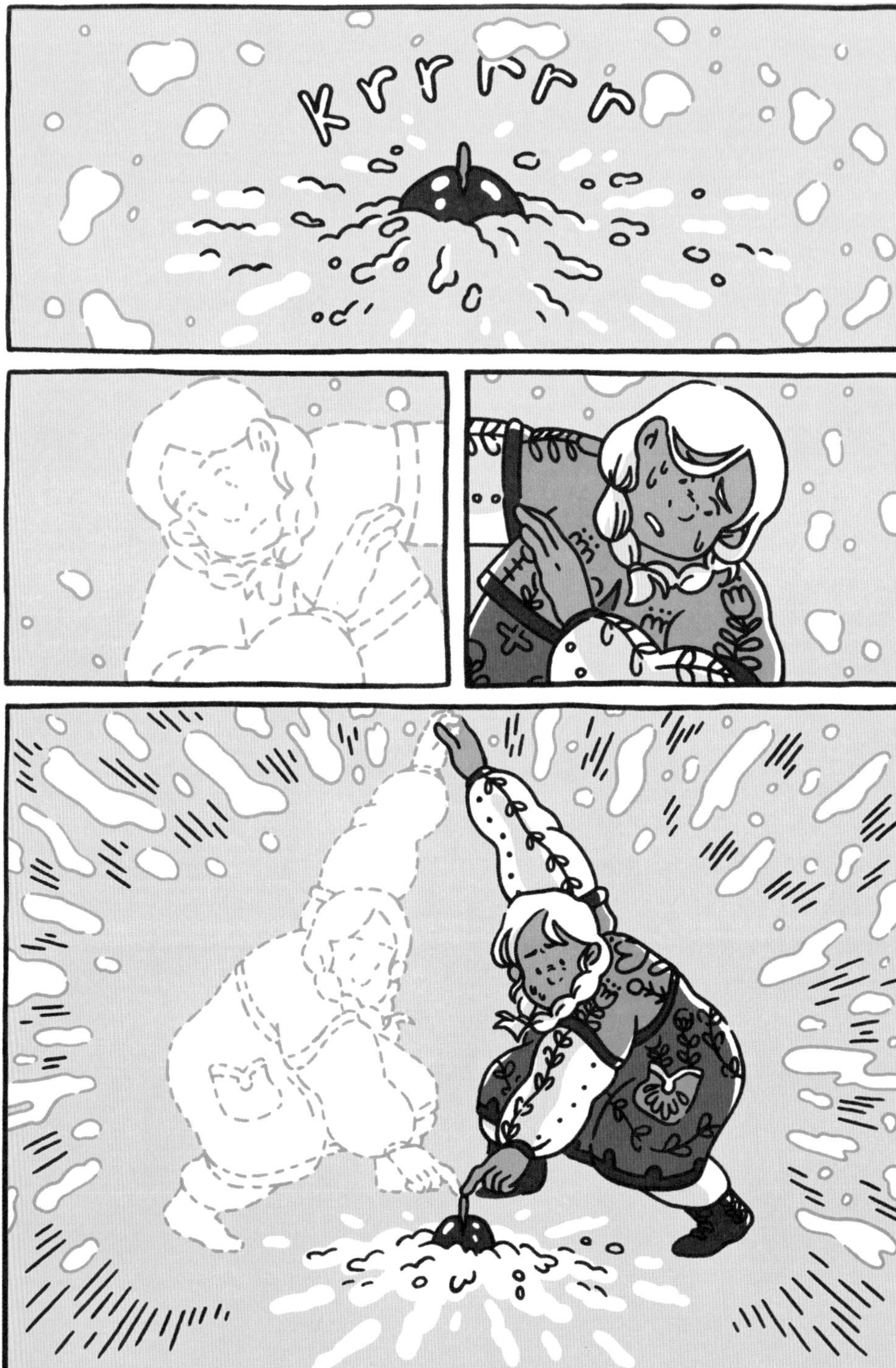
Krrrrrr

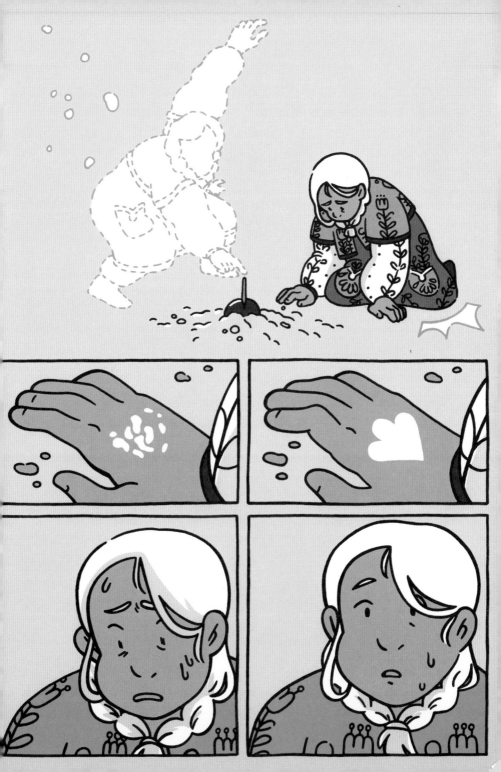

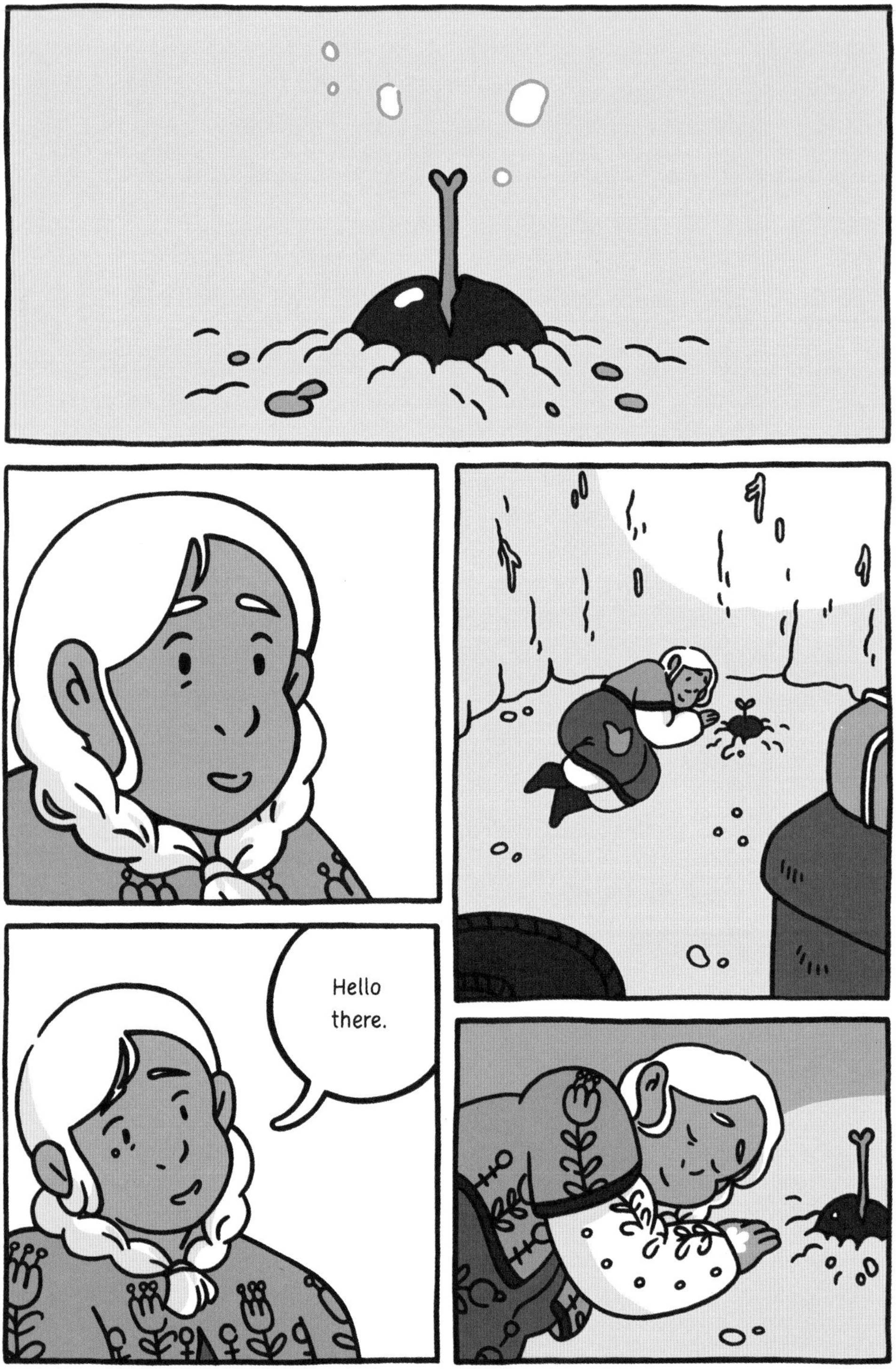
Hello there.

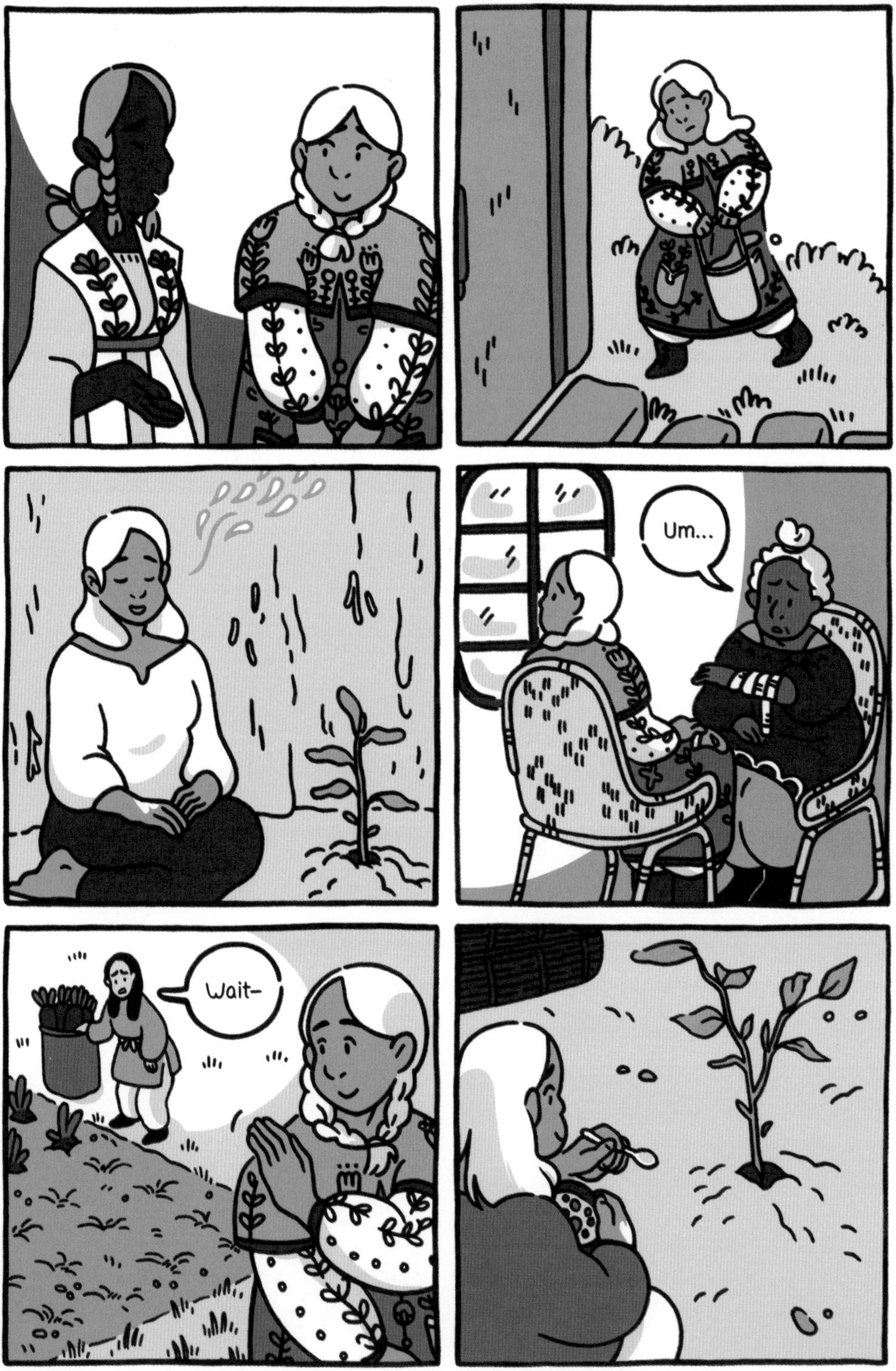
Um...
Wait-

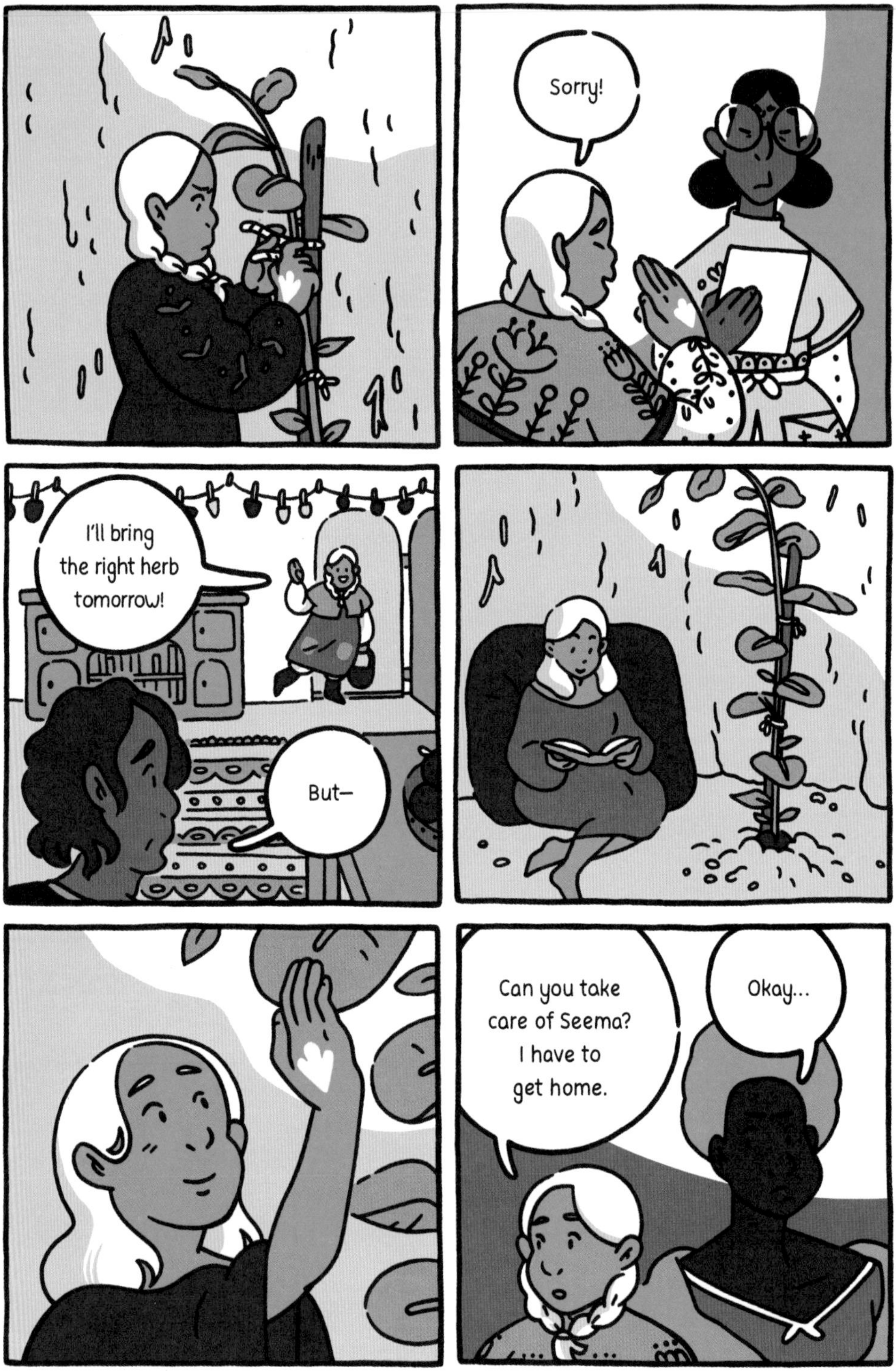
Sorry!
I'll bring the right herb tomorrow!
But—
Can you take care of Seema? I have to get home.
Okay...

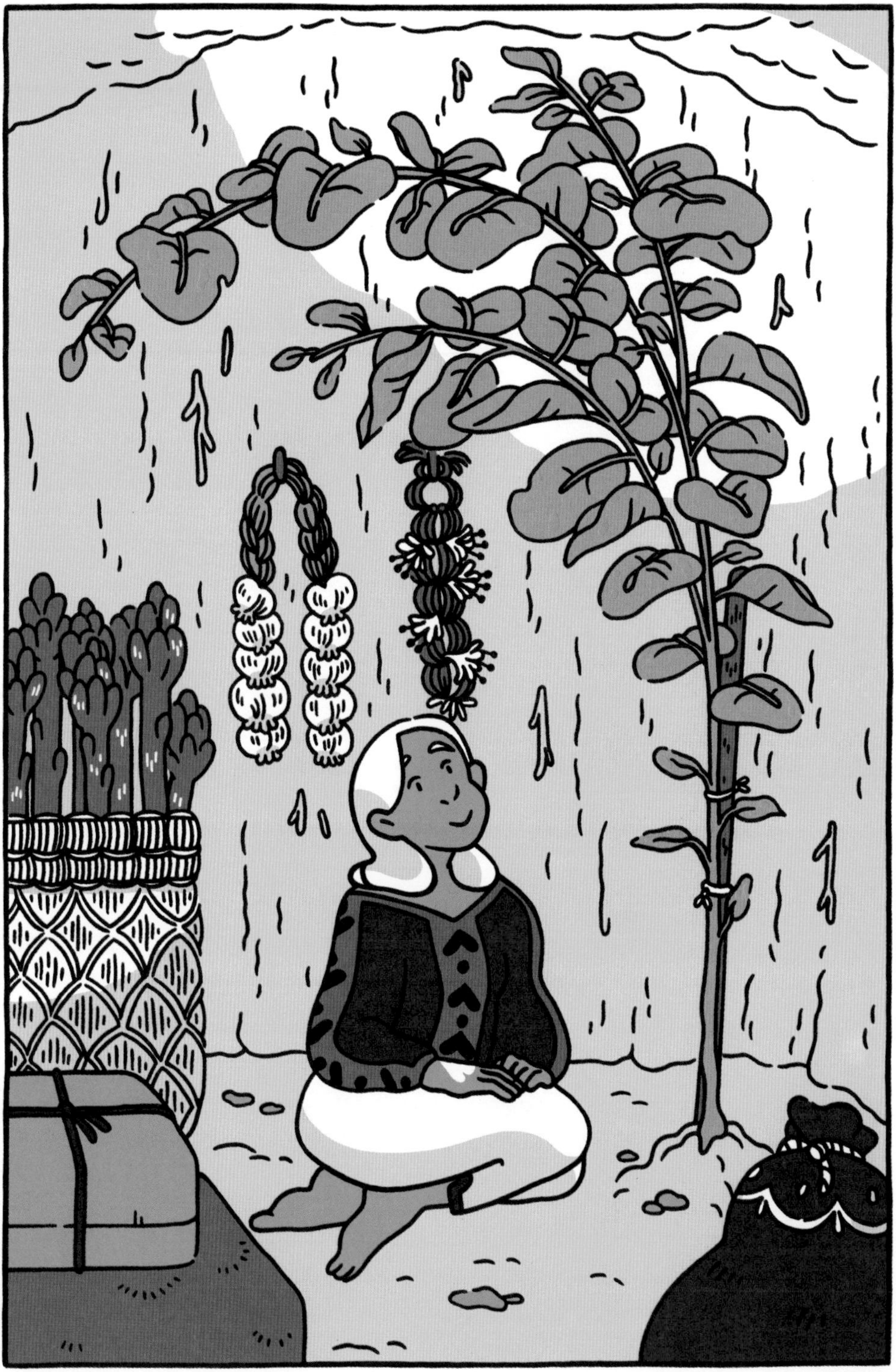

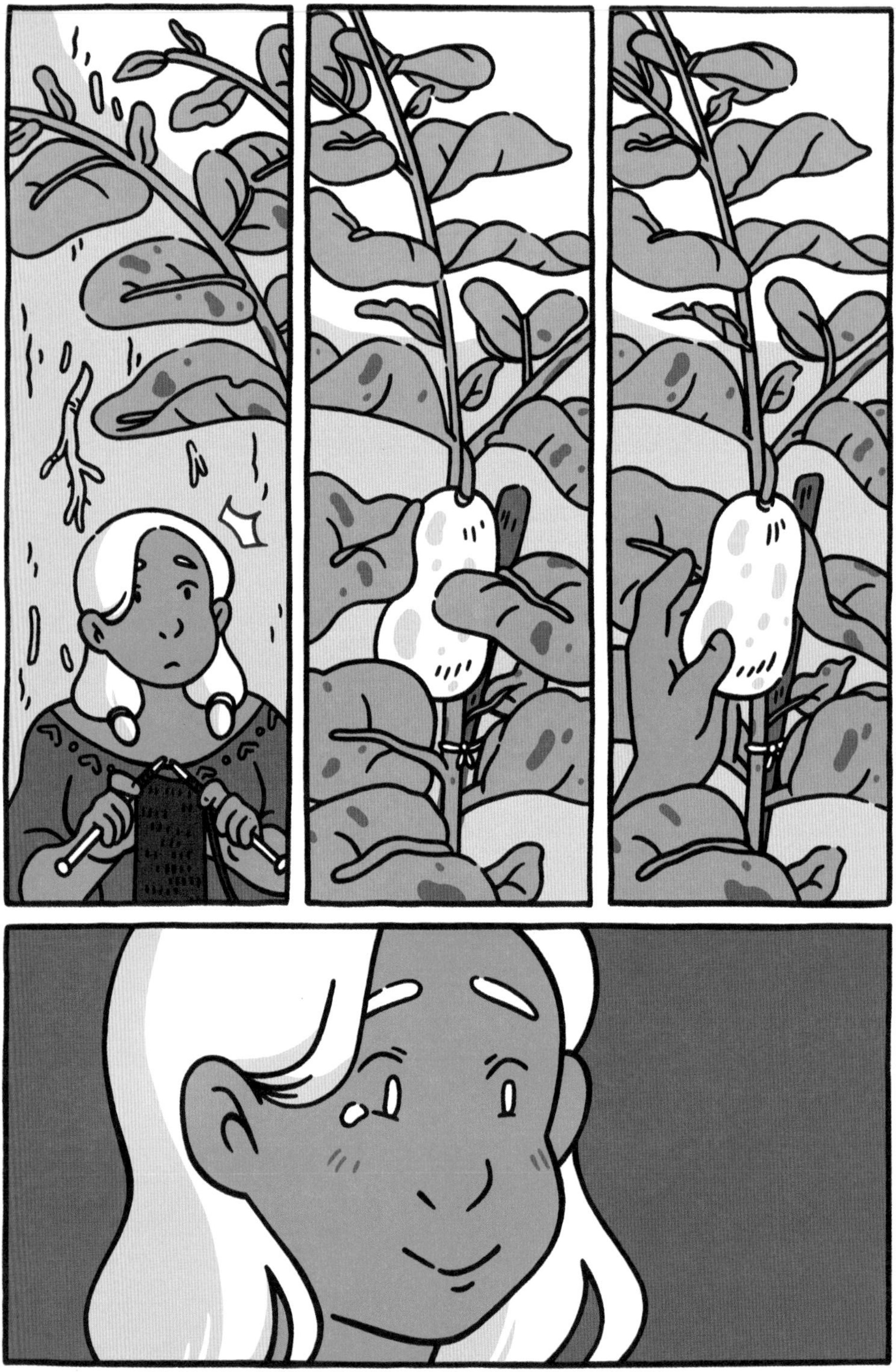

KKrrr

Krrr

rr

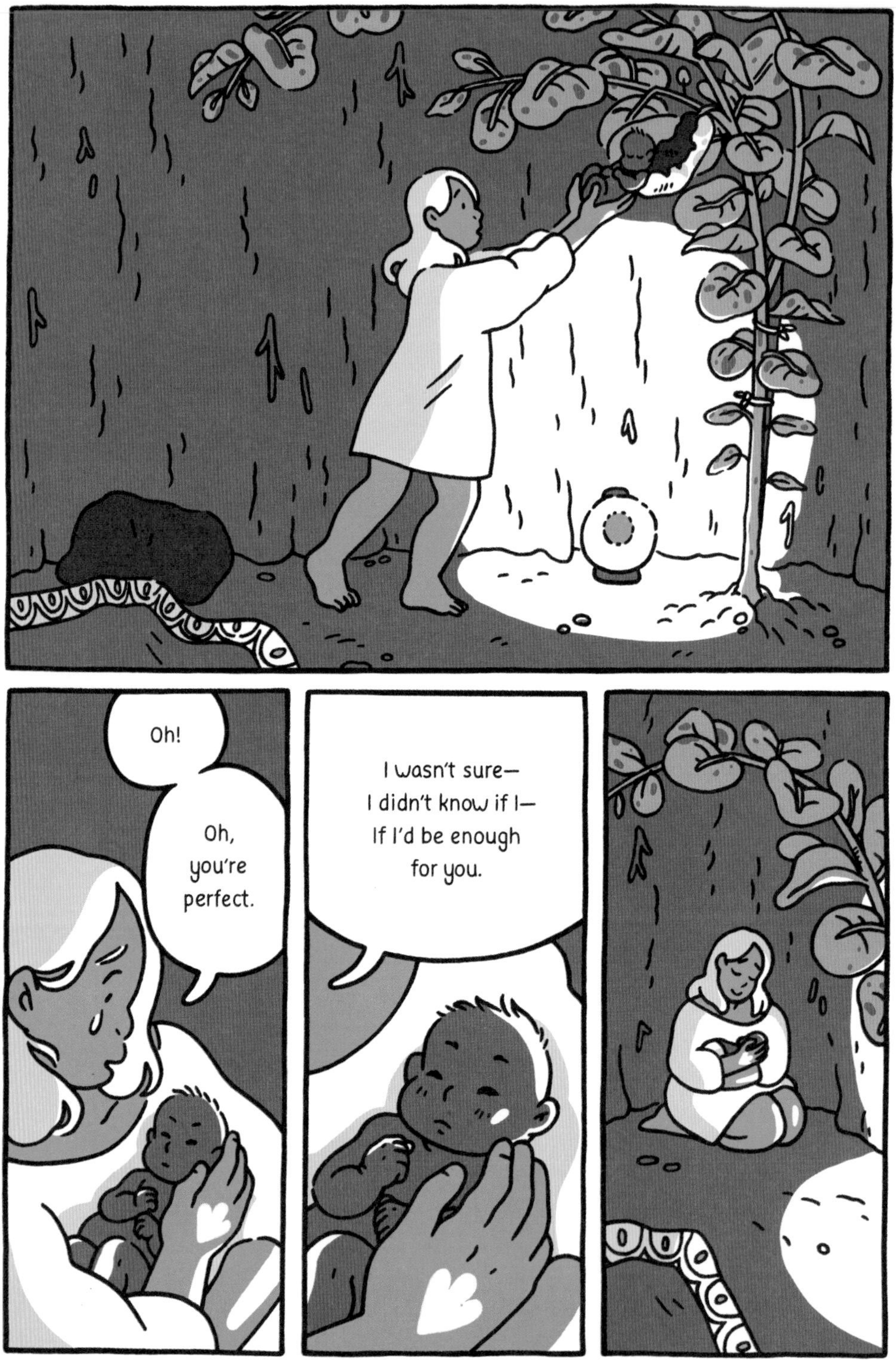
Oh!
Oh, you're perfect.
I wasn't sure— I didn't know if I— If I'd be enough for you.

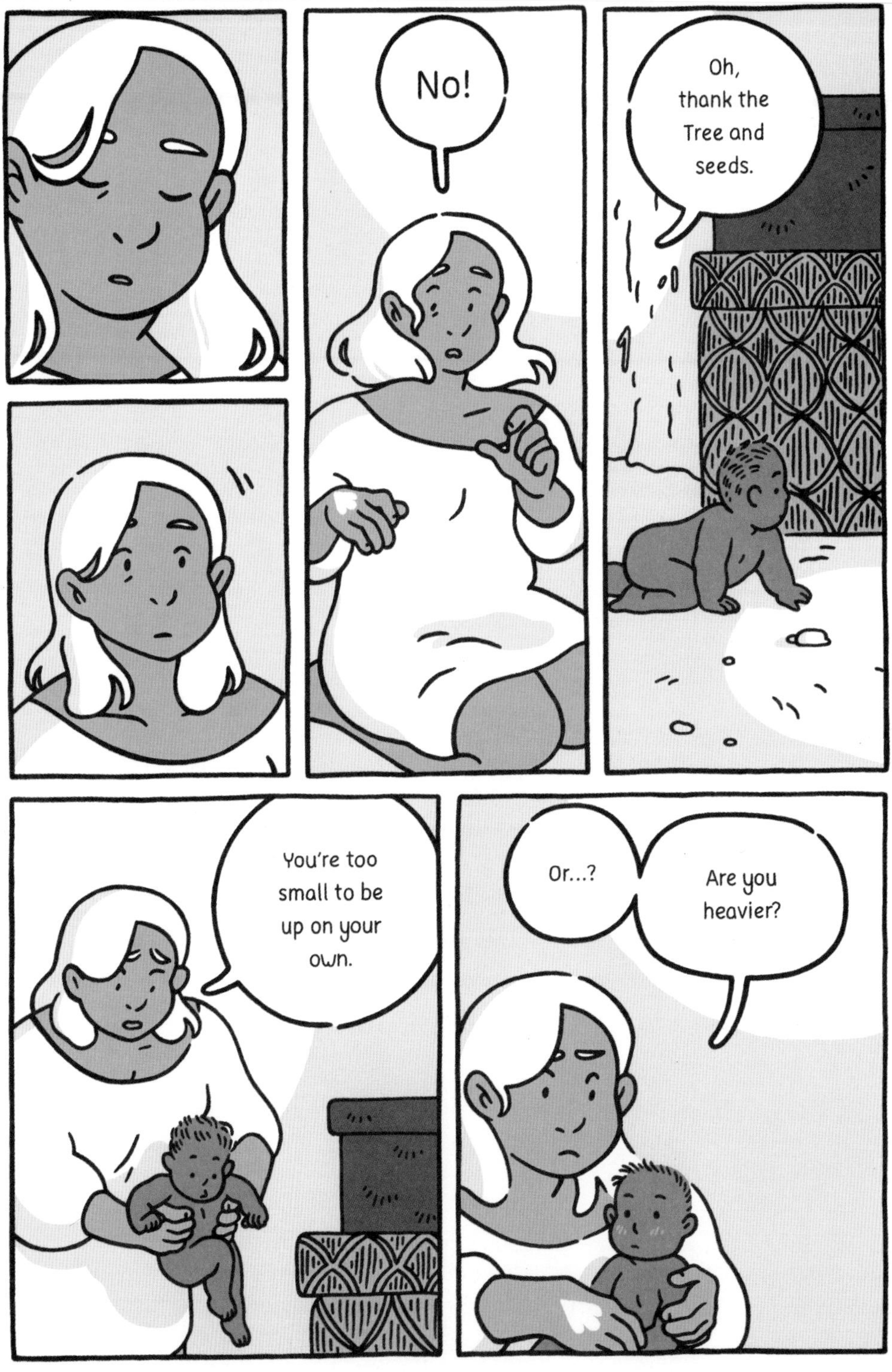
No!
Oh, thank the Tree and seeds.
You're too small to be up on your own.
Or...?
Are you heavier?

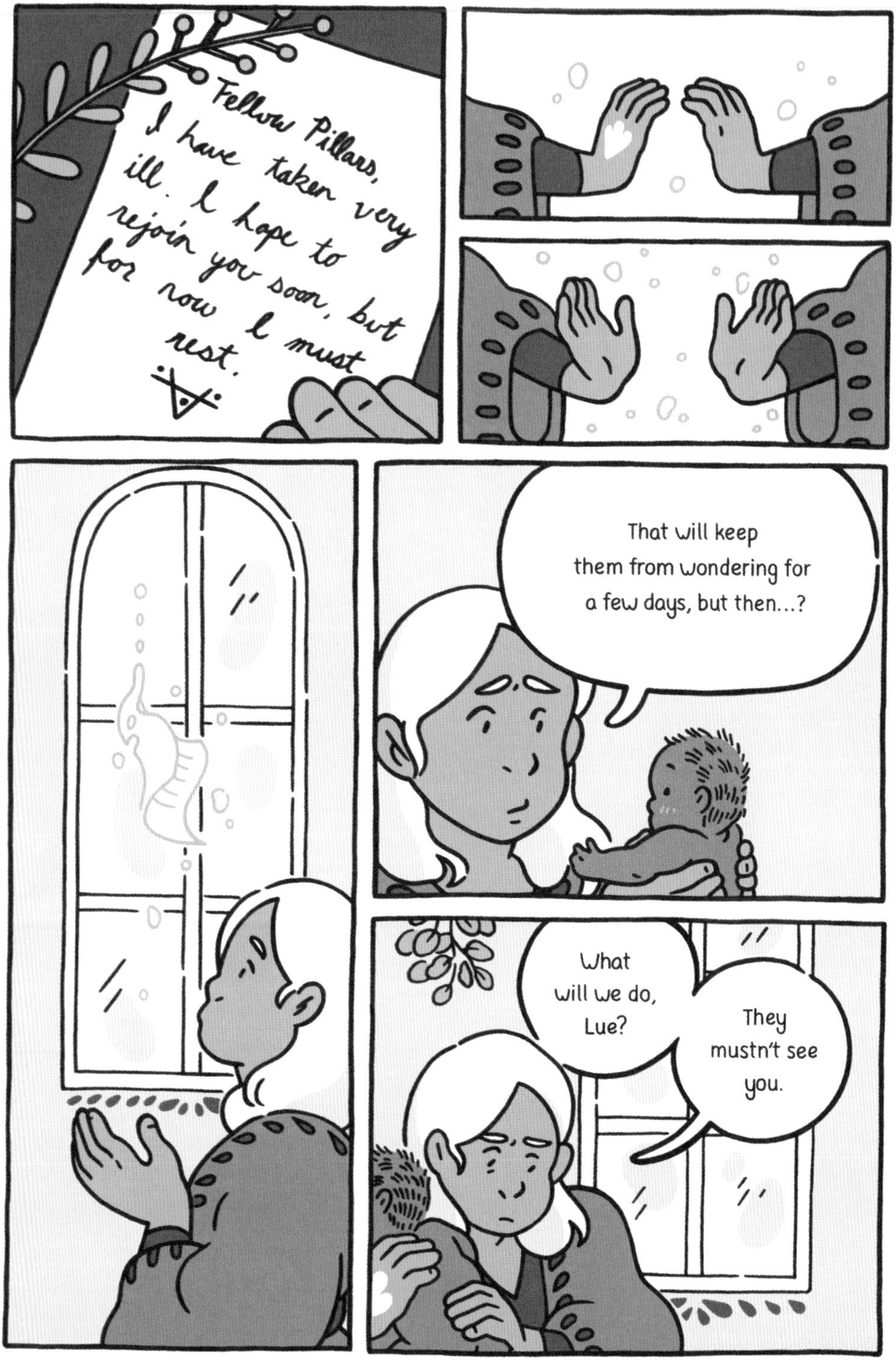
Fellow Pillars,
I have taken very ill. I hope to rejoin you soon, but for now I must rest.
That will keep them from wondering for a few days, but then...?
What will we do, Lue?
They mustn't see you.

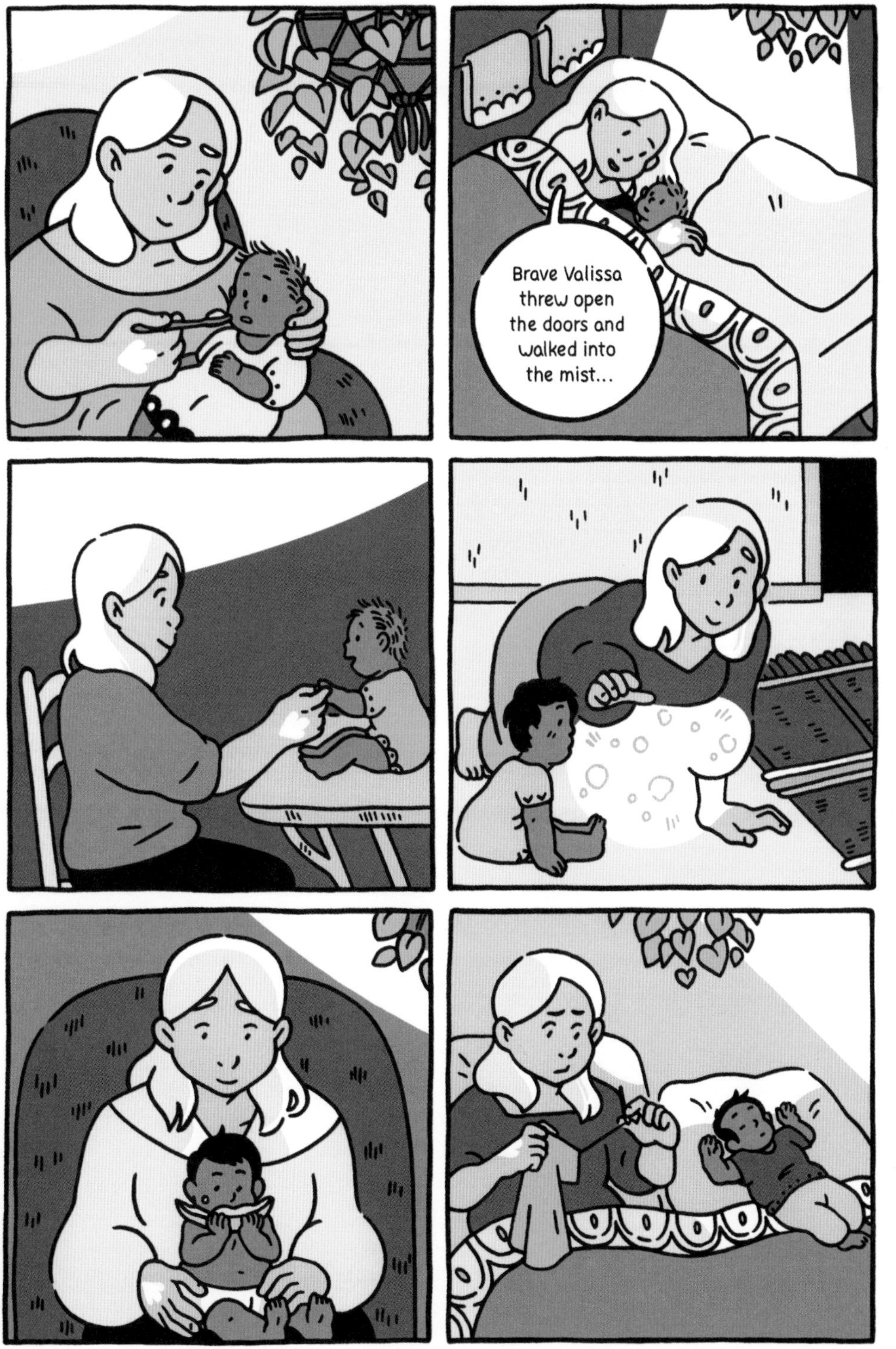
Brave Valissa threw open the doors and walked into the mist...

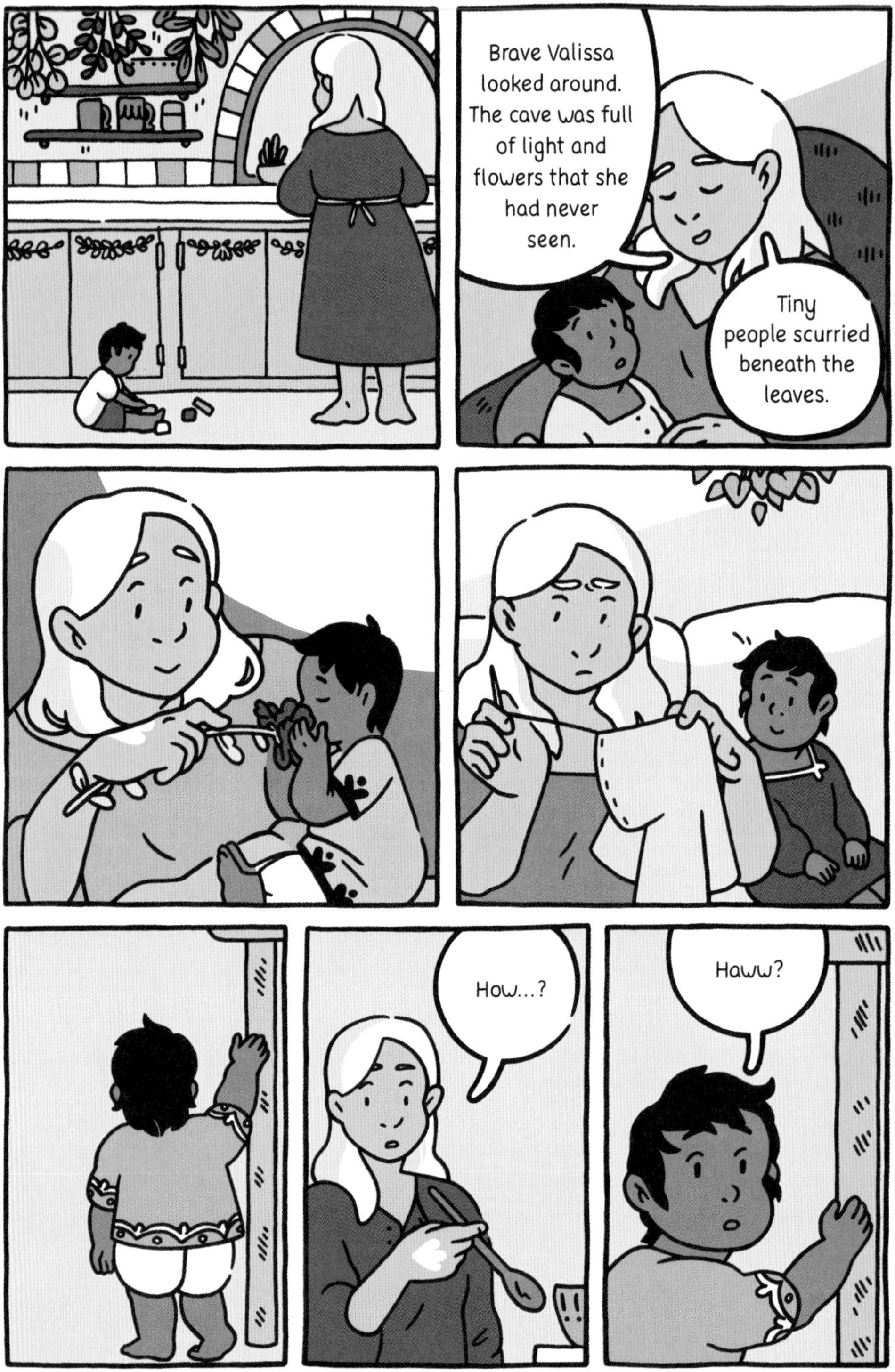
Brave Valissa looked around. The cave was full of light and flowers that she had never seen.
Tiny people scurried beneath the leaves.
How...?
Haww?

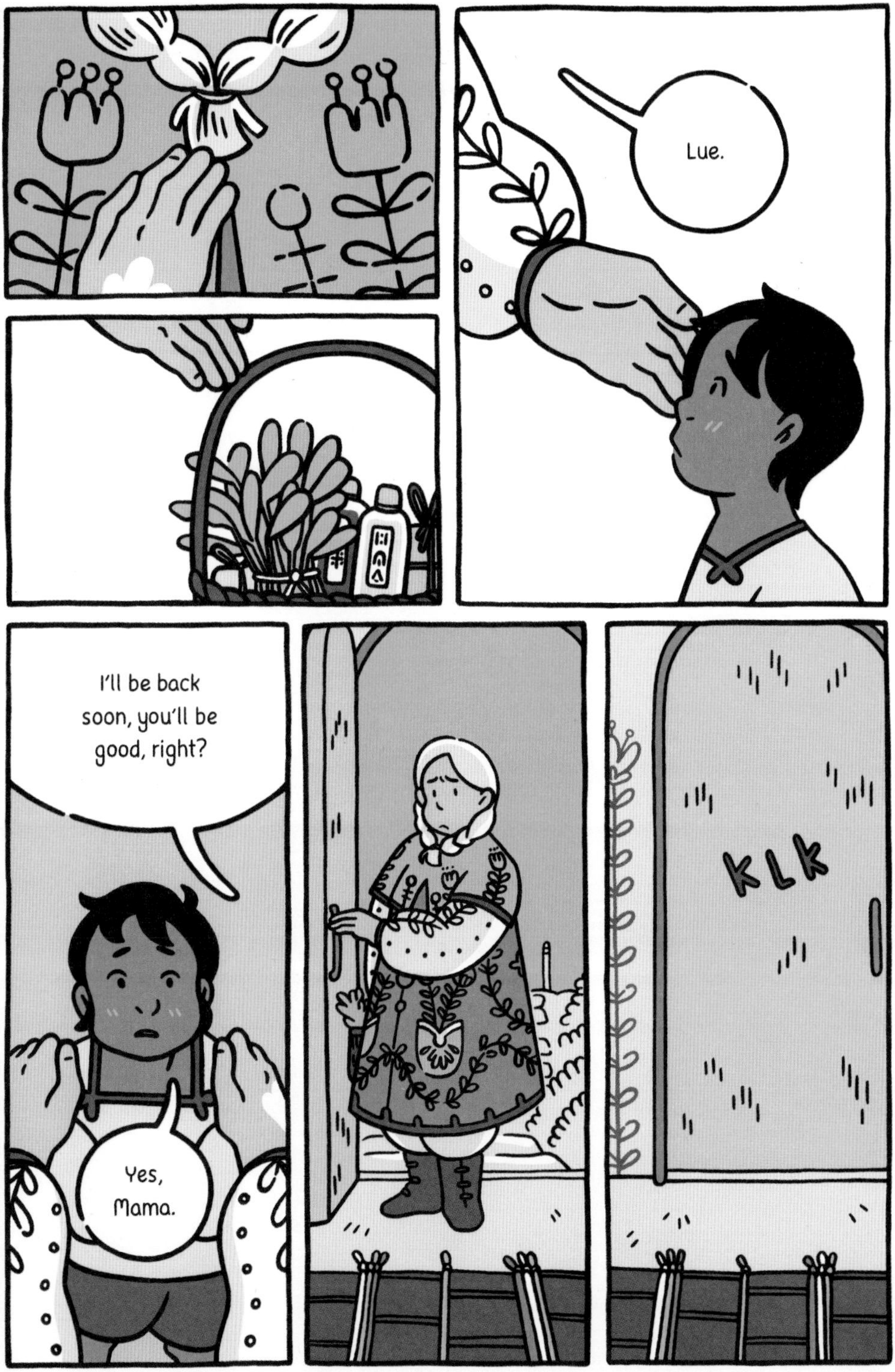
Lue.
I'll be back soon, you'll be good, right?
Yes, Mama.
KLK

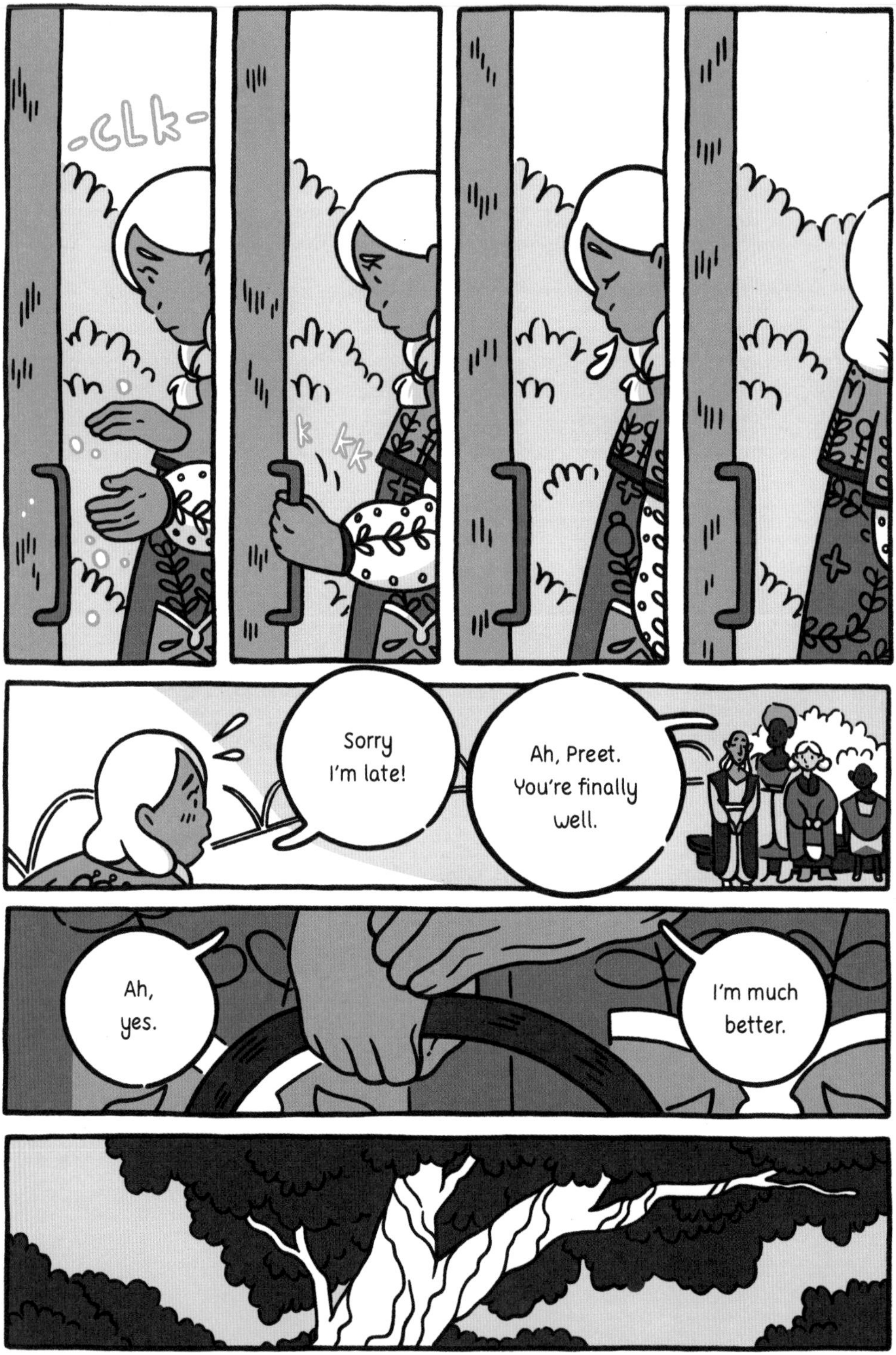
-CLK-
k kk
Sorry I'm late!
Ah, Preet. You're finally well.
Ah, yes.
I'm much better.

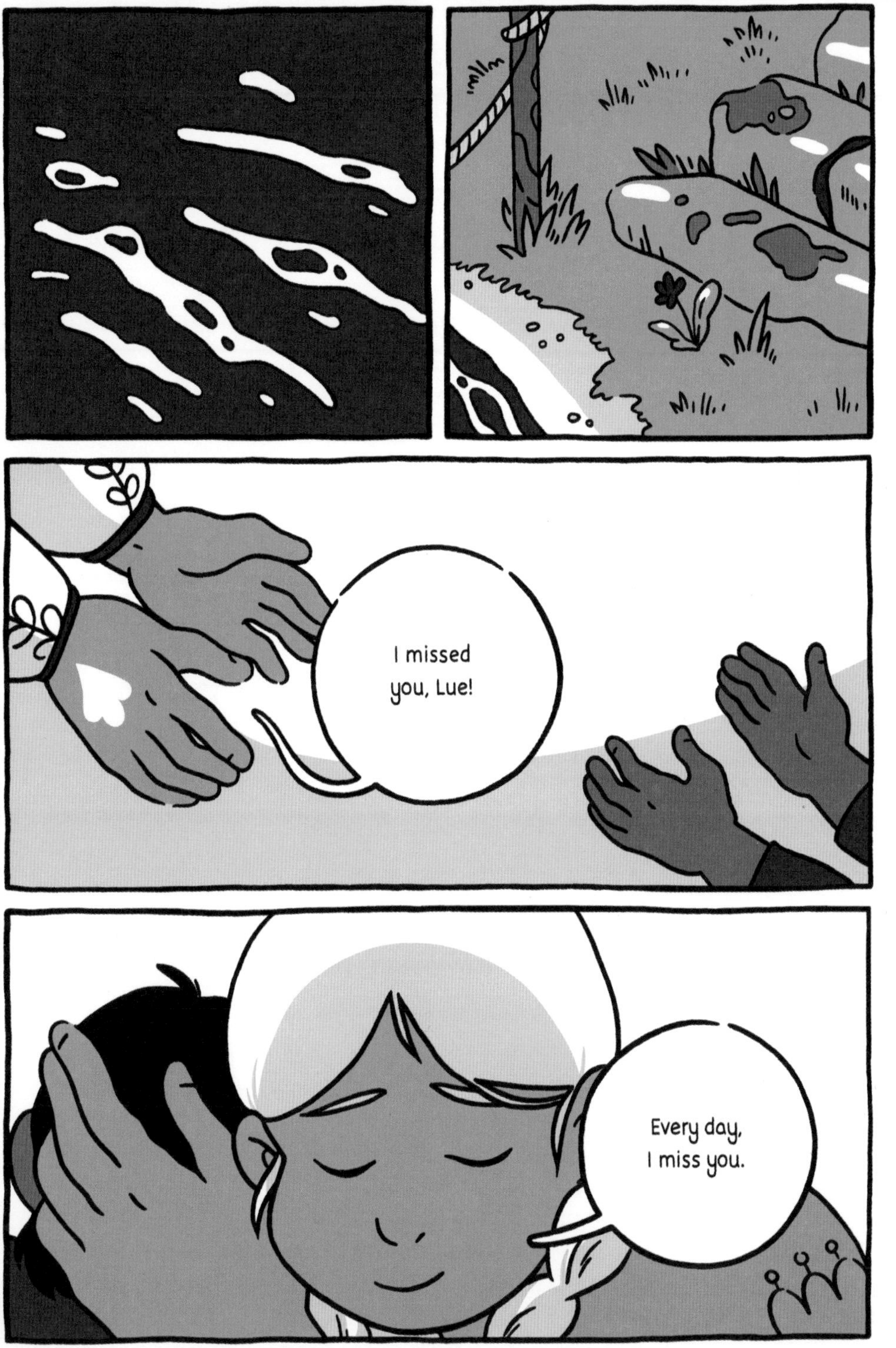
I missed you, Lue!
Every day, I miss you.

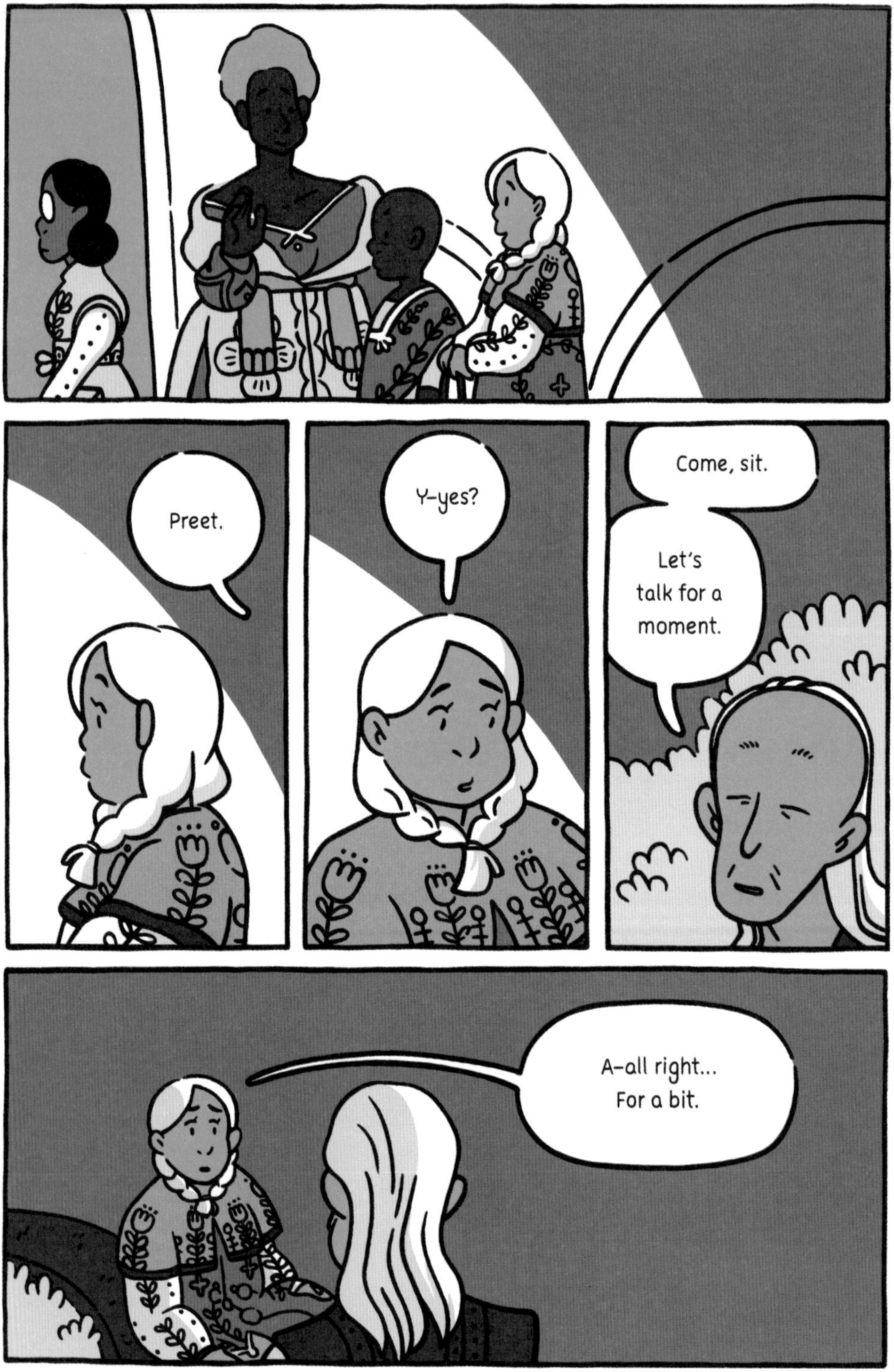
Preet.
Y-yes?
Come, sit.
Let's talk for a moment.
A-all right... For a bit.

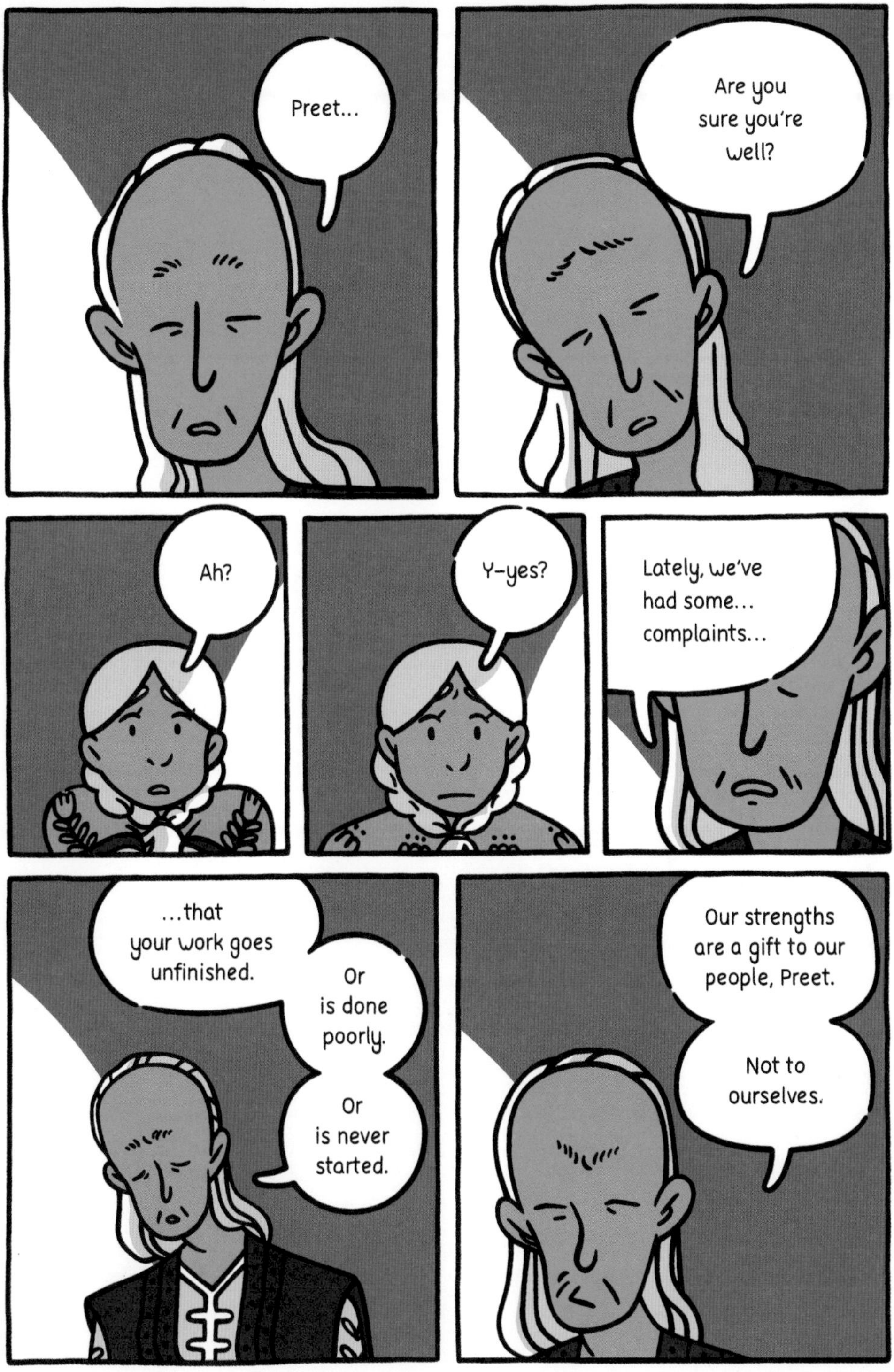
Preet...
Are you sure you're well?
Ah?
Y-yes?
Lately, we've had some... complaints...
...that your work goes unfinished.
Or is done poorly.
Or is never started.
Our strengths are a gift to our people, Preet.
Not to ourselves.

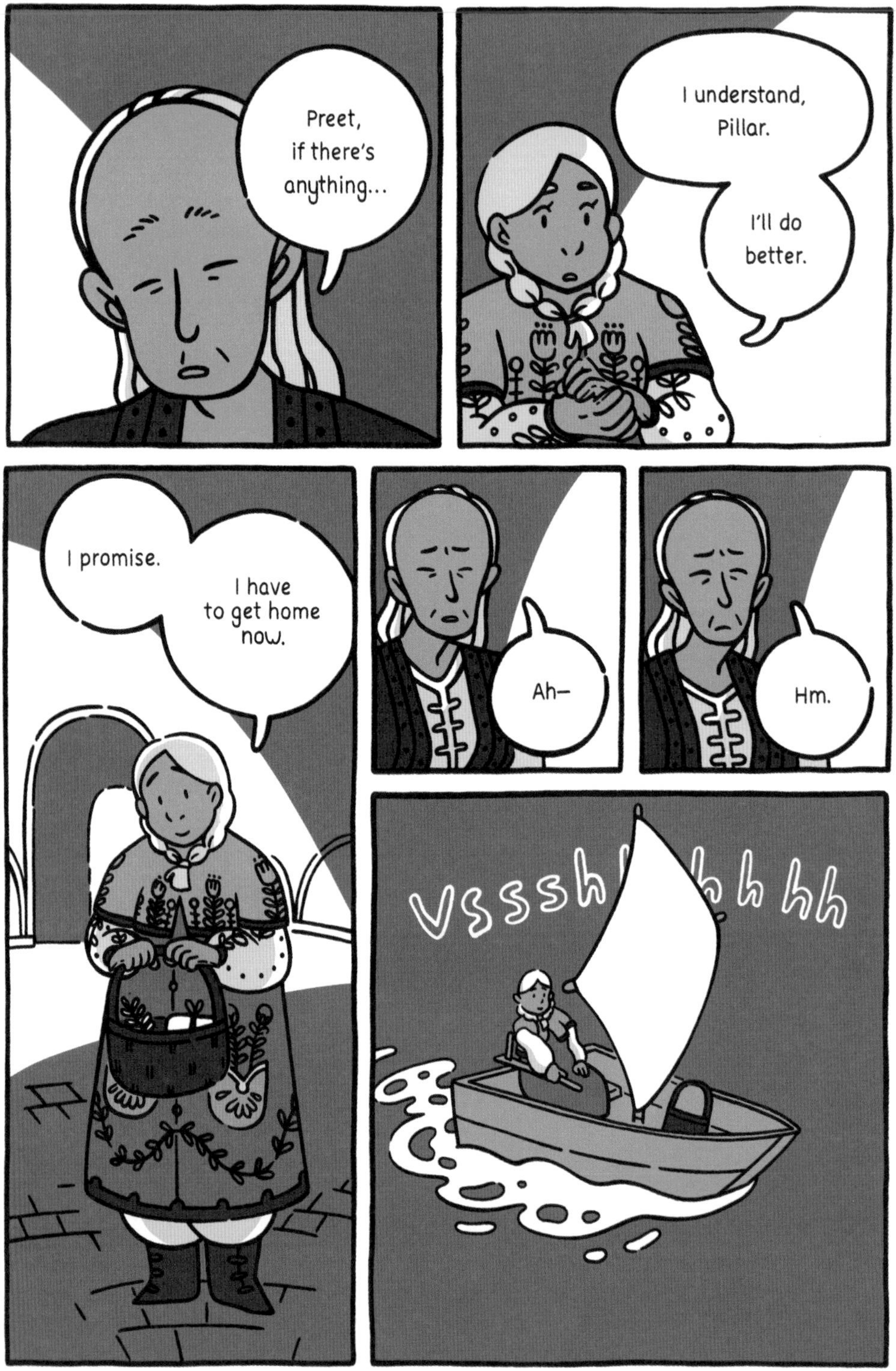
Preet, if there's anything...
I understand, Pillar.
I'll do better.
I promise.
I have to get home now.
Ah–
Hm.
Vsssh hhhh

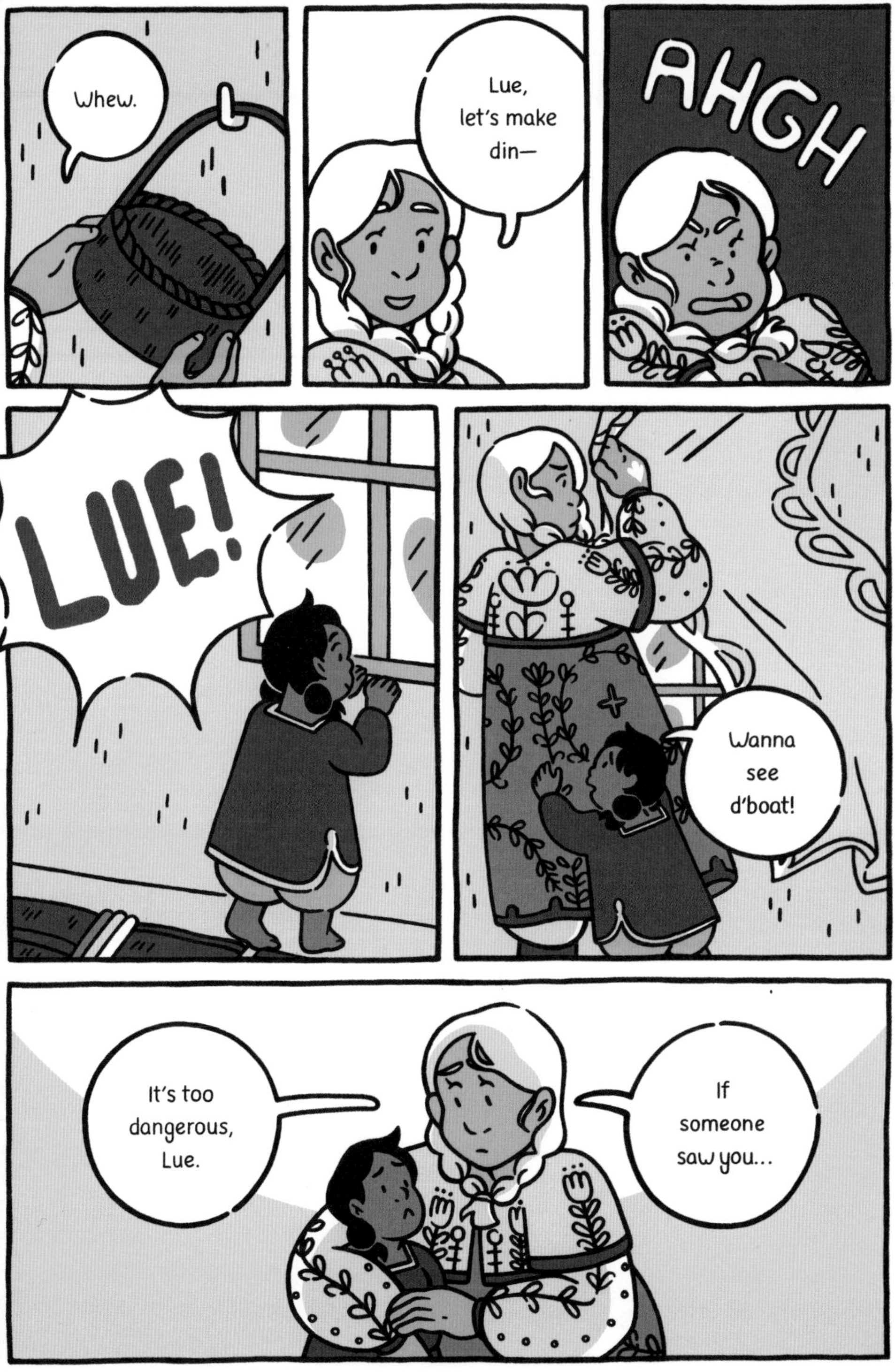
Whew.
Lue, let's make din—
AHGH
LUE!
Wanna see d'boat!
It's too dangerous, Lue.
If someone saw you…

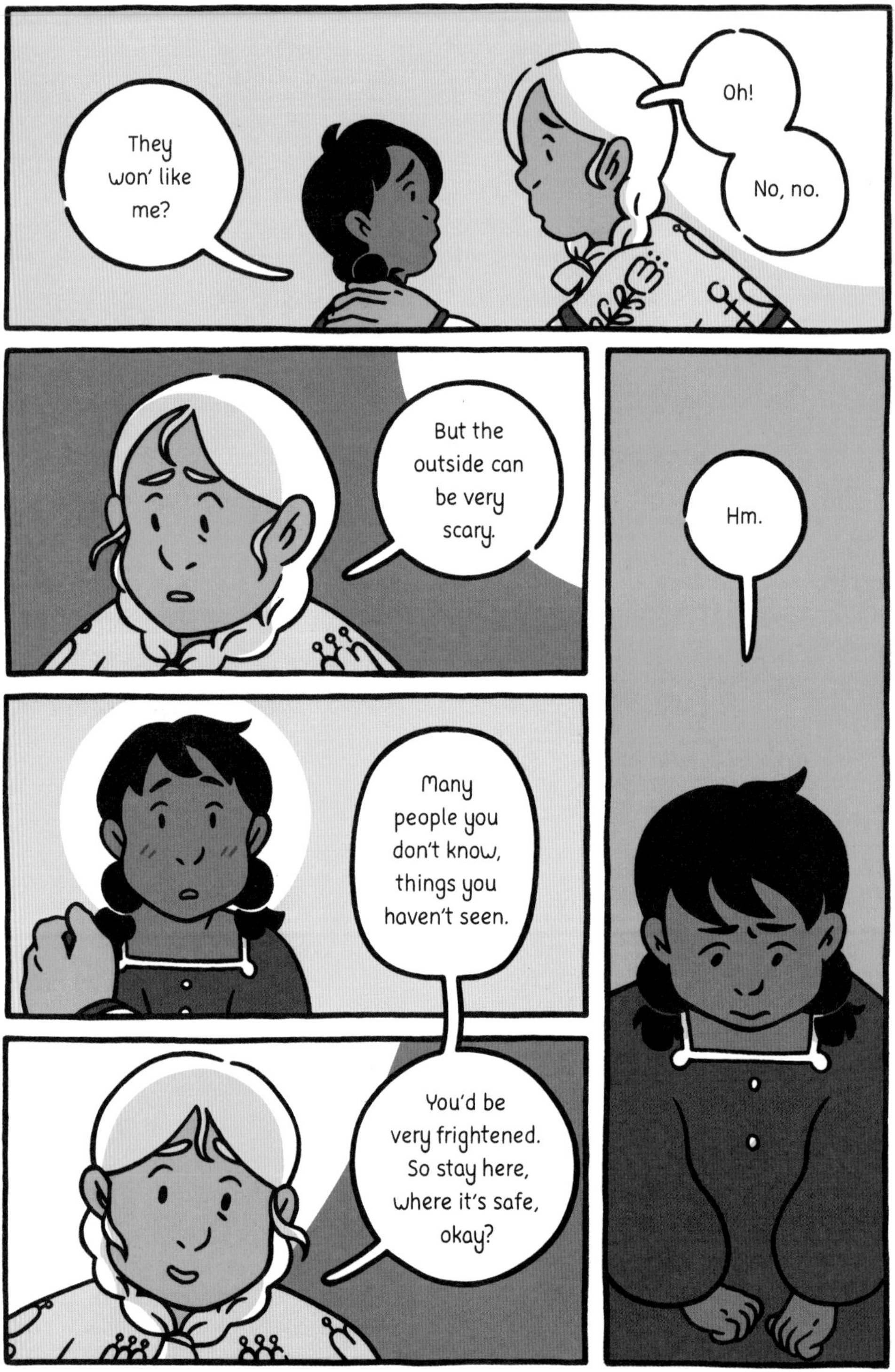
They won' like me?
Oh!
No, no.
But the outside can be very scary.
Hm.
Many people you don't know, things you haven't seen.
You'd be very frightened. So stay here, where it's safe, okay?

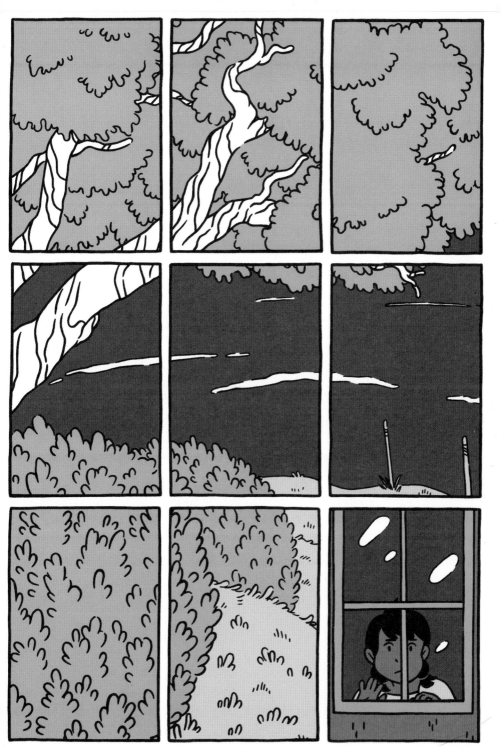

Brave
Lue.

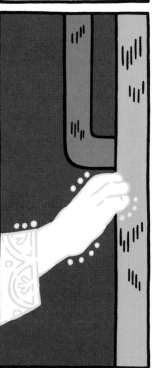

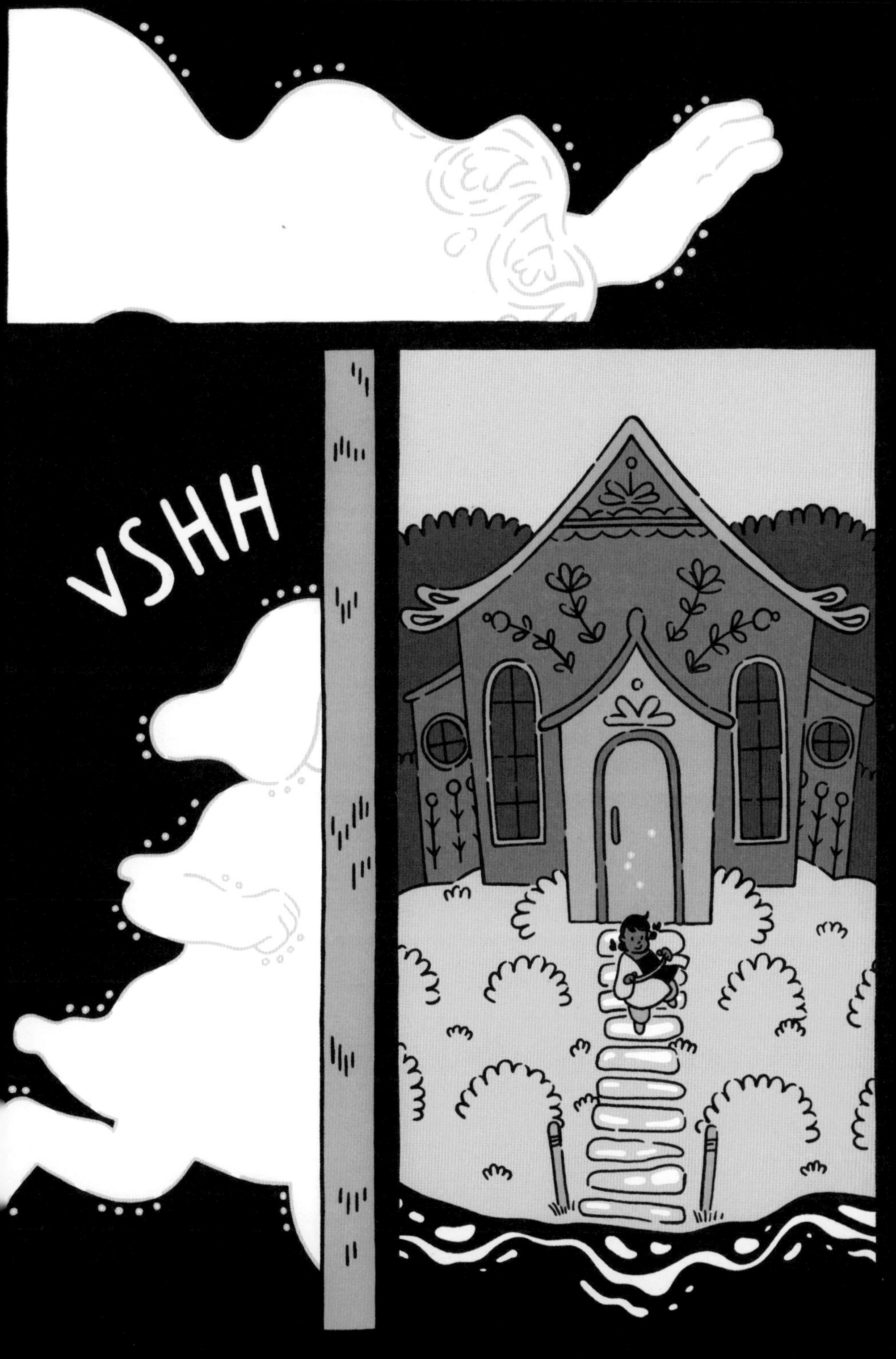
VSHH

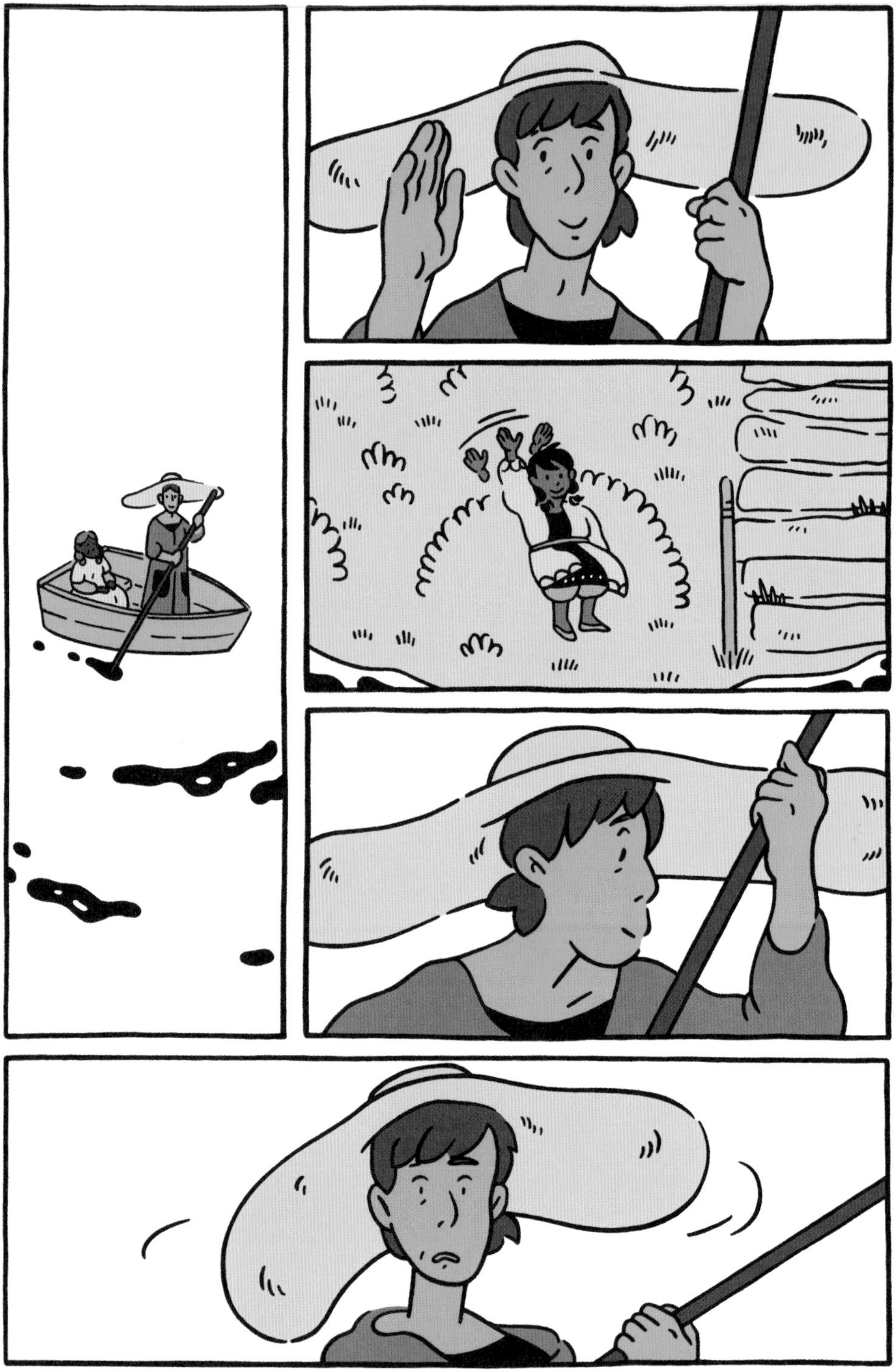

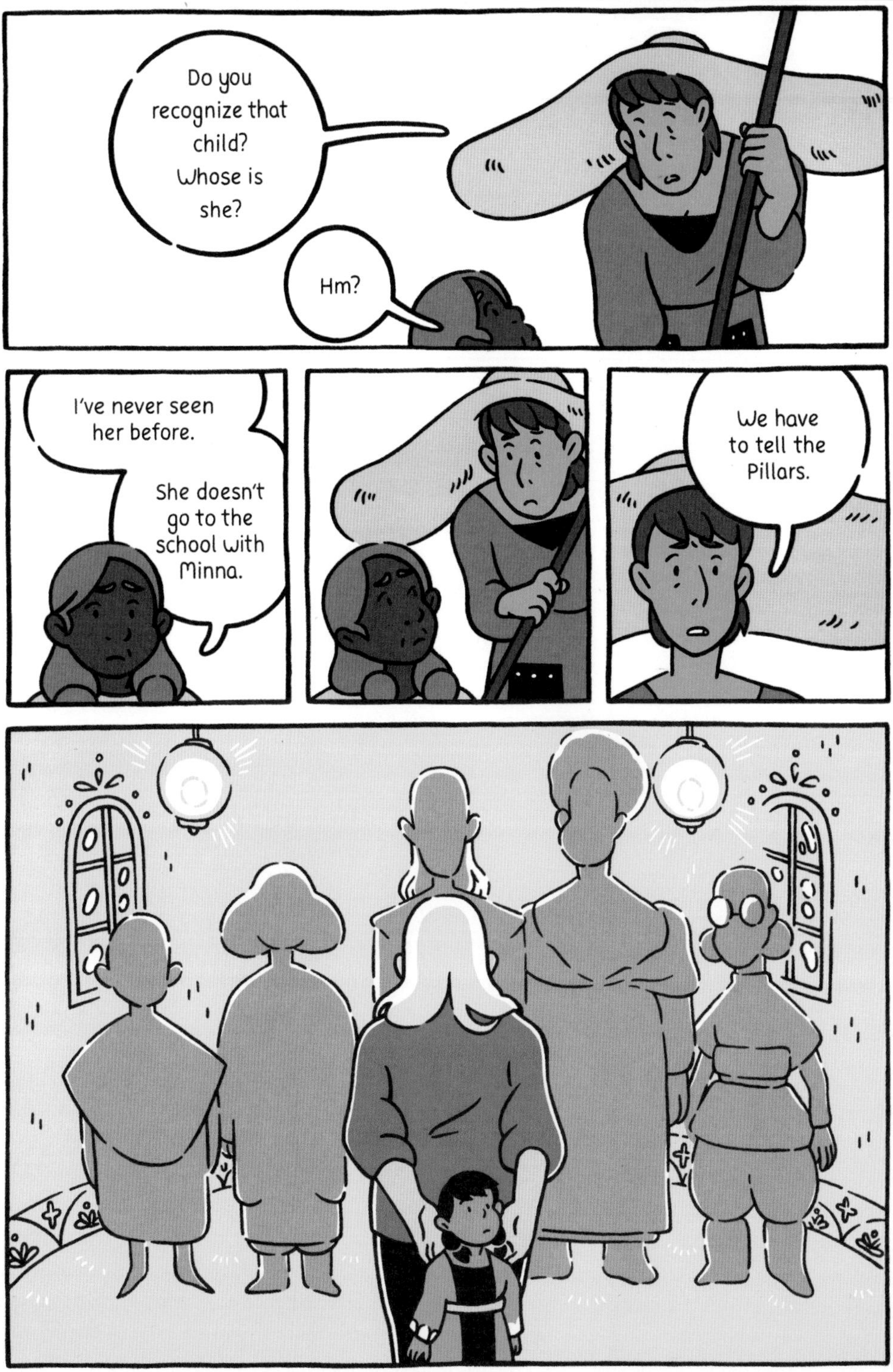
Do you recognize that child? Whose is she?
Hm?
I've never seen her before.
She doesn't go to the school with Minna.
We have to tell the Pillars.

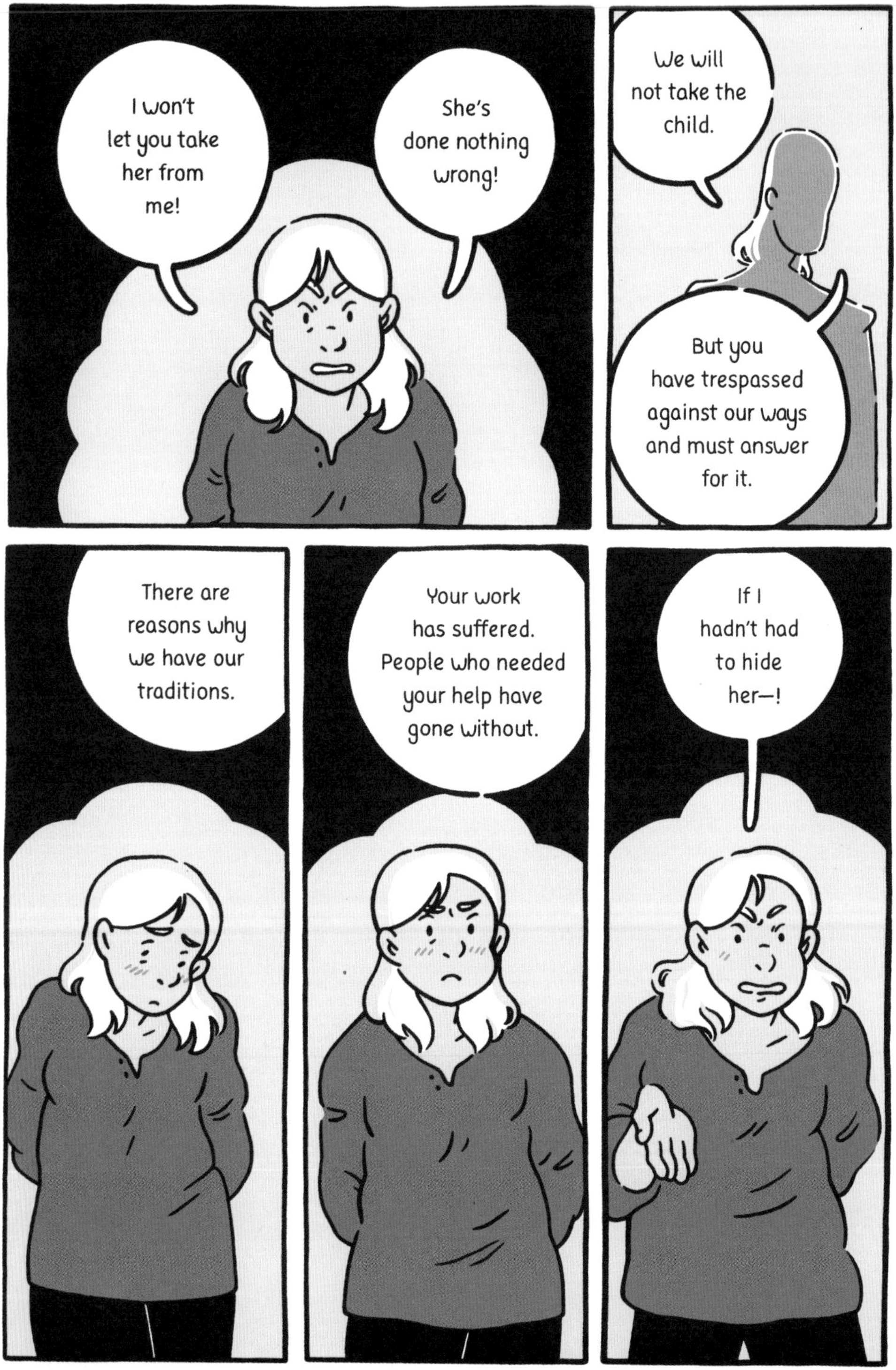
I won't let you take her from me!
She's done nothing wrong!
We will not take the child.
But you have trespassed against our ways and must answer for it.
There are reasons why we have our traditions.
Your work has suffered. People who needed your help have gone without.
If I hadn't had to hide her—!

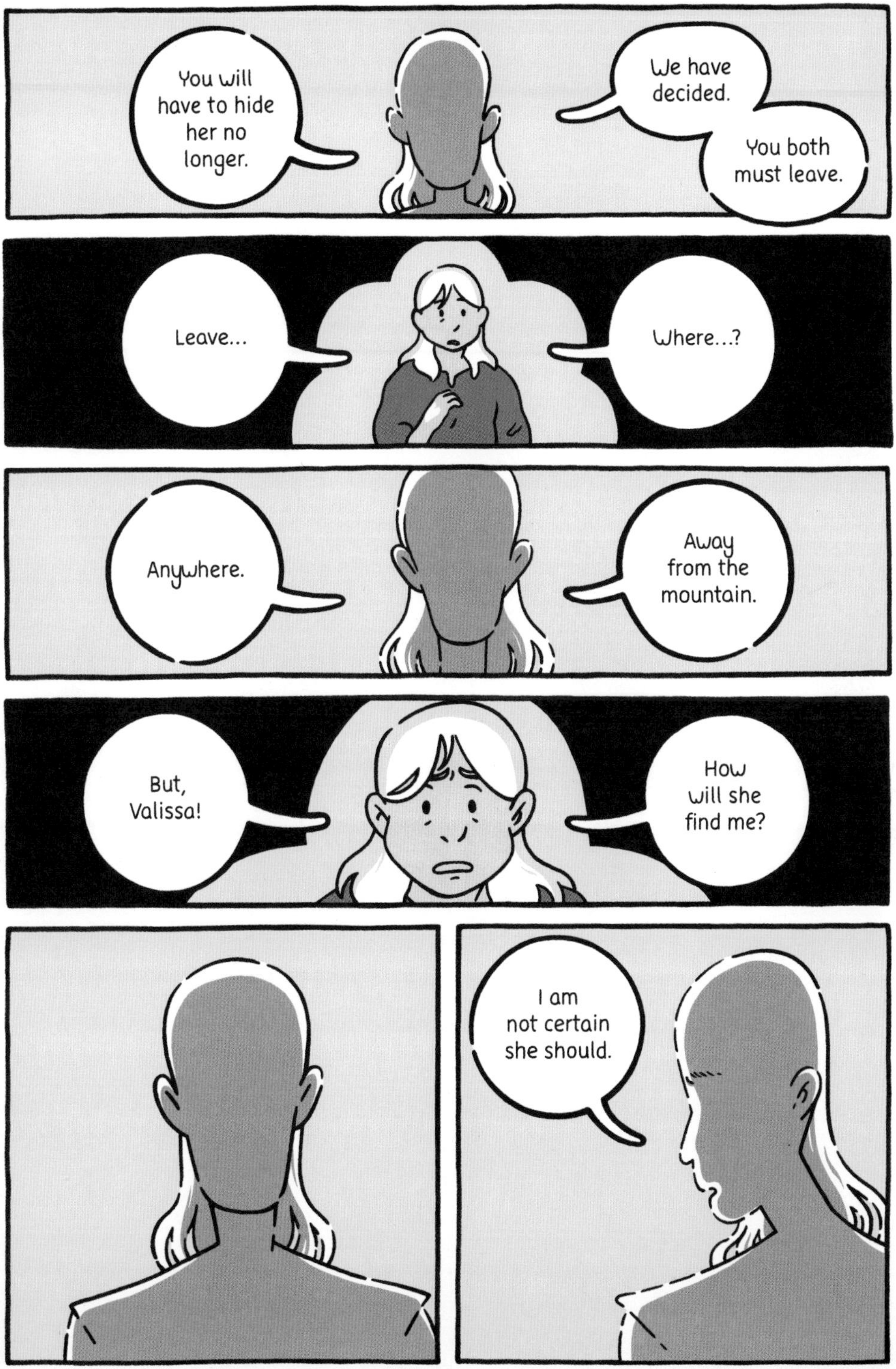
You will have to hide her no longer.
We have decided.
You both must leave.
Leave...
Where...?
Anywhere.
Away from the mountain.
But, Valissa!
How will she find me?
I am not certain she should.

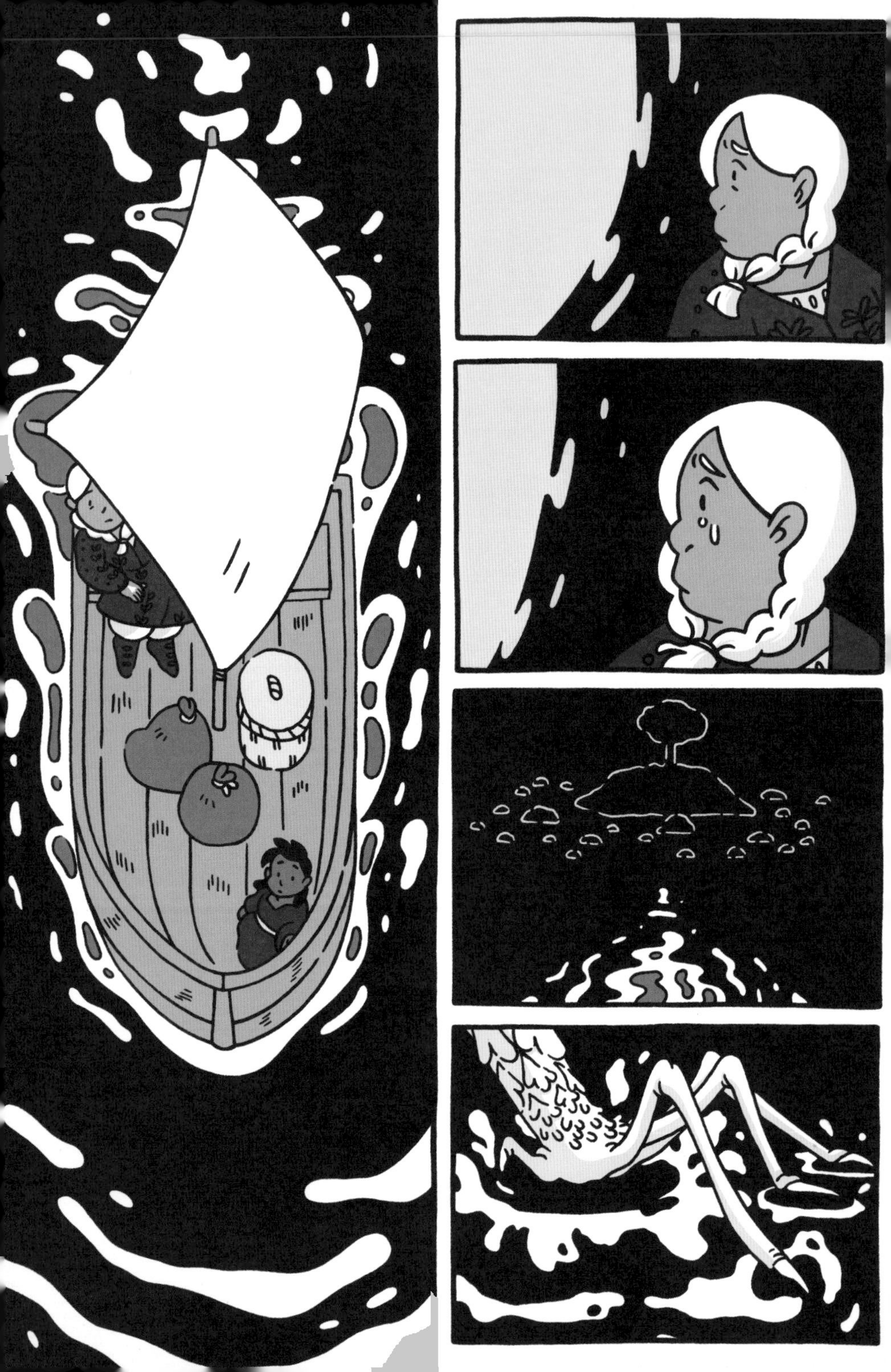

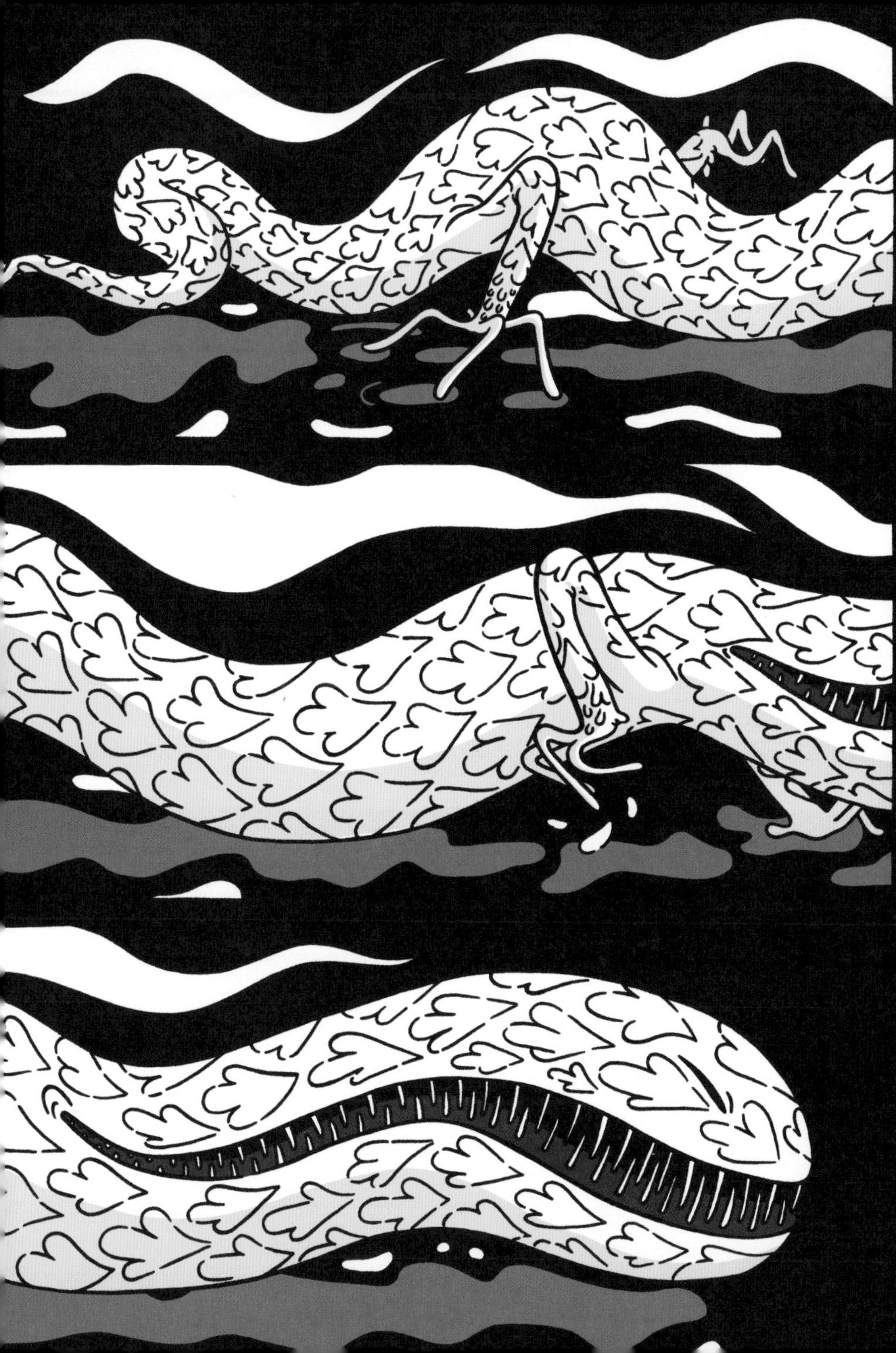

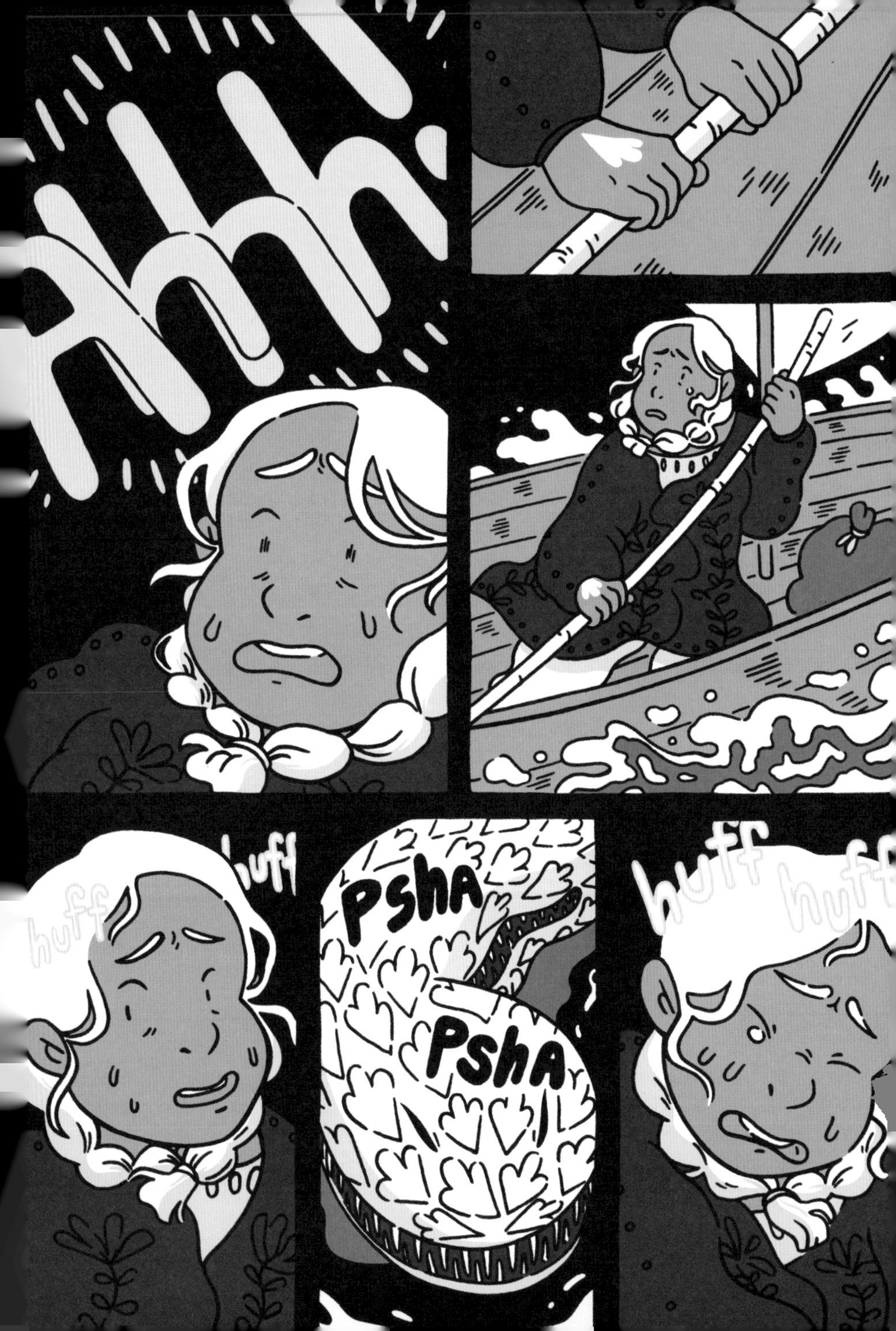
huff
huff
Psha
Psha
huff
huff

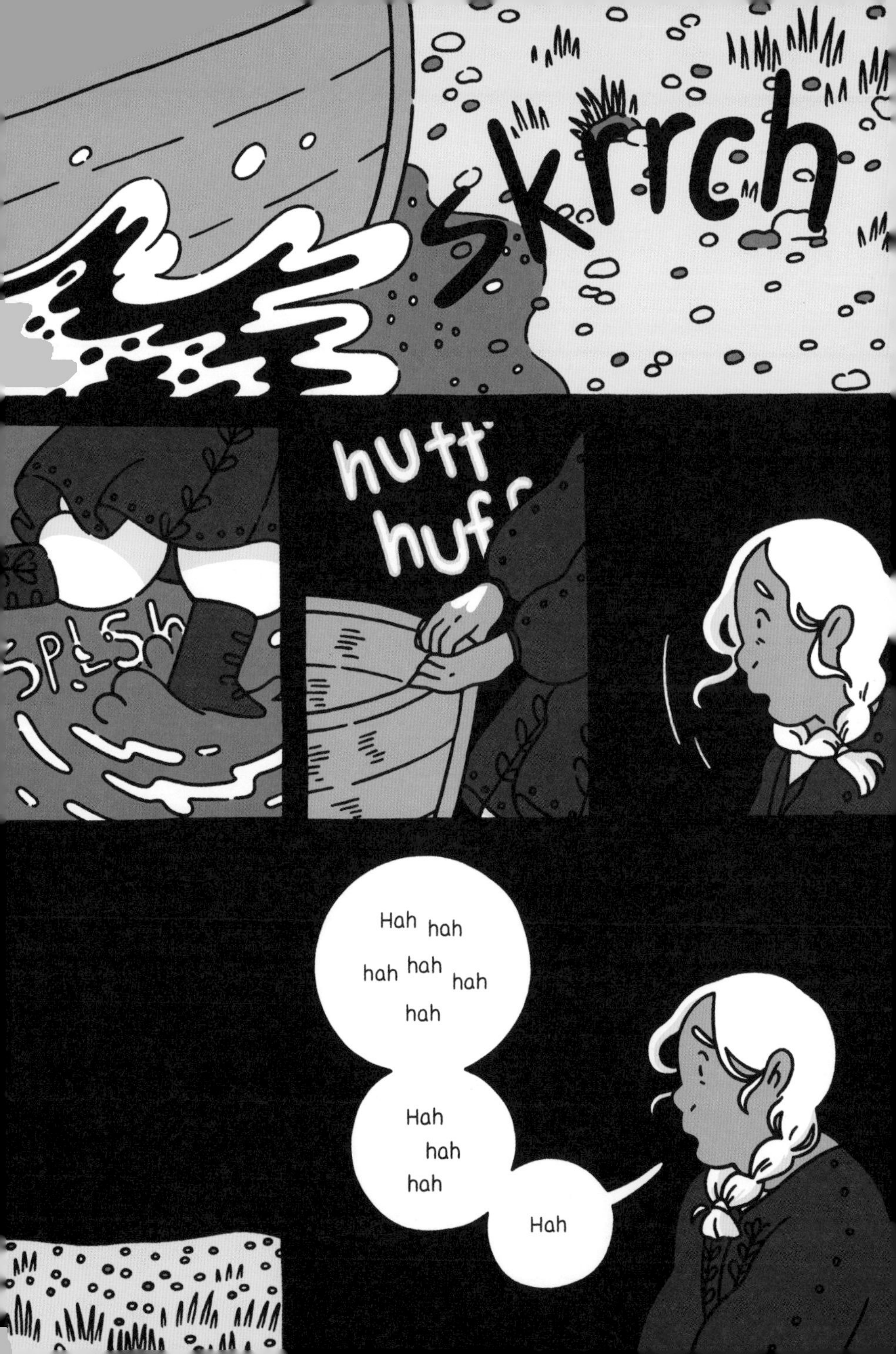

Skrrch
SPLSh
huff
huff
Hah hah hah hah hah hah
Hah hah hah
Hah

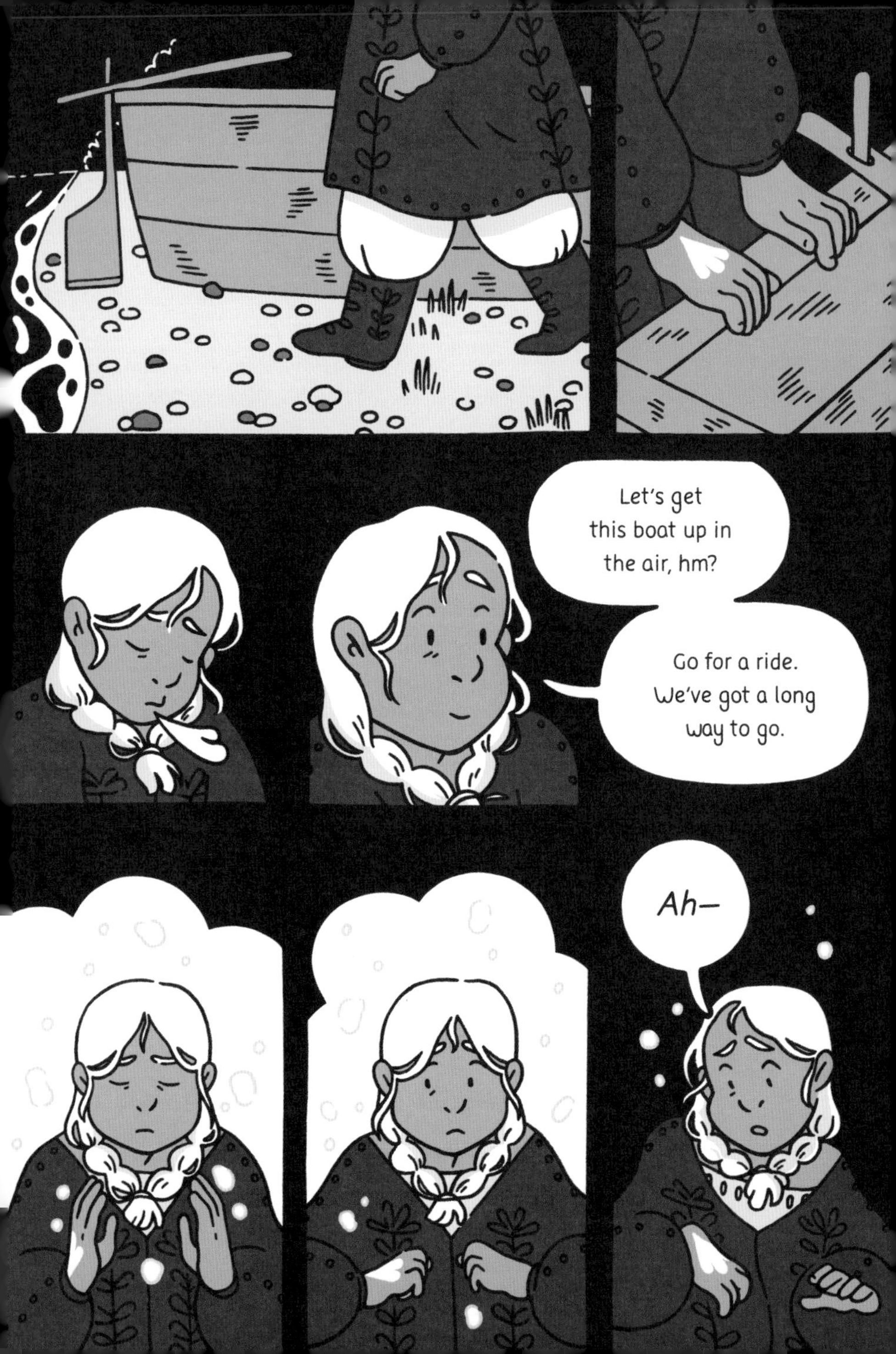
Let's get this boat up in the air, hm?
Go for a ride. We've got a long way to go.
Ah–

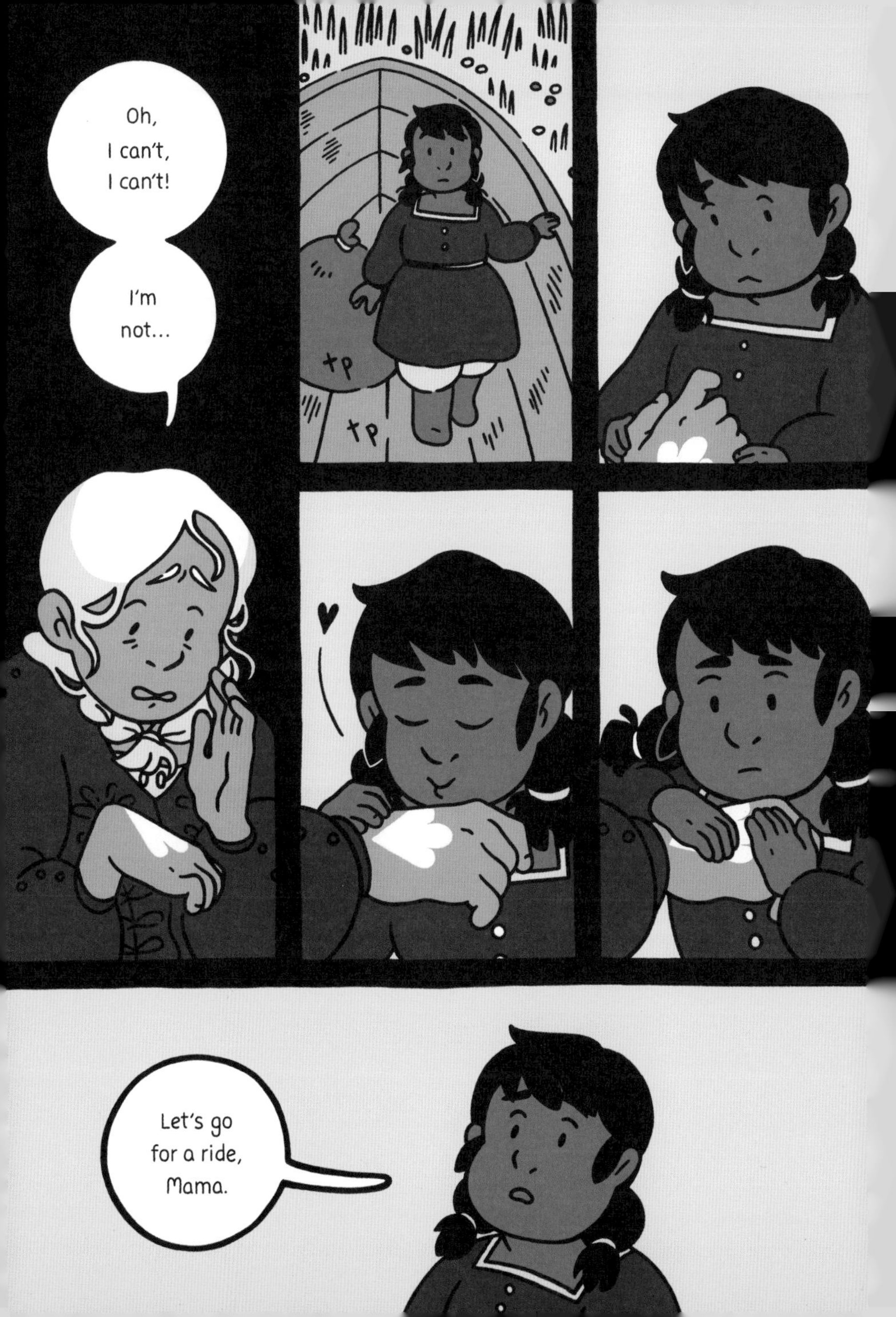
Oh, I can't, I can't!
I'm not...
tp
tp
Let's go for a ride, Mama.

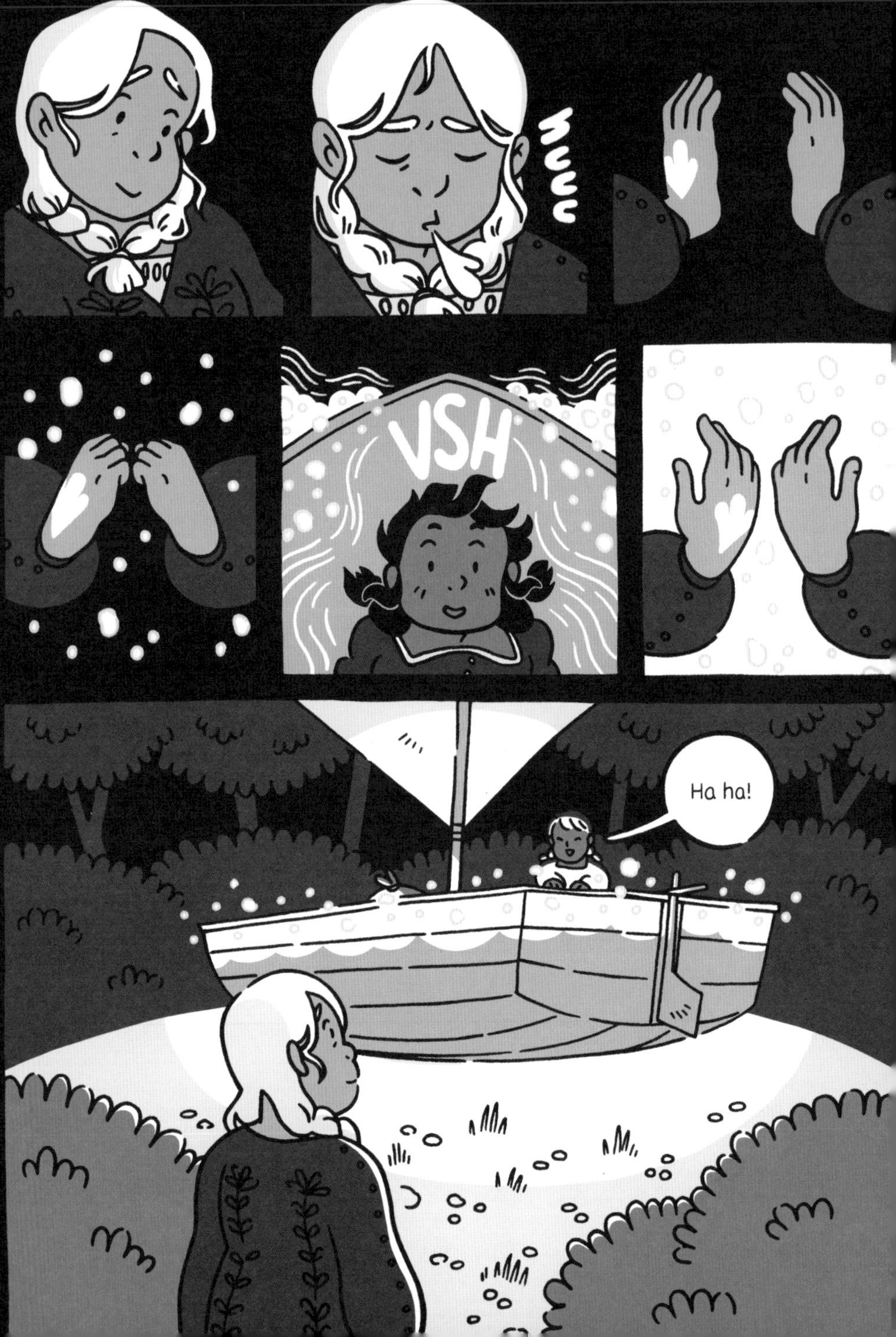

huuu
VSH
Ha ha!

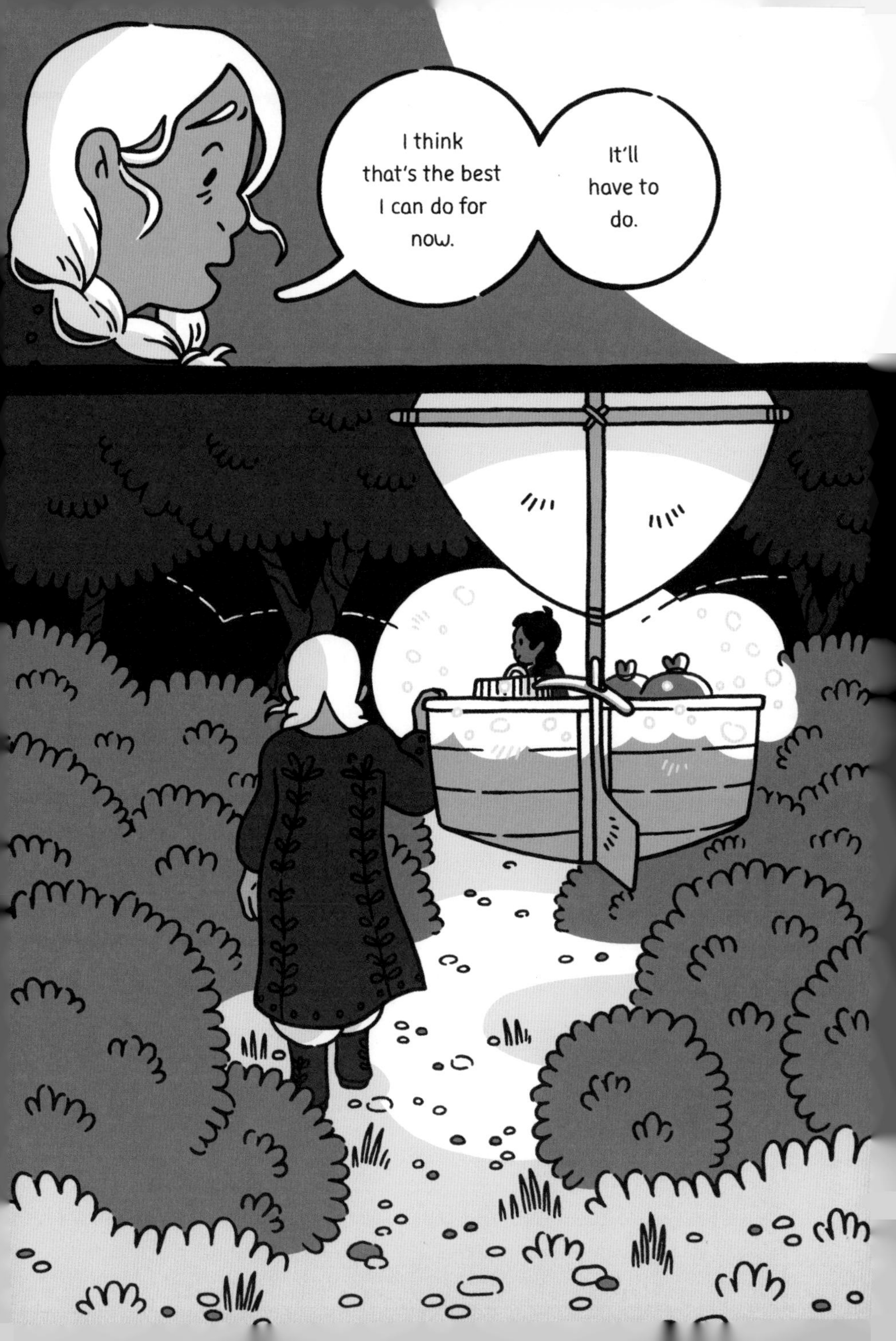
I think that's the best I can do for now.
It'll have to do.

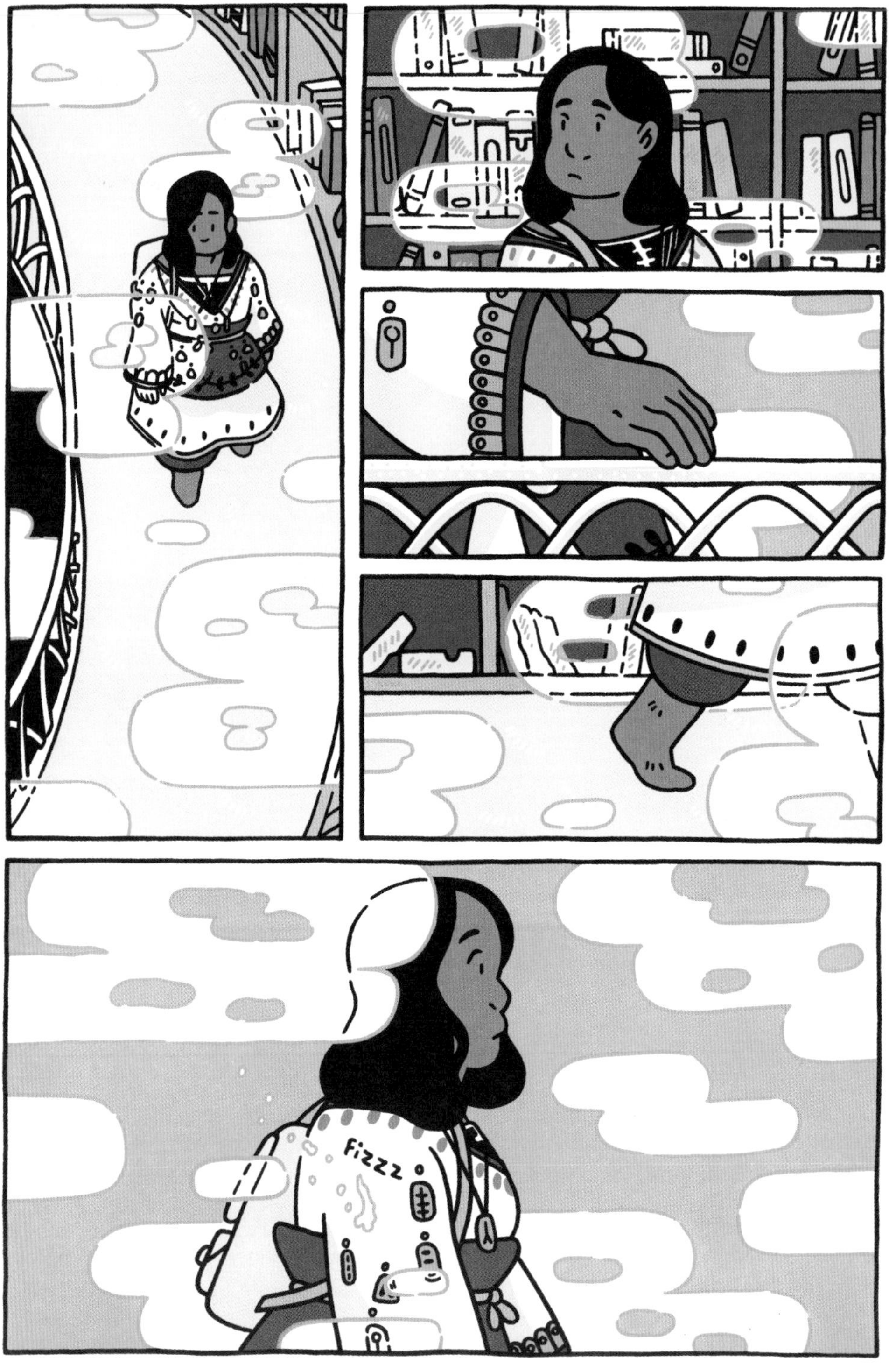
Fizzz

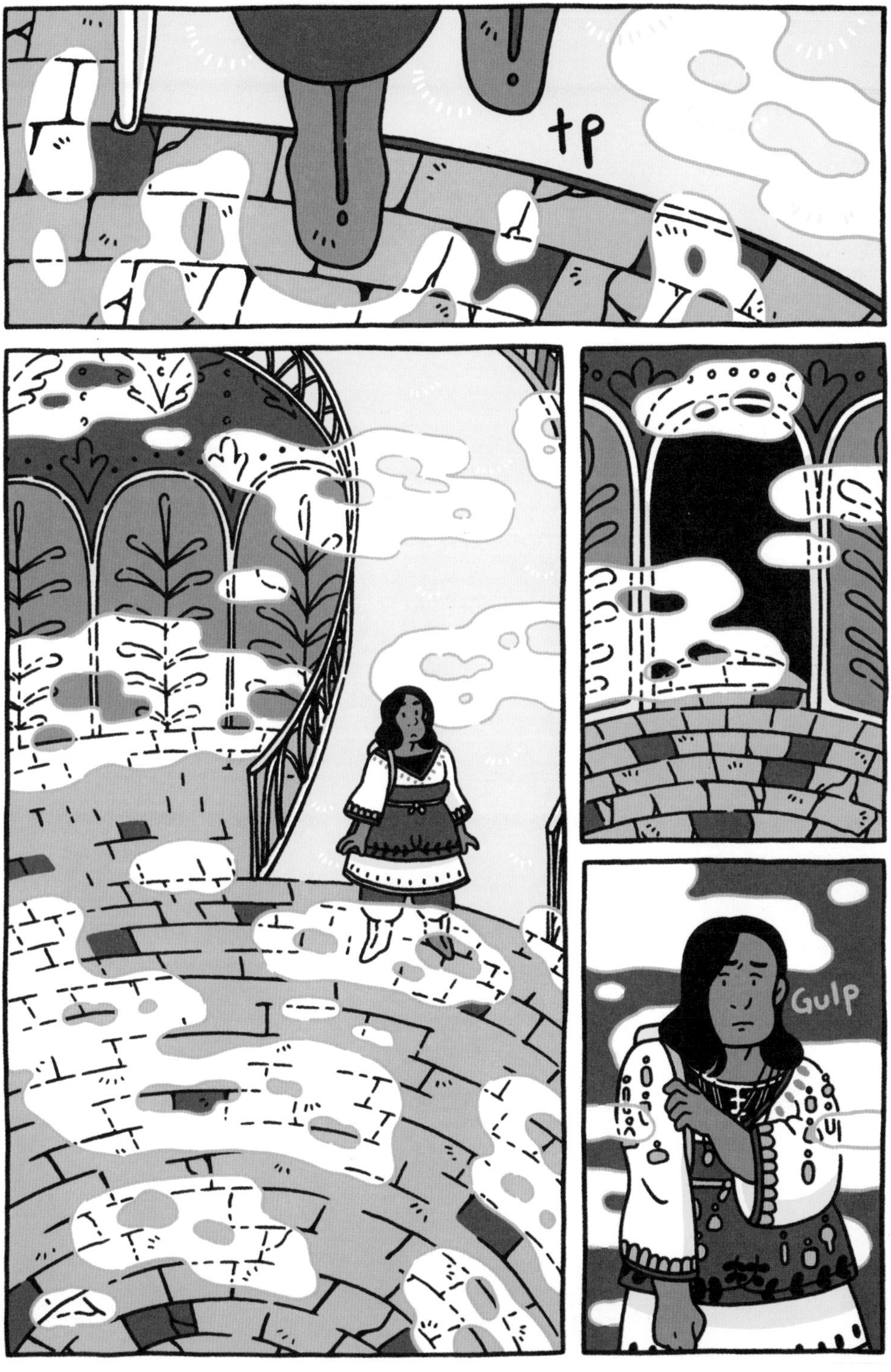
tp
GULP

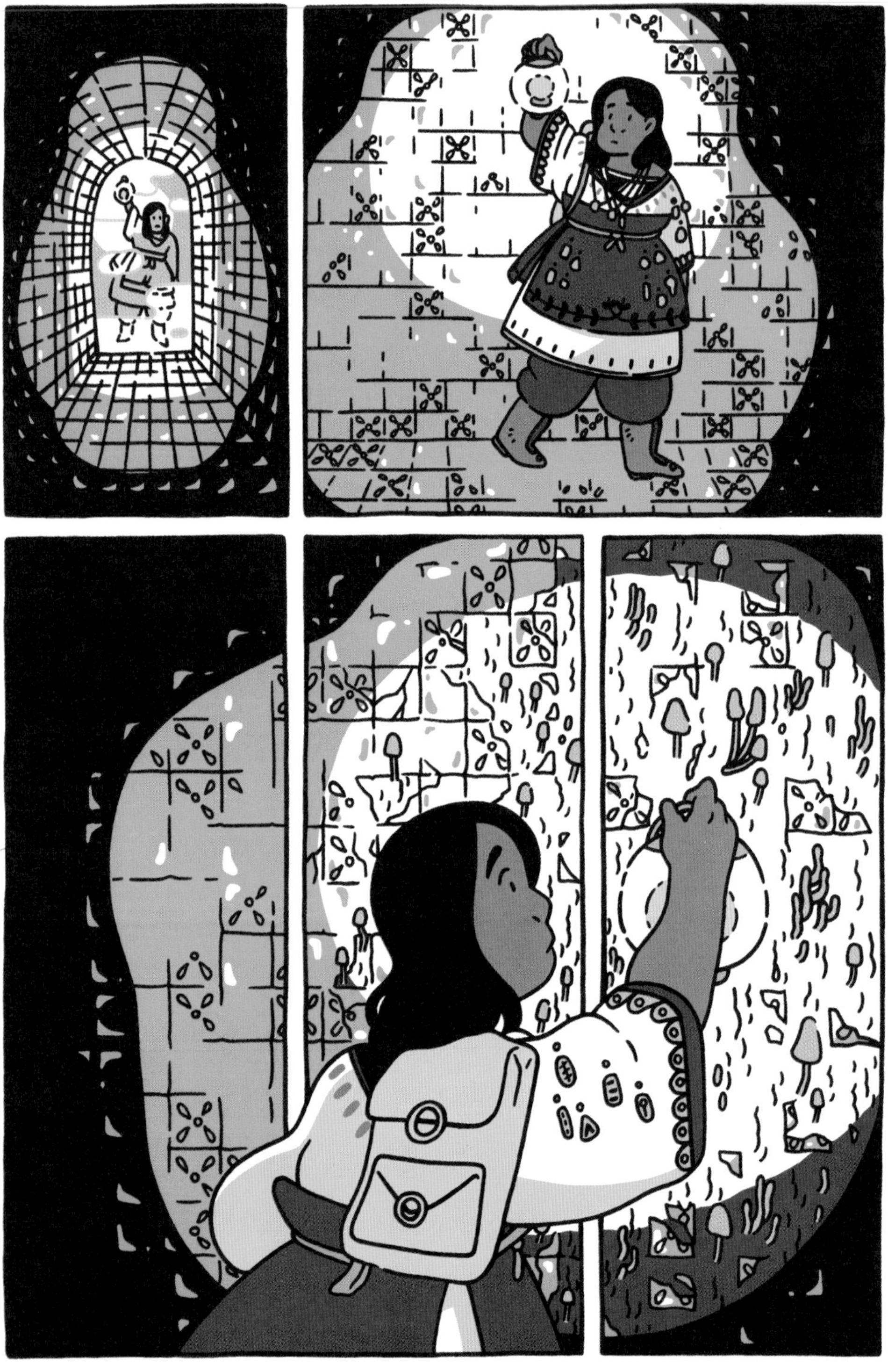

streeetch
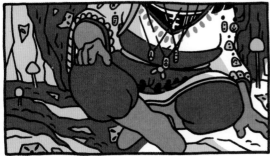

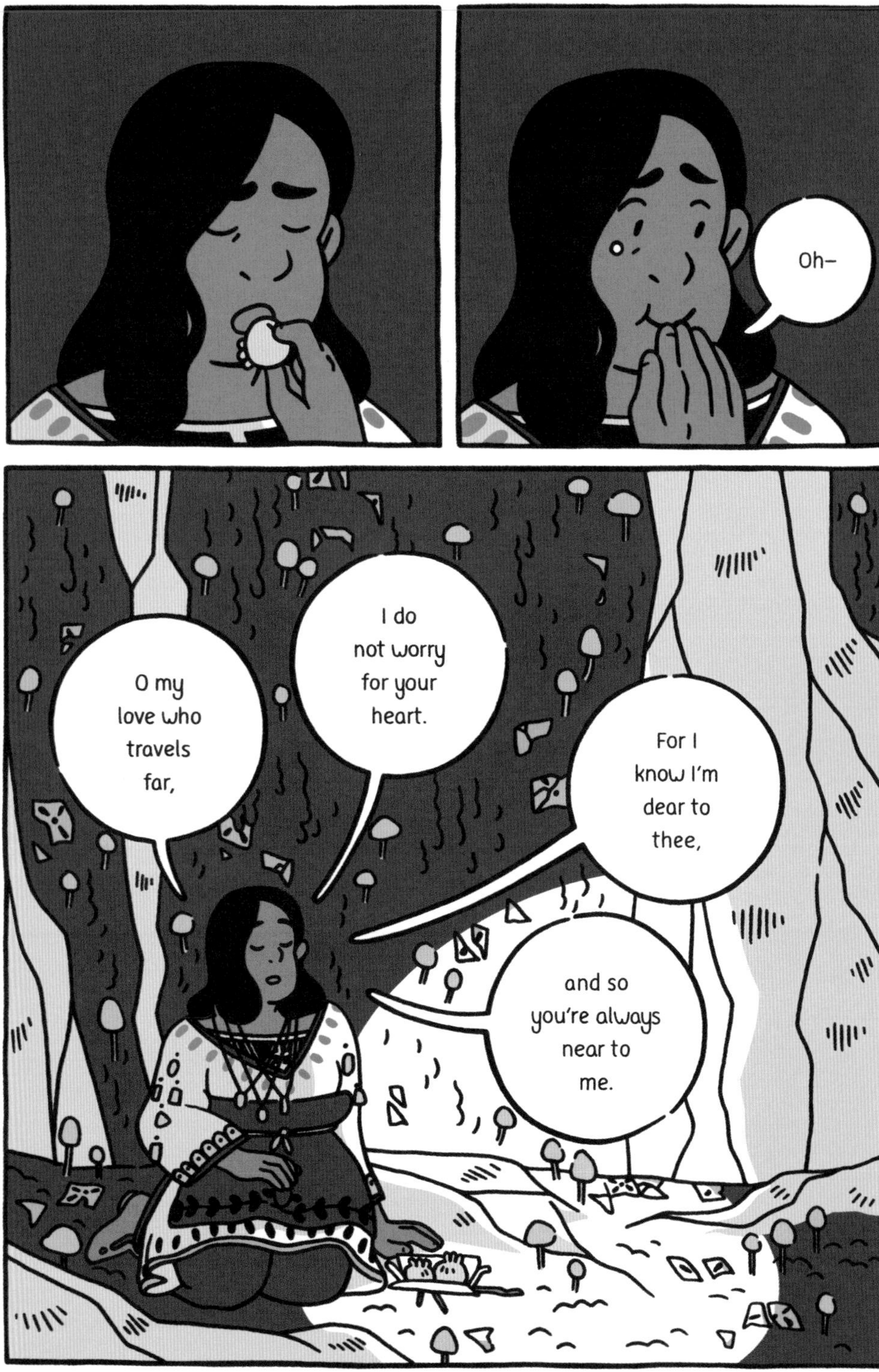
Oh–
O my love who travels far,
I do not worry for your heart.
For I know I'm dear to thee,
and so you're always near to me.

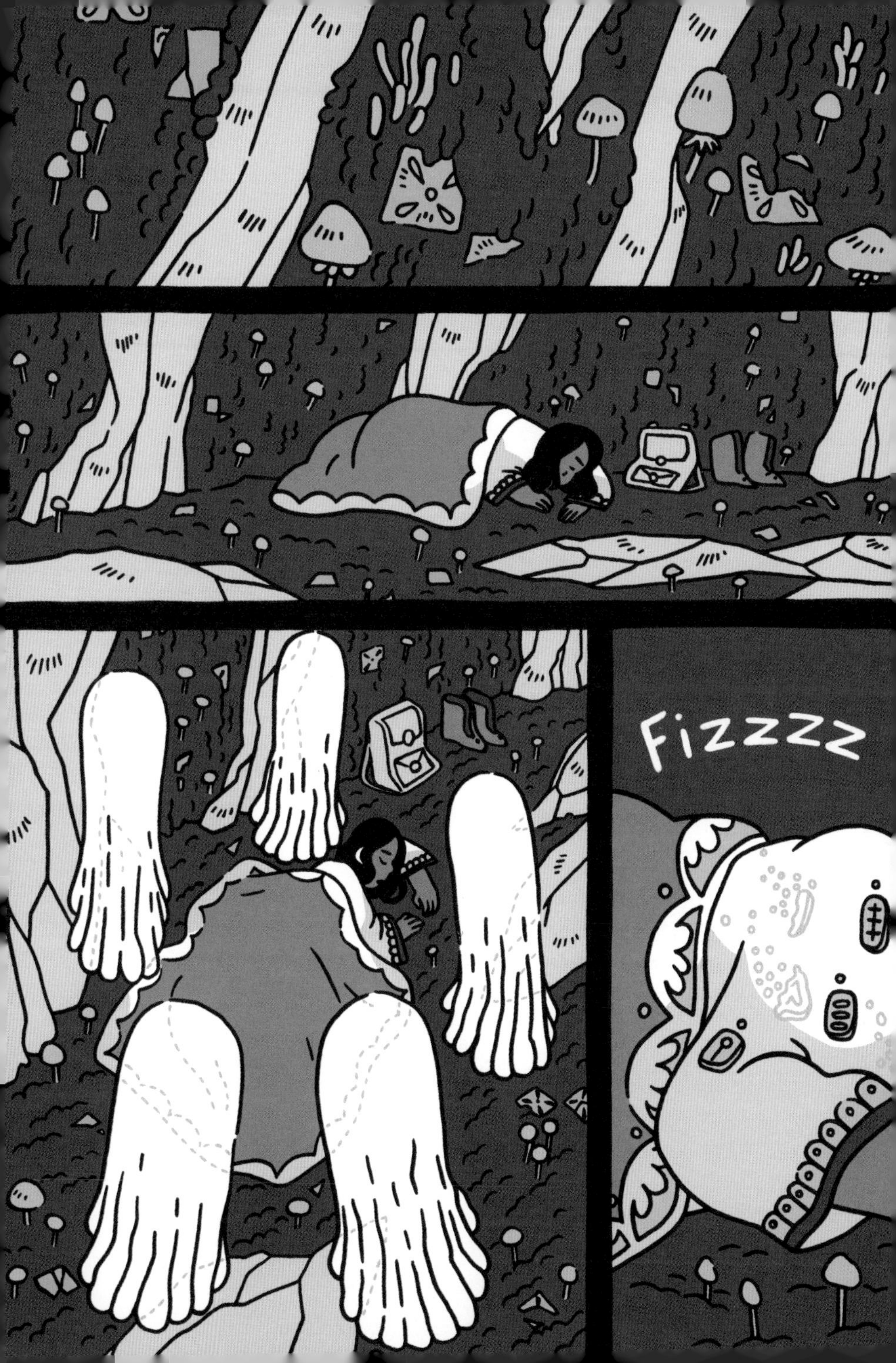
Fizzzz

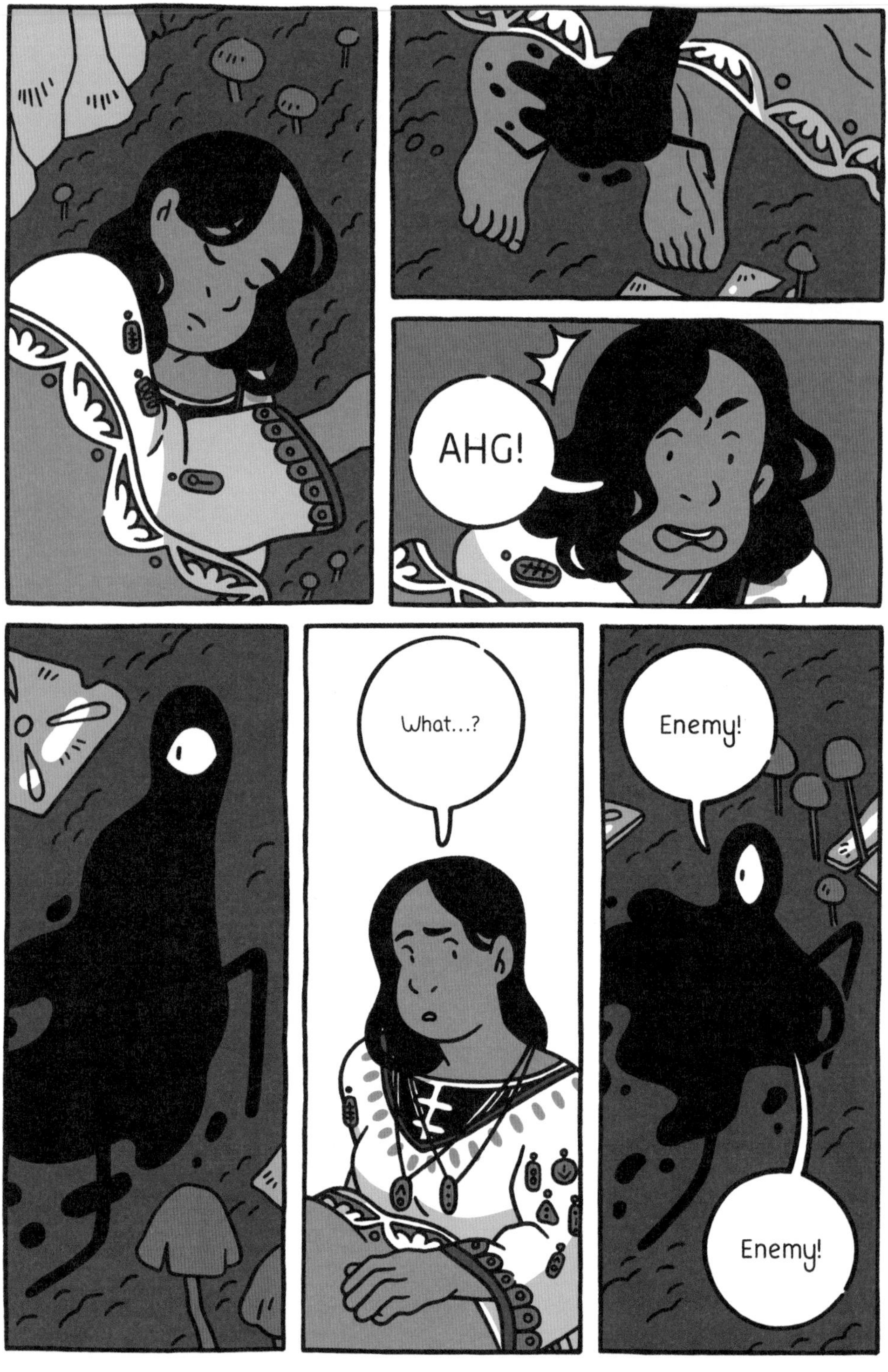
AHG!
What...?
Enemy!
Enemy!

Curses, already?

Enemy!

Your. Your!

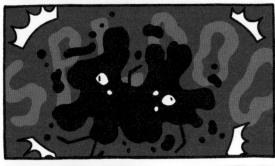

Your enemy!

Your enemy!

Eh?

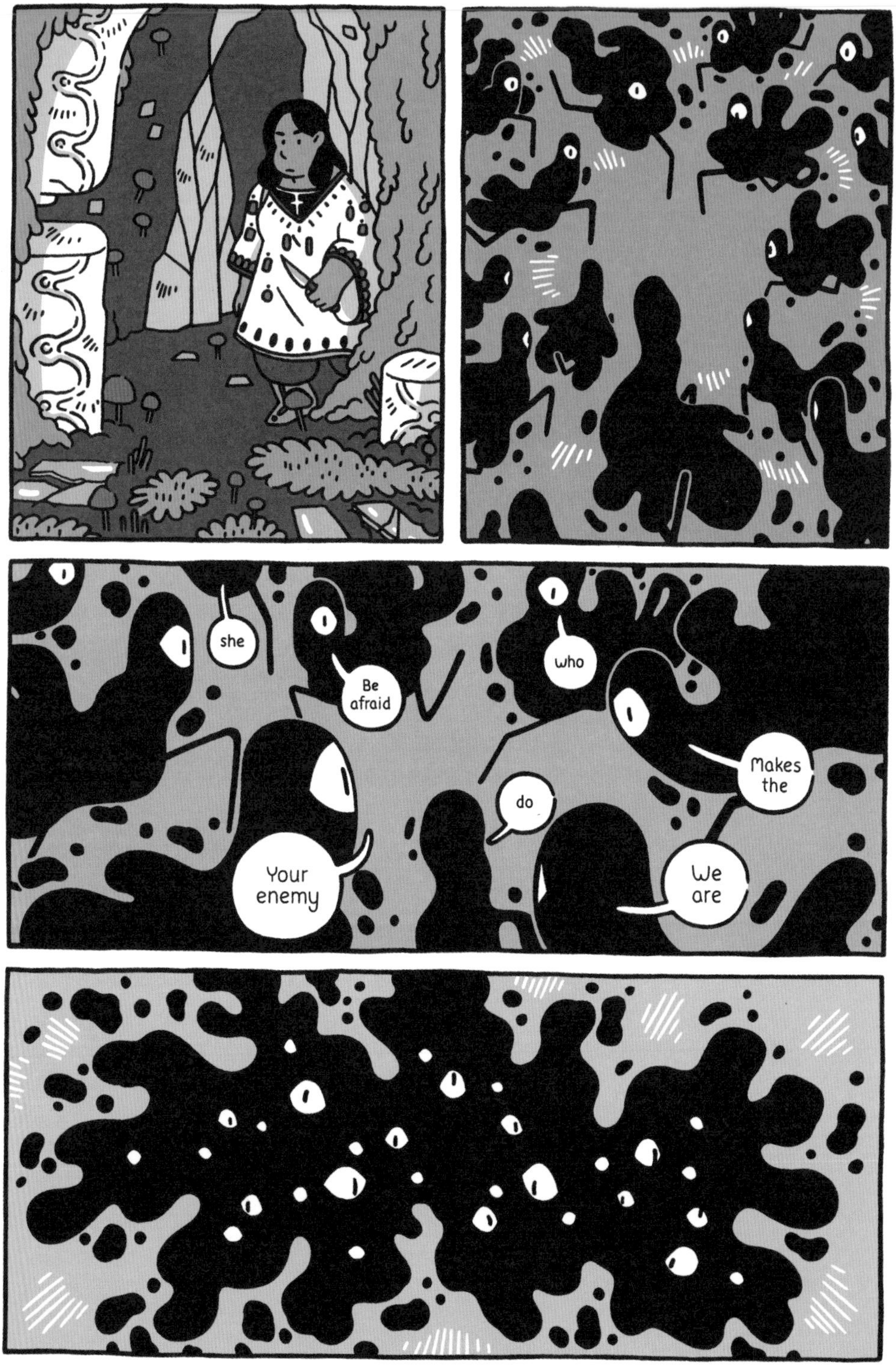
she
Be afraid
who
Makes the
do
Your enemy
We are

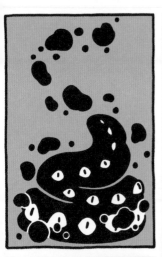

Do not
be afraid.
We are not
your enemy.

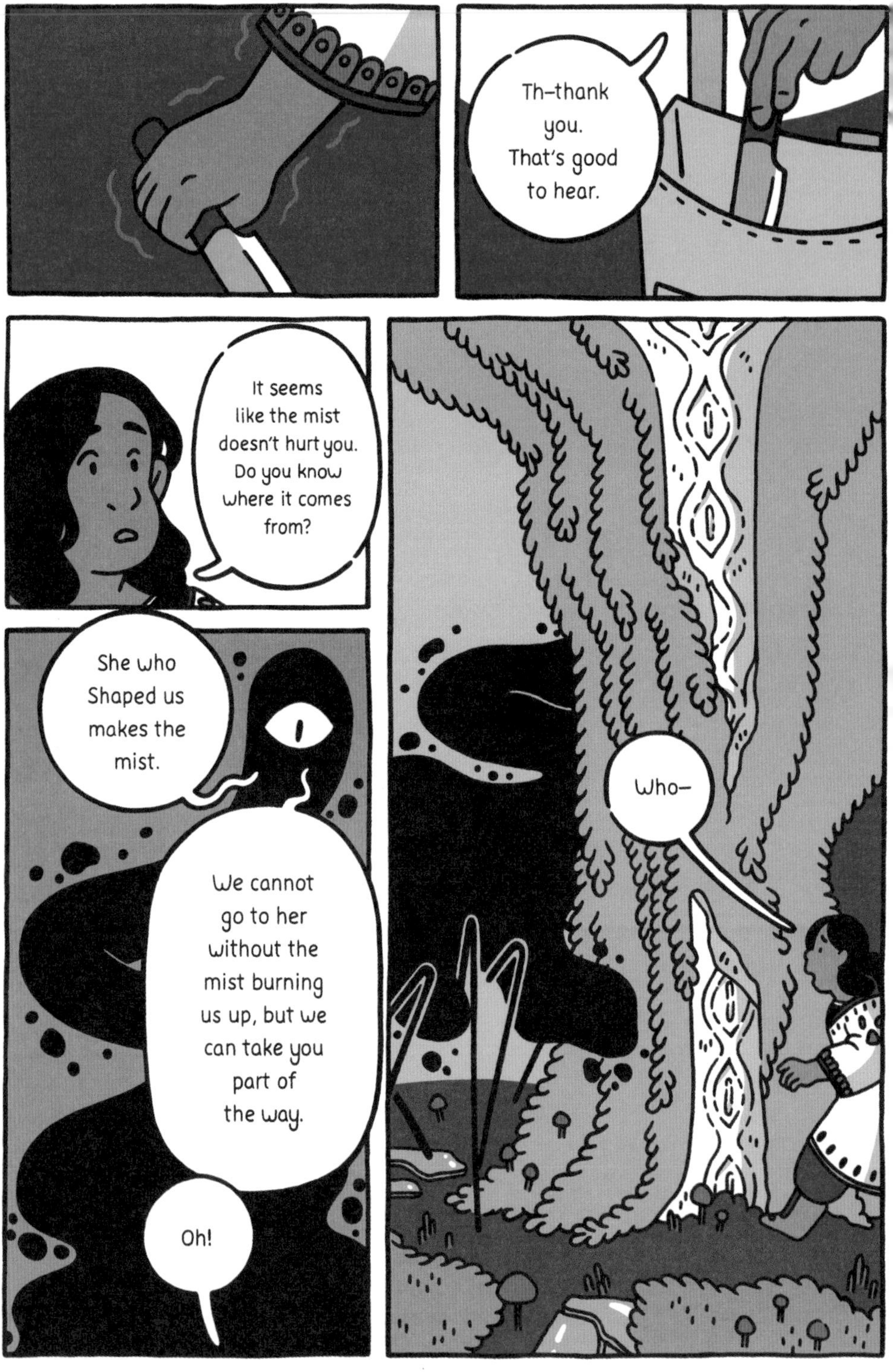
Th–thank you. That's good to hear.
It seems like the mist doesn't hurt you. Do you know where it comes from?
She who Shaped us makes the mist.
We cannot go to her without the mist burning us up, but we can take you part of the way.
Oh!
Who–

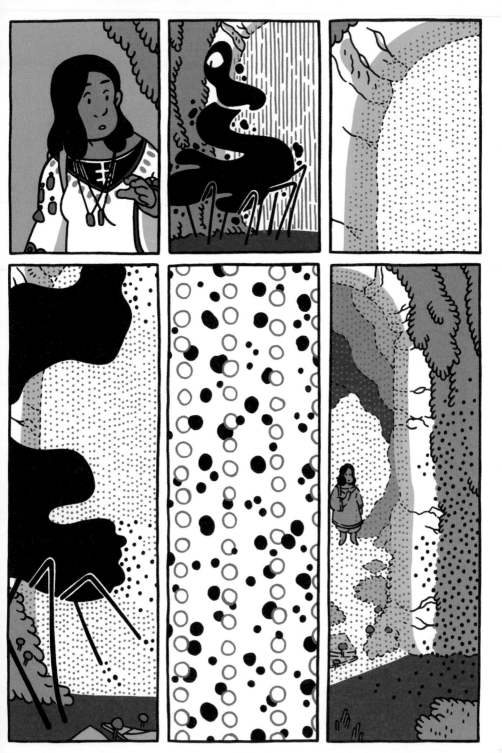

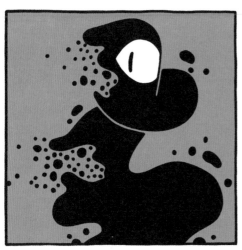

Come through. It is safe.

Ah, I don't think I can.

I don't have the power to change and split apart like you do.

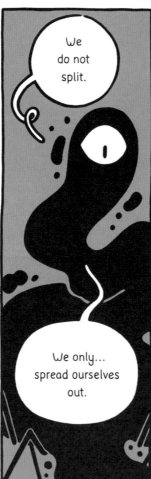

We do not split.

We only... spread ourselves out.

But you can be many different things!

I can't do that, I'm only me. Just one.

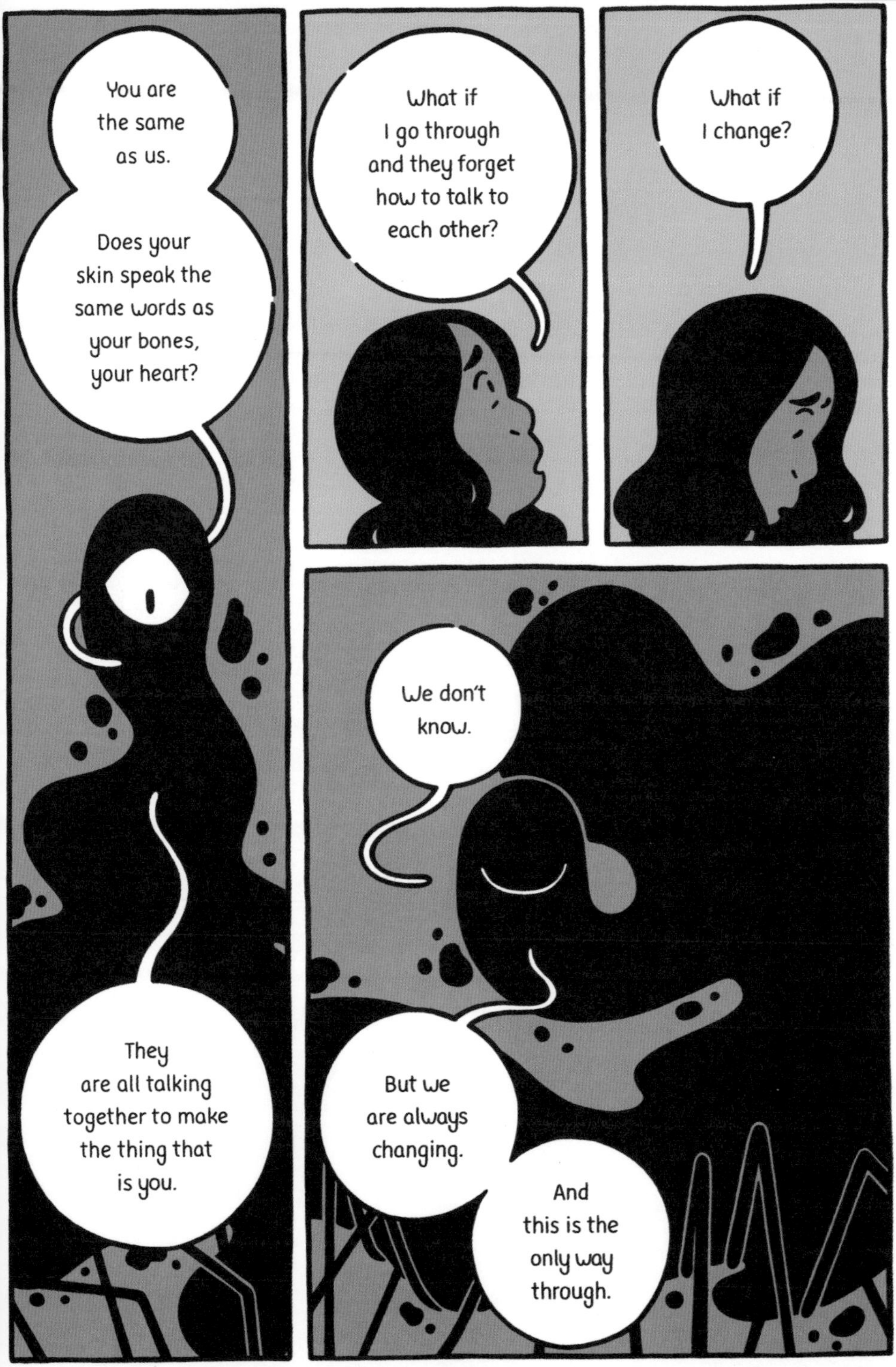
You are the same as us.
Does your skin speak the same words as your bones, your heart?
They are all talking together to make the thing that is you.
What if I go through and they forget how to talk to each other?
What if I change?
We don't know.
But we are always changing.
And this is the only way through.

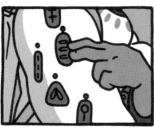

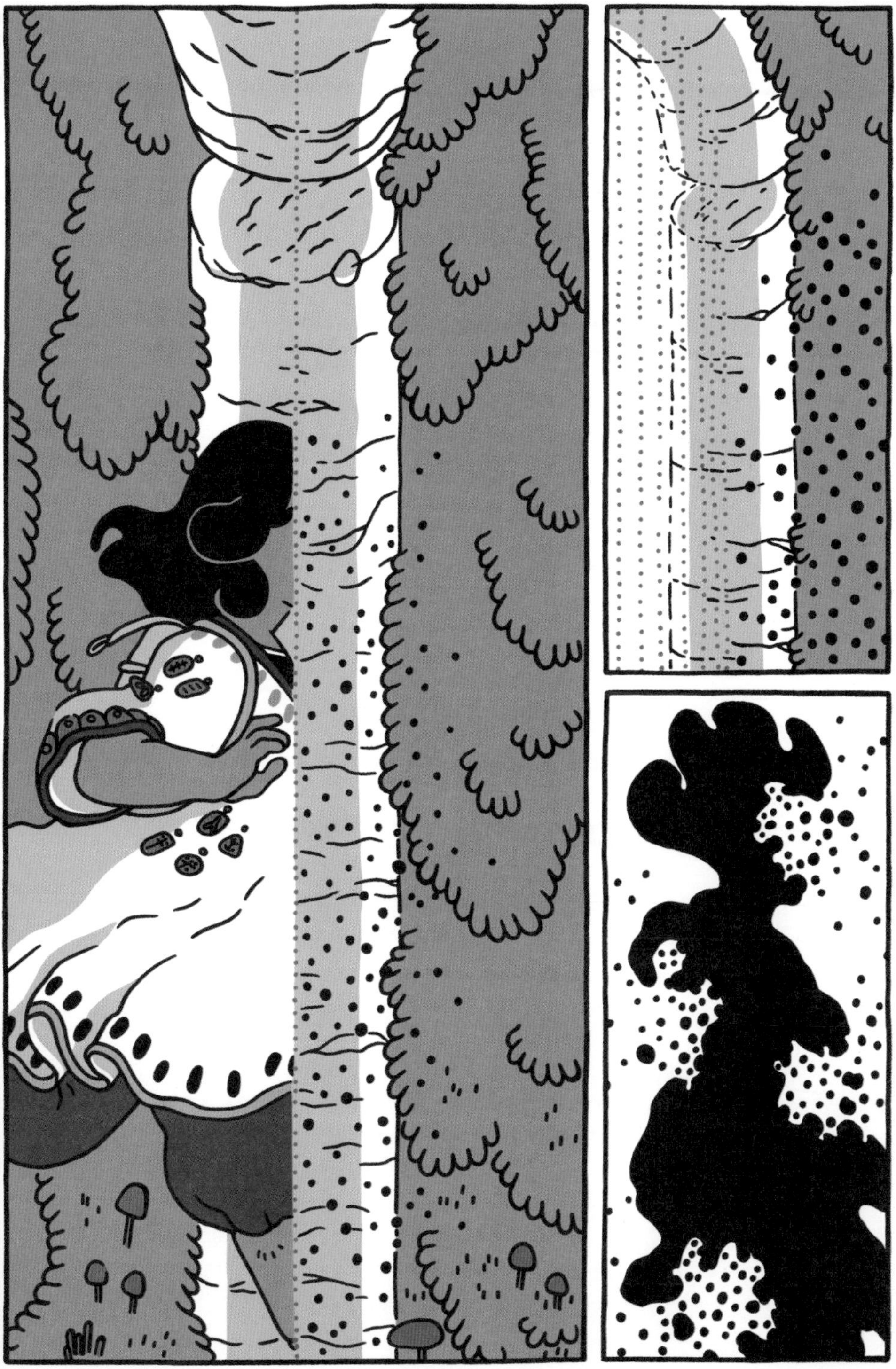

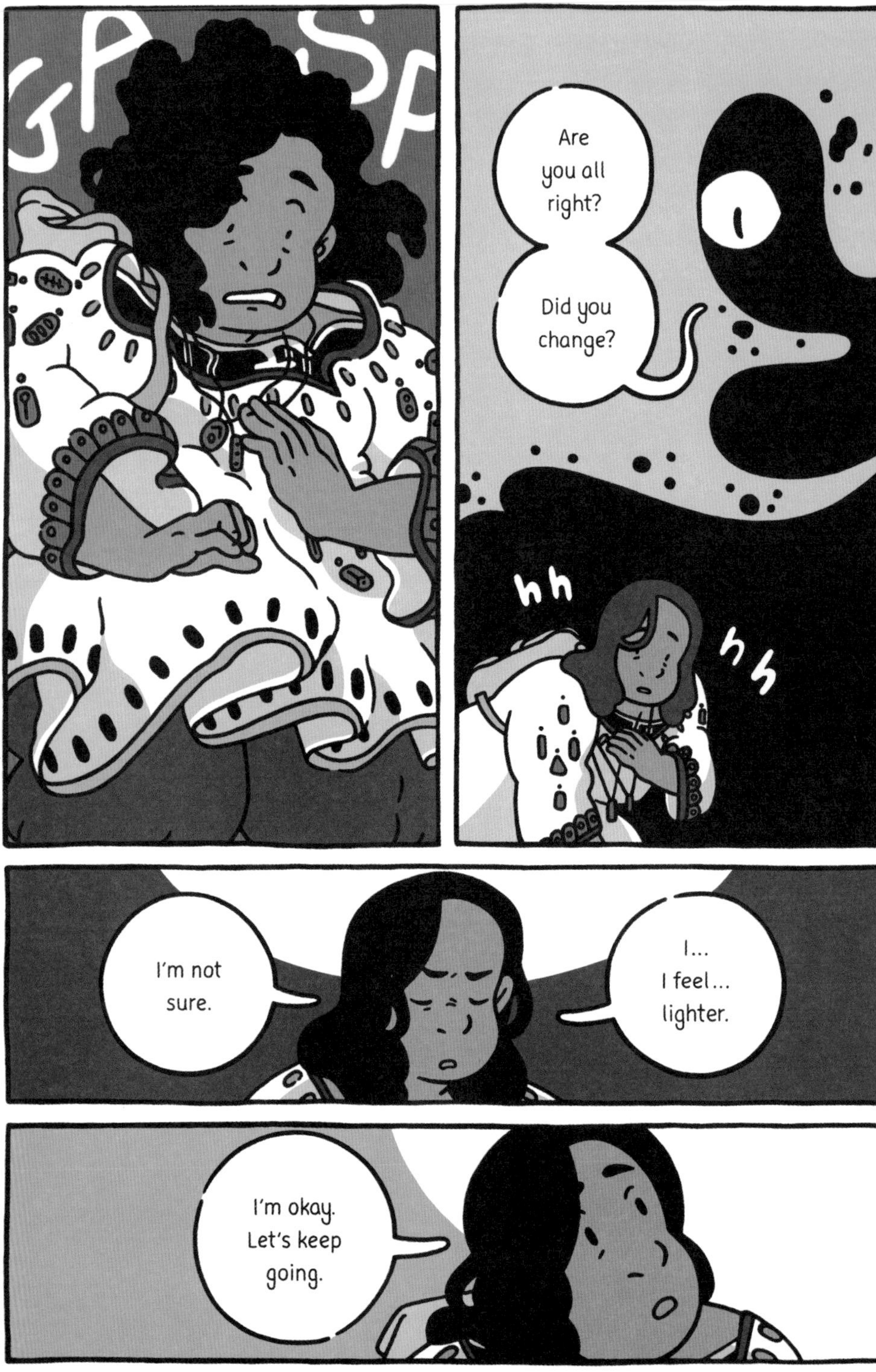
GASP
Are you all right?
Did you change?
hh
hh
I'm not sure.
I... I feel... lighter.
I'm okay. Let's keep going.

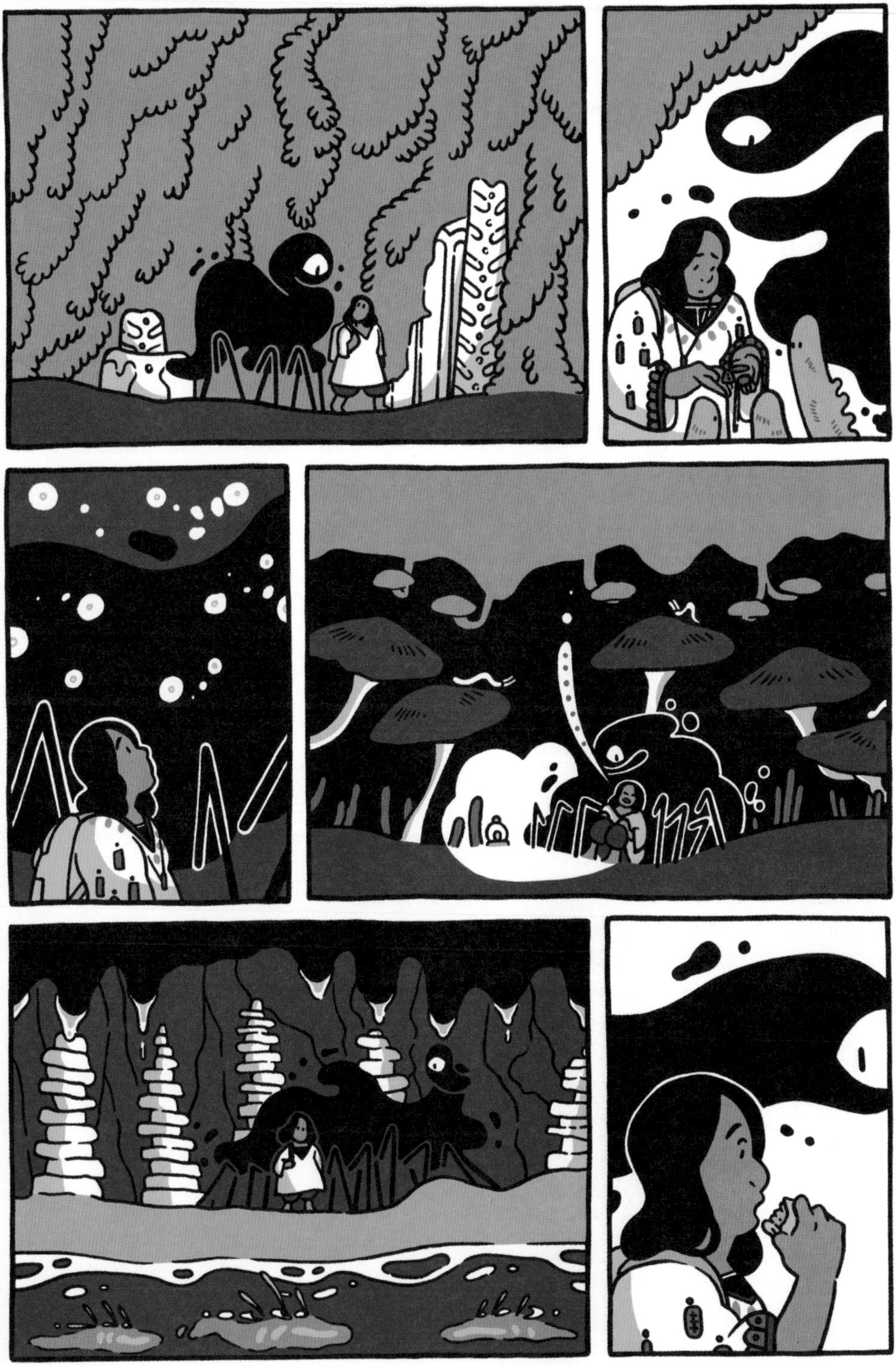

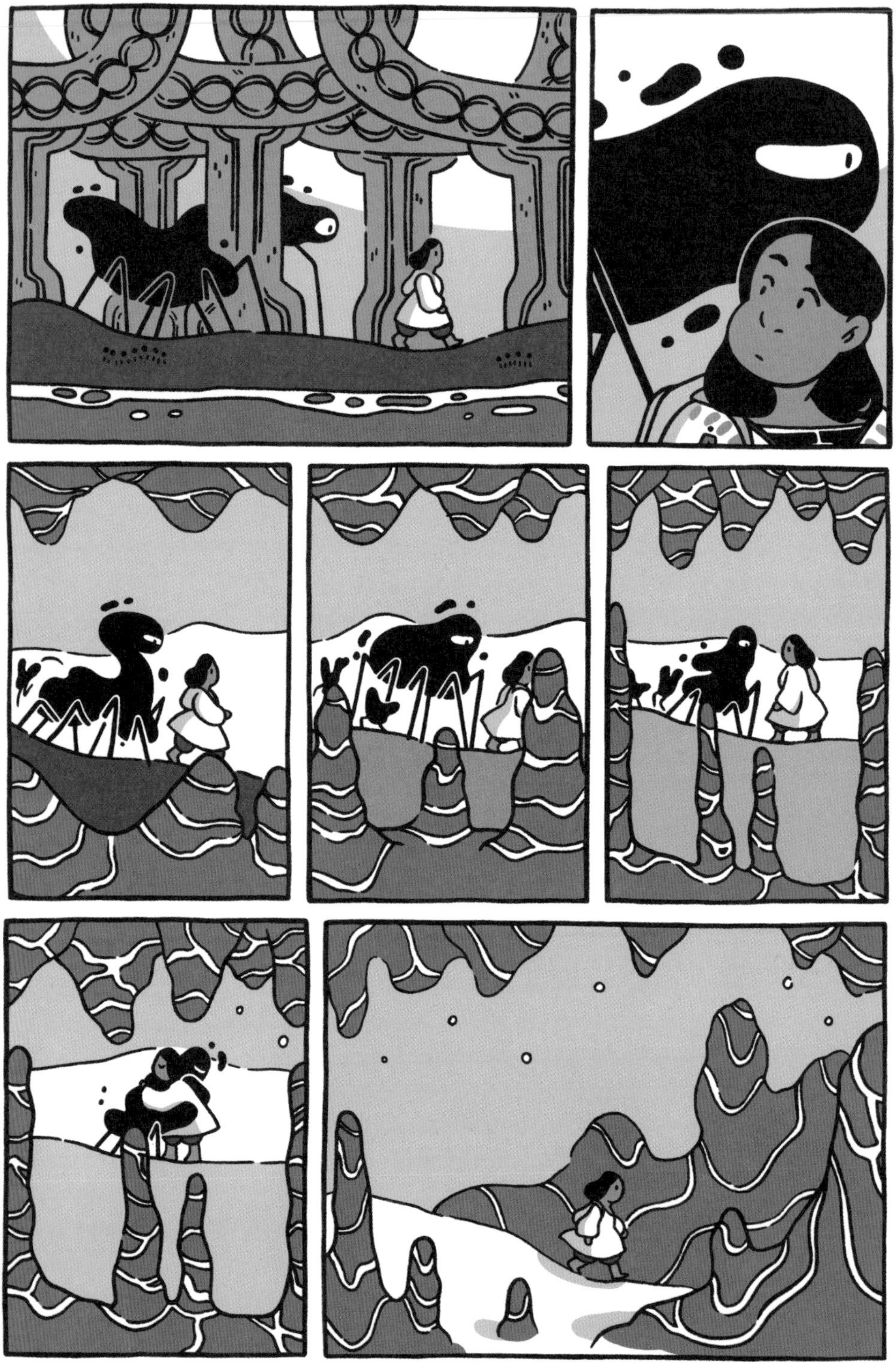

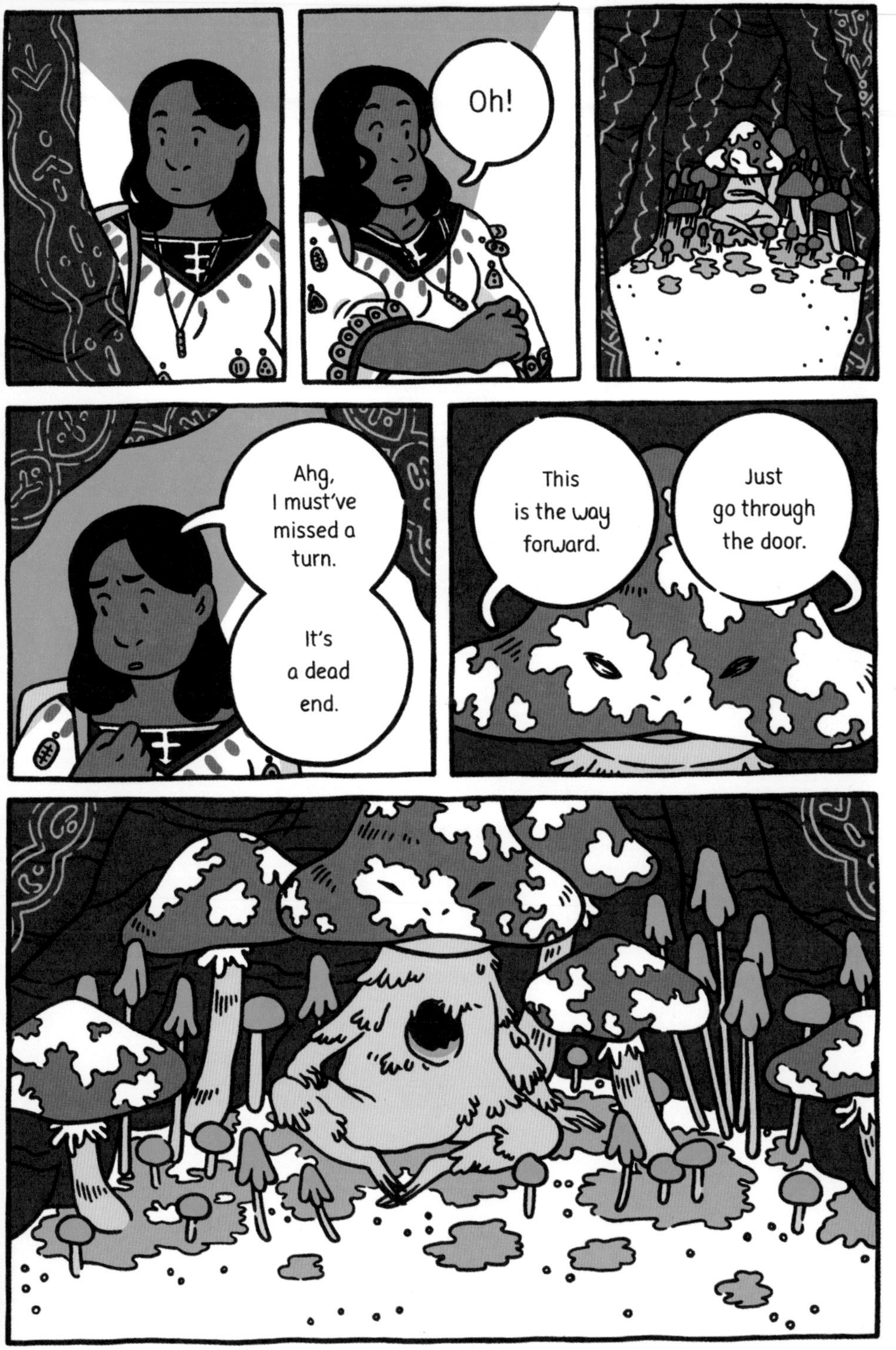
Oh!
Ahg, I must've missed a turn.
It's a dead end.
This is the way forward.
Just go through the door.

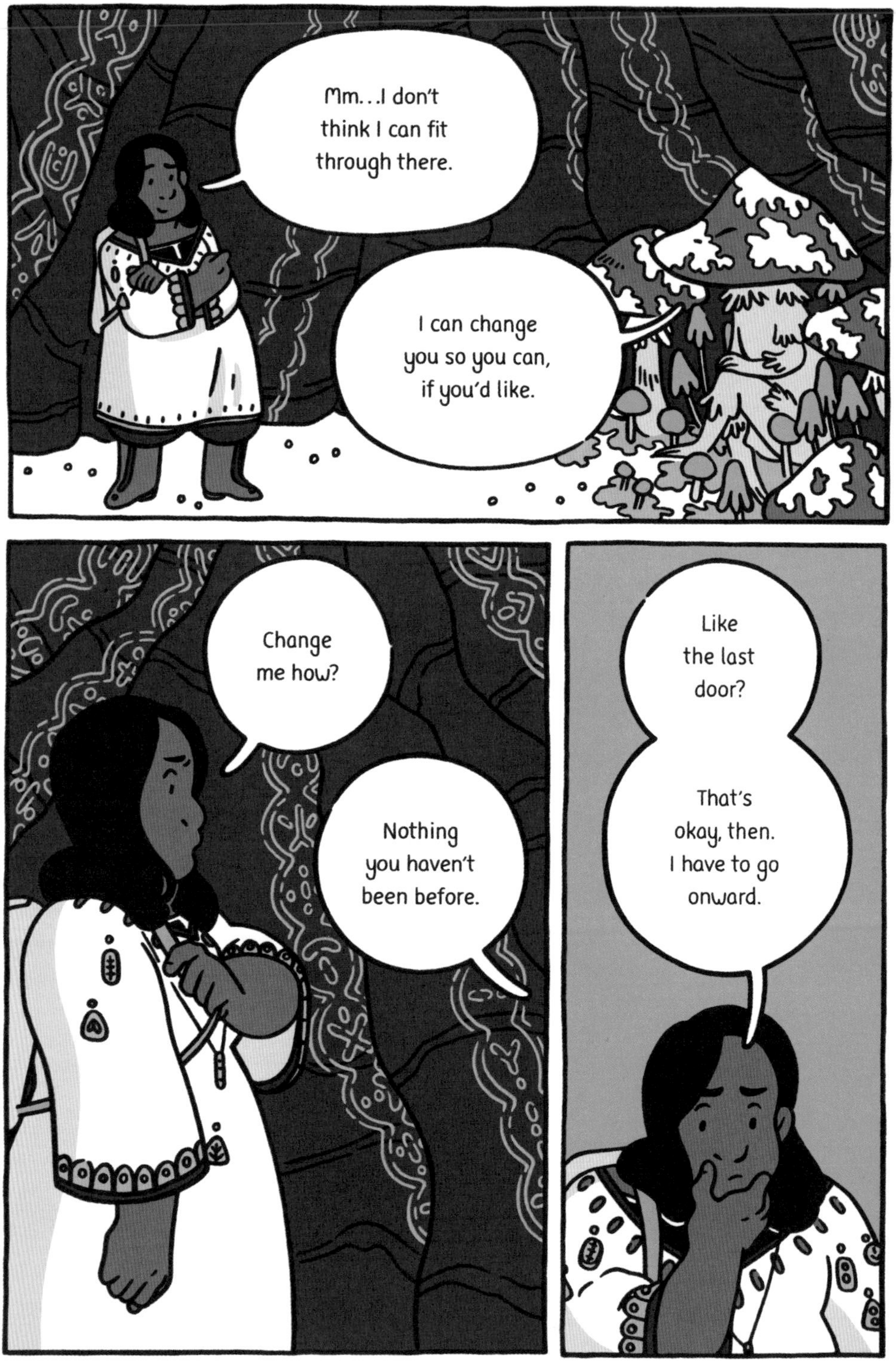
Mm...I don't think I can fit through there.
I can change you so you can, if you'd like.
Change me how?
Nothing you haven't been before.
Like the last door?
That's okay, then. I have to go onward.

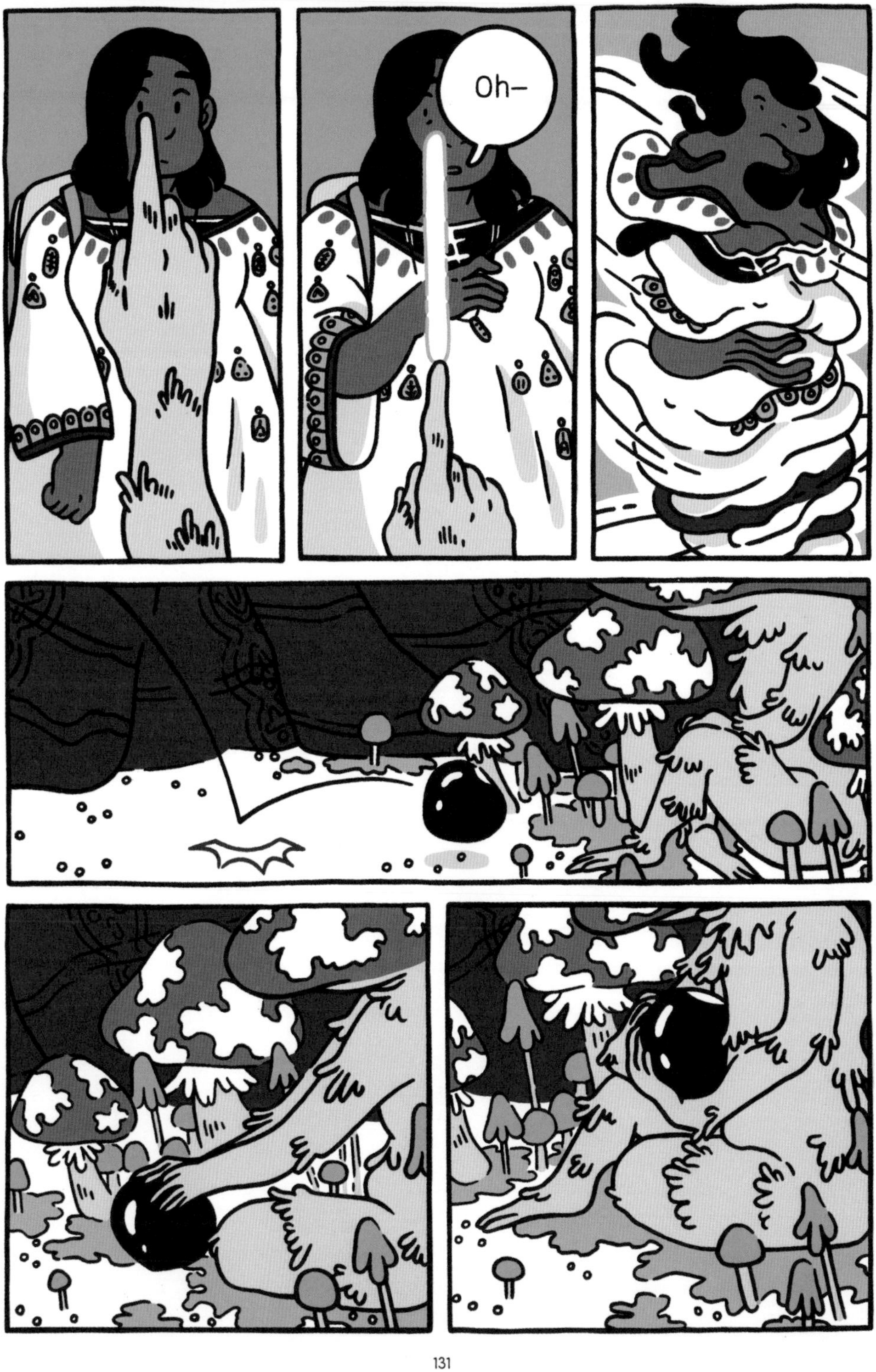
Oh–

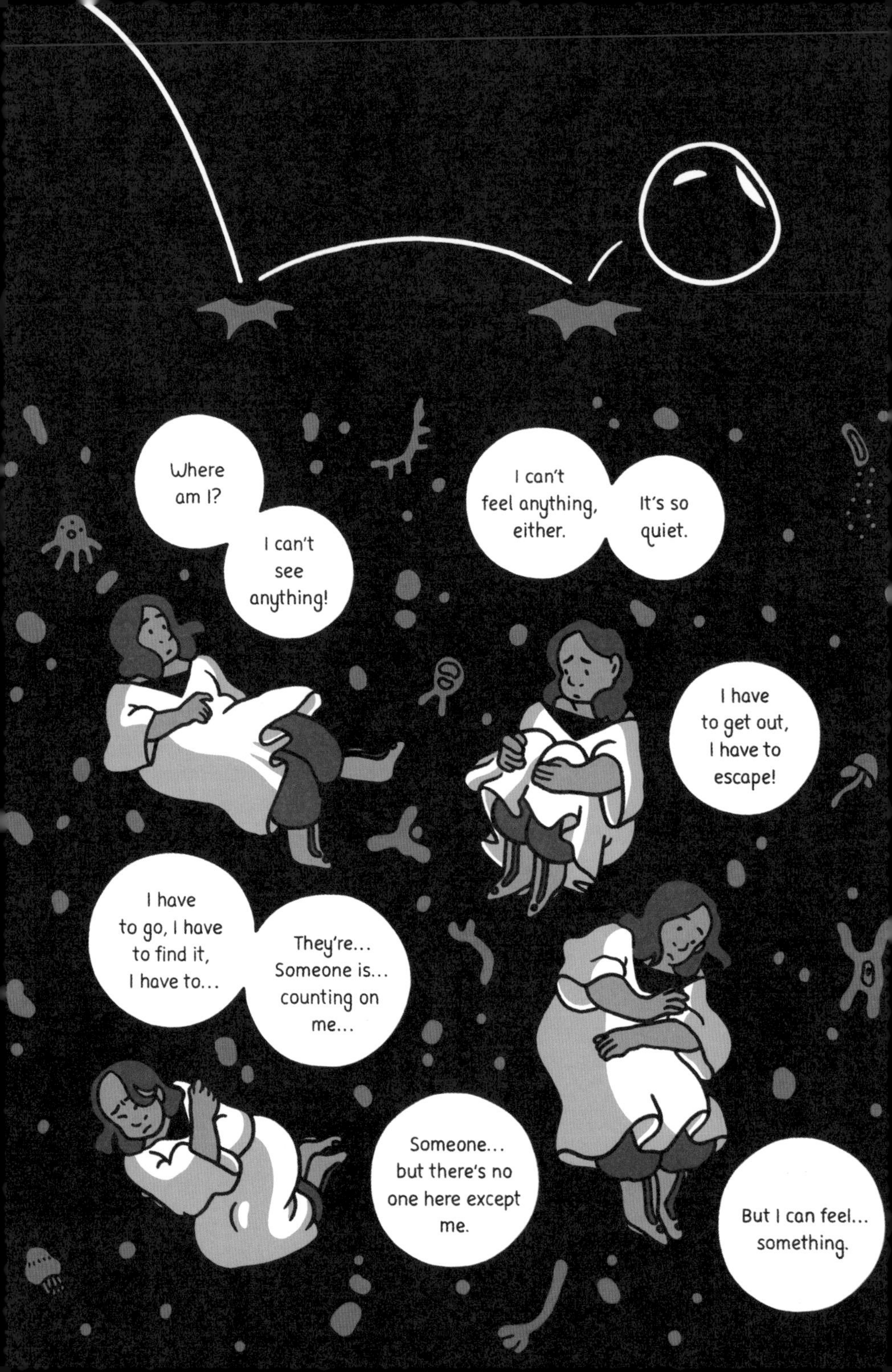
Where am I?
I can't see anything!
I can't feel anything, either.
It's so quiet.
I have to get out, I have to escape!
I have to go, I have to find it, I have to...
They're... Someone is... counting on me...
Someone... but there's no one here except me.
But I can feel... something.

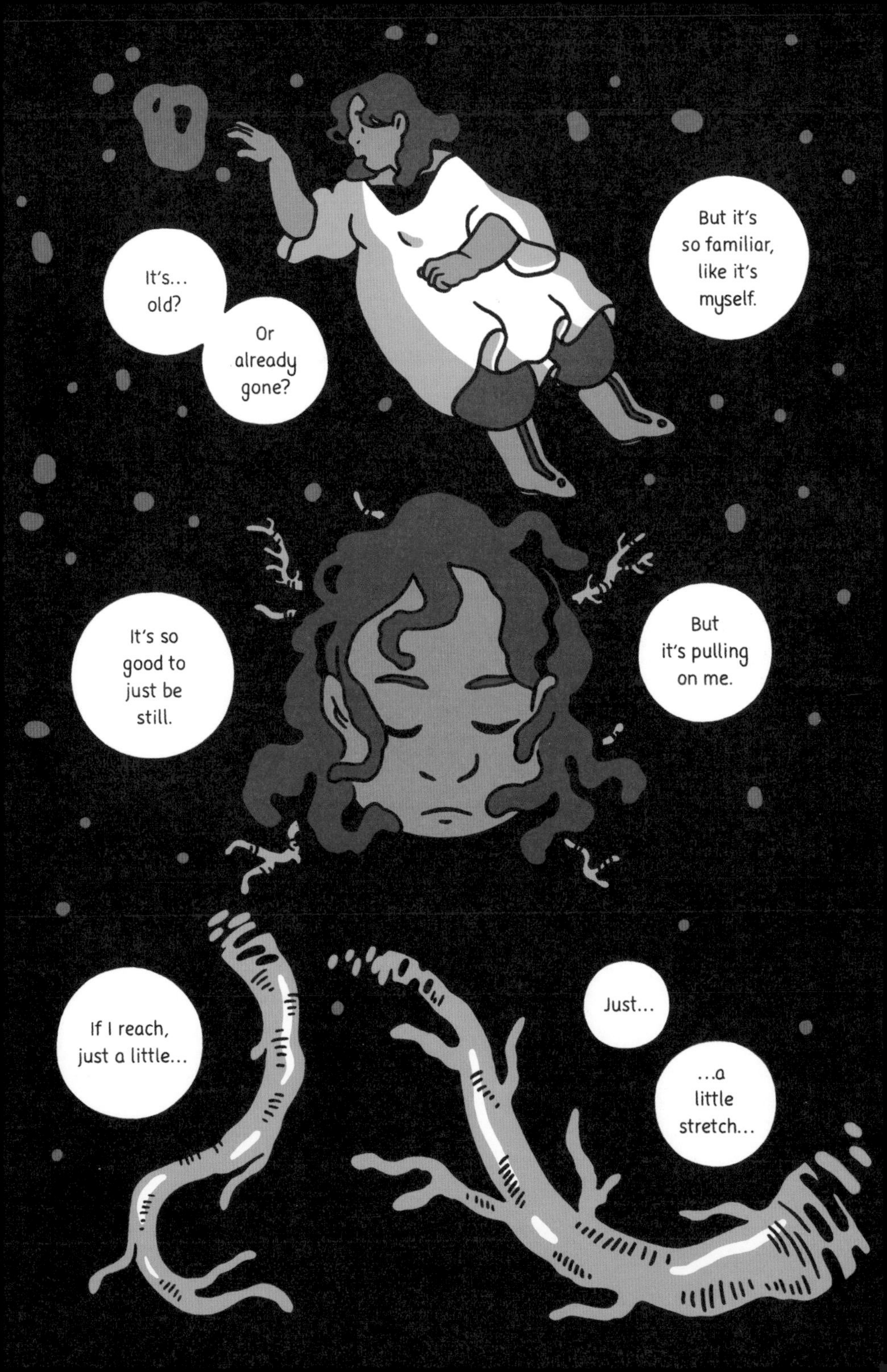
It's... old?
Or already gone?
But it's so familiar, like it's myself.
It's so good to just be still.
But it's pulling on me.
If I reach, just a little...
Just...
...a little stretch...

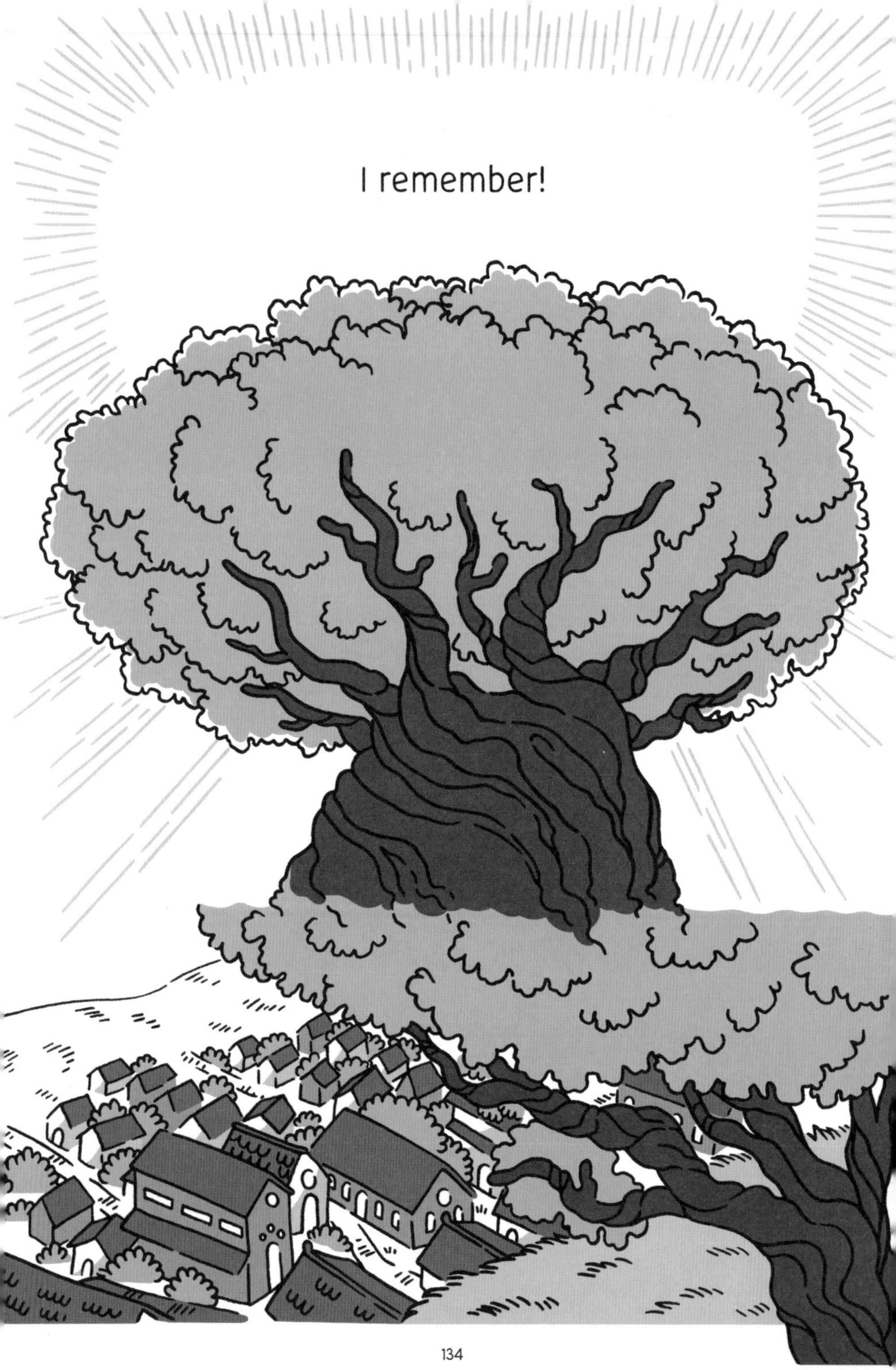
I remember!

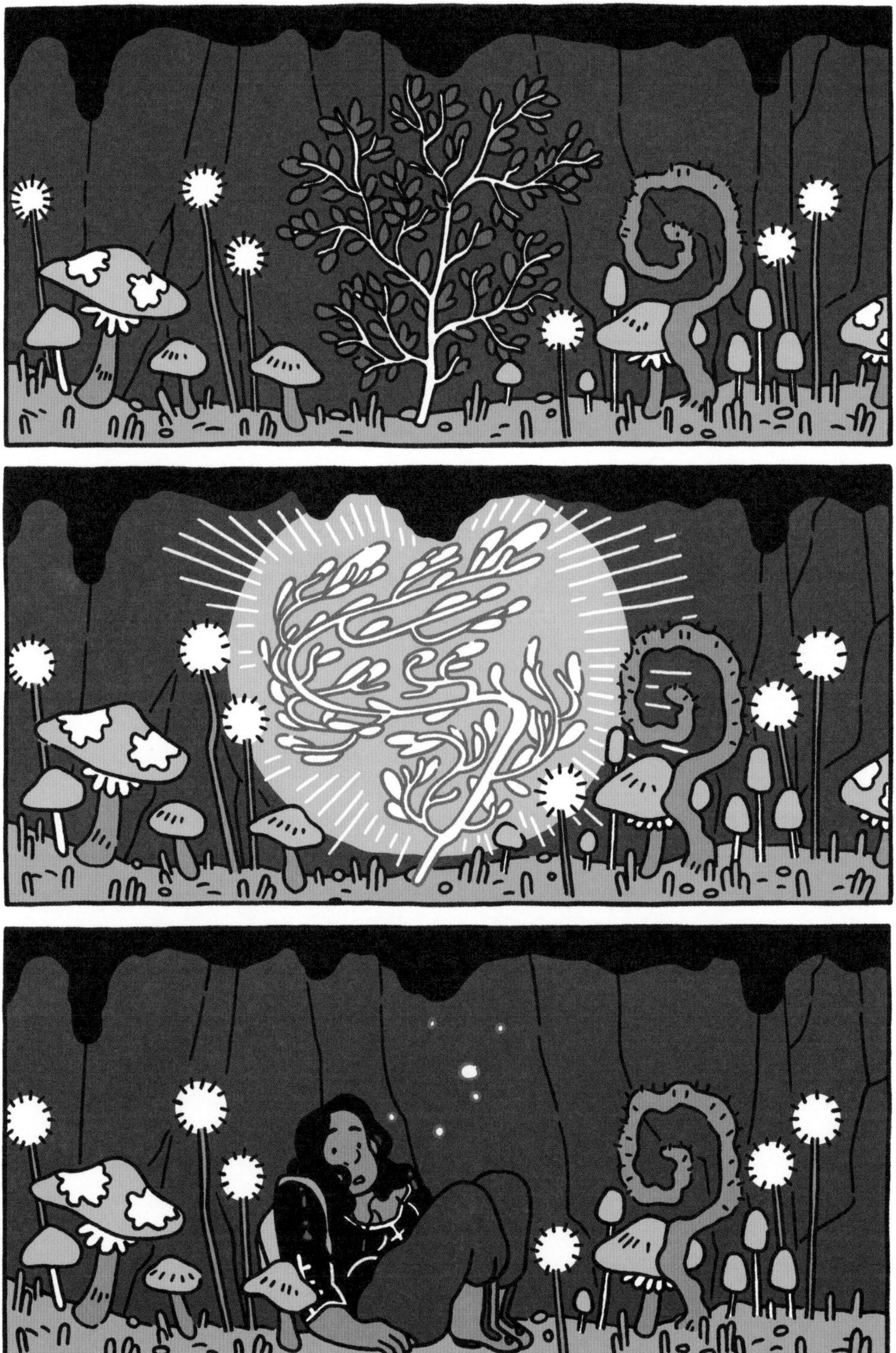

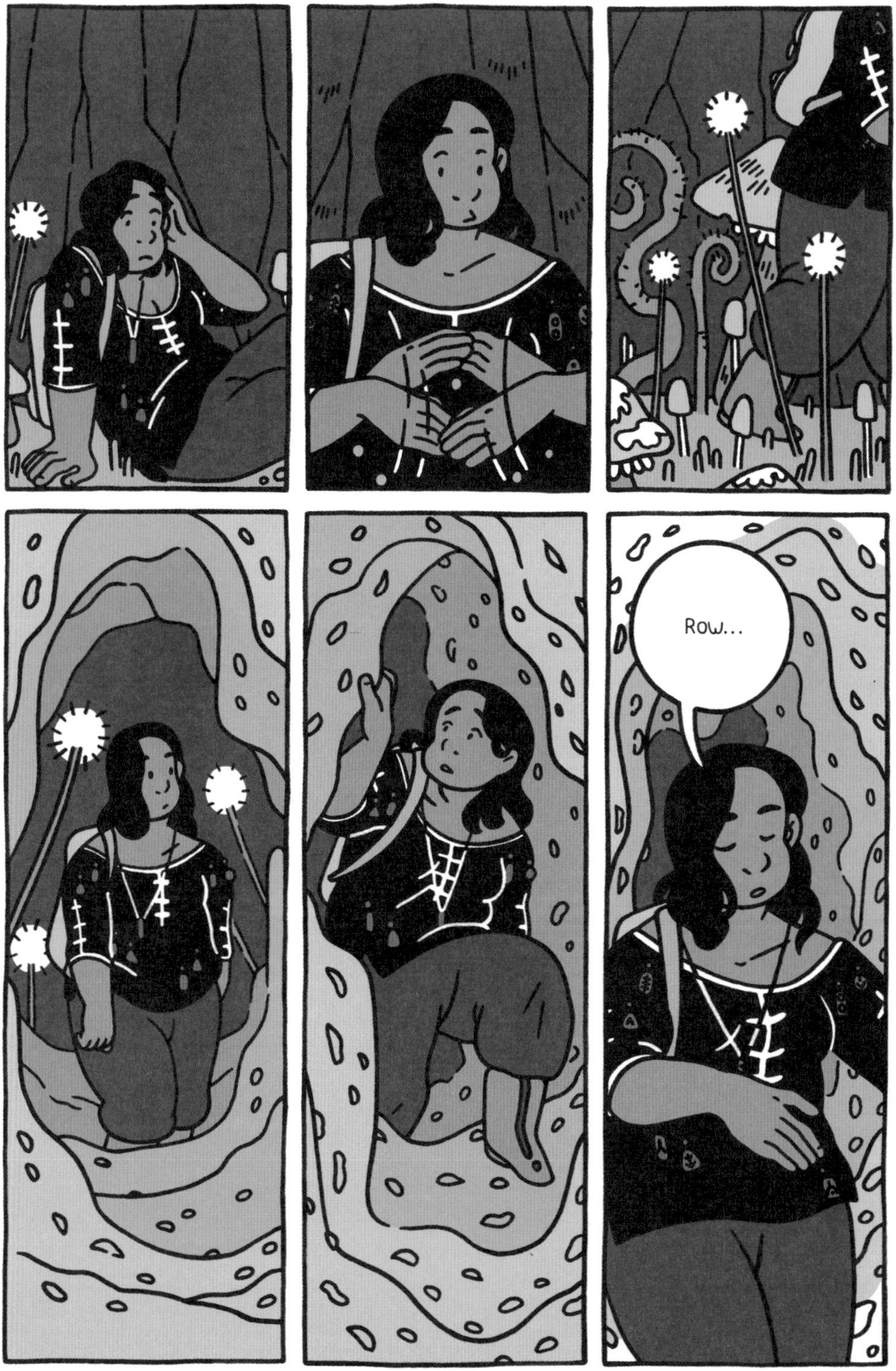
Row...

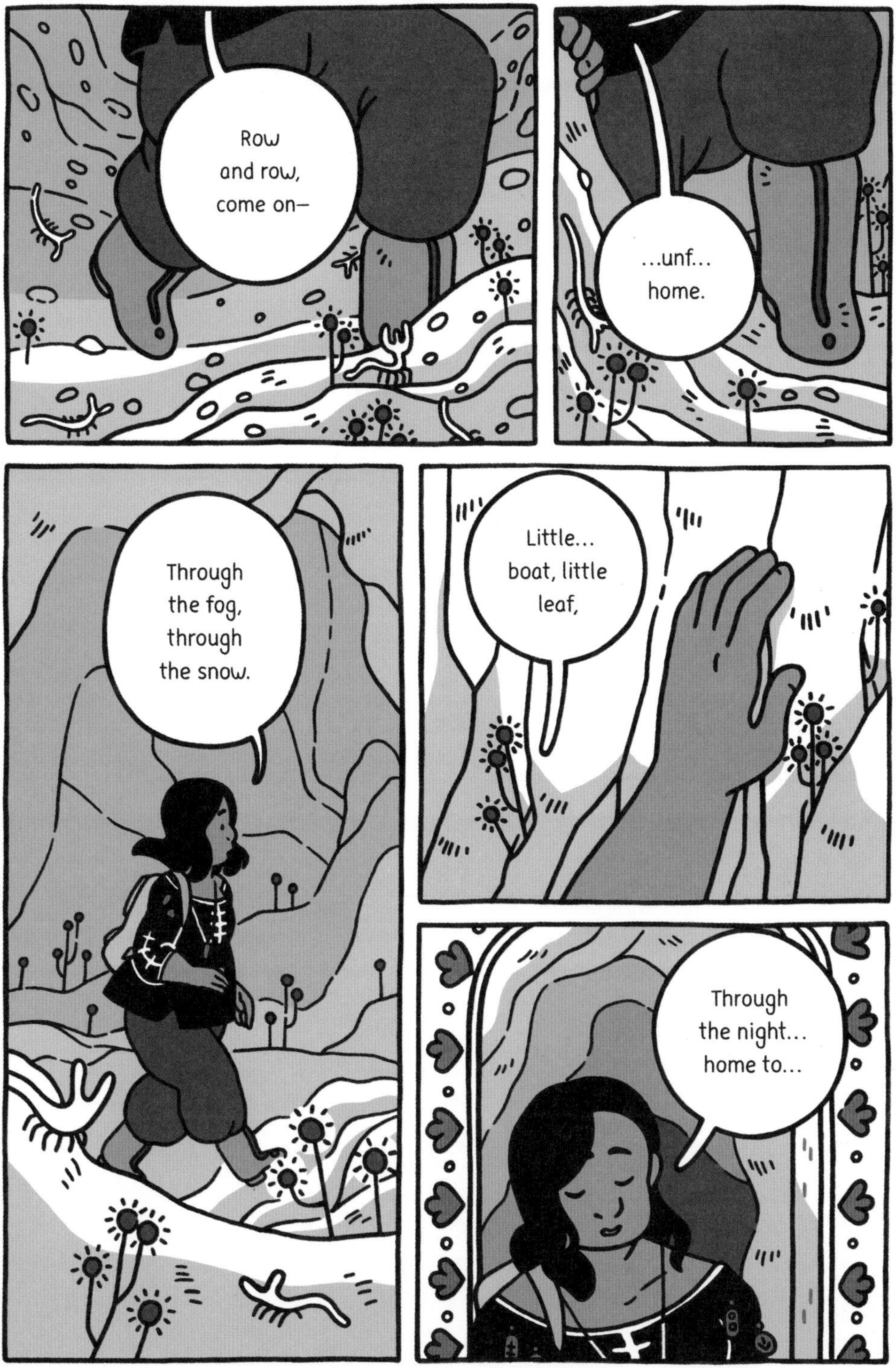
Row and row, come on—
...unf... home.
Through the fog, through the snow.
Little... boat, little leaf,
Through the night... home to...

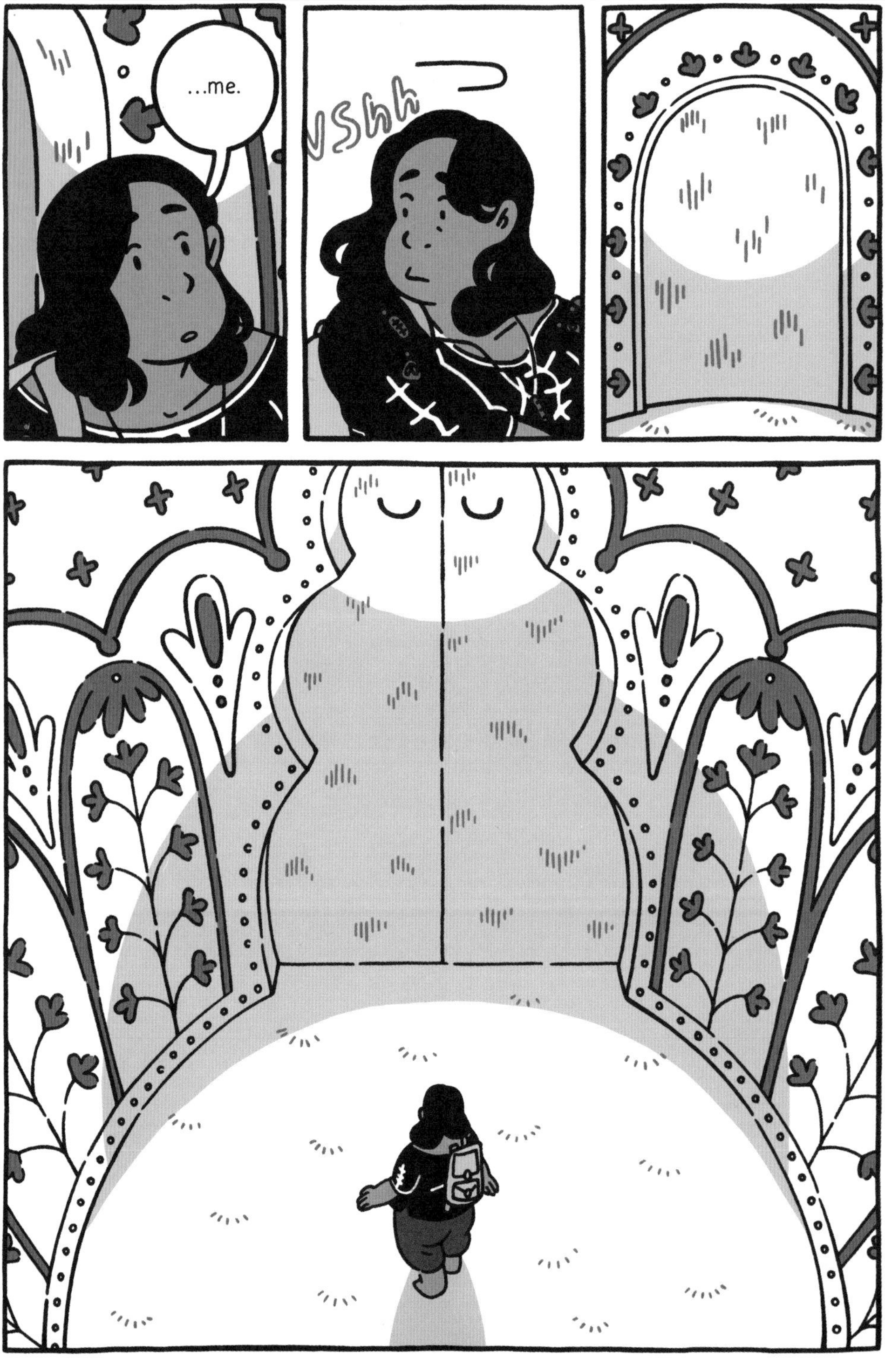
...me.
VSHH

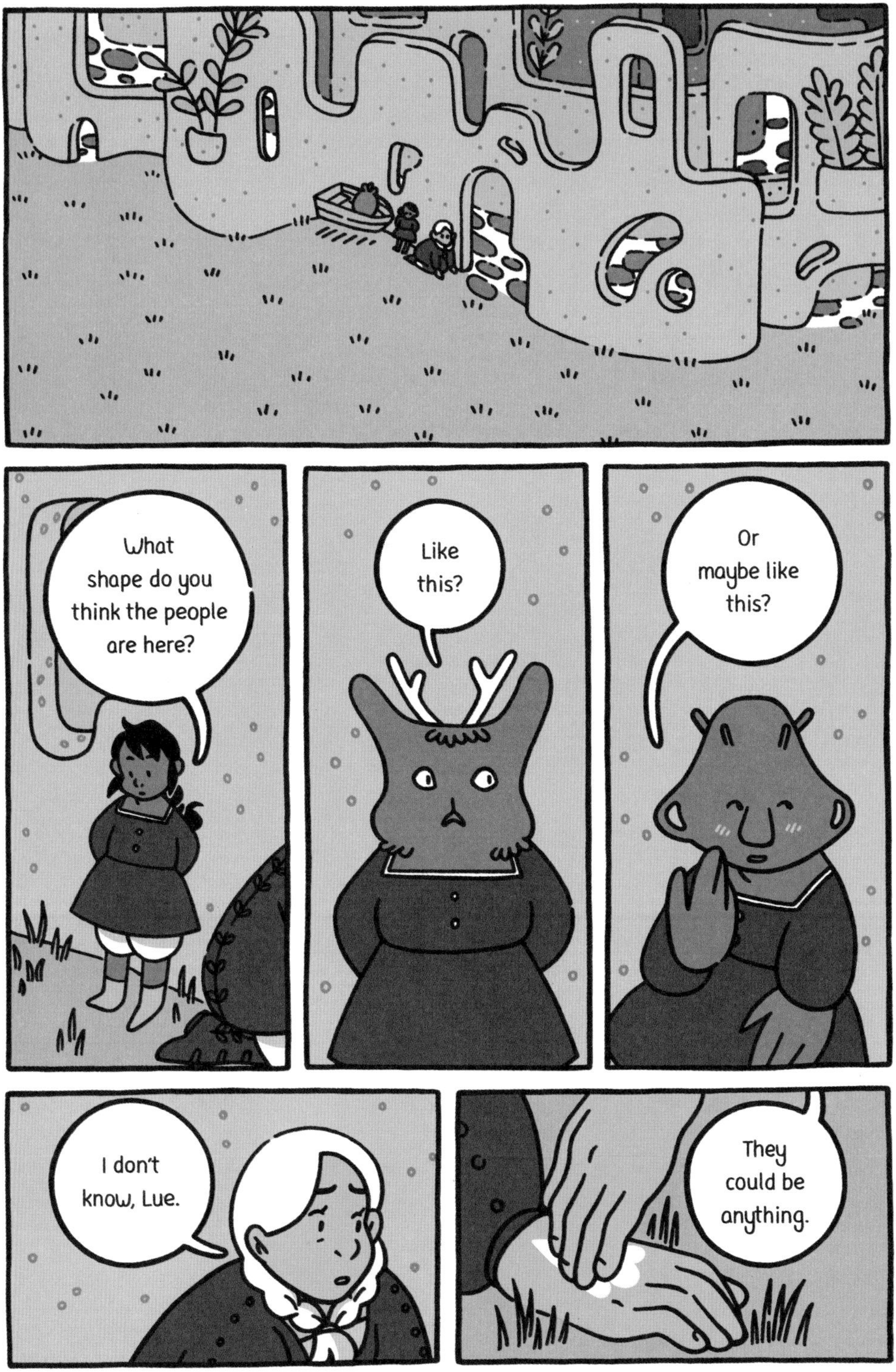

What shape do you think the people are here?
Like this?
Or maybe like this?
I don't know, Lue.
They could be anything.

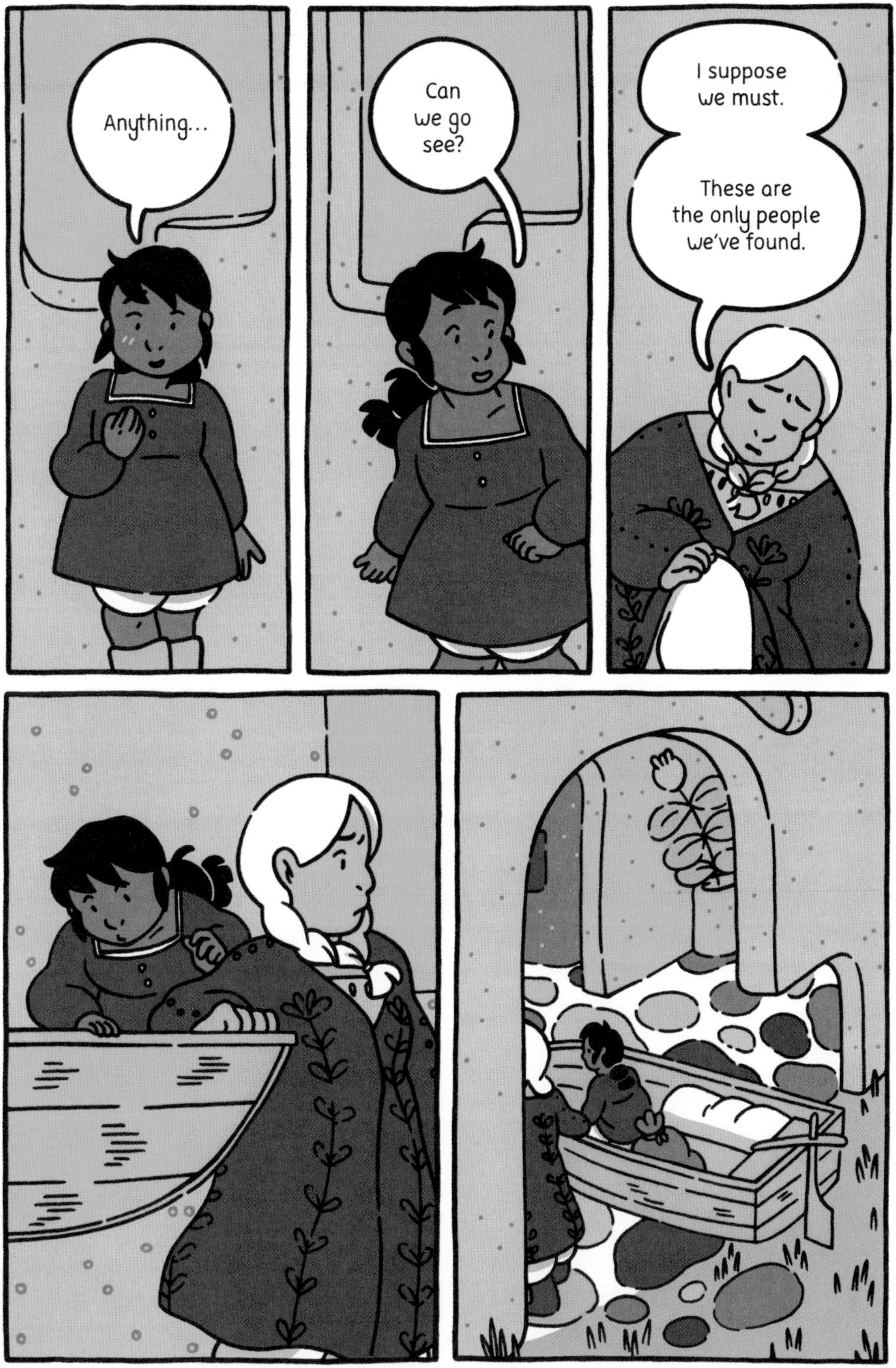
Anything...
Can we go see?
I suppose we must.
These are the only people we've found.

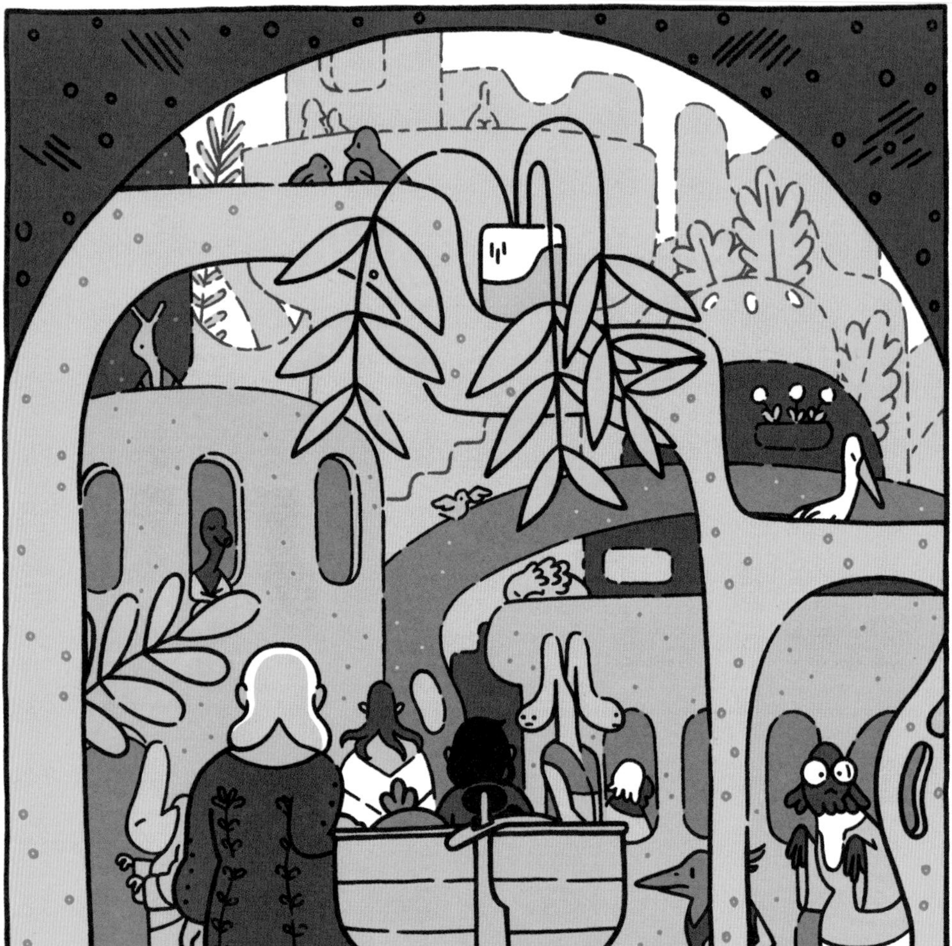

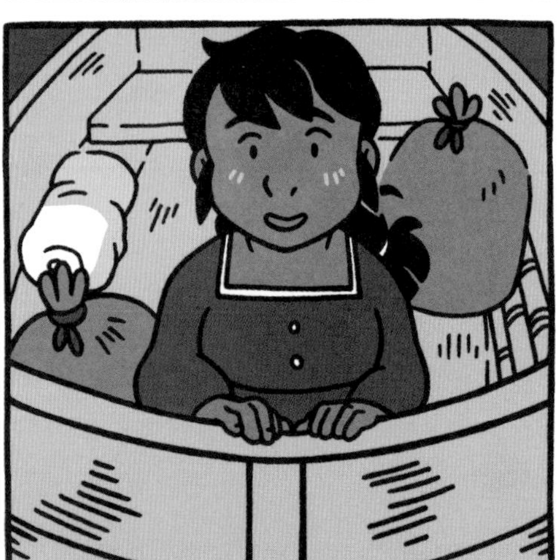

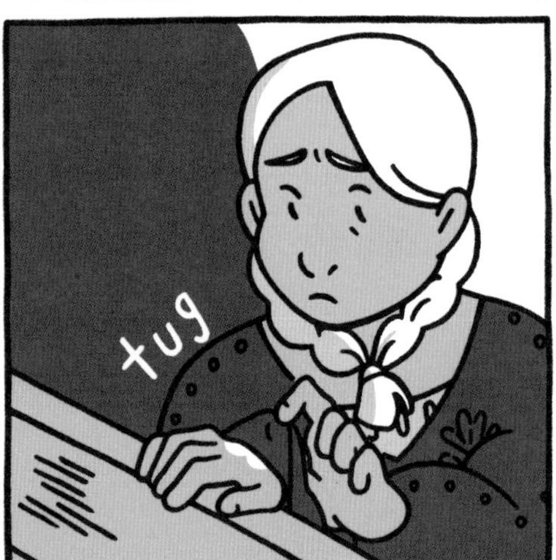
tug

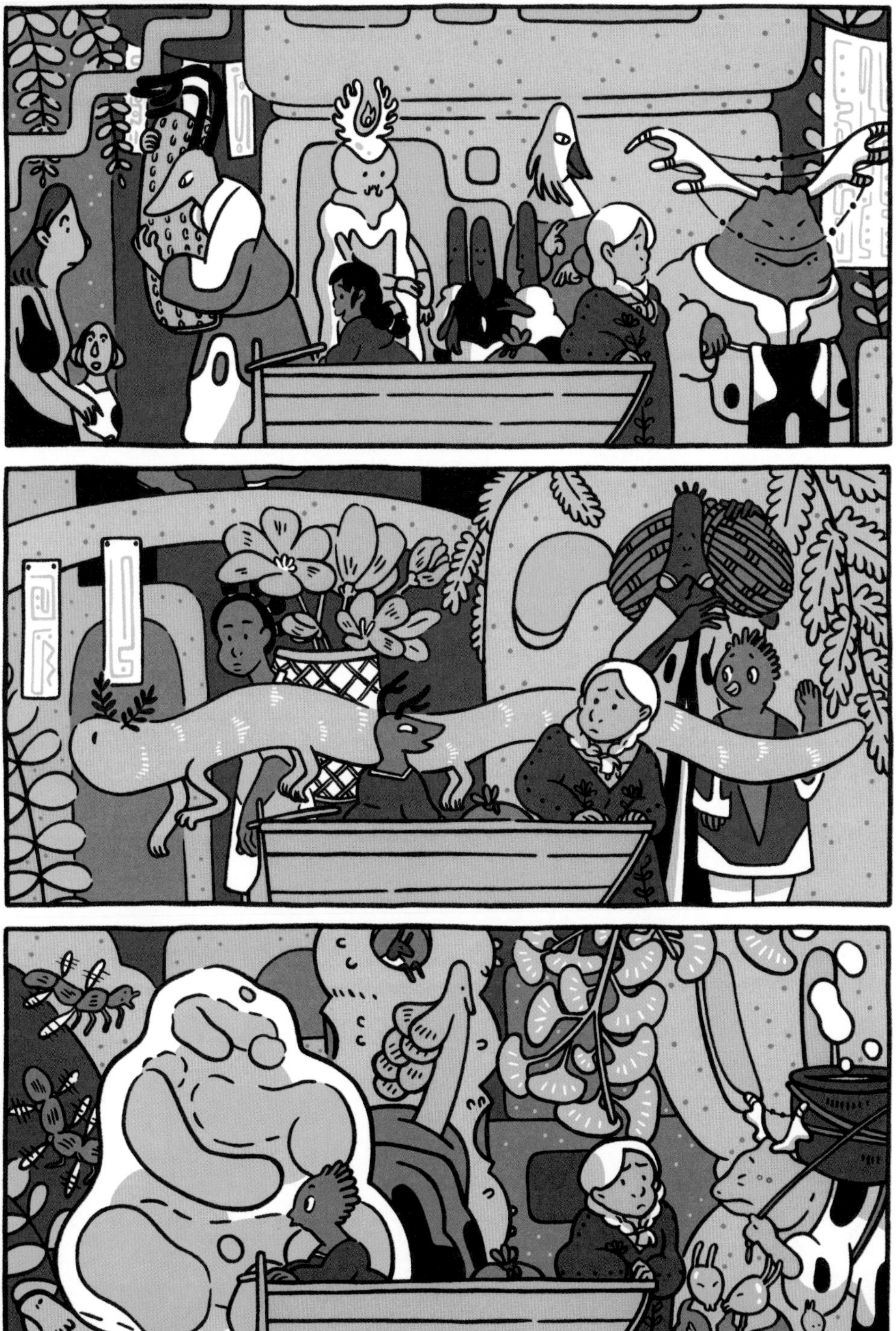

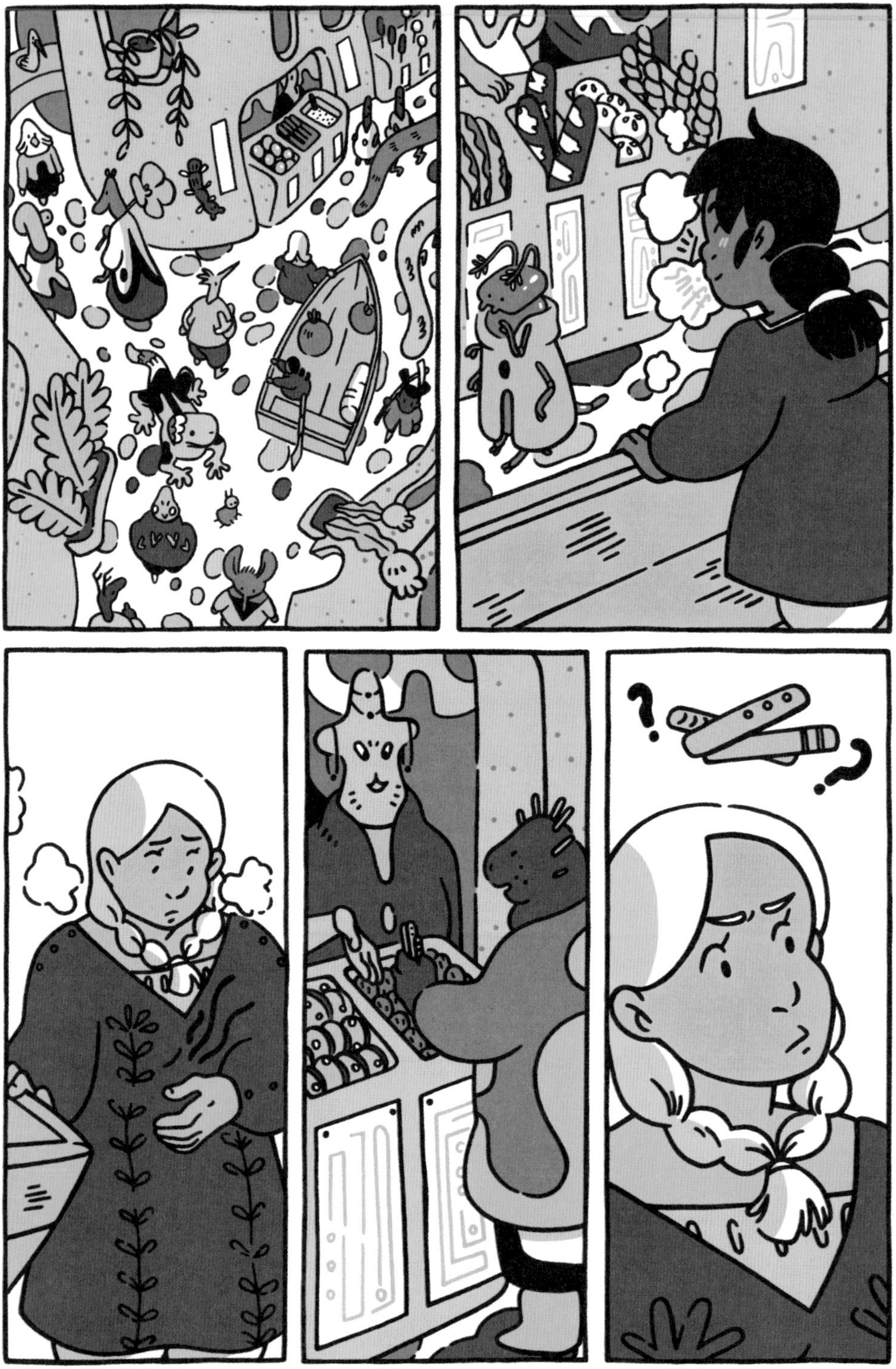
sniff

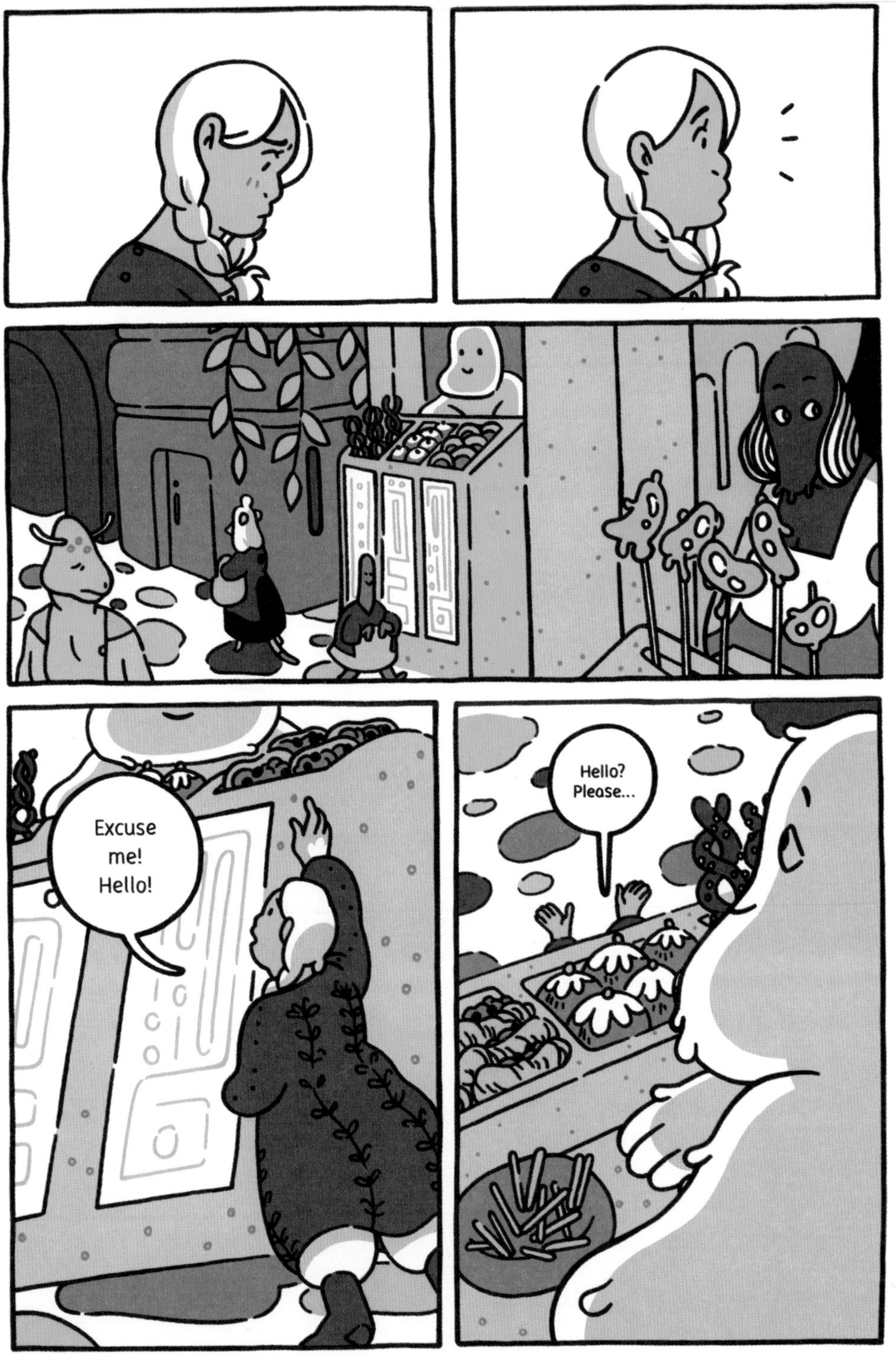
Excuse me! Hello!
Hello? Please...

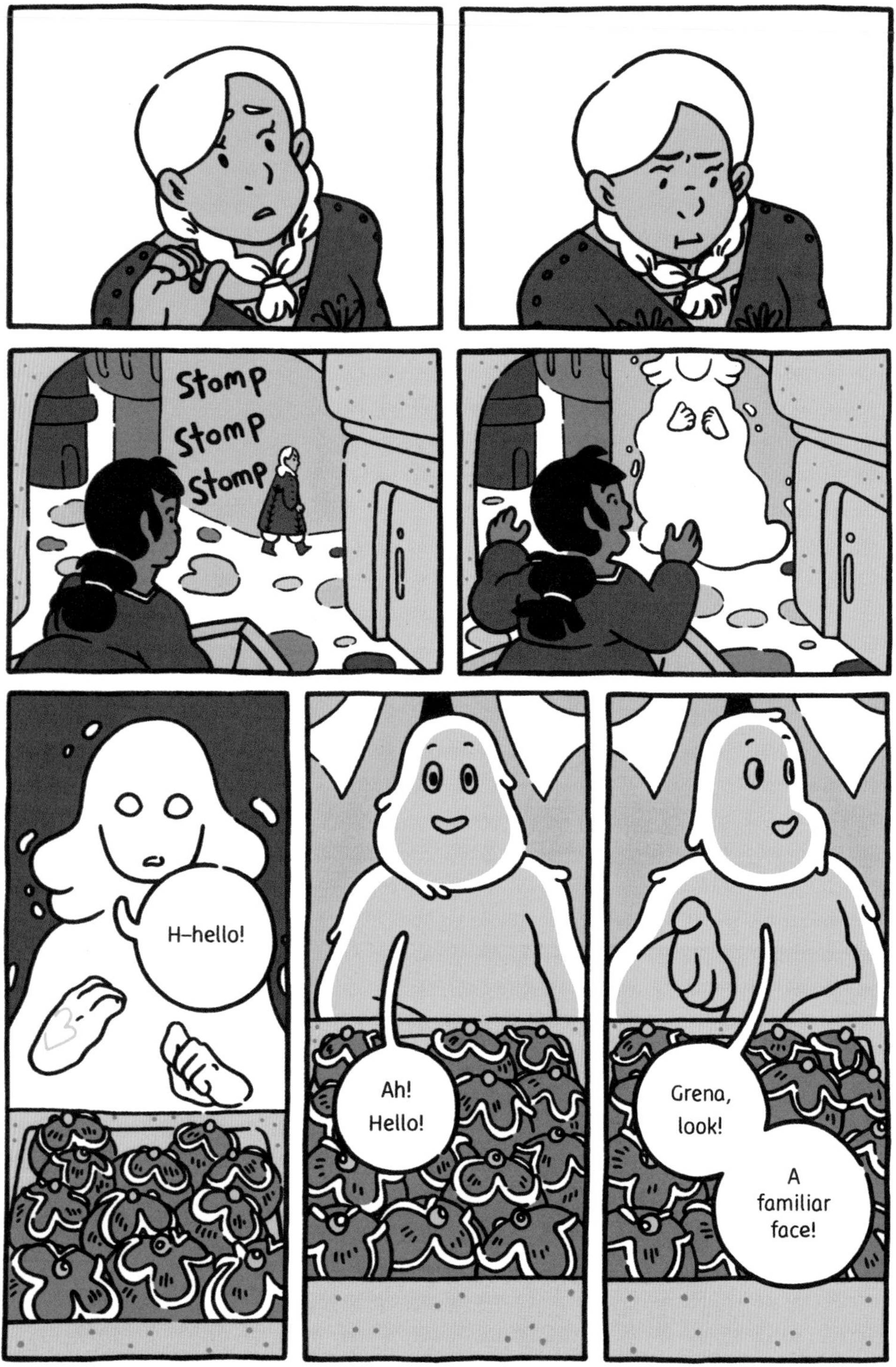
Stomp
Stomp
Stomp
H–hello!
Ah! Hello!
Grena, look!
A familiar face!

Well, well! We don't see folks like us often.

What brings you here?

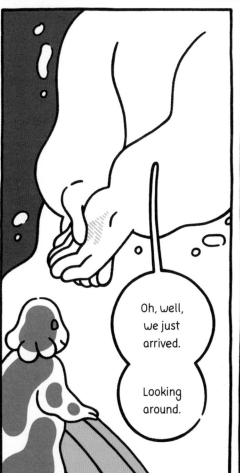

Oh, well, we just arrived.

Looking around.

Welcome, then!

Here, have a pastry, on the house.

Oh!

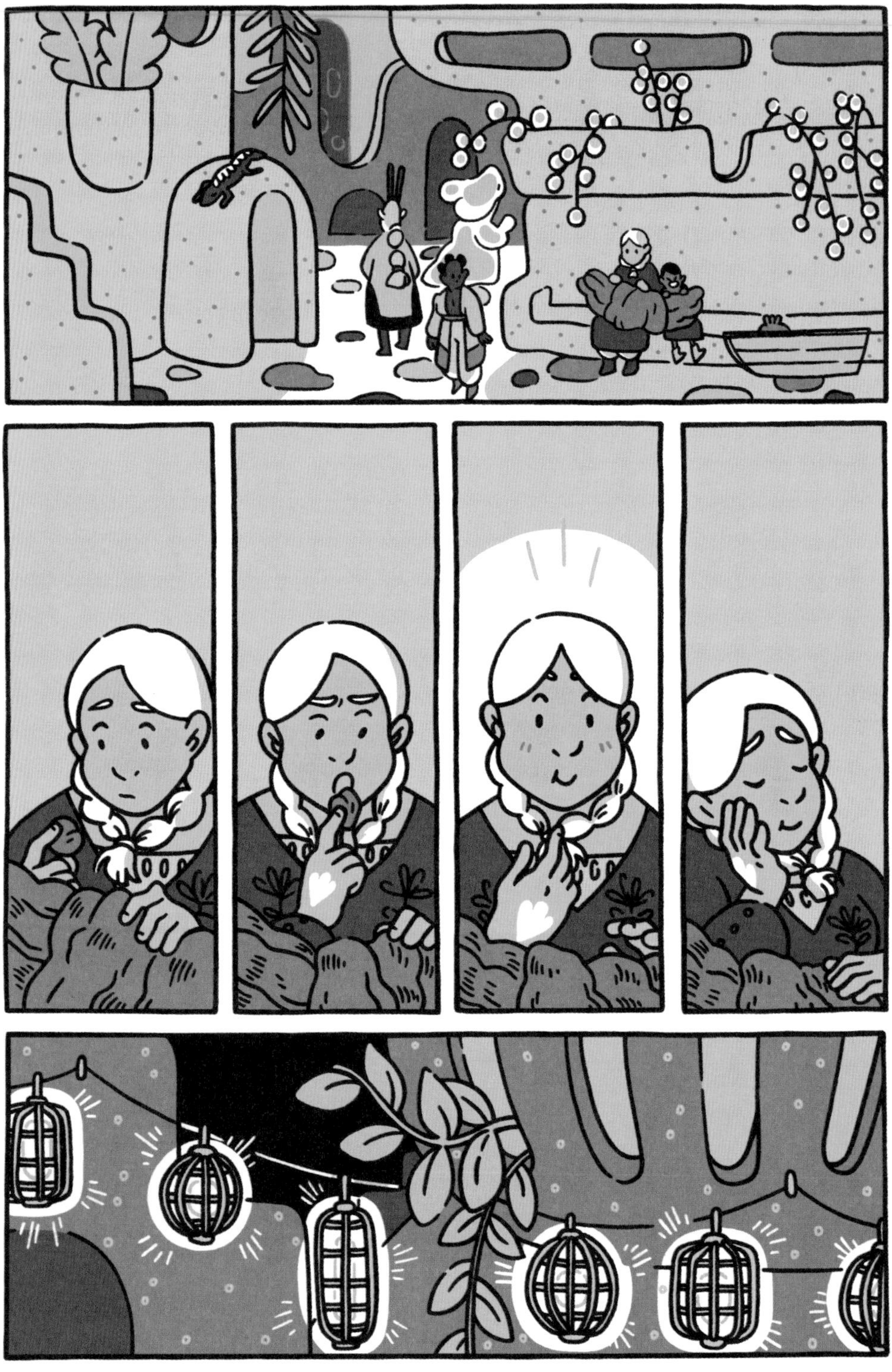

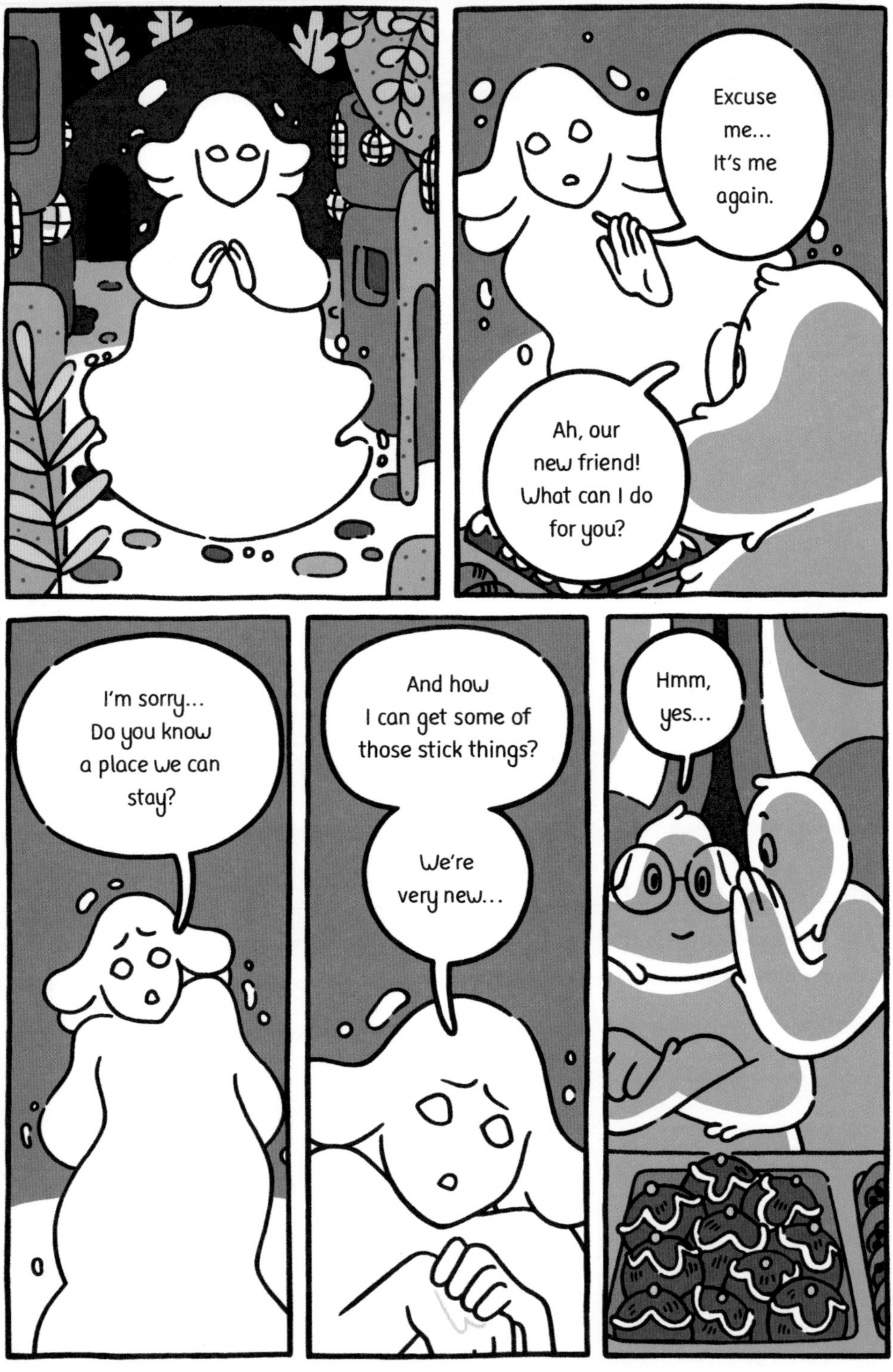
Excuse me... It's me again.
Ah, our new friend! What can I do for you?
I'm sorry... Do you know a place we can stay?
And how I can get some of those stick things?
We're very new...
Hmm, yes...

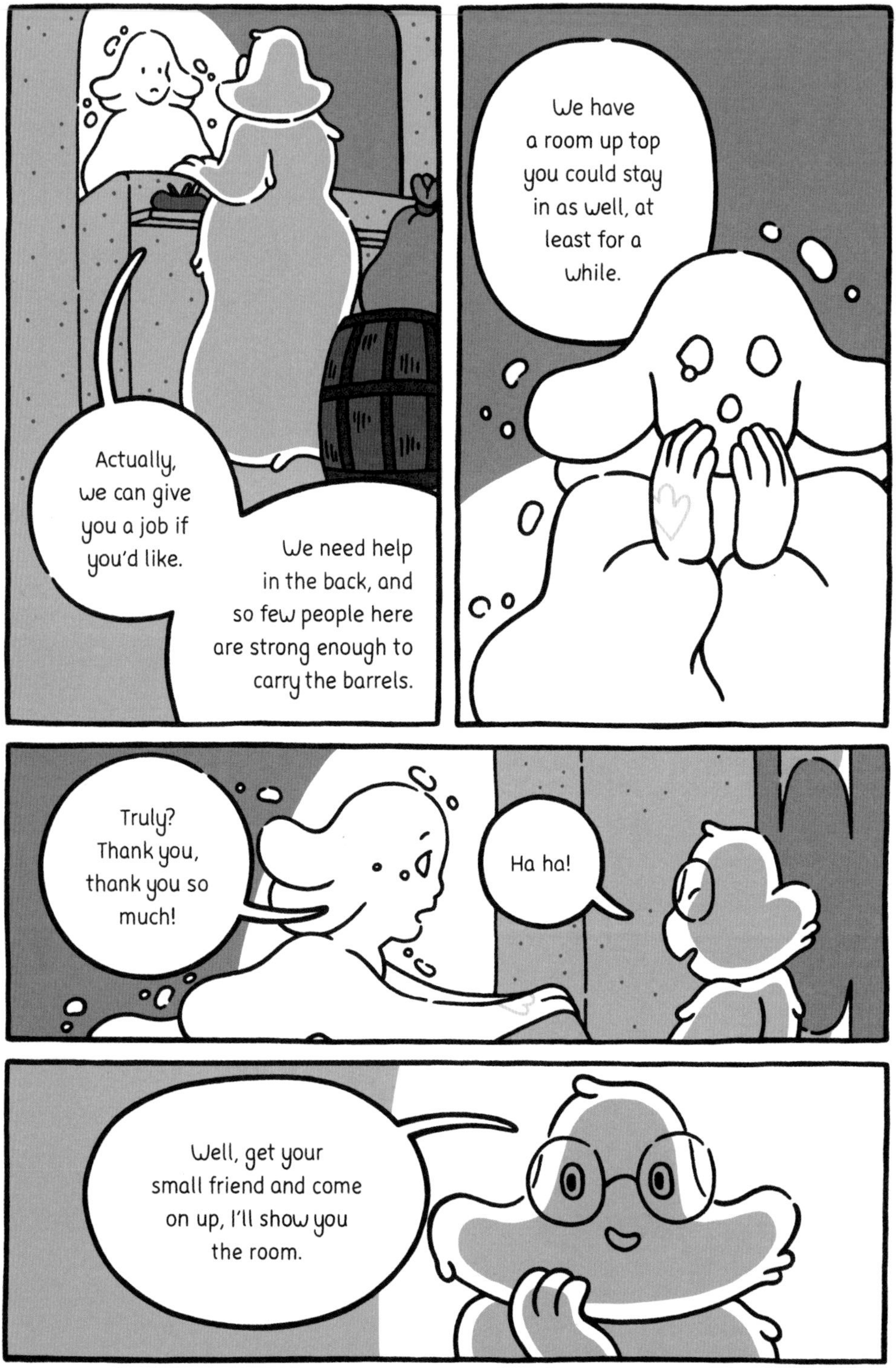
Actually, we can give you a job if you'd like.
We need help in the back, and so few people here are strong enough to carry the barrels.
We have a room up top you could stay in as well, at least for a while.
Truly? Thank you, thank you so much!
Ha ha!
Well, get your small friend and come on up, I'll show you the room.

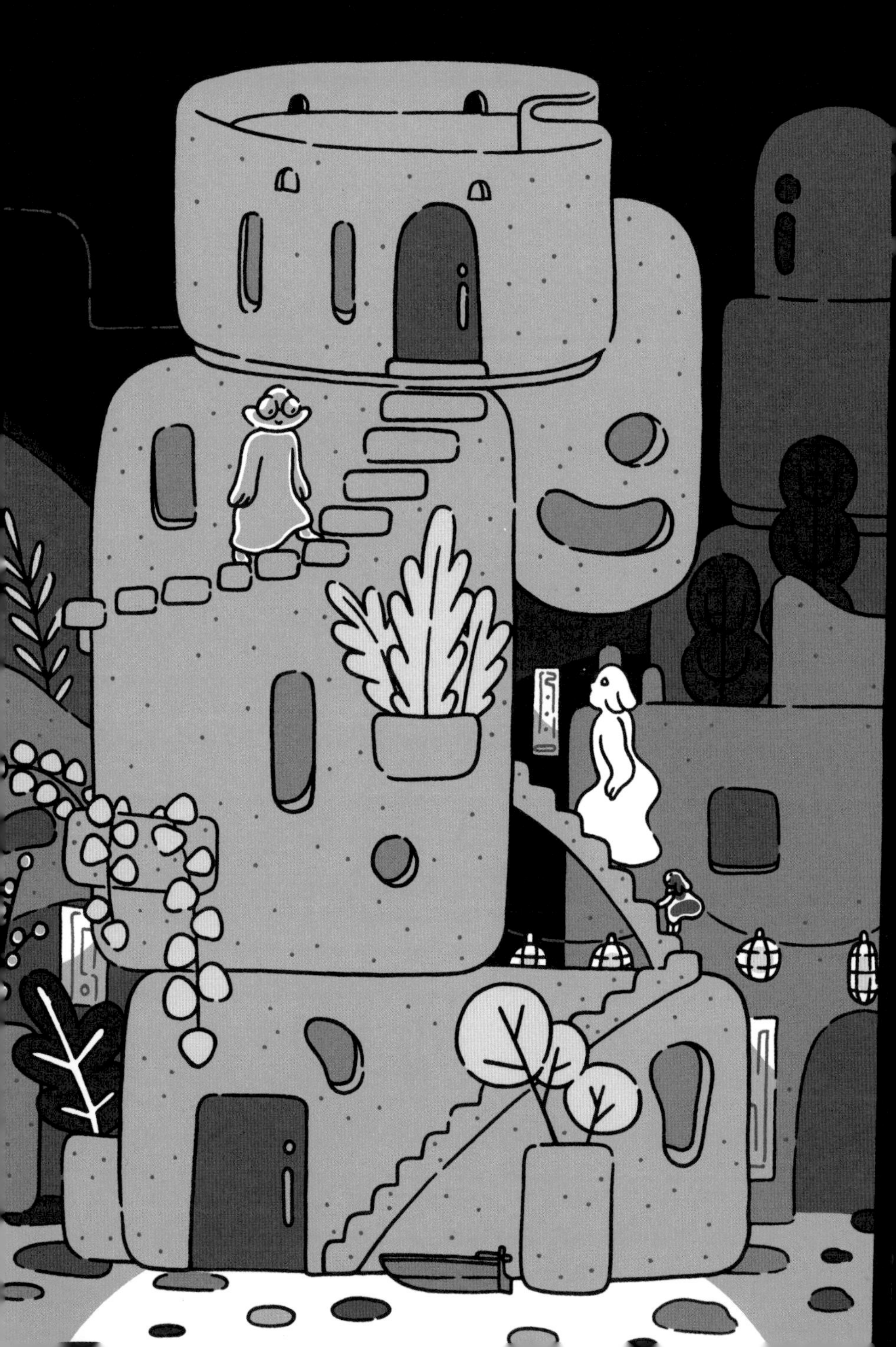

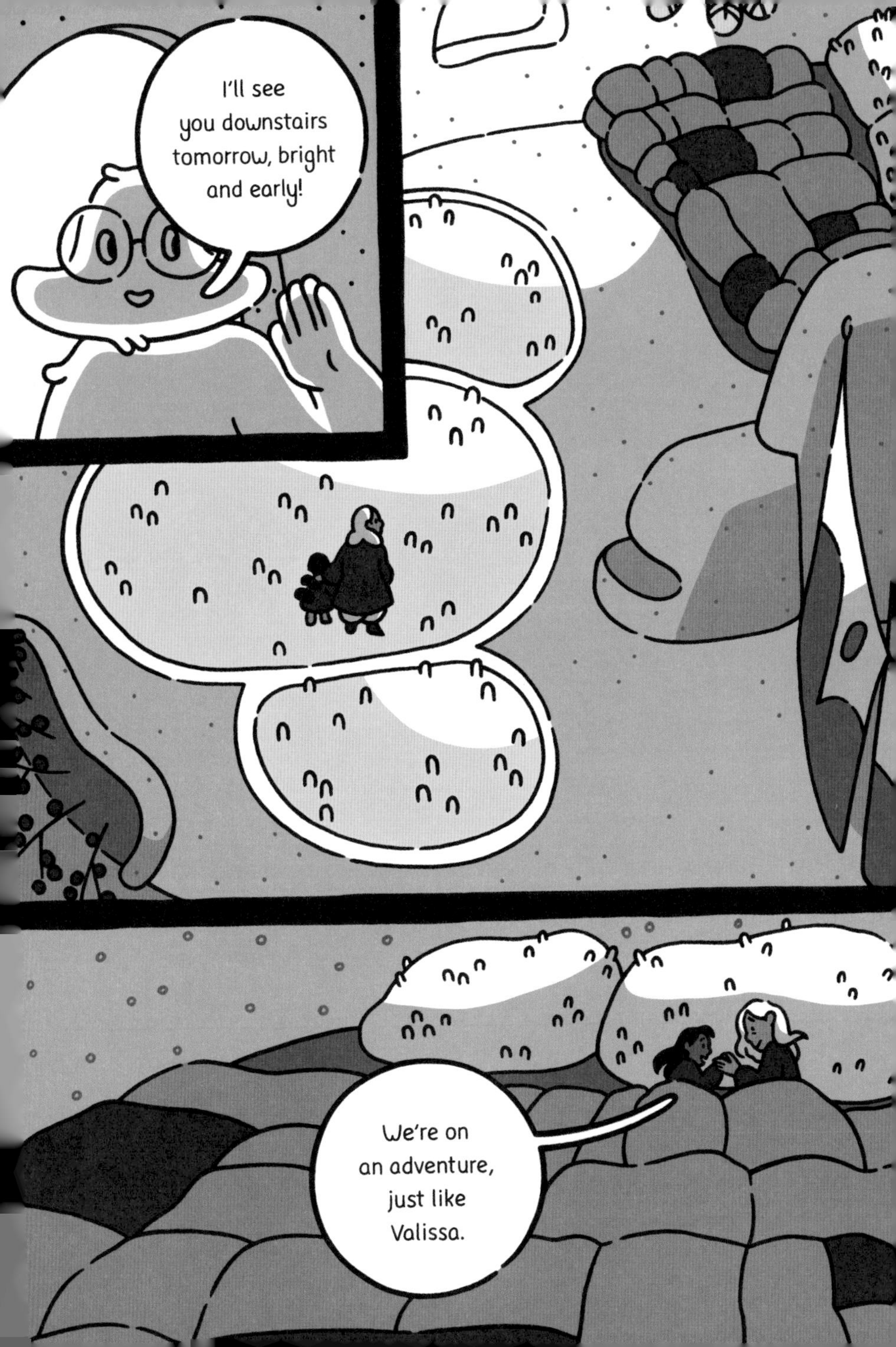
I'll see you downstairs tomorrow, bright and early!
We're on an adventure, just like Valissa.

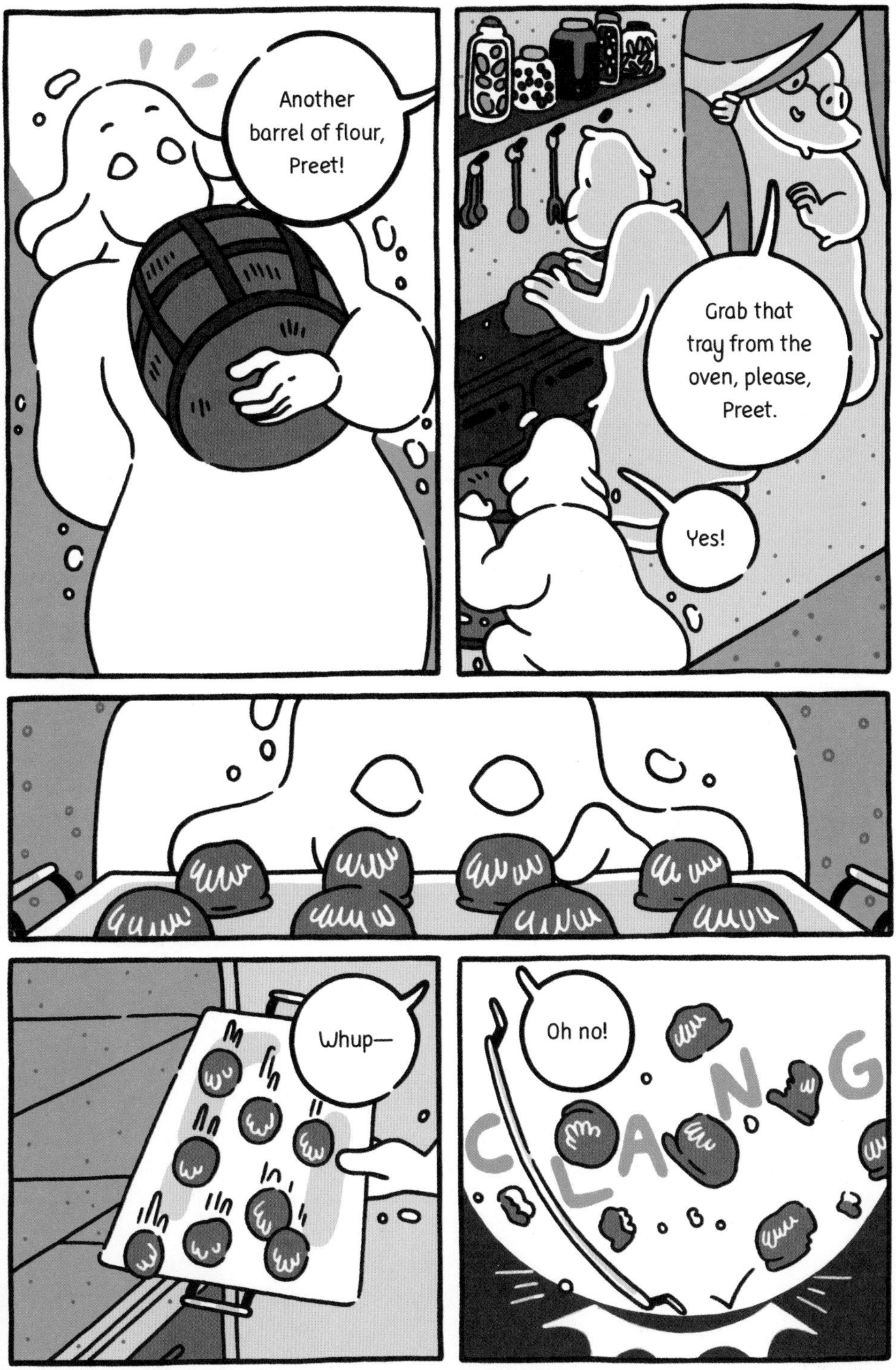

Another barrel of flour, Preet!
Grab that tray from the oven, please, Preet.
Yes!
Whup—
Oh no!
CLANG

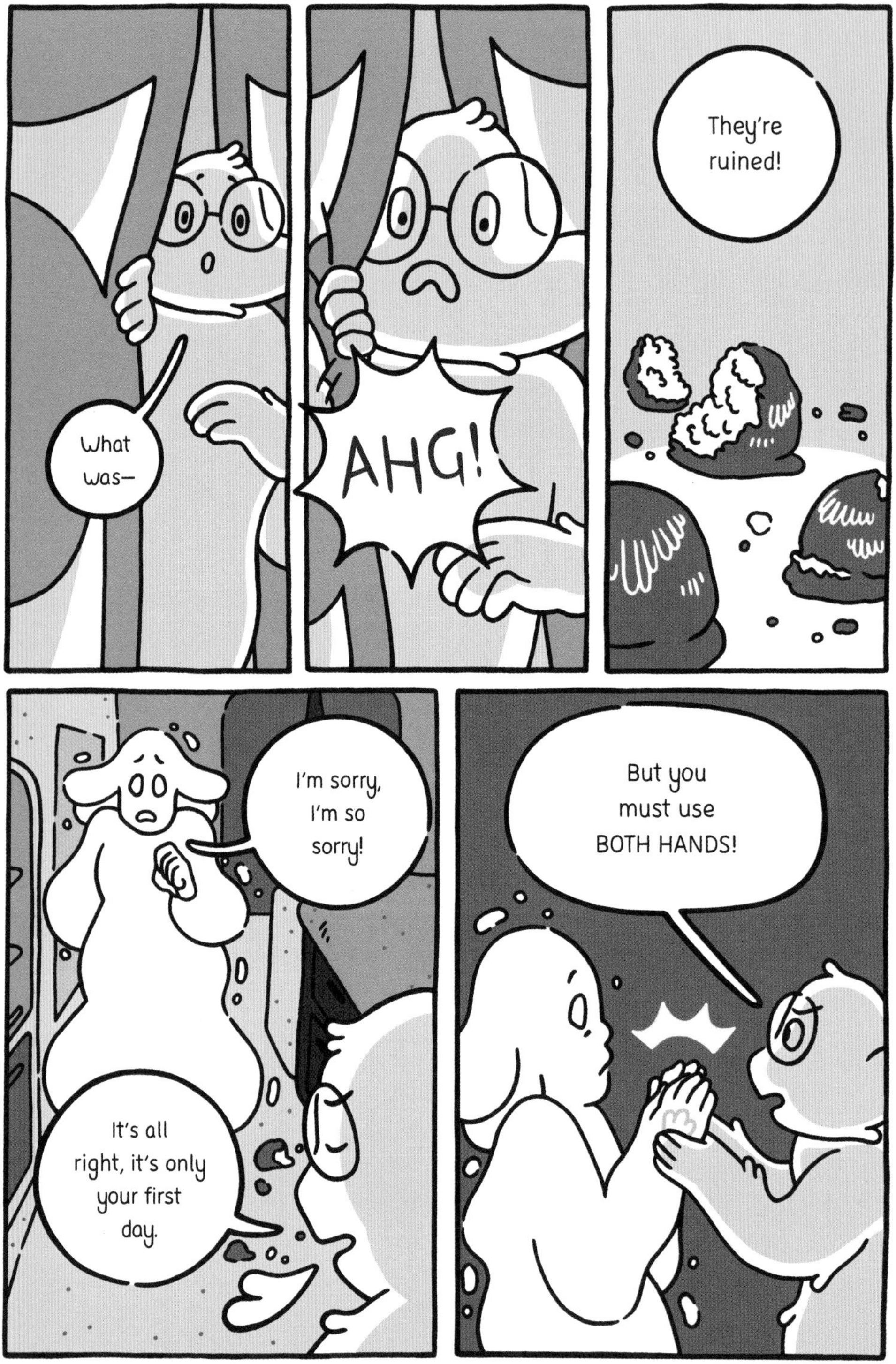
What was—
AHG!
They're ruined!
I'm sorry, I'm so sorry!
It's all right, it's only your first day.
But you must use BOTH HANDS!

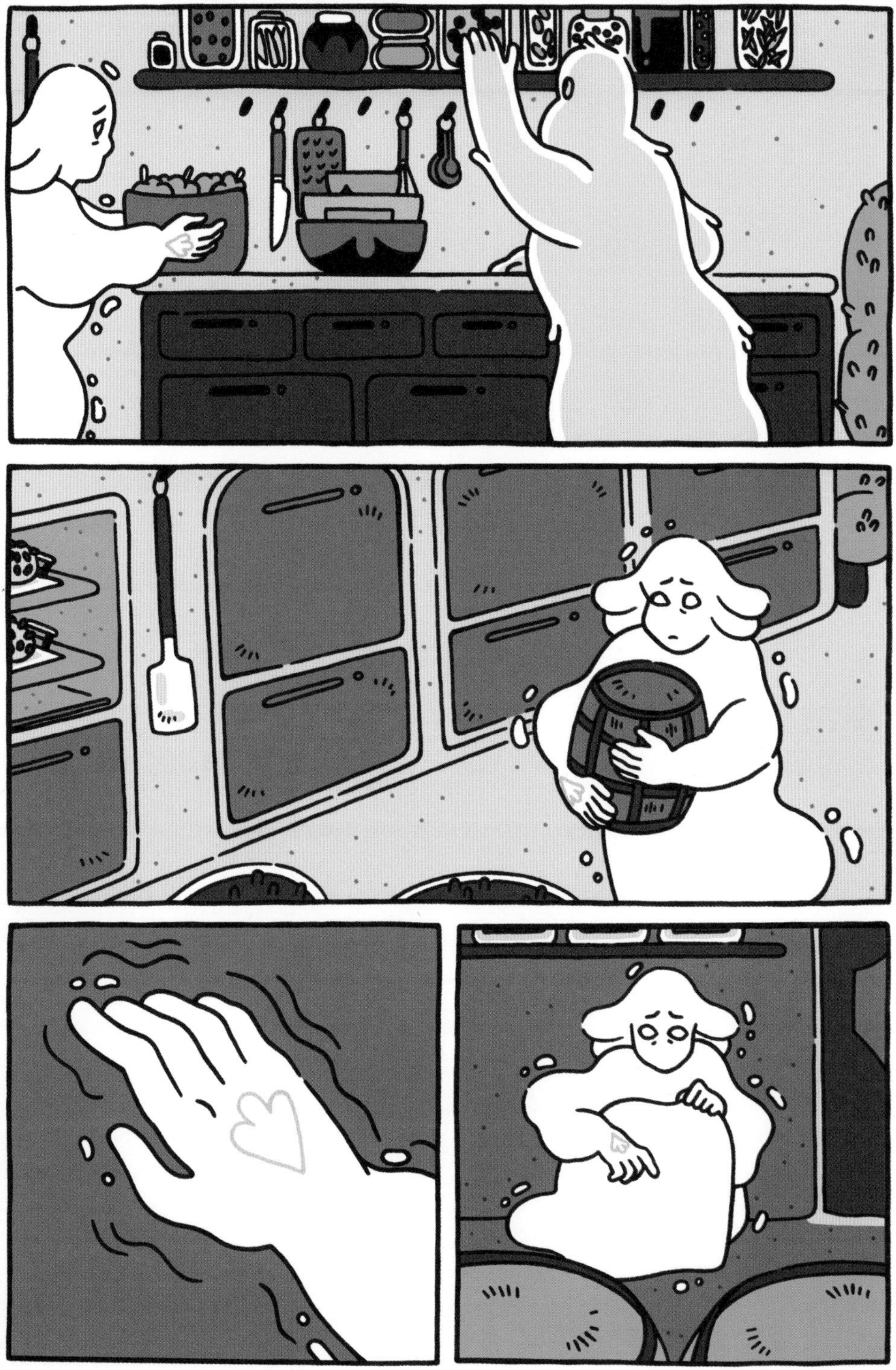

Here you go!
Thanks—

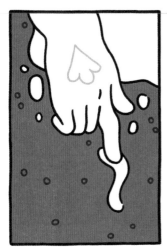

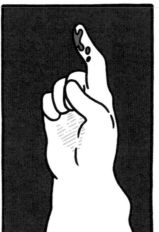

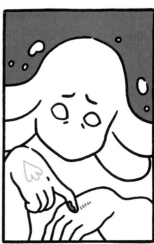

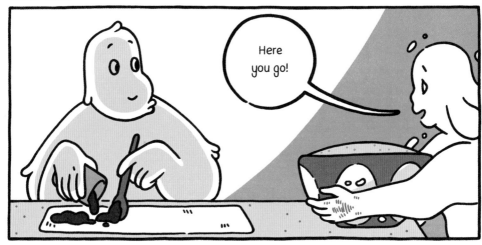

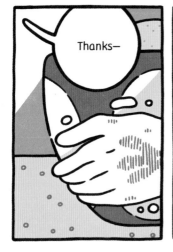

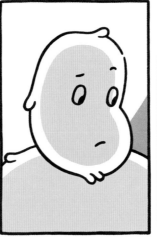

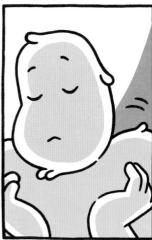

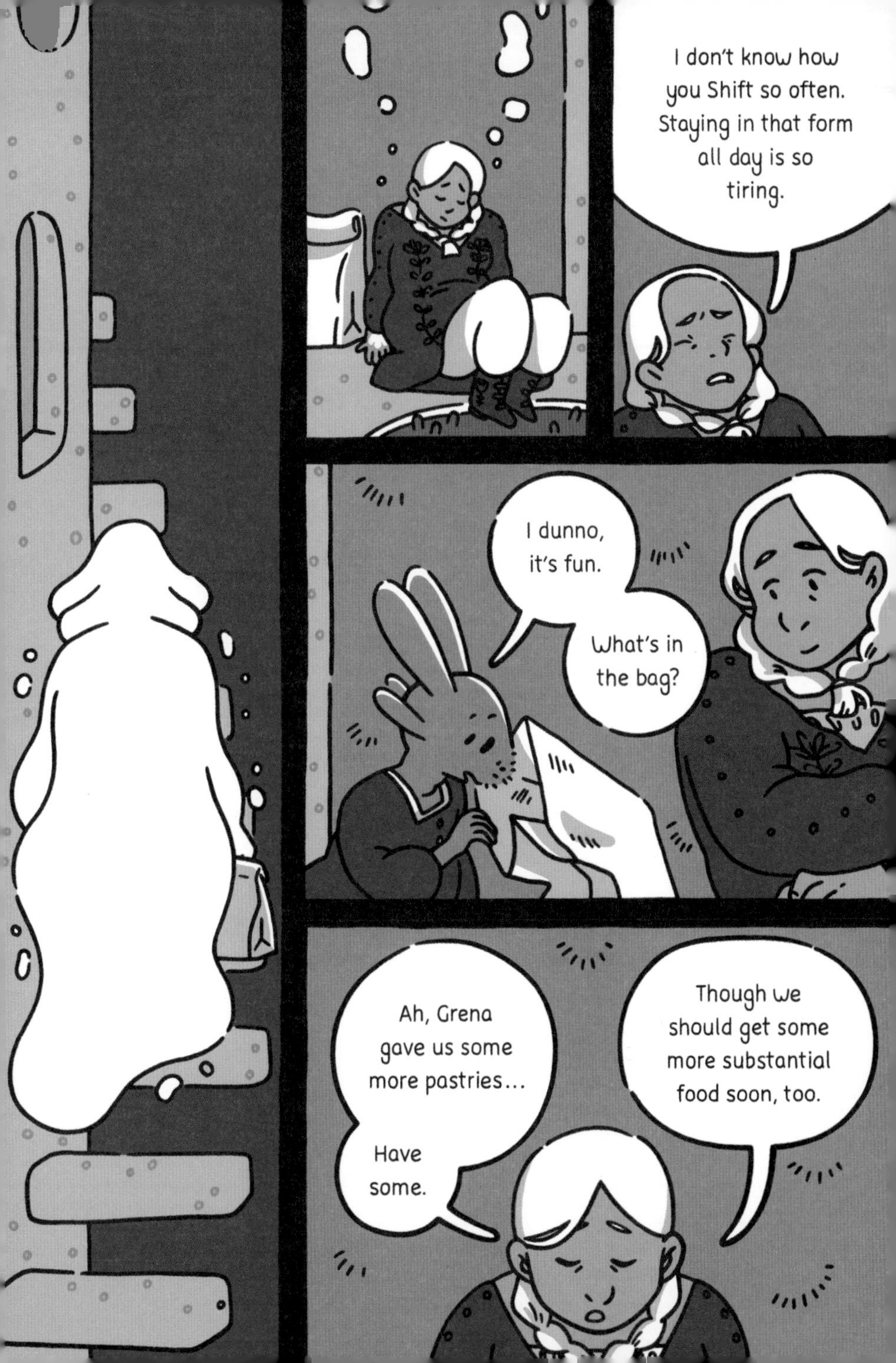
I don't know how you Shift so often. Staying in that form all day is so tiring.
I dunno, it's fun.
What's in the bag?
Ah, Grena gave us some more pastries...
Have some.
Though we should get some more substantial food soon, too.

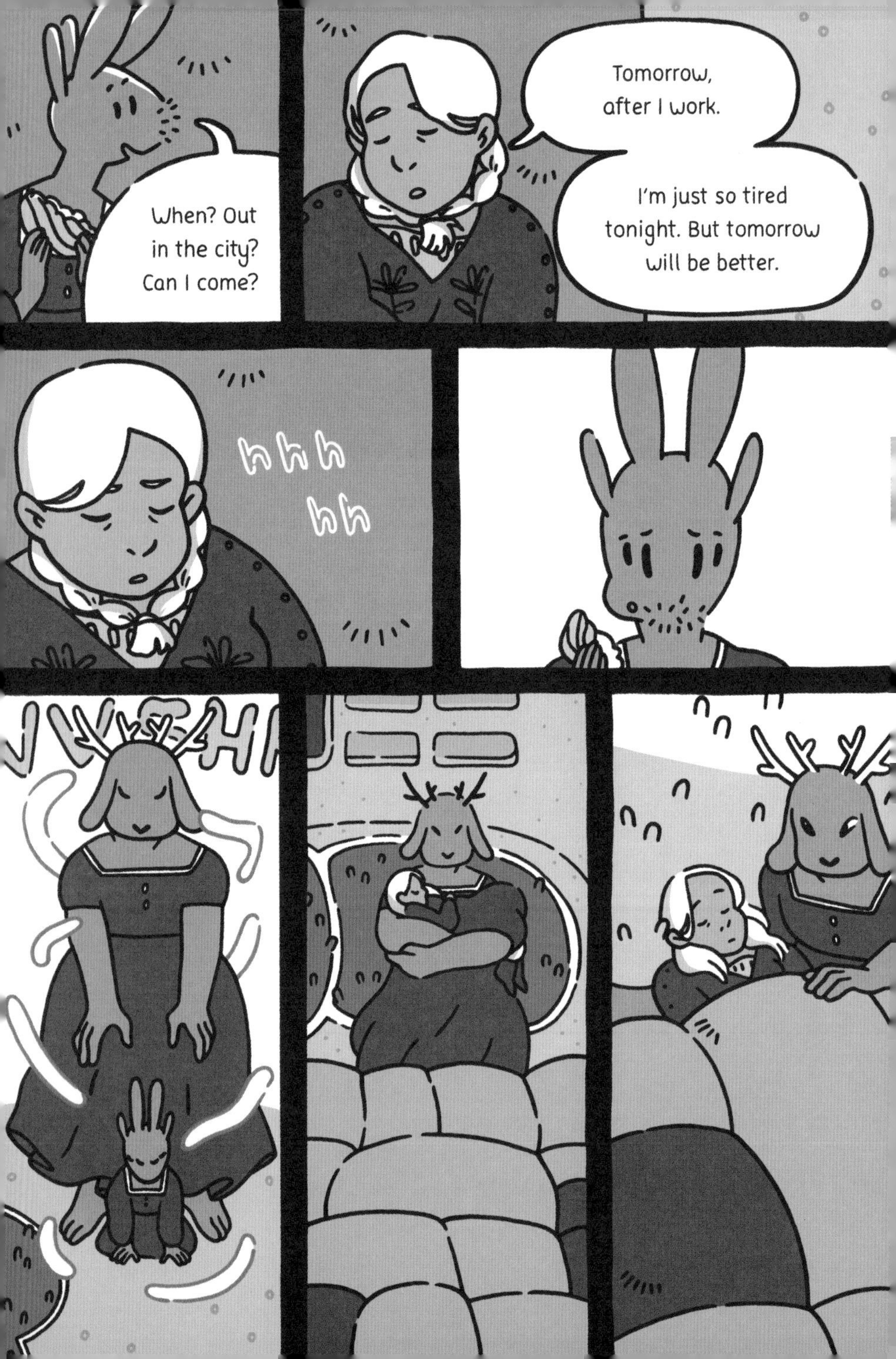
When? Out in the city? Can I come?
Tomorrow, after I work.
I'm just so tired tonight. But tomorrow will be better.
hhh
hh

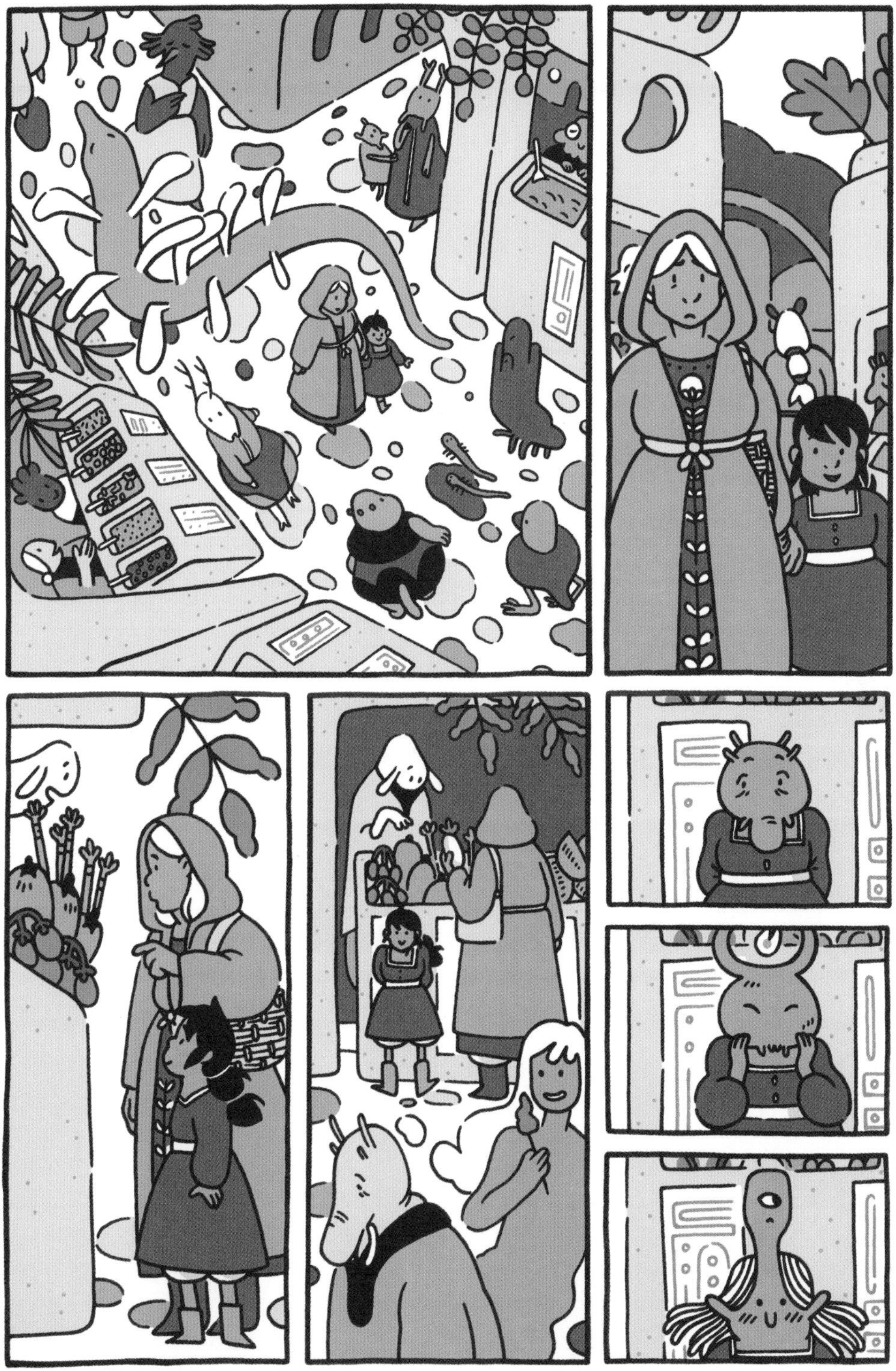

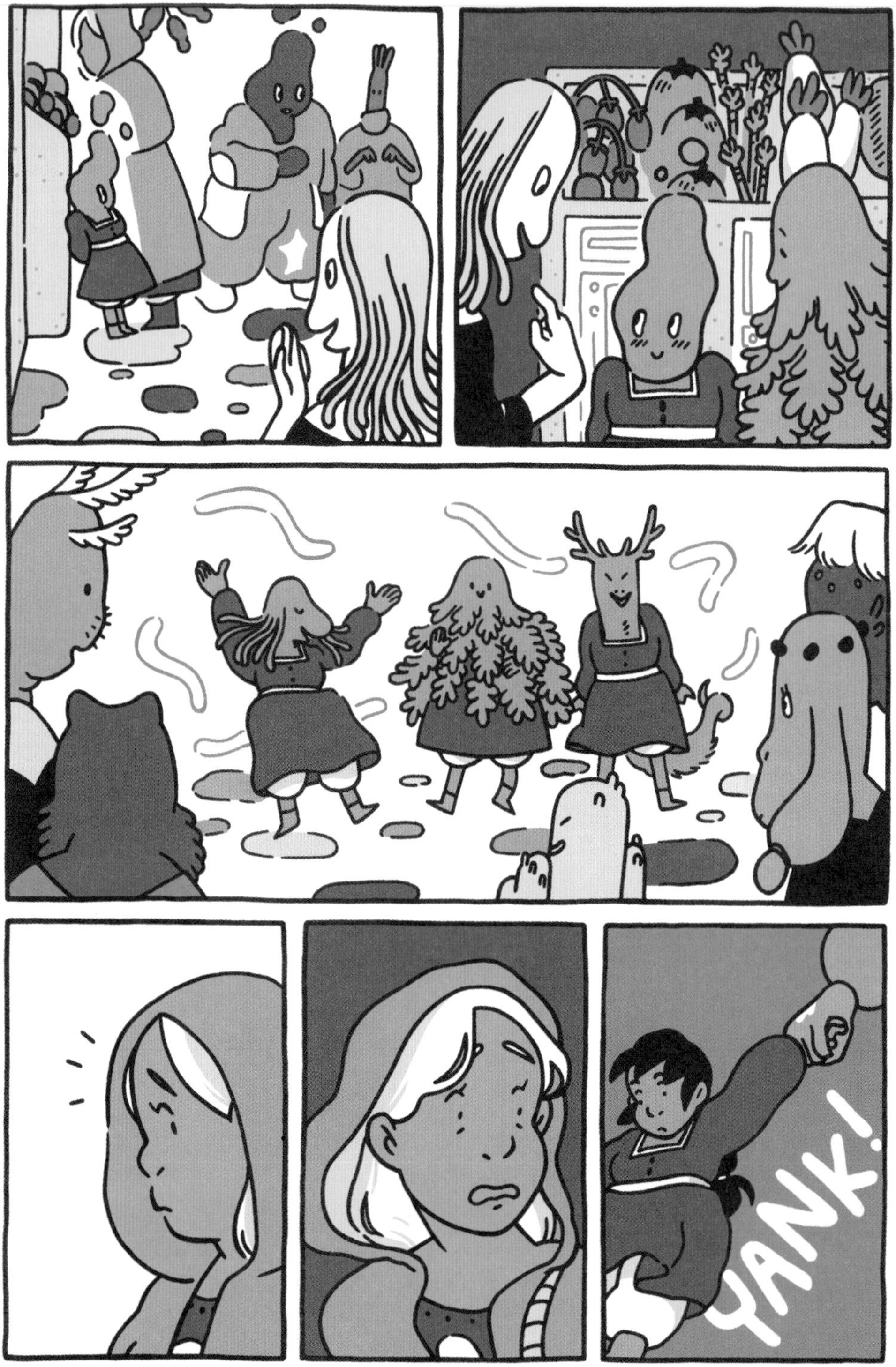
YANK!

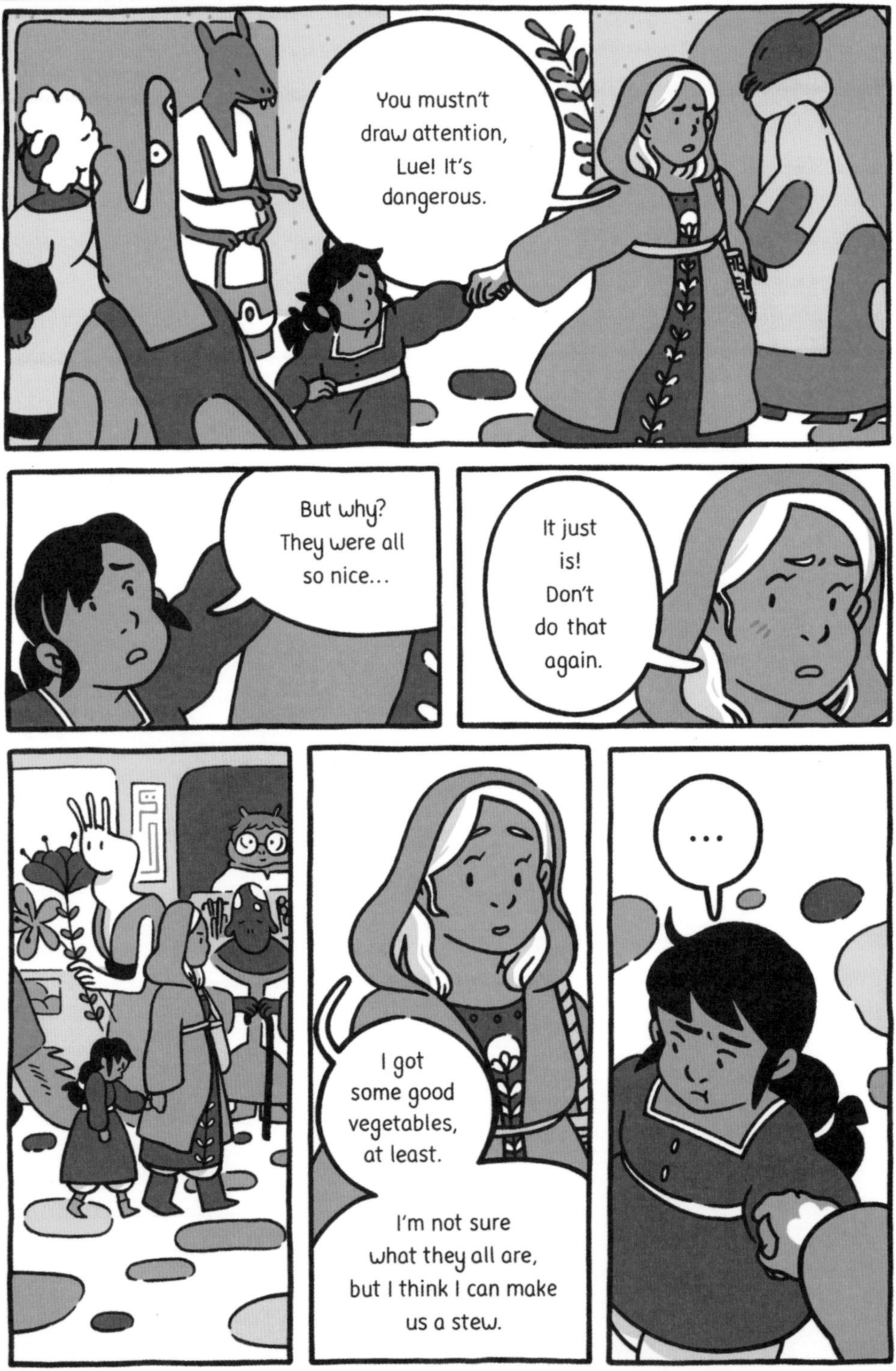
You mustn't draw attention, Lue! It's dangerous.
But why? They were all so nice...
It just is! Don't do that again.
I got some good vegetables, at least.
I'm not sure what they all are, but I think I can make us a stew.
...

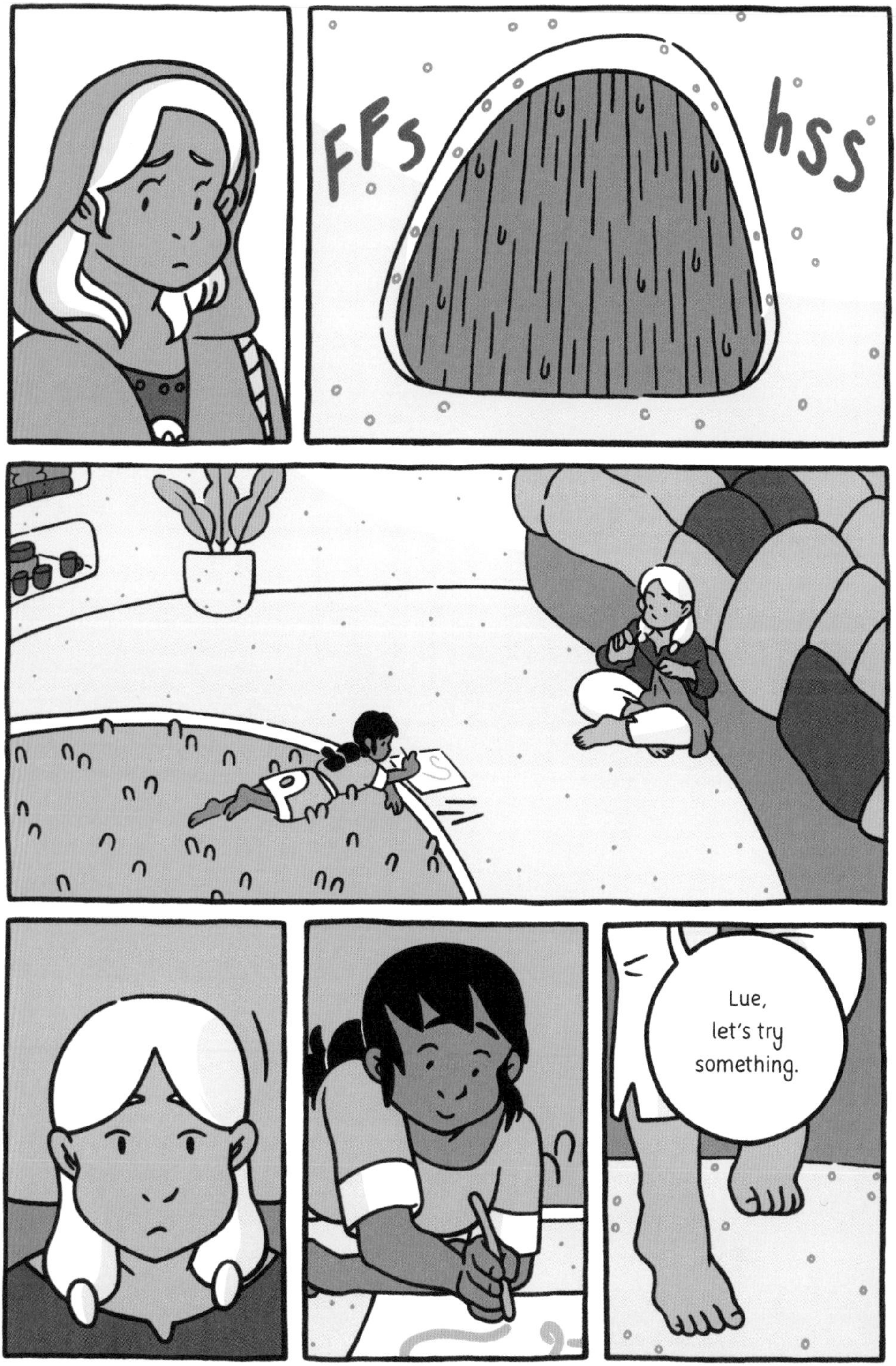
FFs
hss
Lue,
let's try
something.

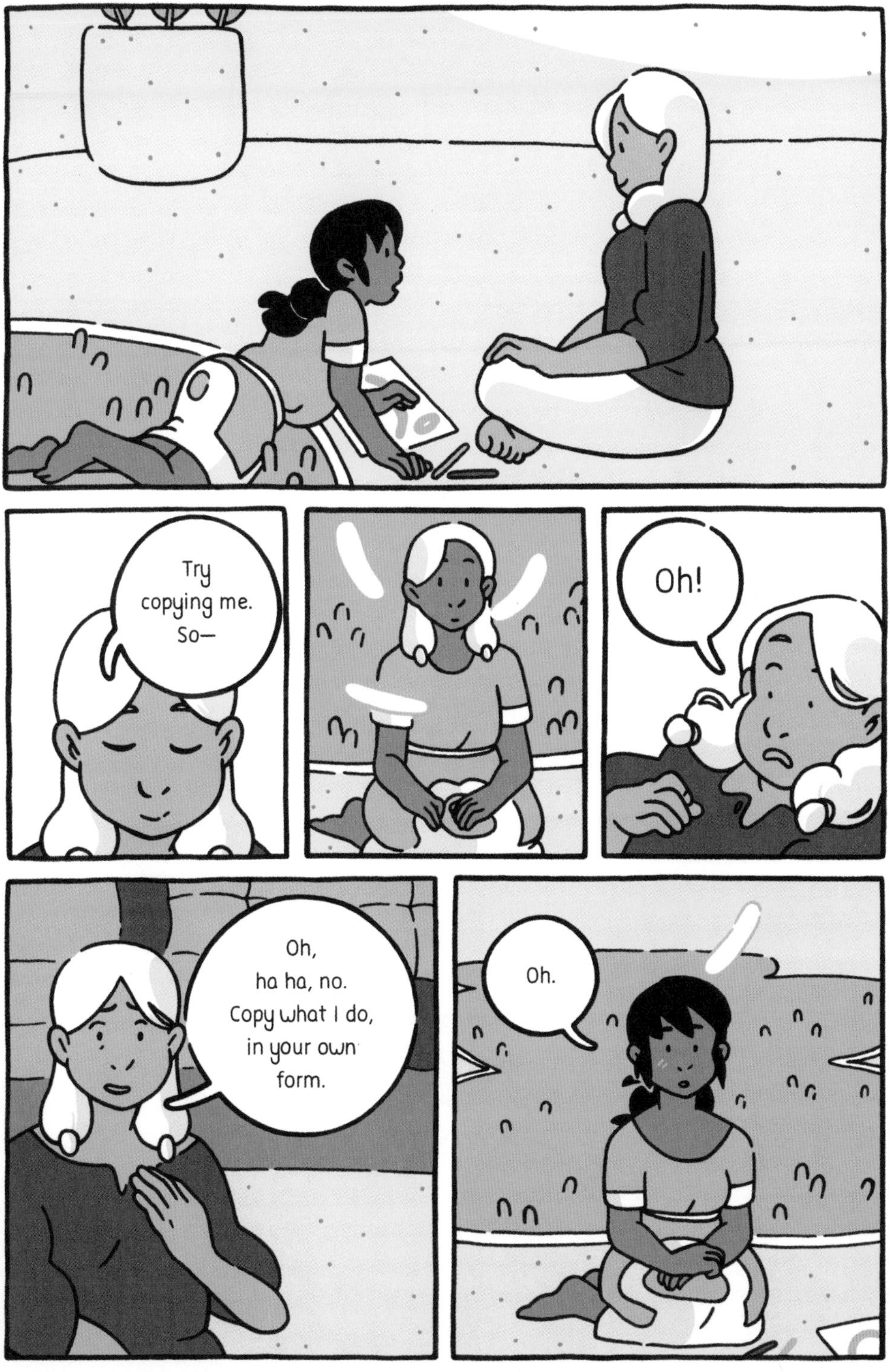
Try copying me. So—
Oh!
Oh, ha ha, no. Copy what I do, in your own form.
Oh.

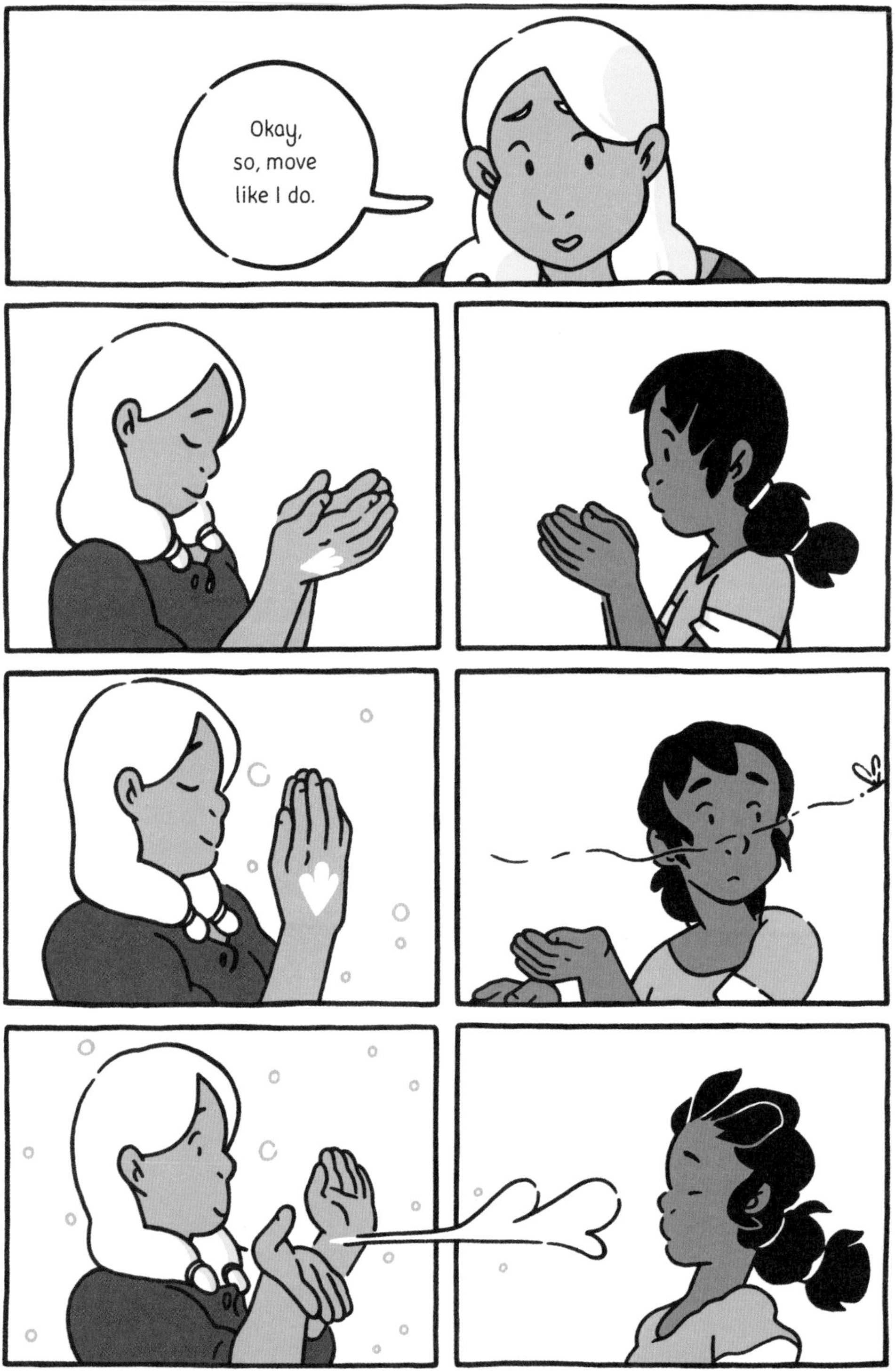
Okay, so, move like I do.

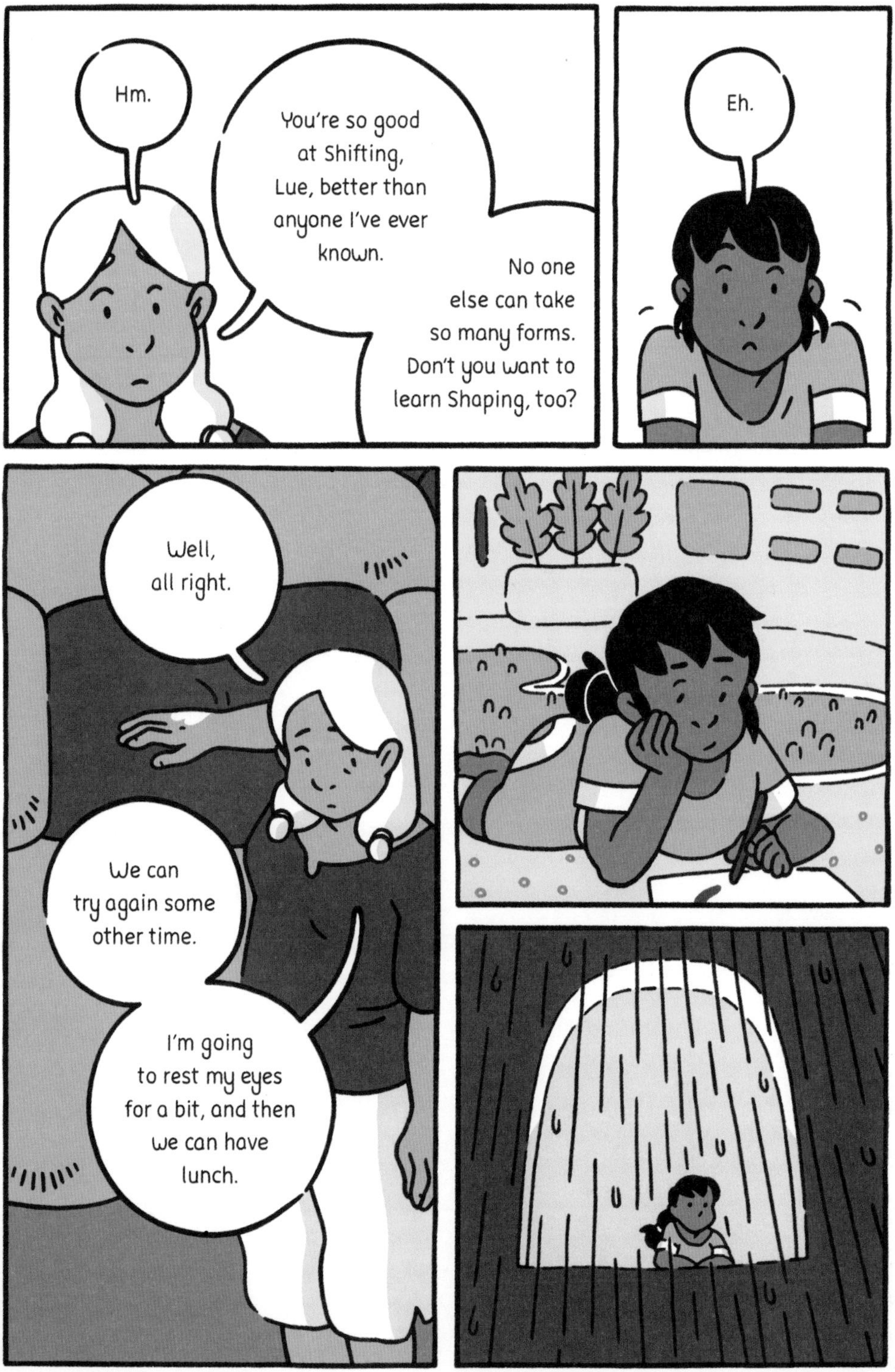
Hm.
You're so good at Shifting, Lue, better than anyone I've ever known.
No one else can take so many forms. Don't you want to learn Shaping, too?
Eh.
Well, all right.
We can try again some other time.
I'm going to rest my eyes for a bit, and then we can have lunch.

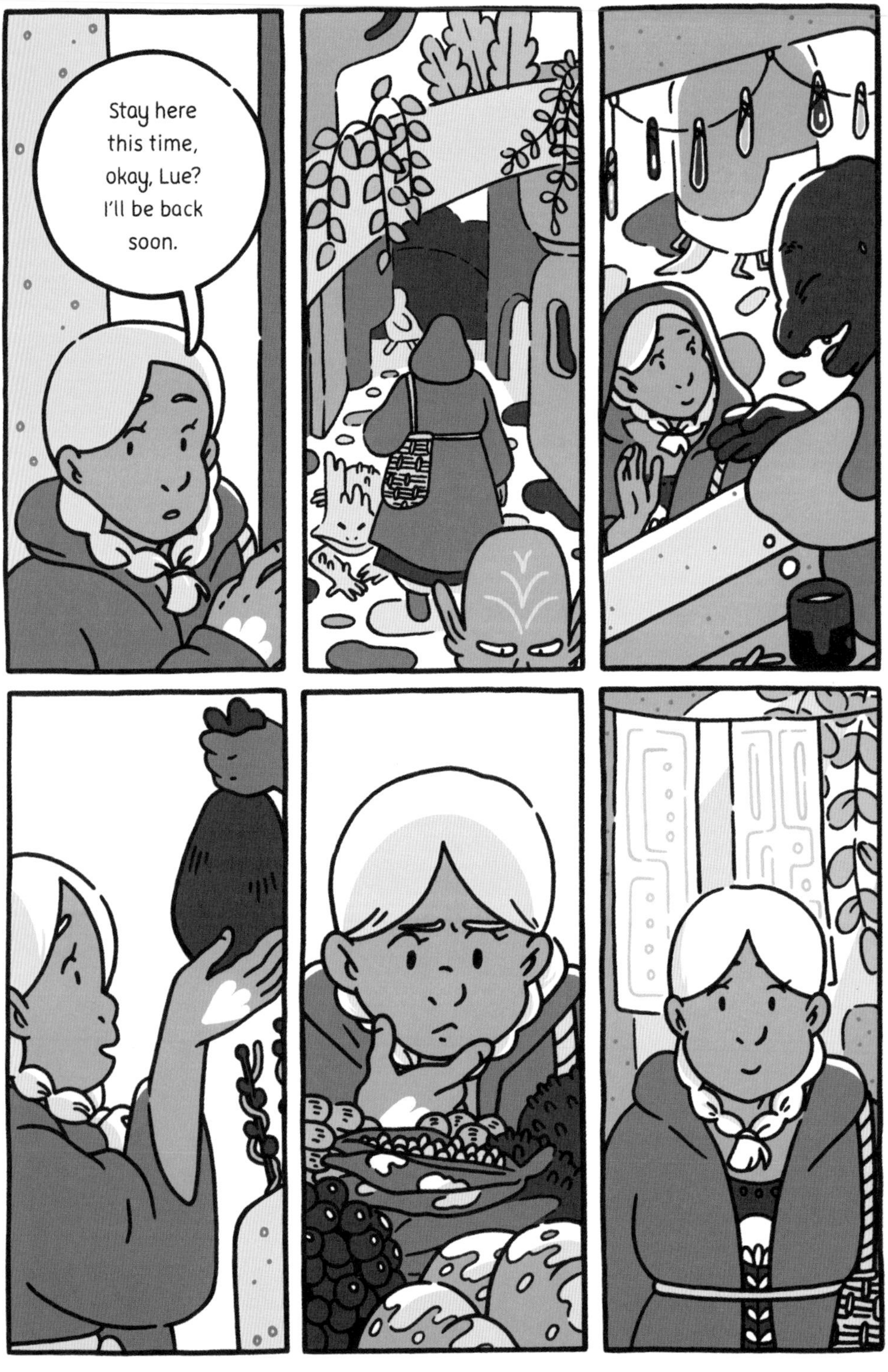
Stay here this time, okay, Lue? I'll be back soon.

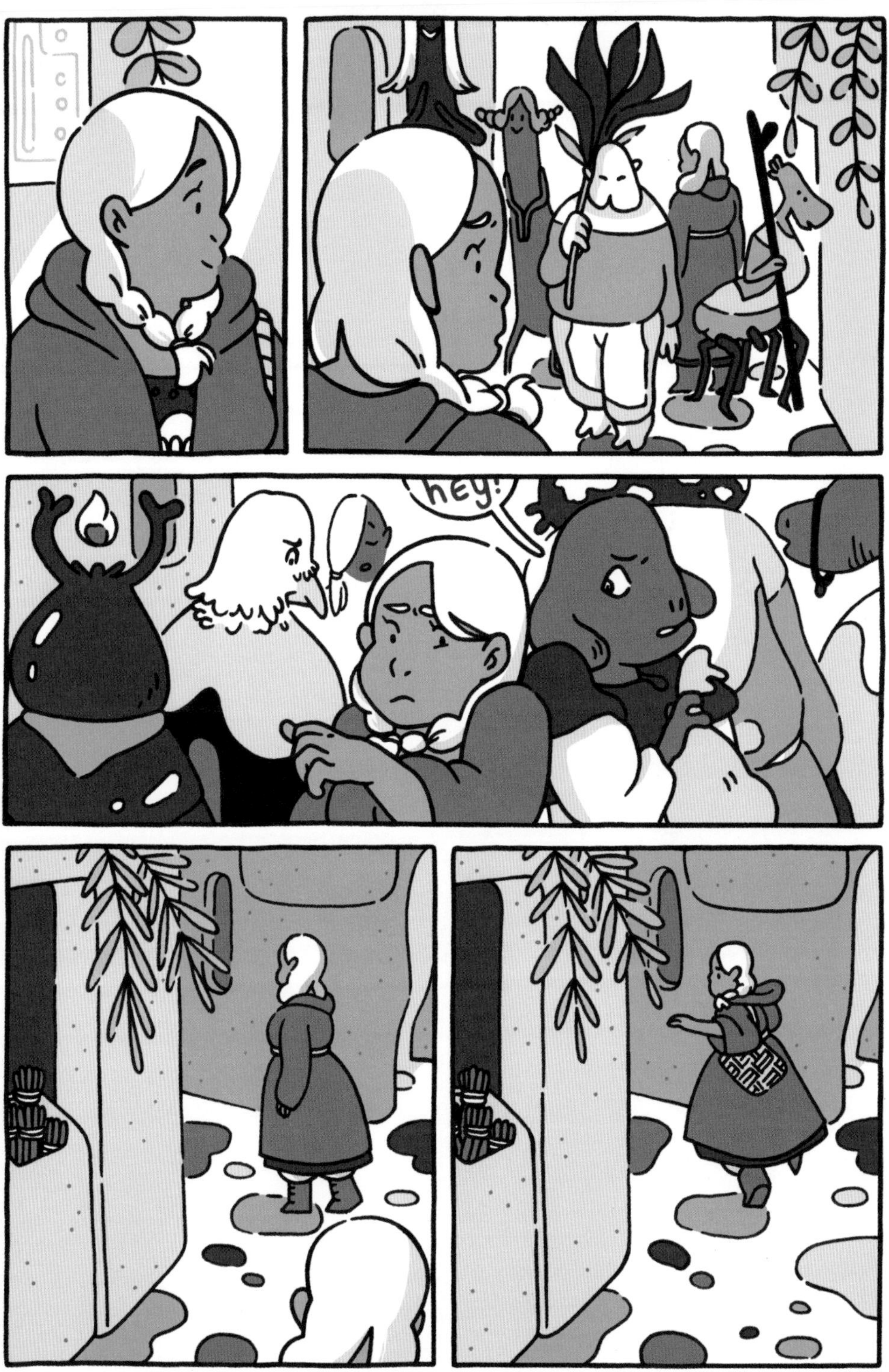
hey!

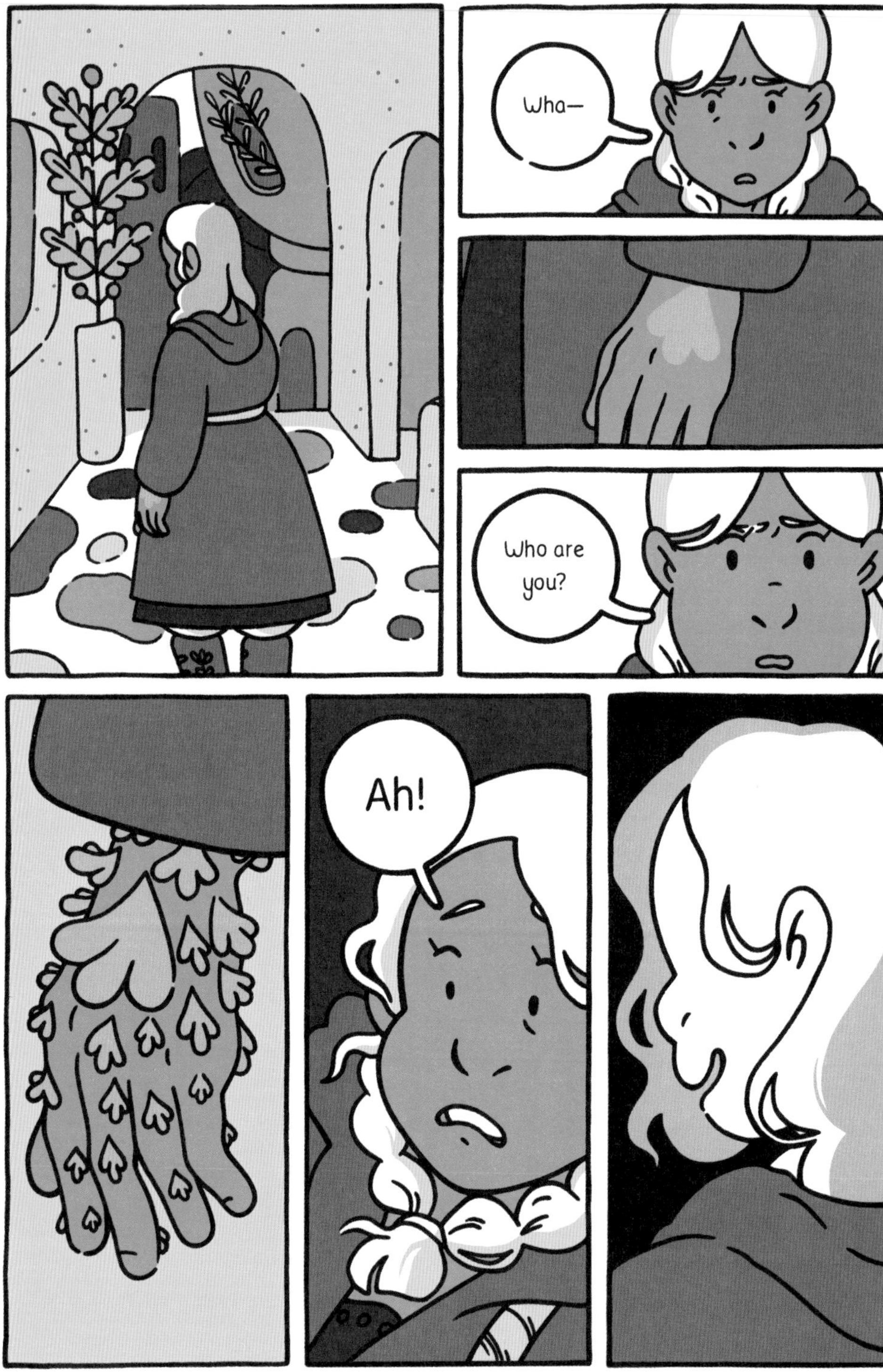
Wha—
Who are you?
Ah!

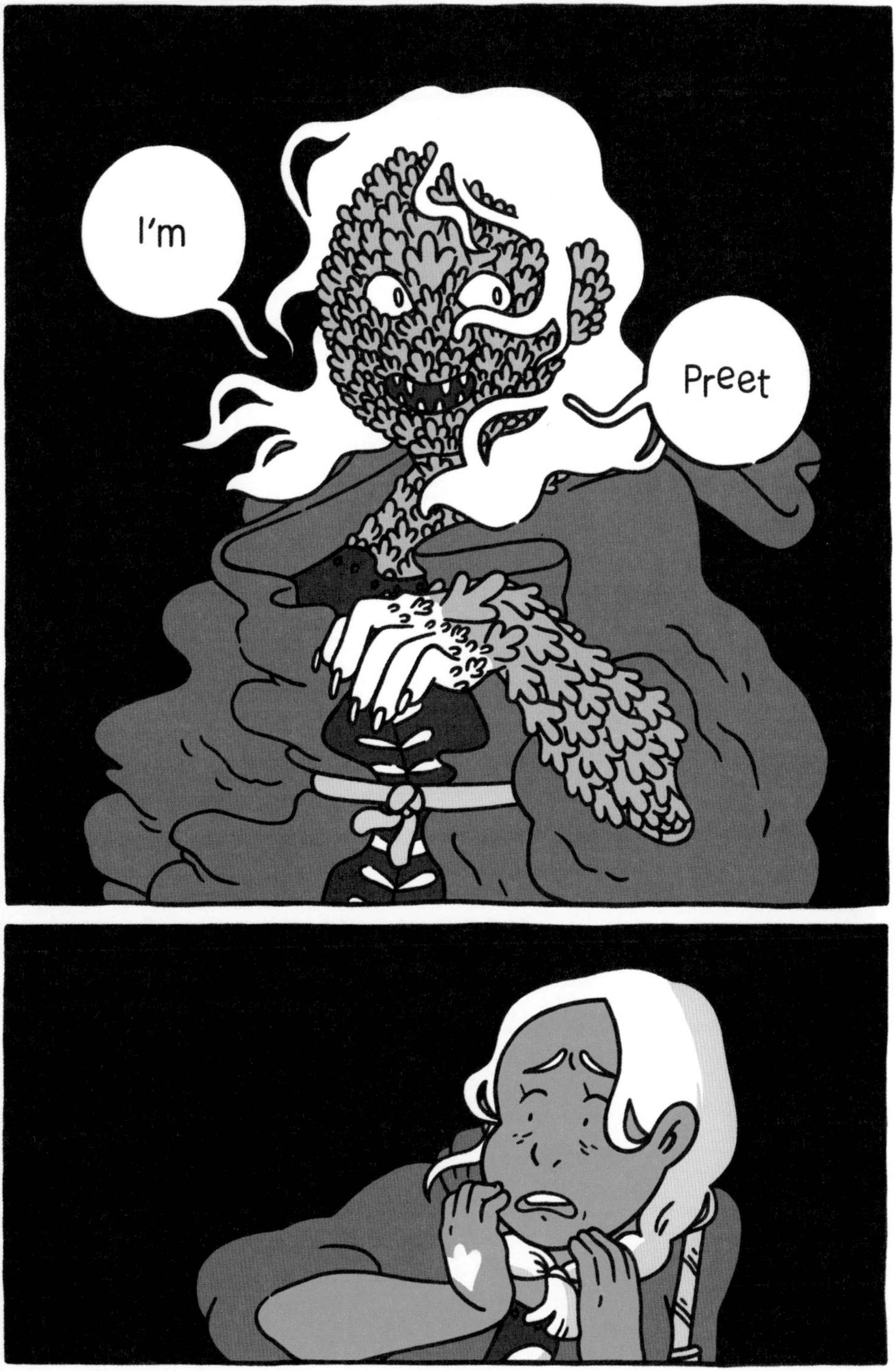
I'm
Preet

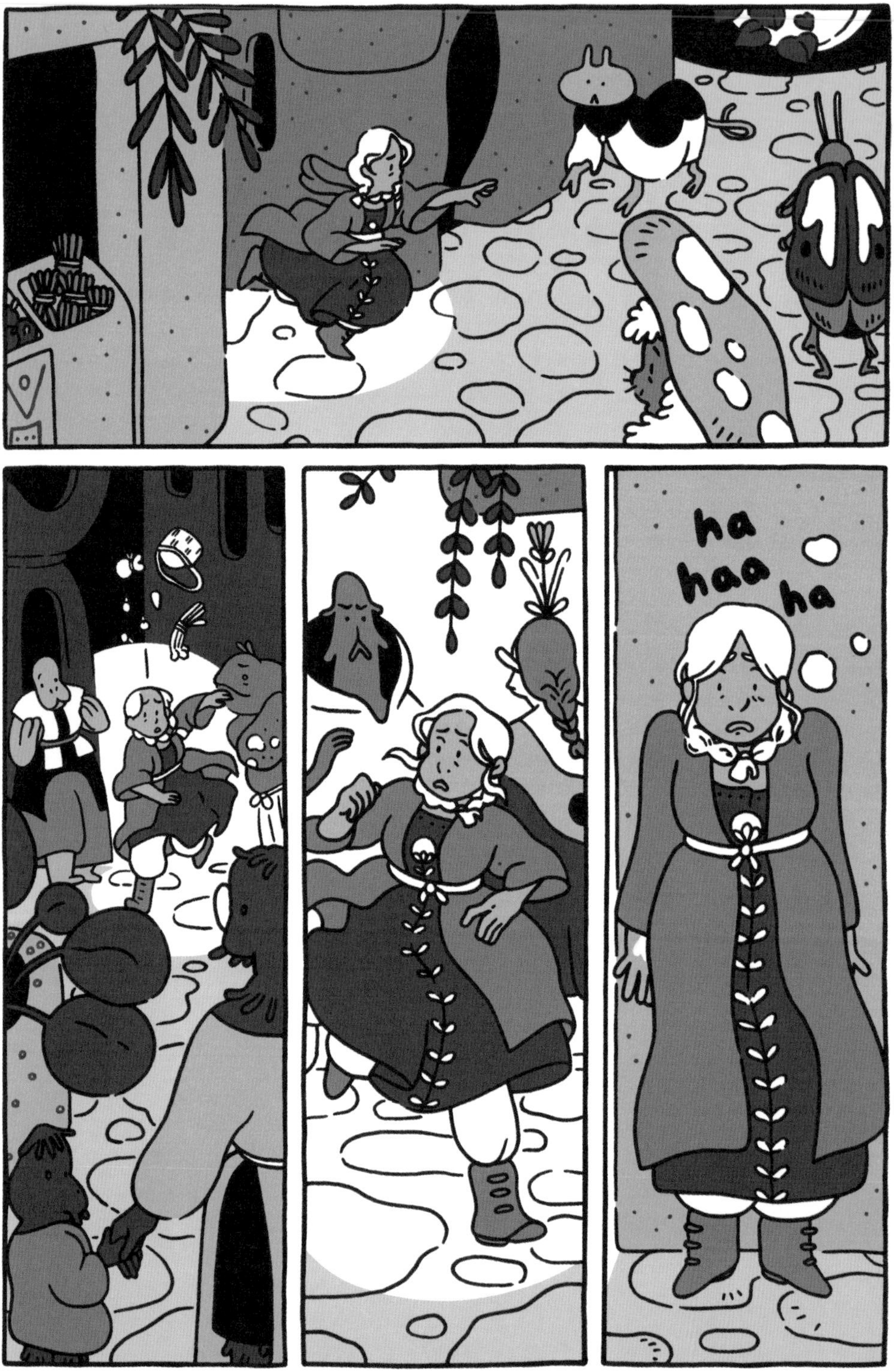
ha
haa
ha

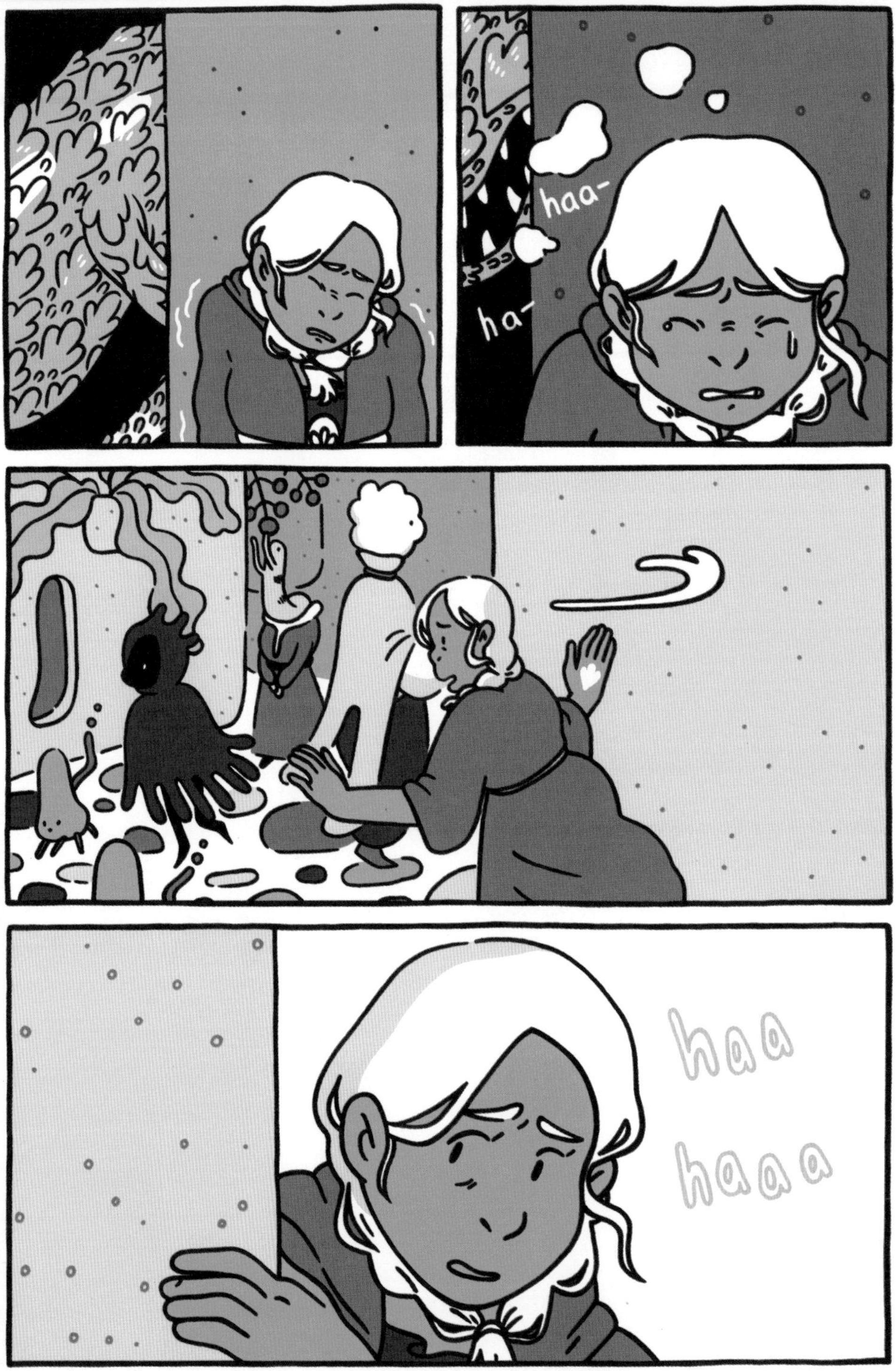
haa-
ha-
haa
haaa

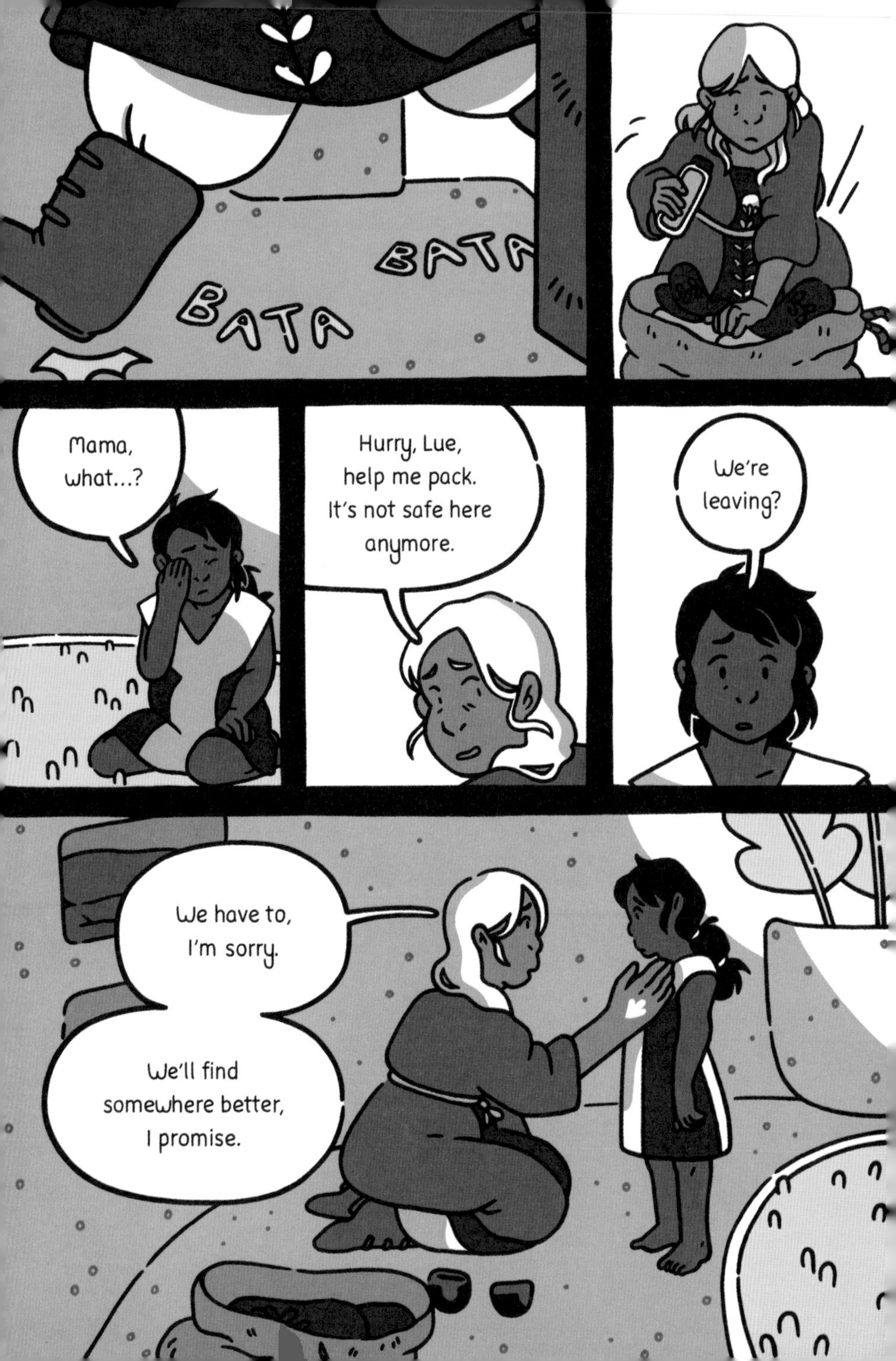
BATA
BATA
Mama, what...?
Hurry, Lue, help me pack. It's not safe here anymore.
We're leaving?
We have to, I'm sorry.
We'll find somewhere better, I promise.

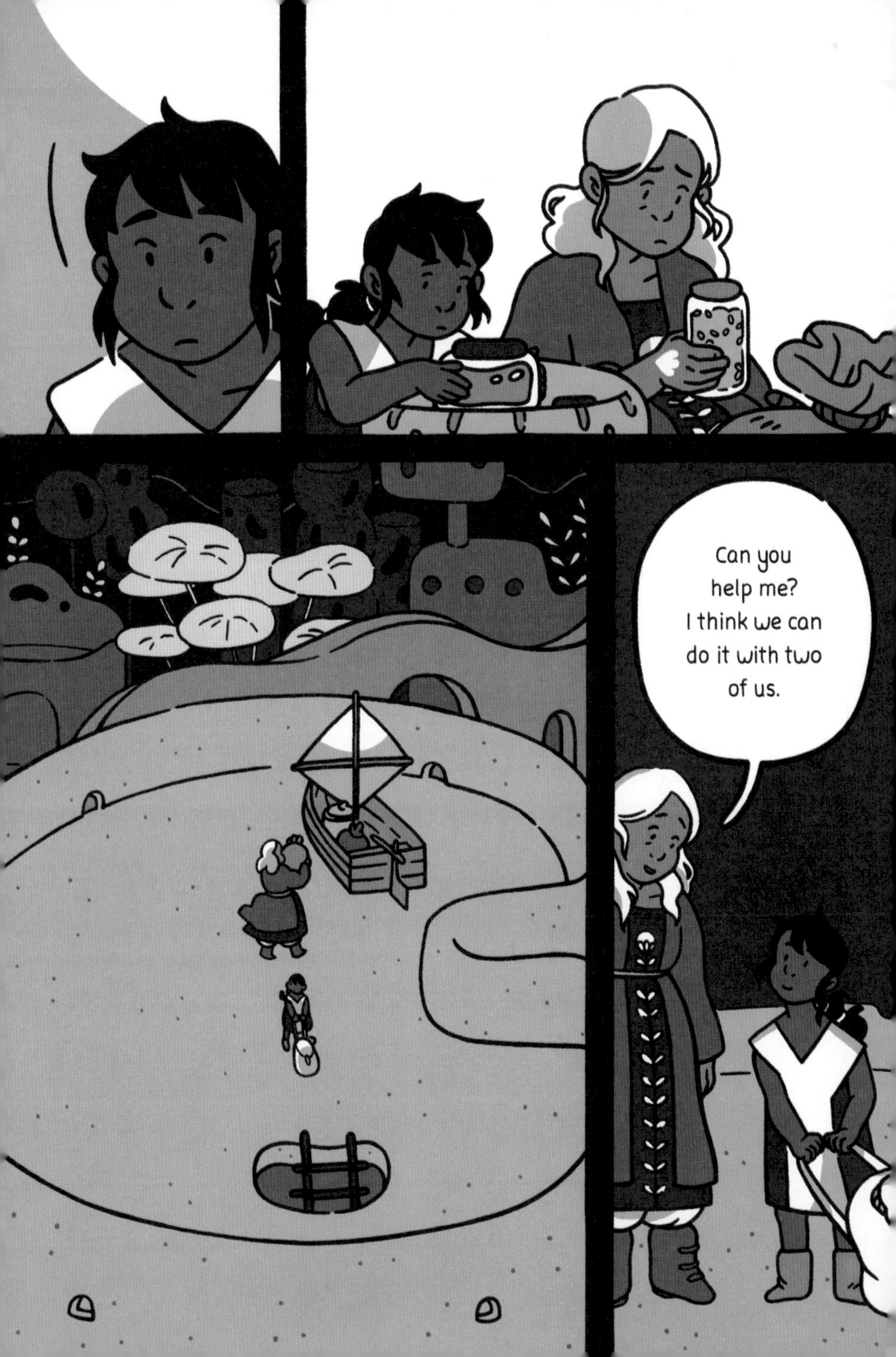
Can you help me? I think we can do it with two of us.

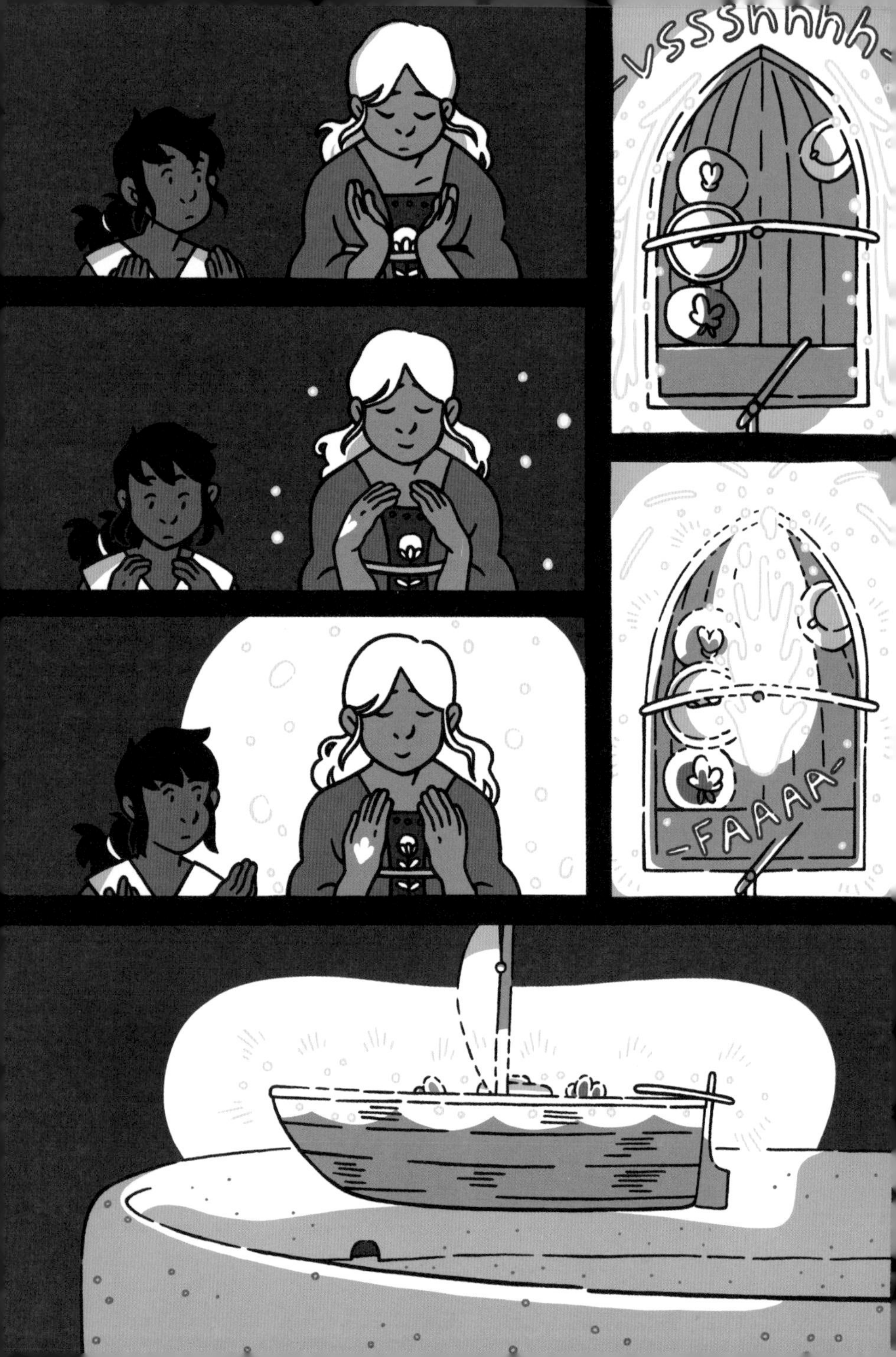
-VSSSHHHH-
-FAAAA-

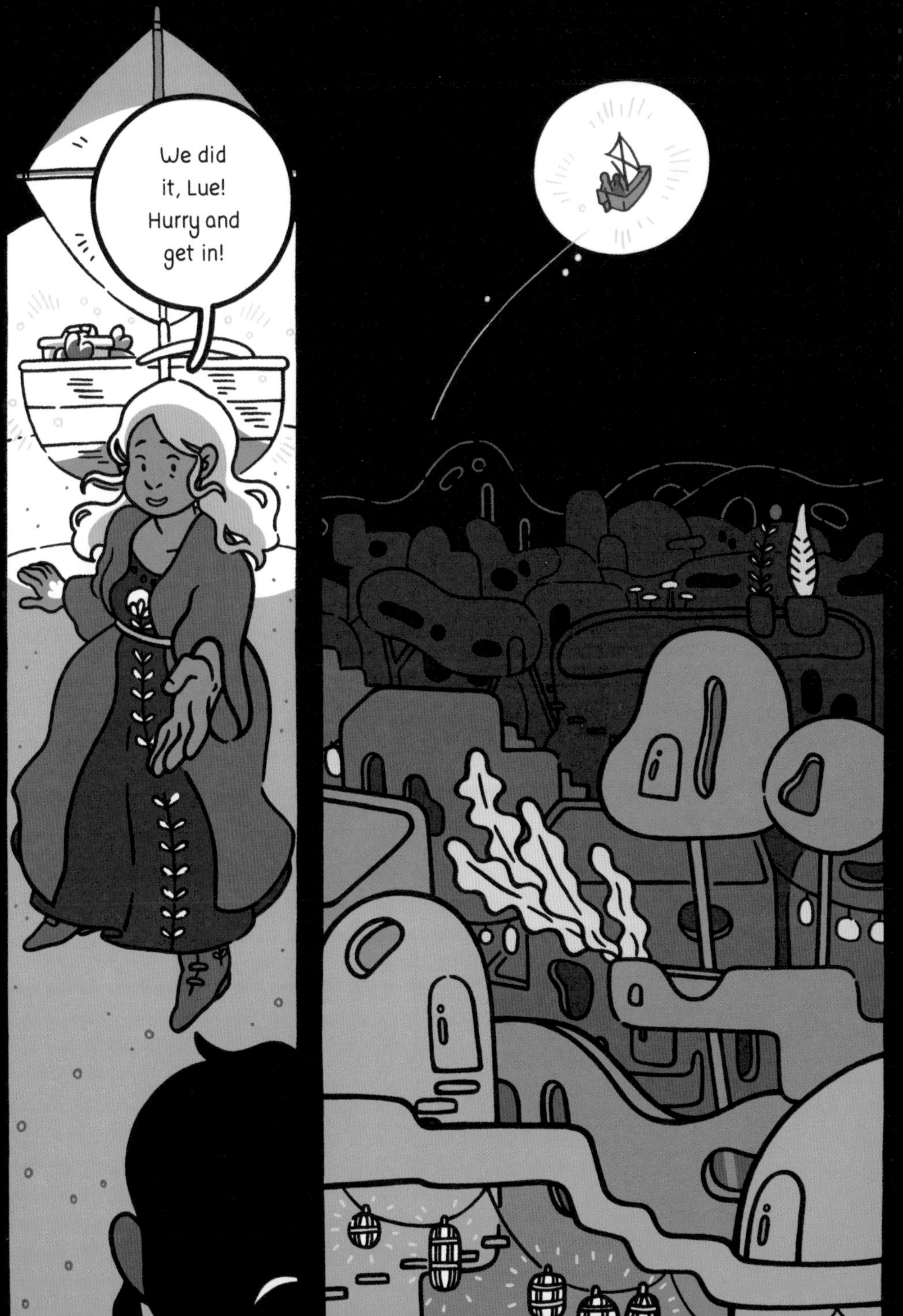
We did it, Lue! Hurry and get in!

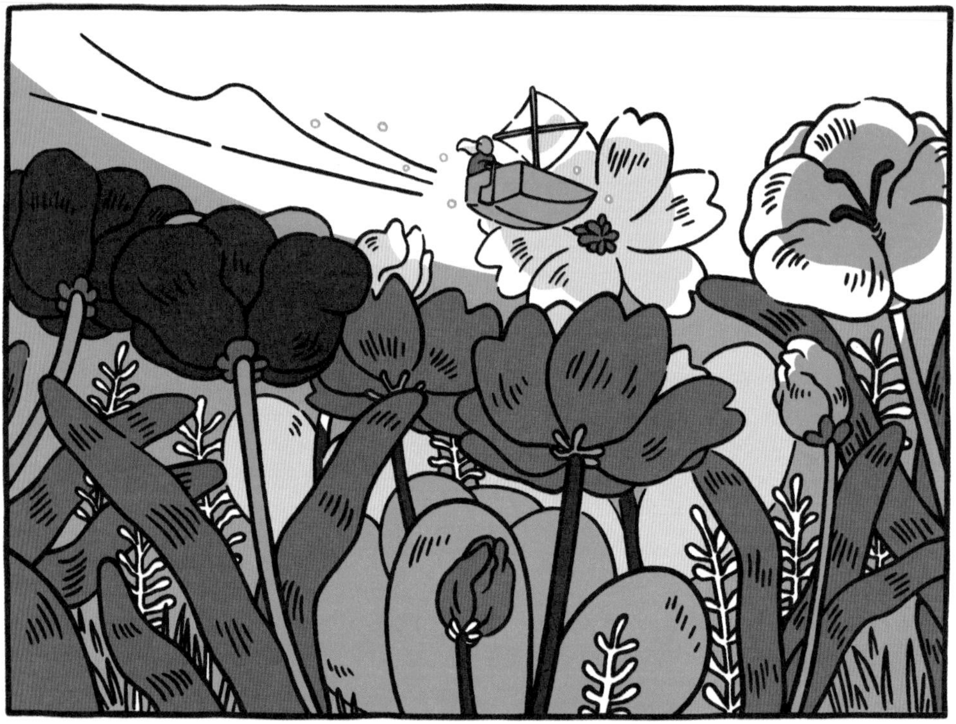

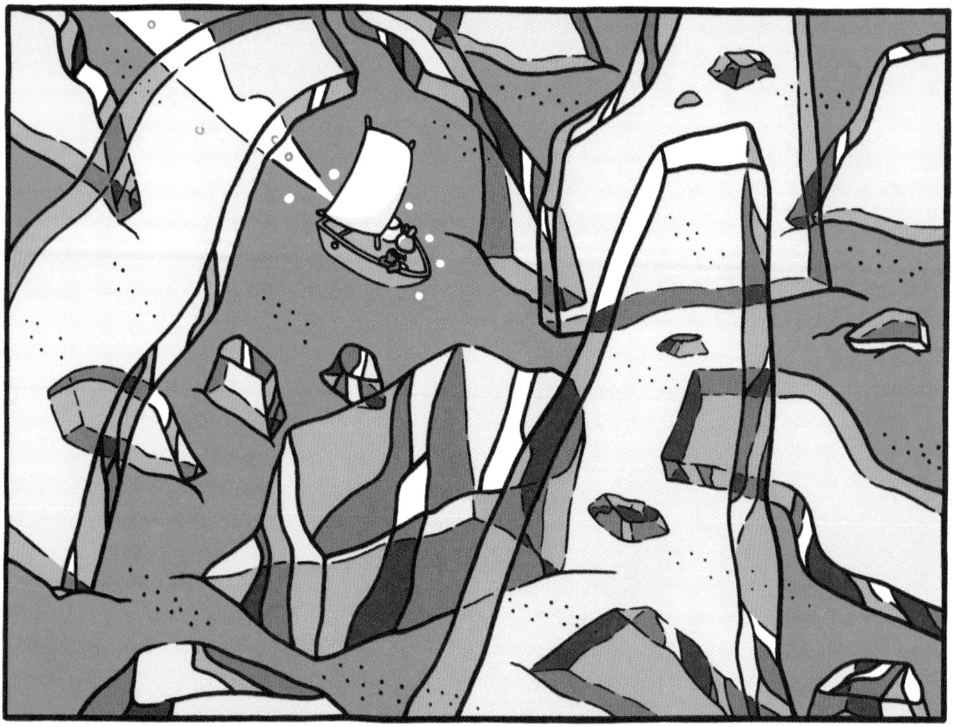

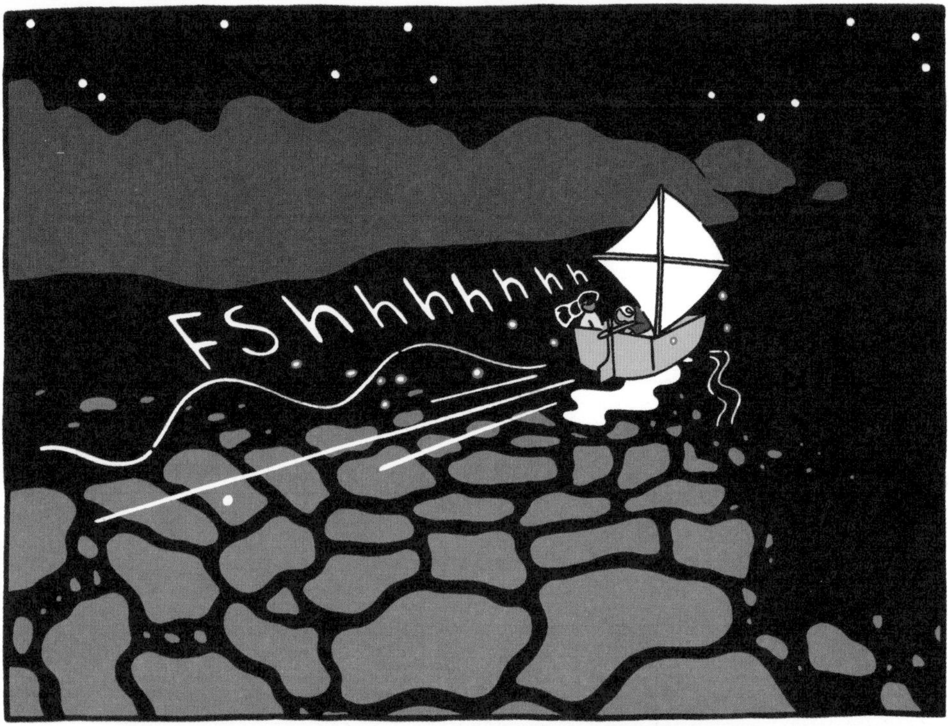
FShhhhhhh

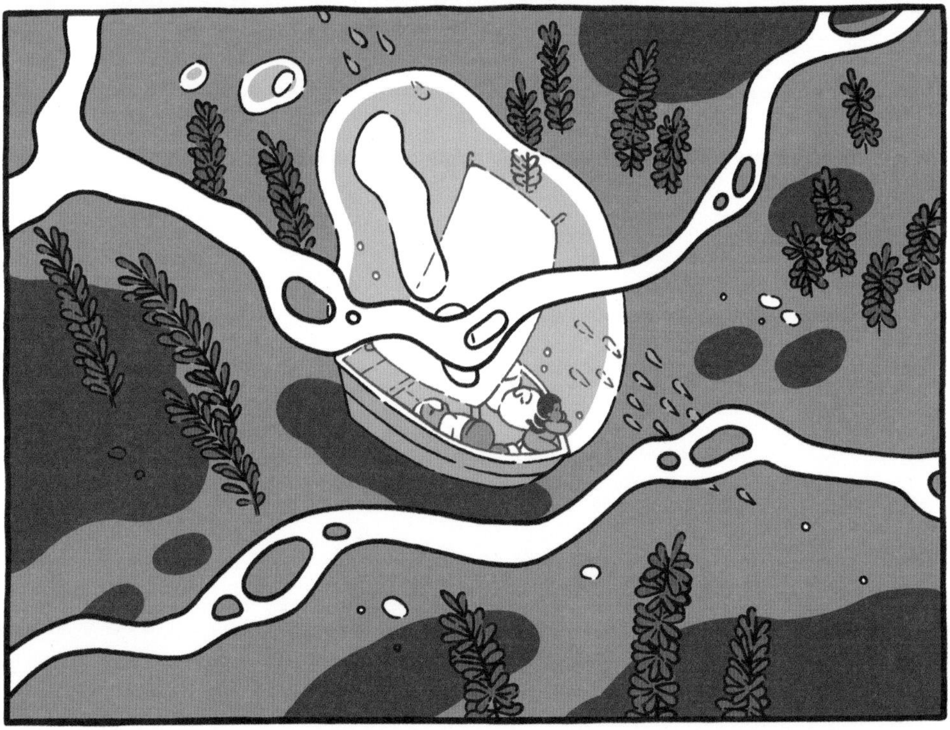

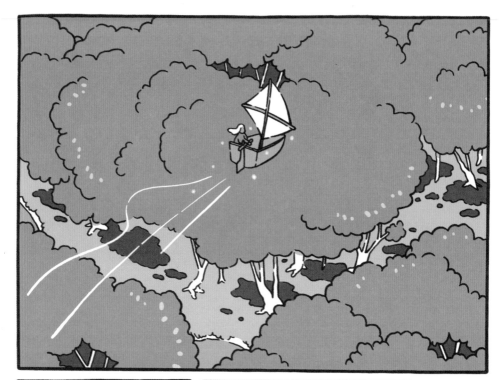

This feels... right.

It's not like home, but it's similar.

It feels safe. Protected.

We can make a home here, Lue.

Just the two of us.

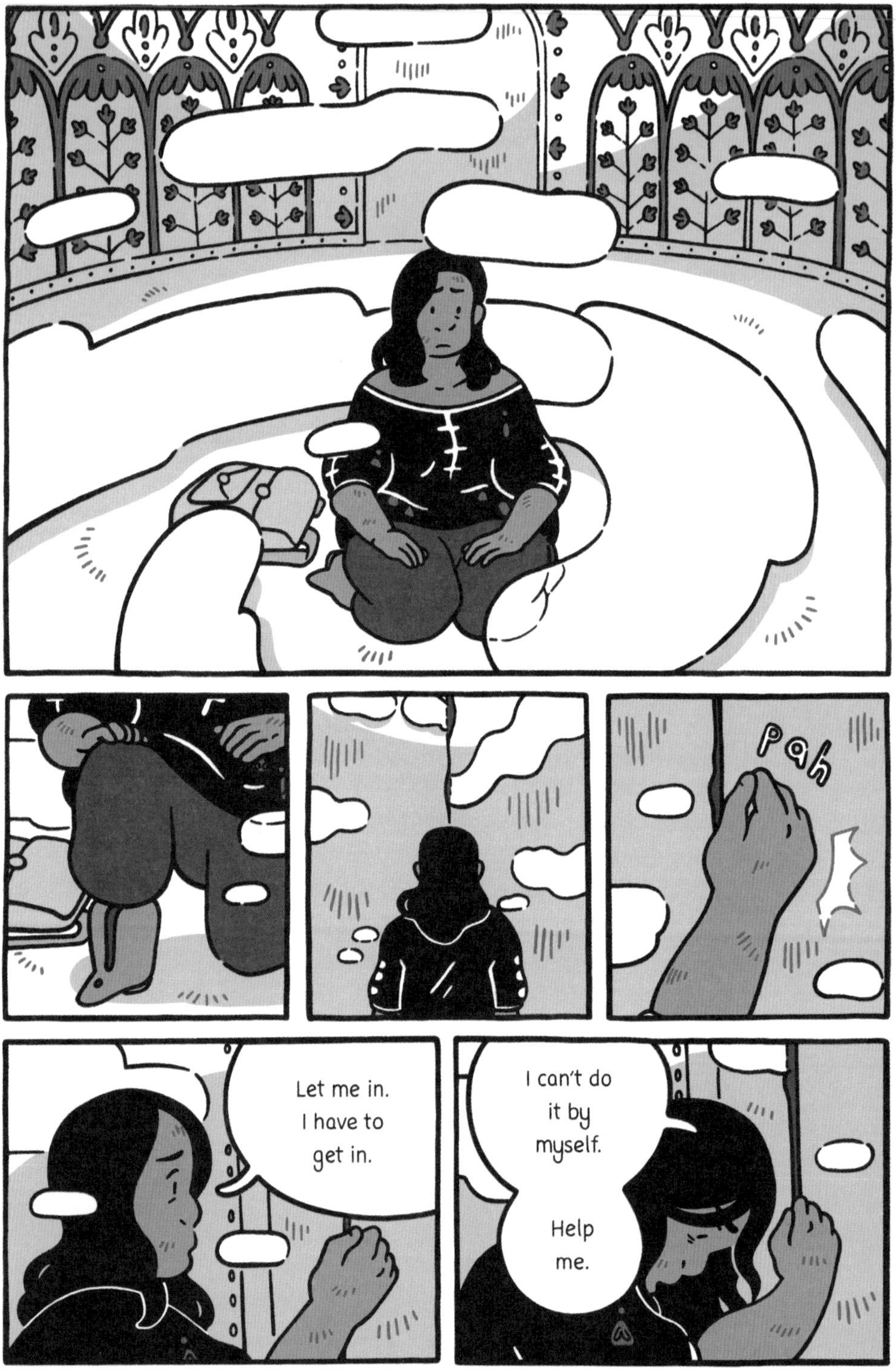
pah
Let me in.
I have to
get in.
I can't do
it by
myself.
Help
me.

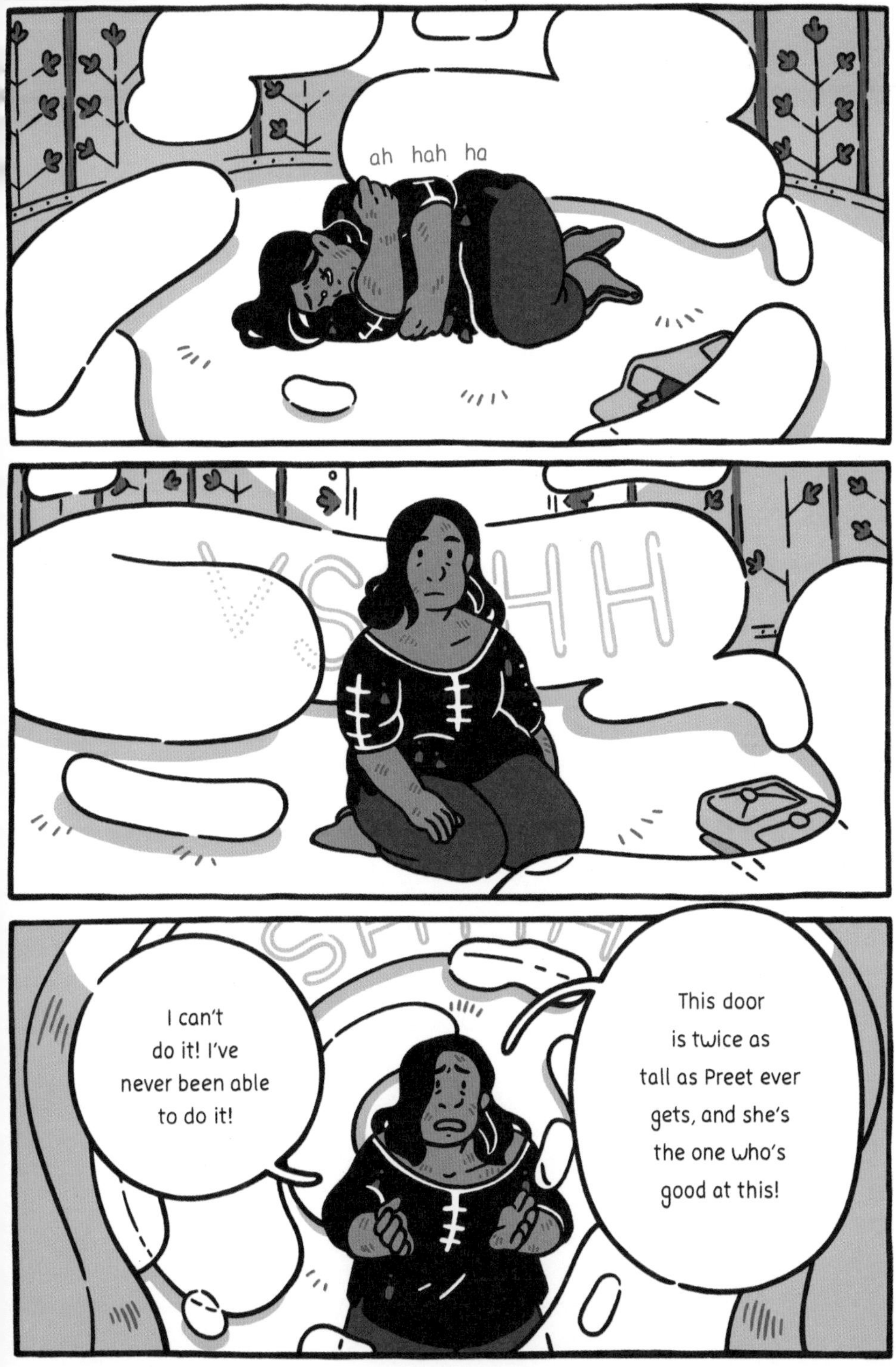
ah hah ha
VSHH
I can't do it! I've never been able to do it!
This door is twice as tall as Preet ever gets, and she's the one who's good at this!

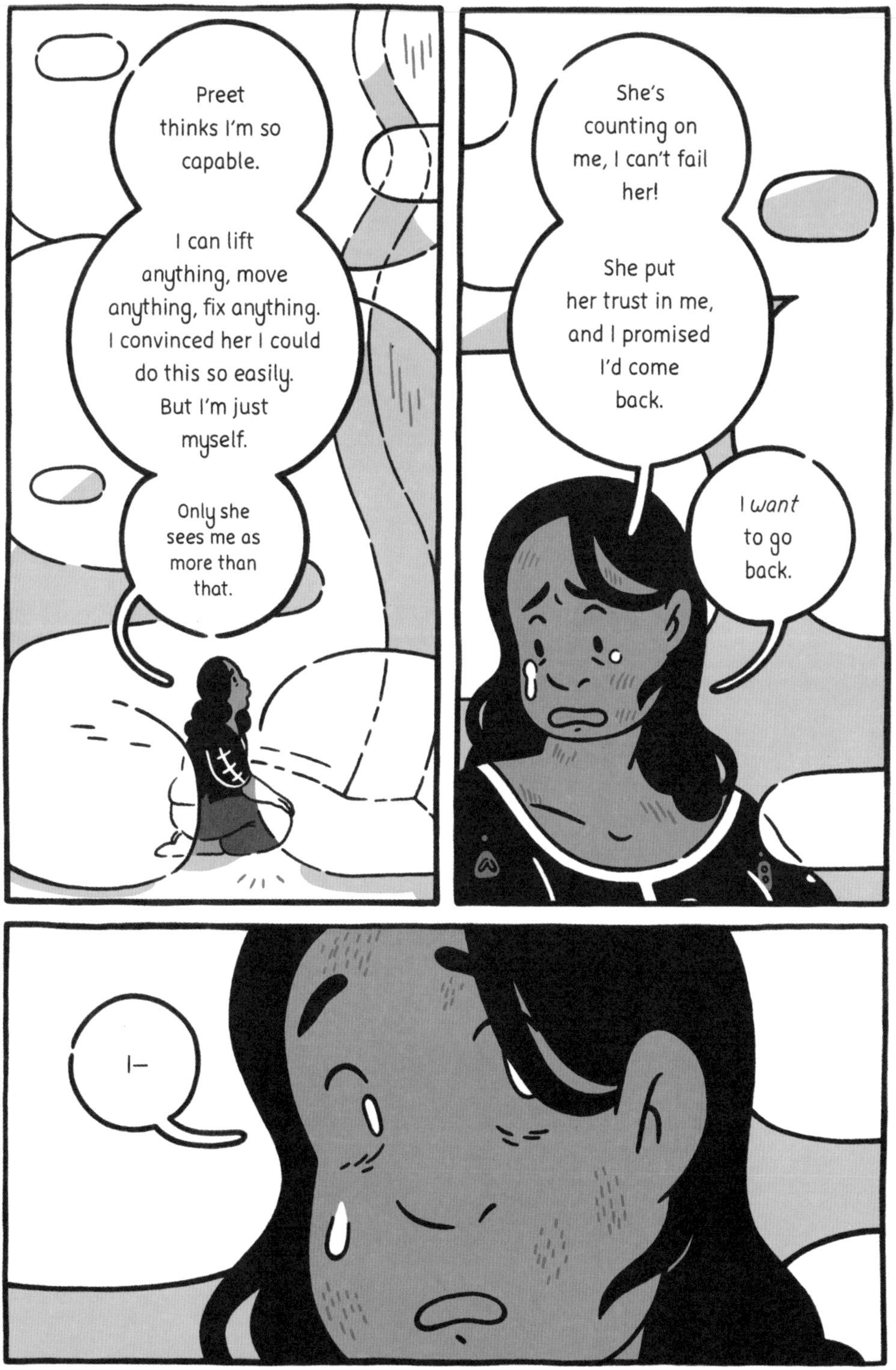
Preet thinks I'm so capable.
I can lift anything, move anything, fix anything. I convinced her I could do this so easily. But I'm just myself.
Only she sees me as more than that.
She's counting on me, I can't fail her!
She put her trust in me, and I promised I'd come back.
I *want* to go back.
I—

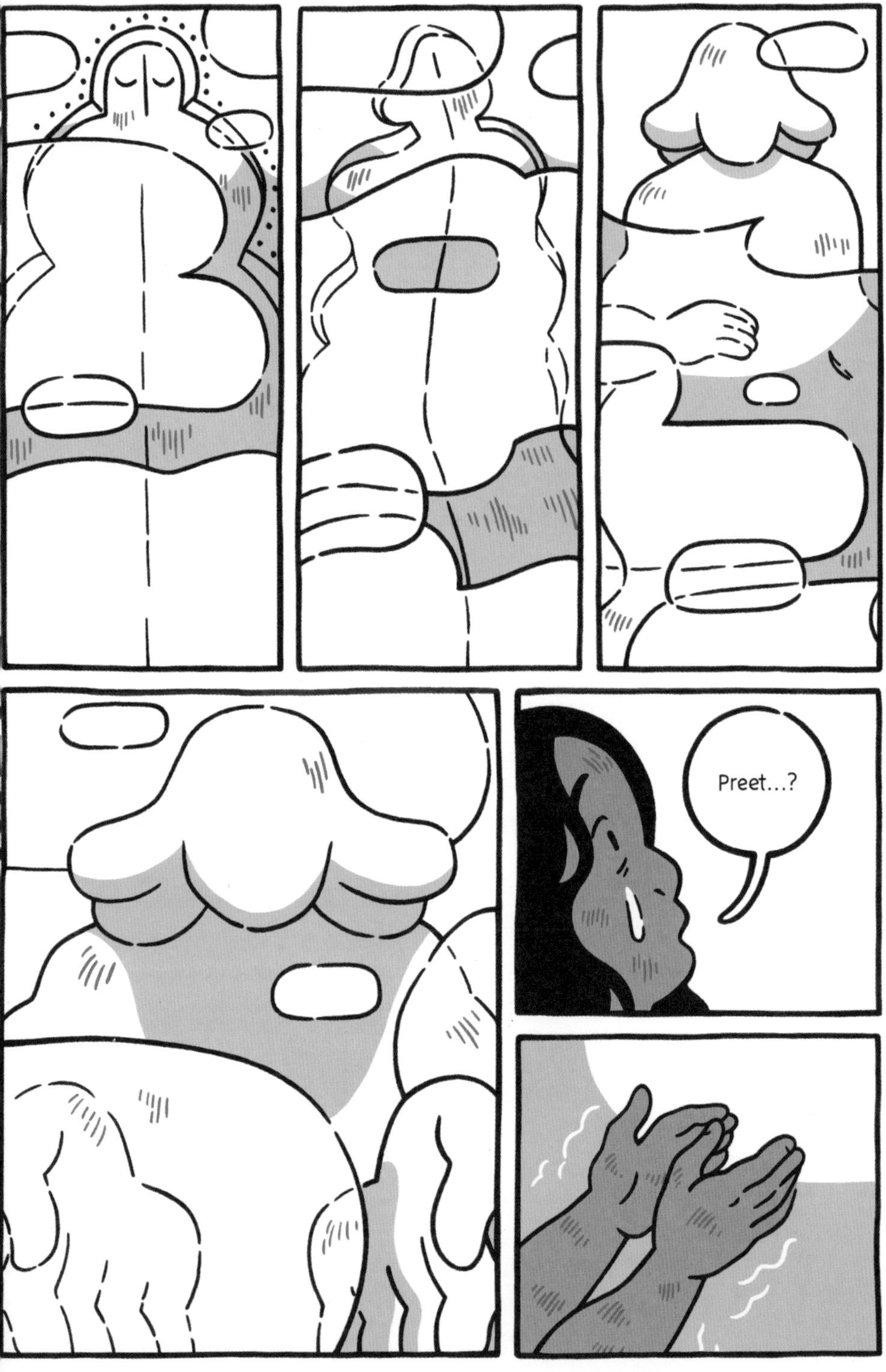
Preet...?

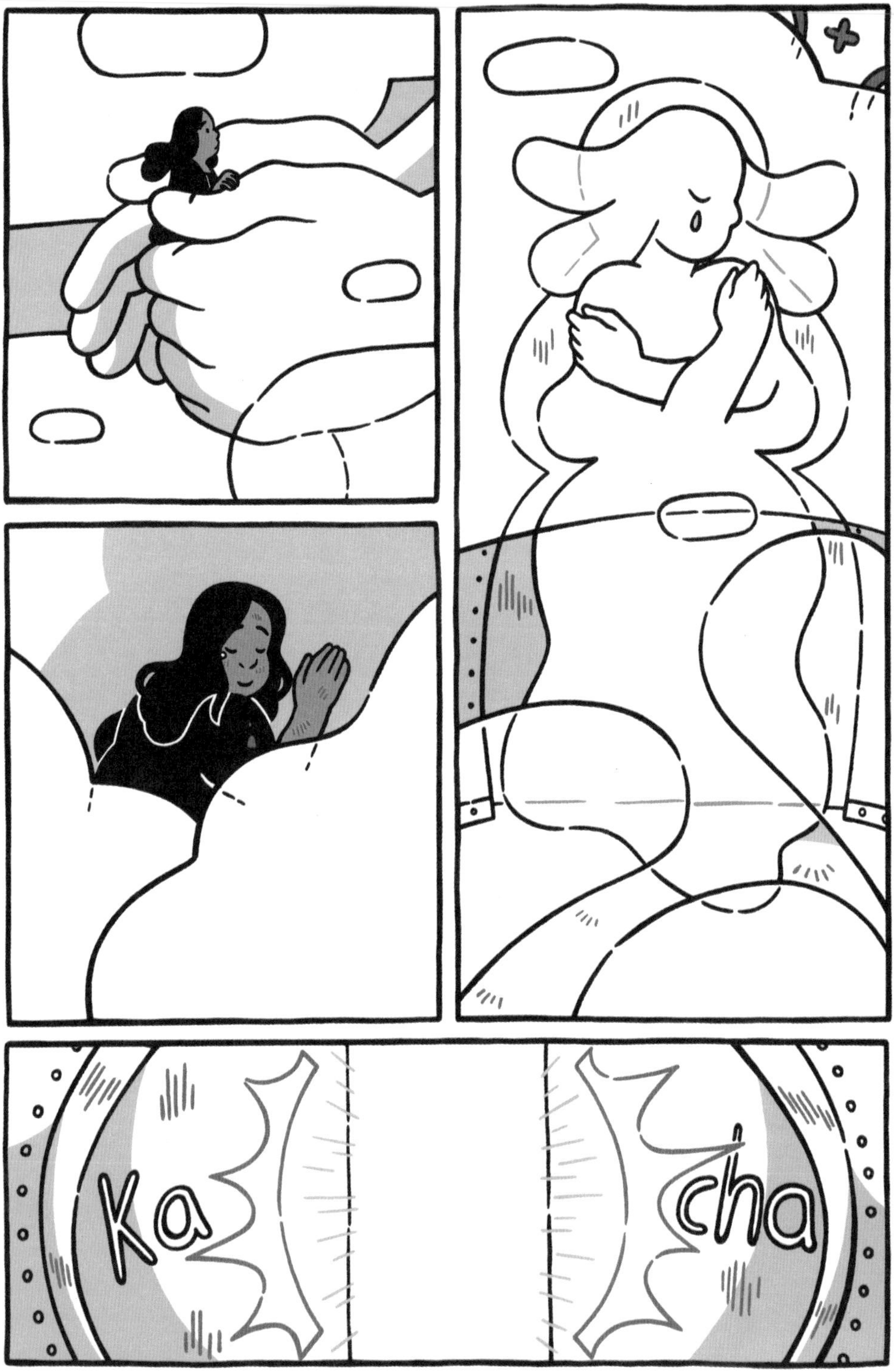
Ka
cha

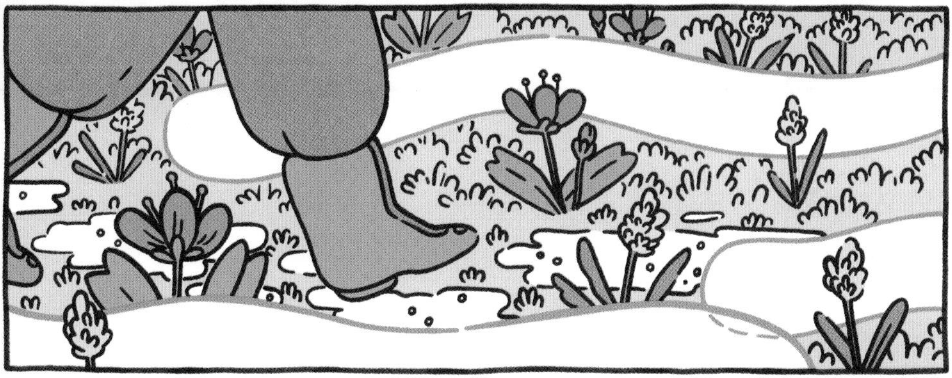

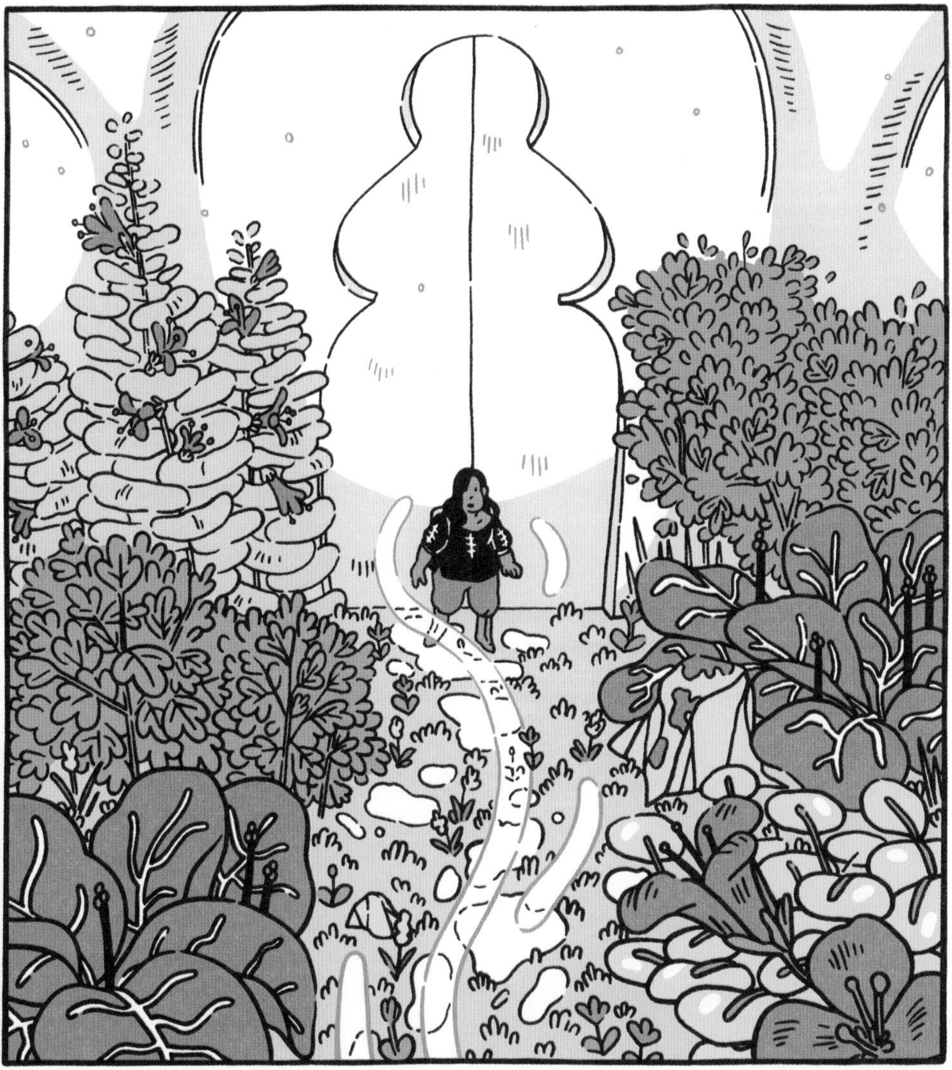

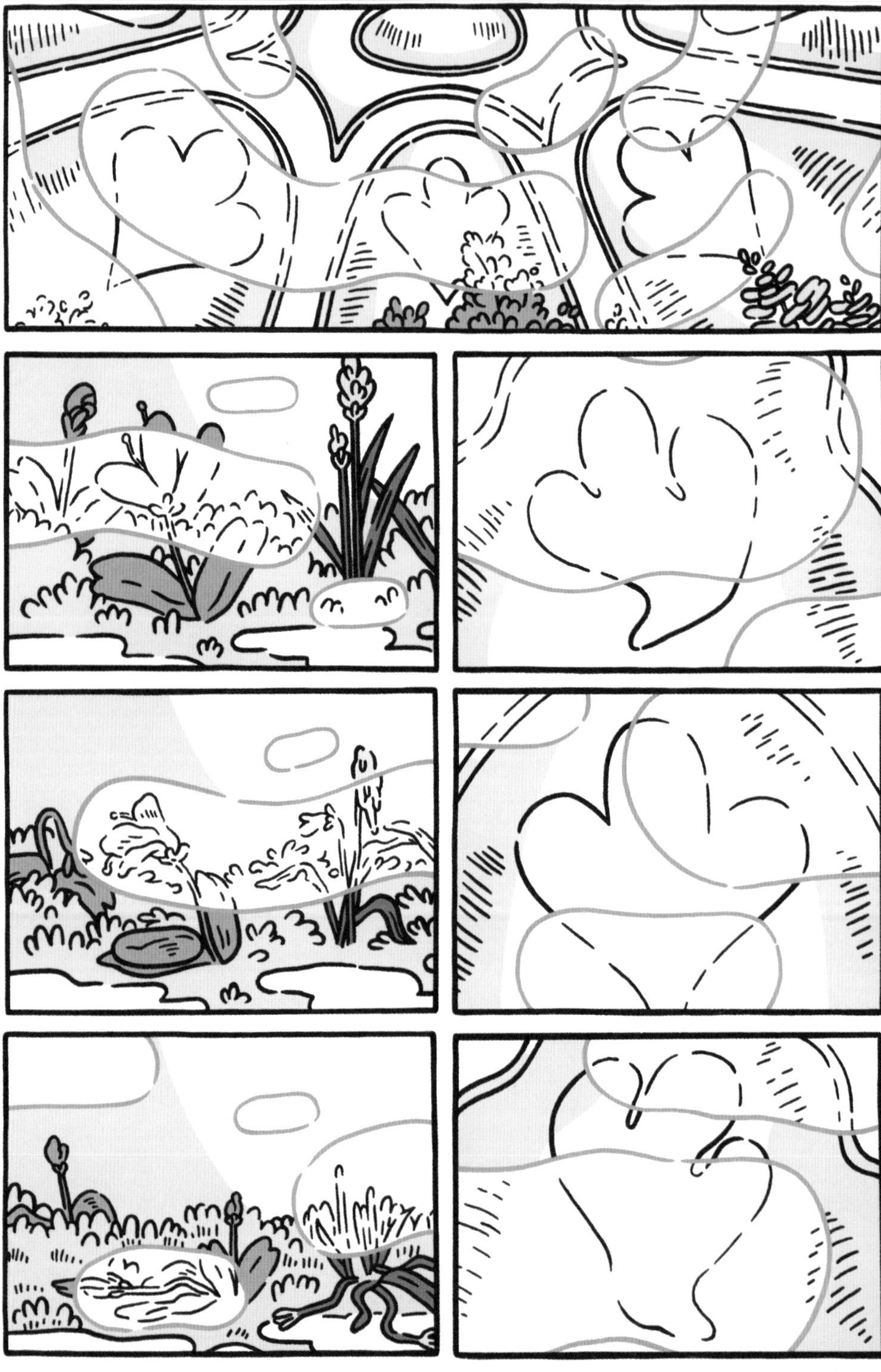

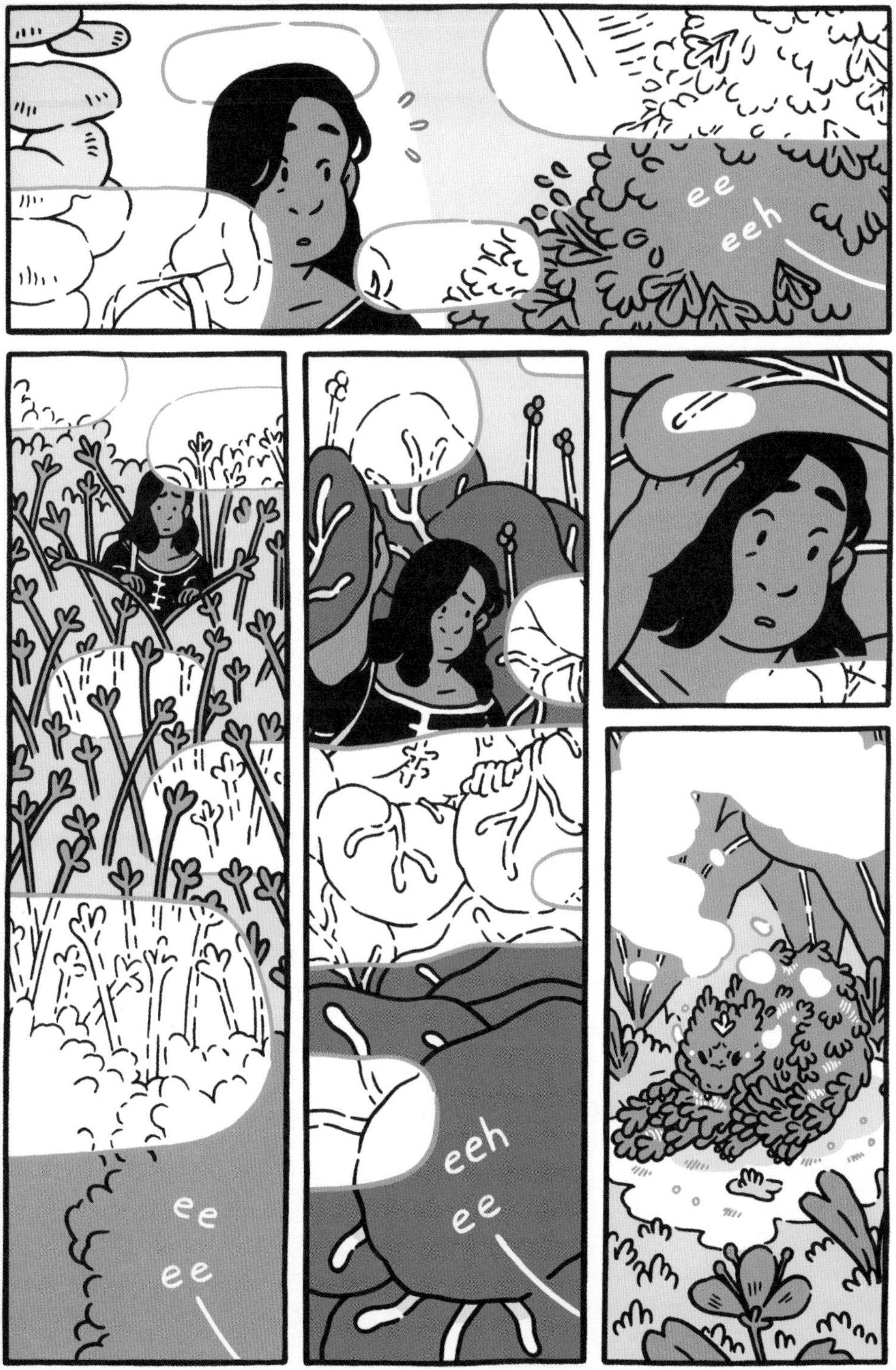
ee
eeh
ee
ee
eeh
ee

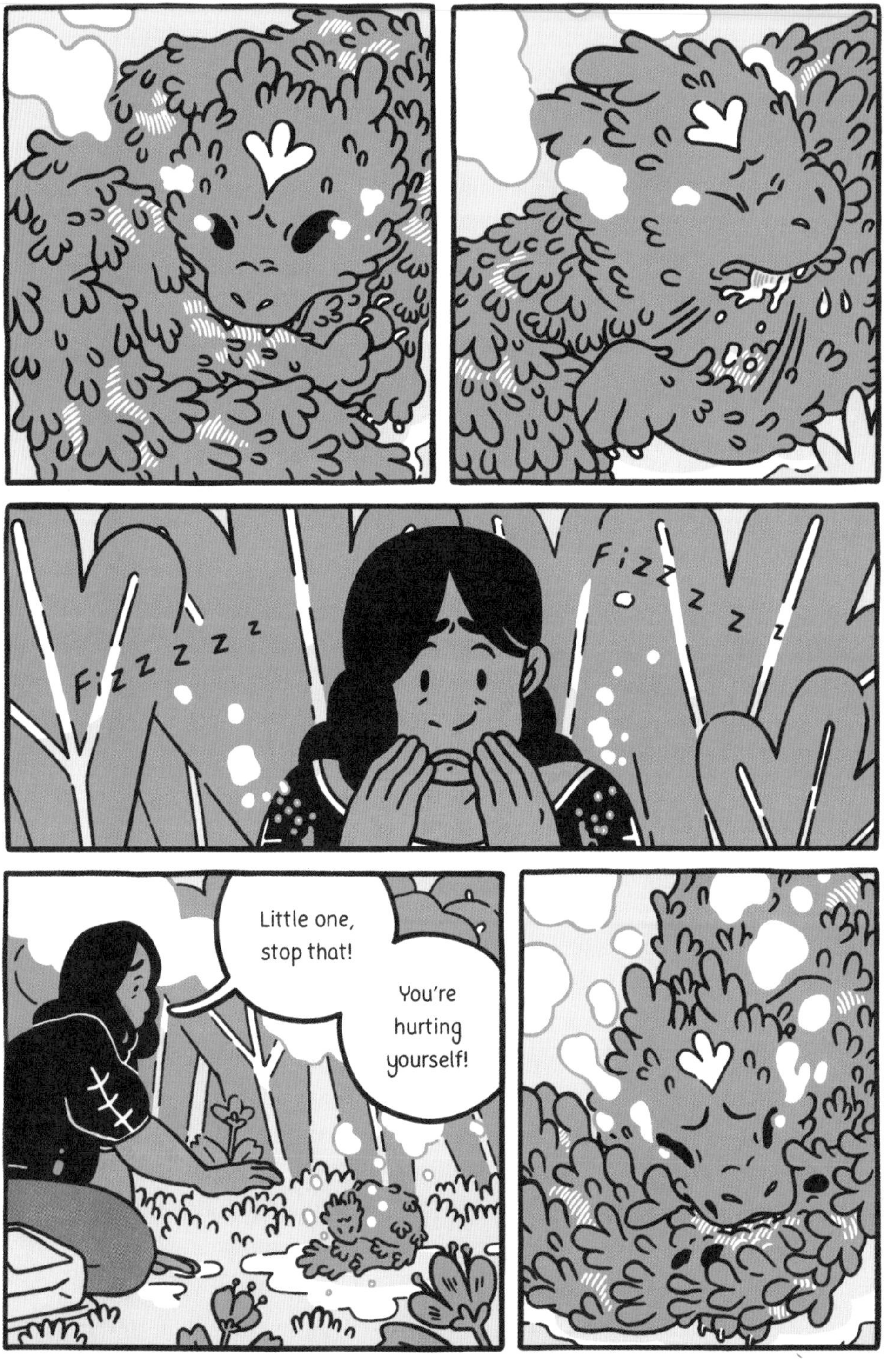
Fizzzzz
Fizzzzz
Little one, stop that!
You're hurting yourself!

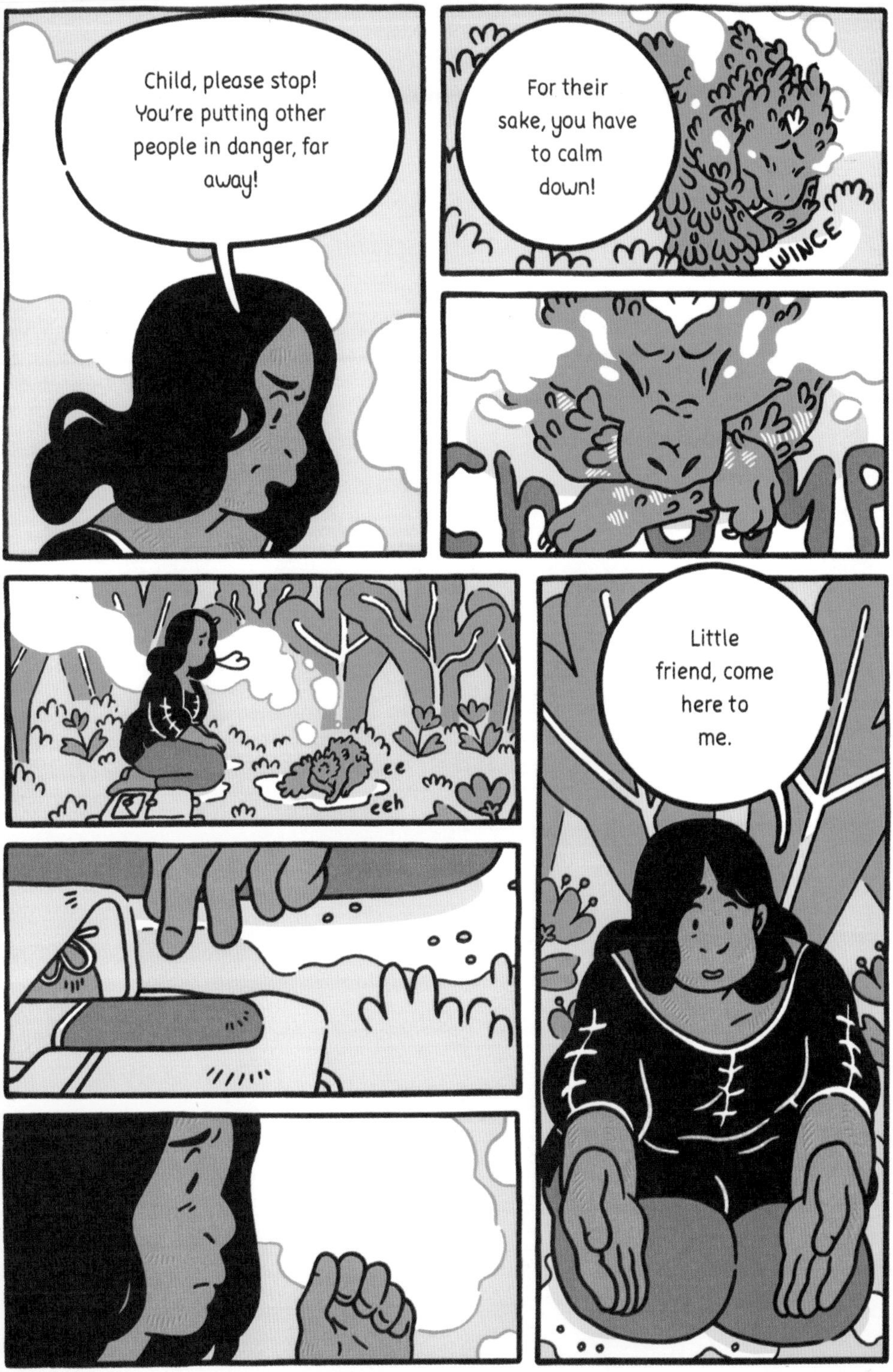
Child, please stop! You're putting other people in danger, far away!
For their sake, you have to calm down!
WINCE
ee
eeh
Little friend, come here to me.

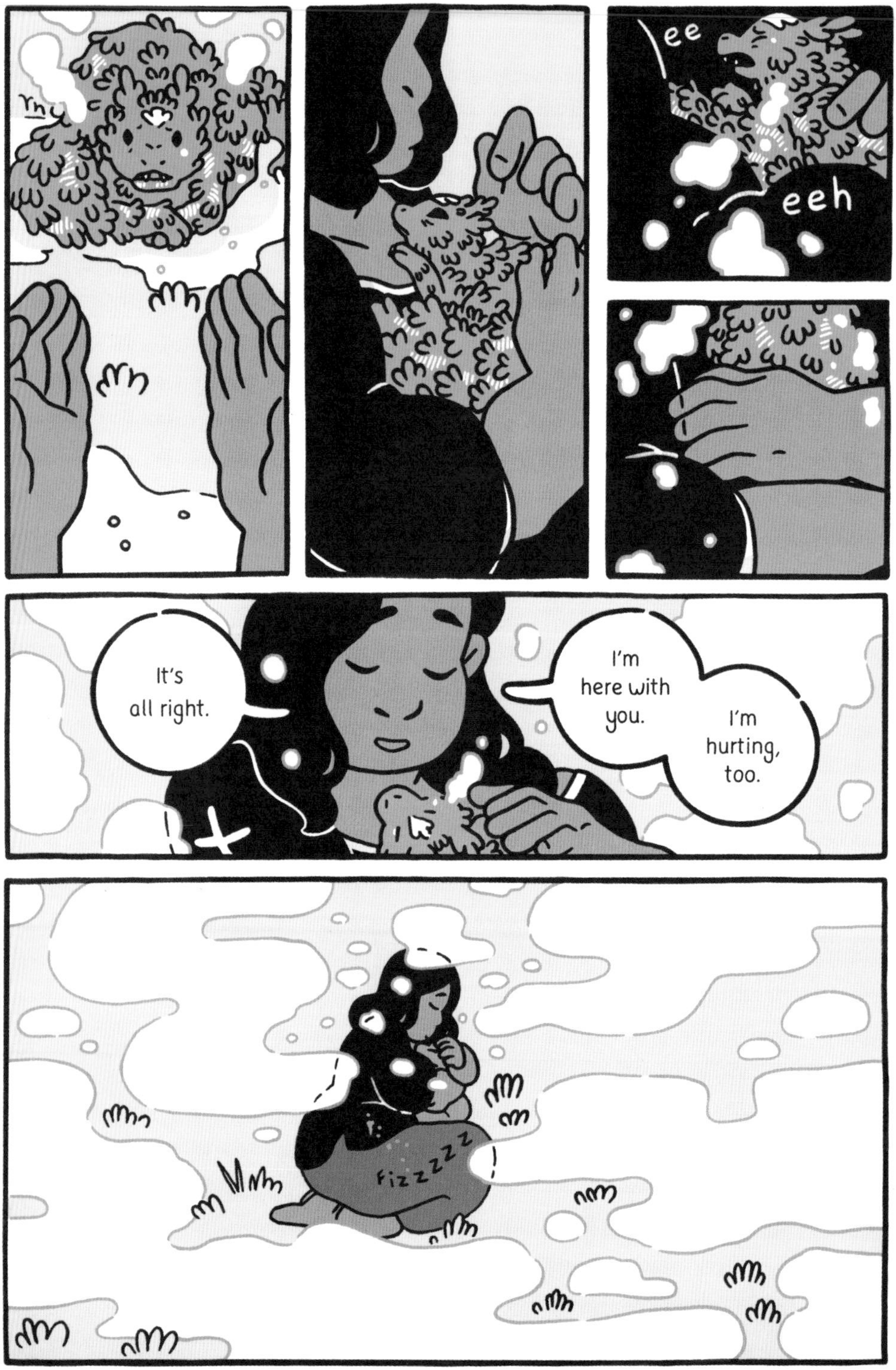

ee
eeh
It's all right.
I'm here with you.
I'm hurting, too.
Fizzzzz

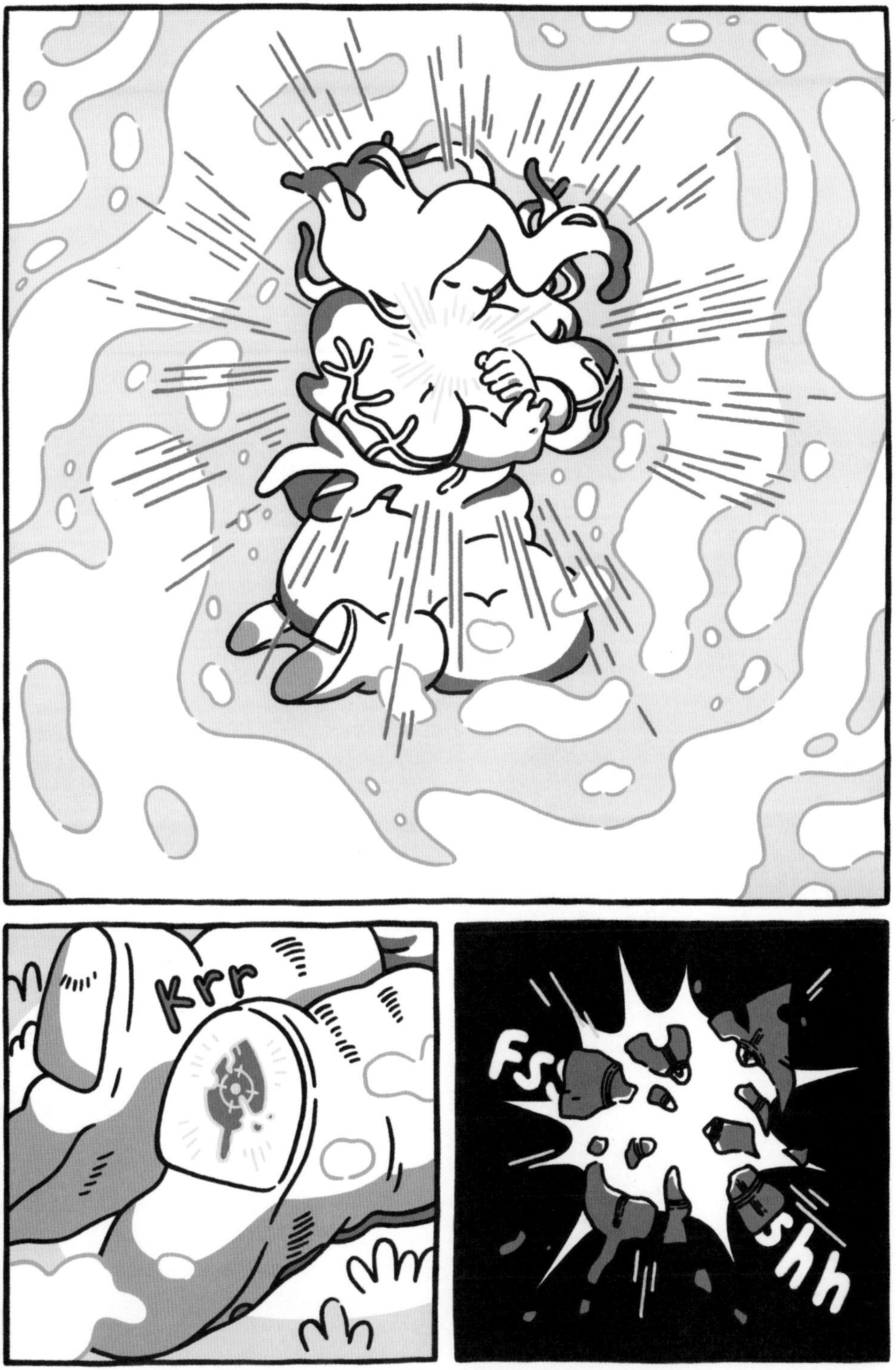
krr
FSS
shh

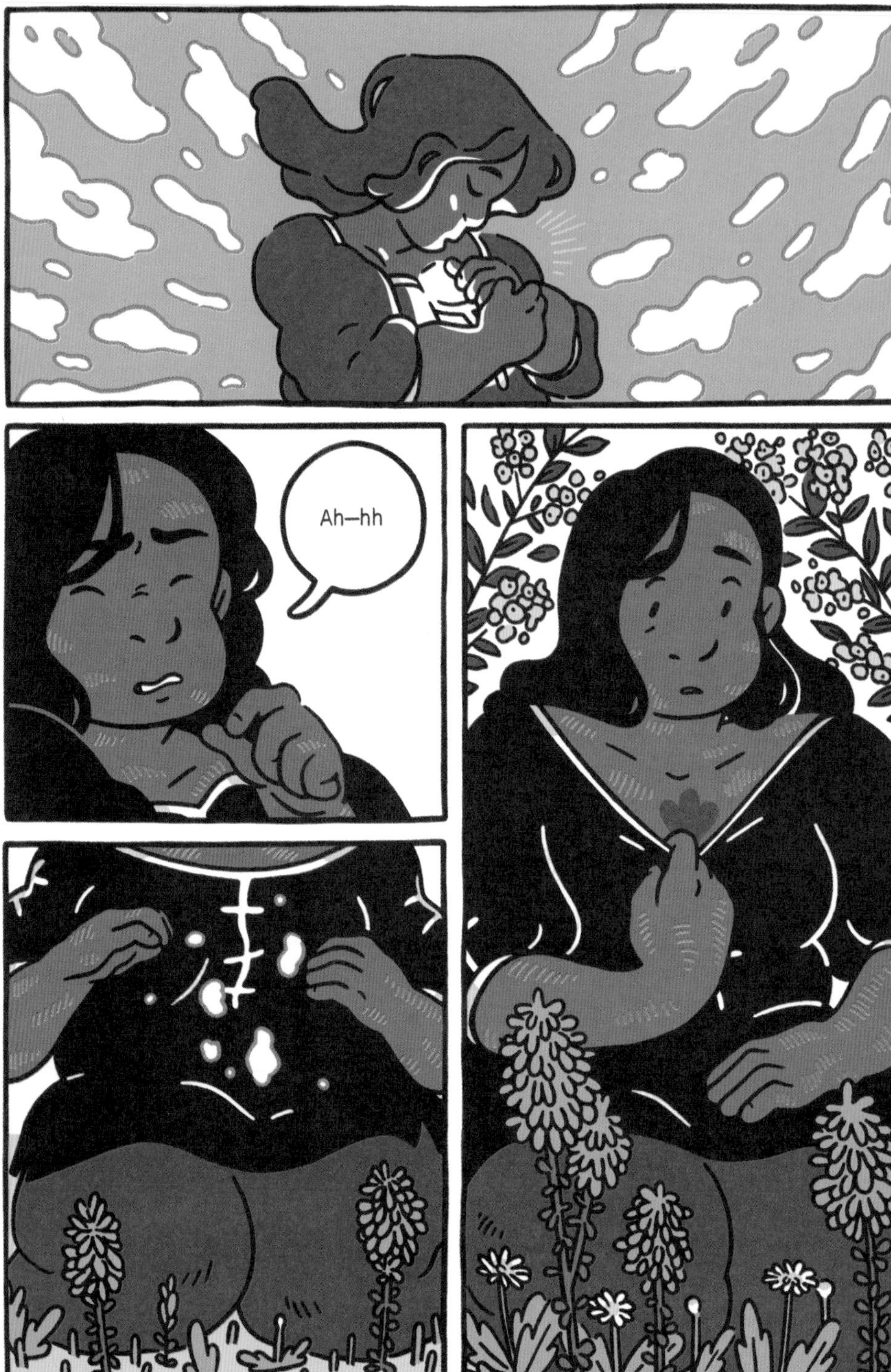
Ah—hh

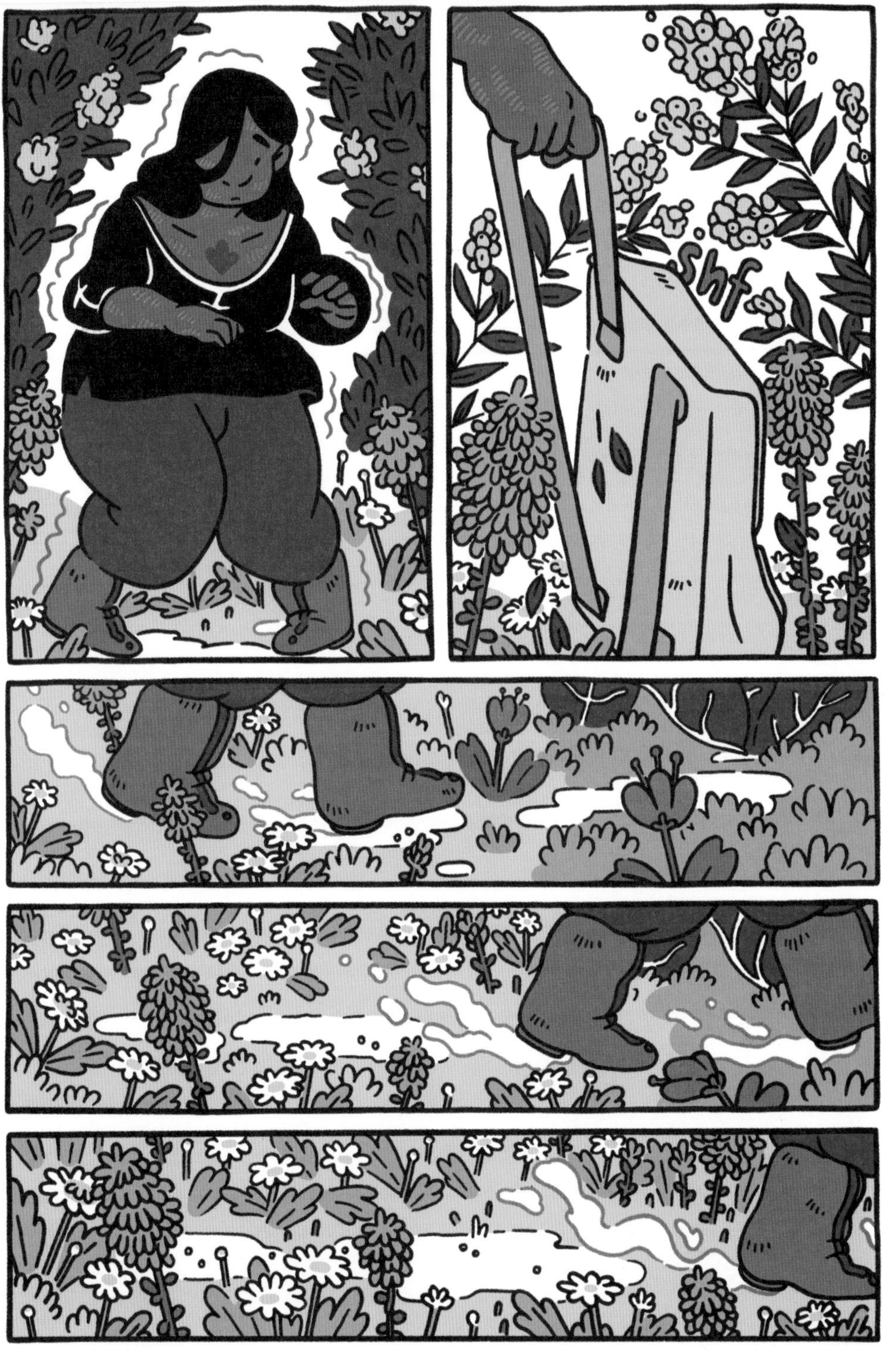
shf

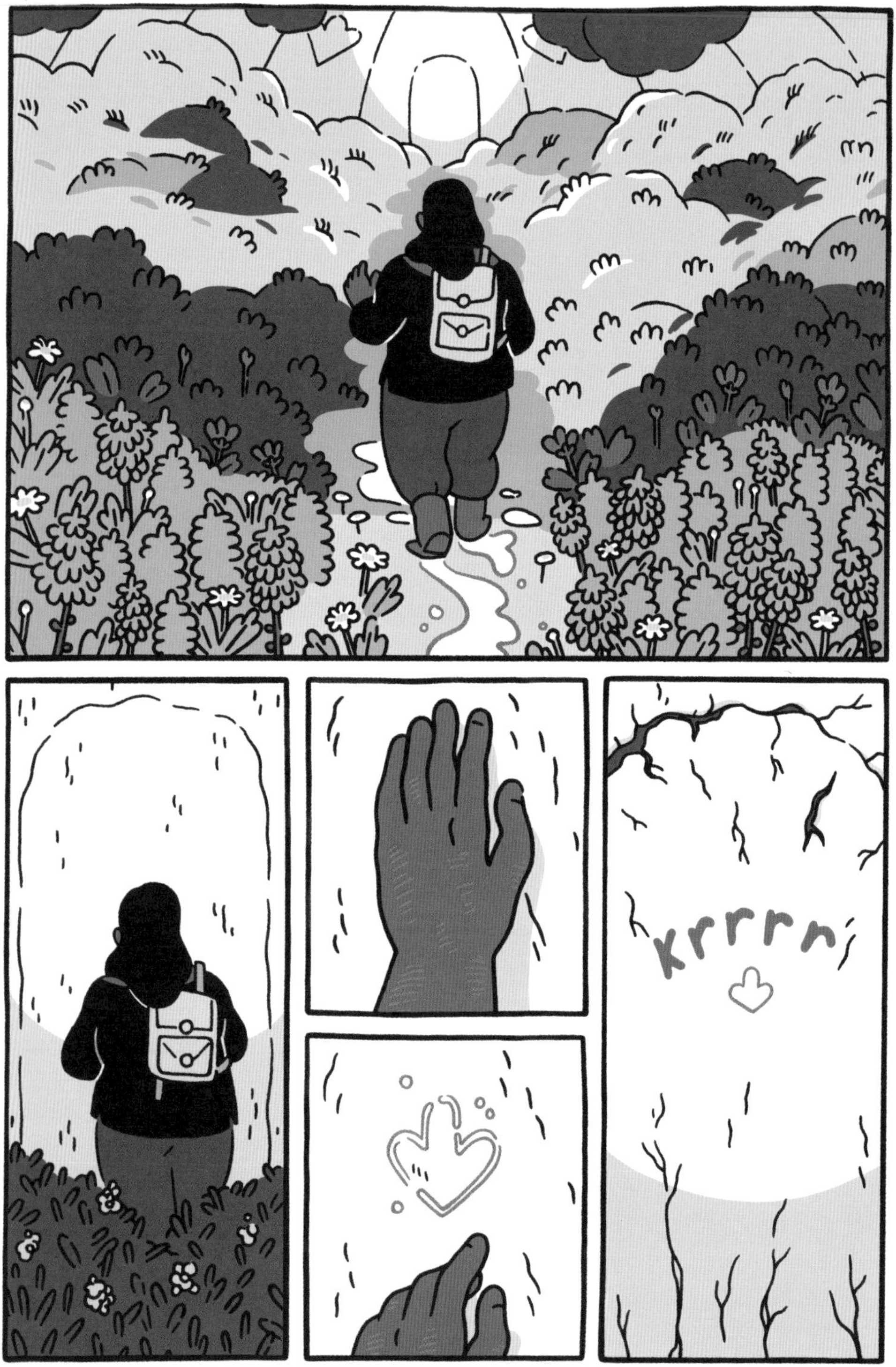
krrrn

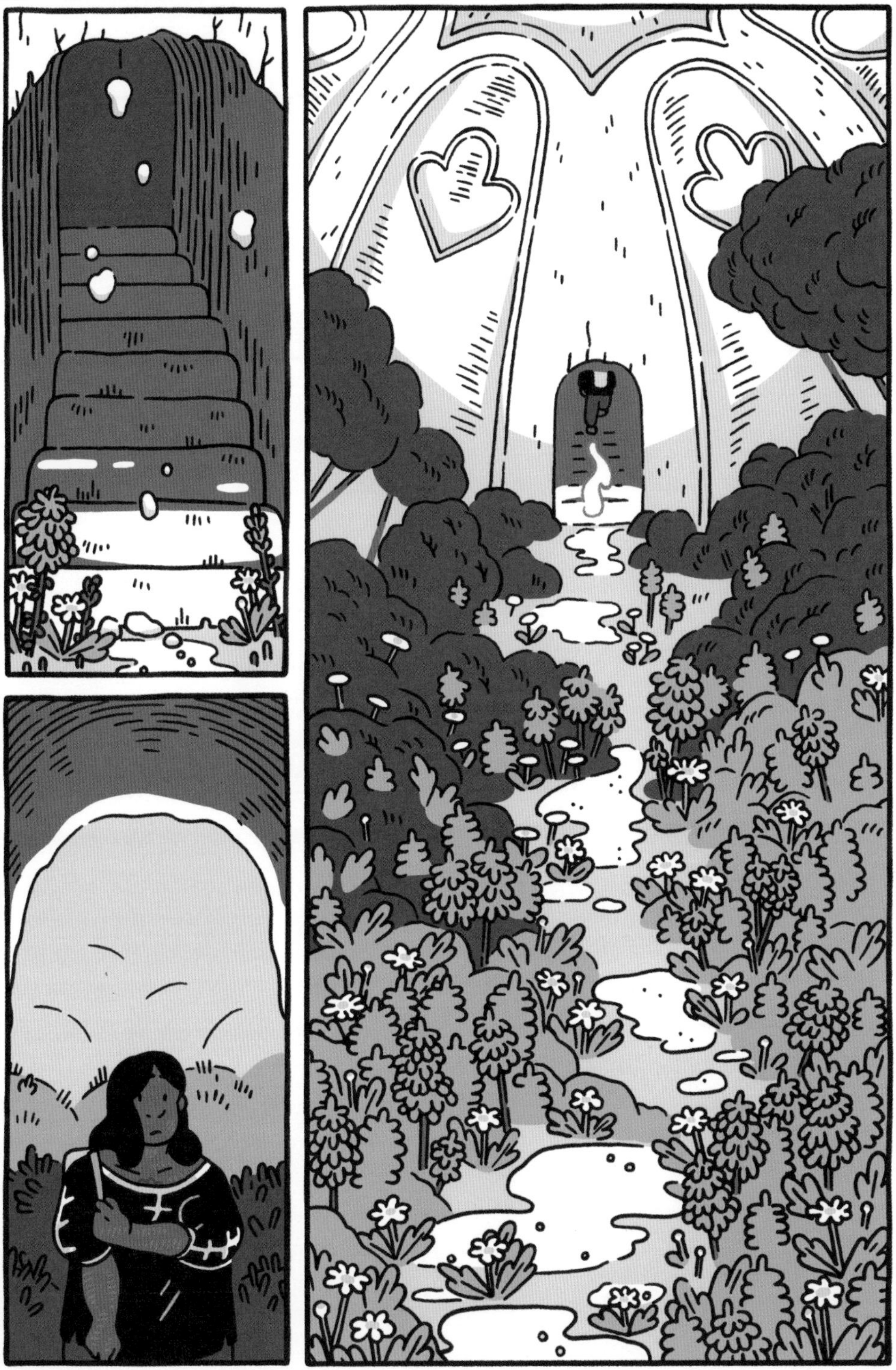

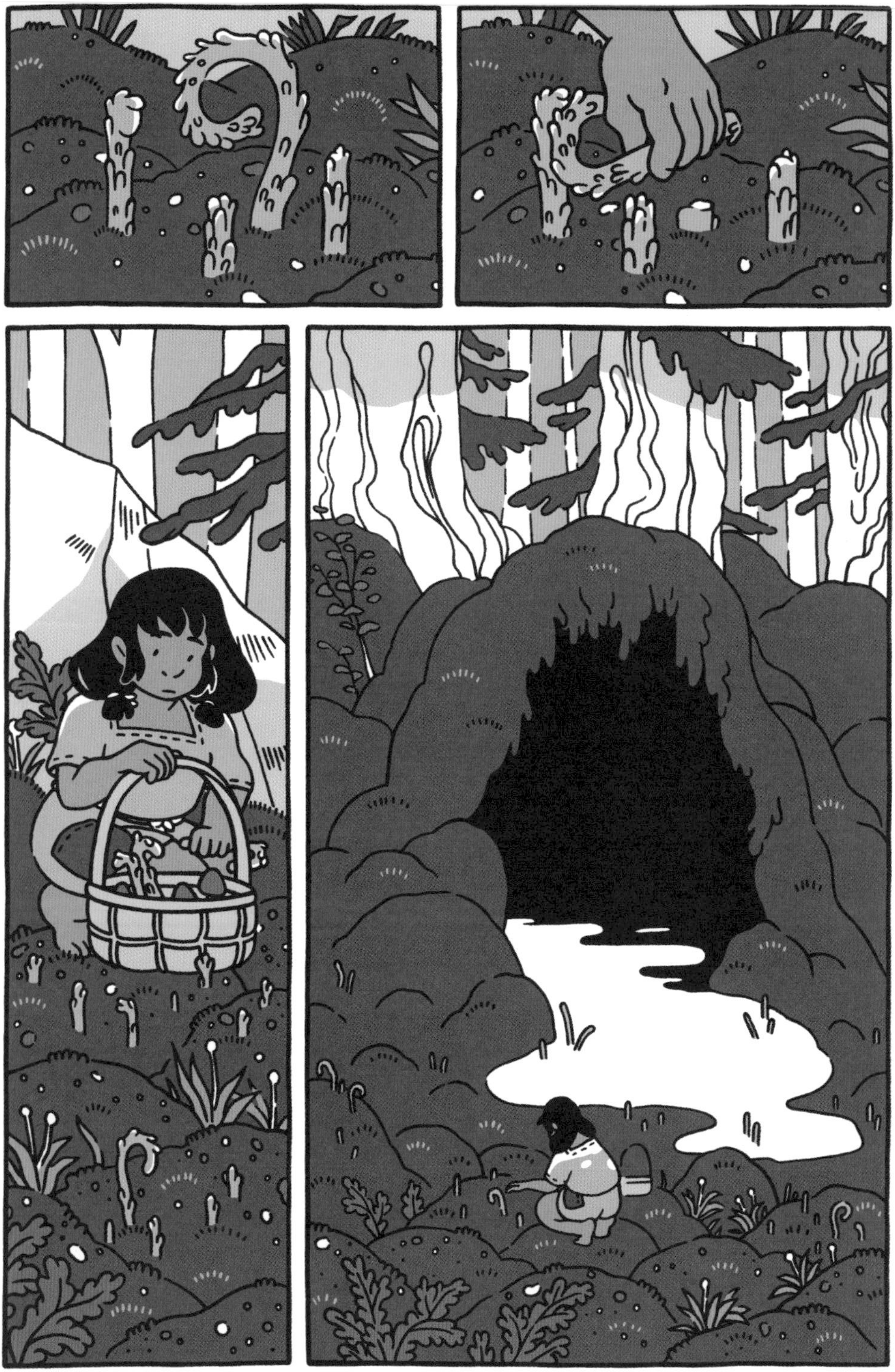

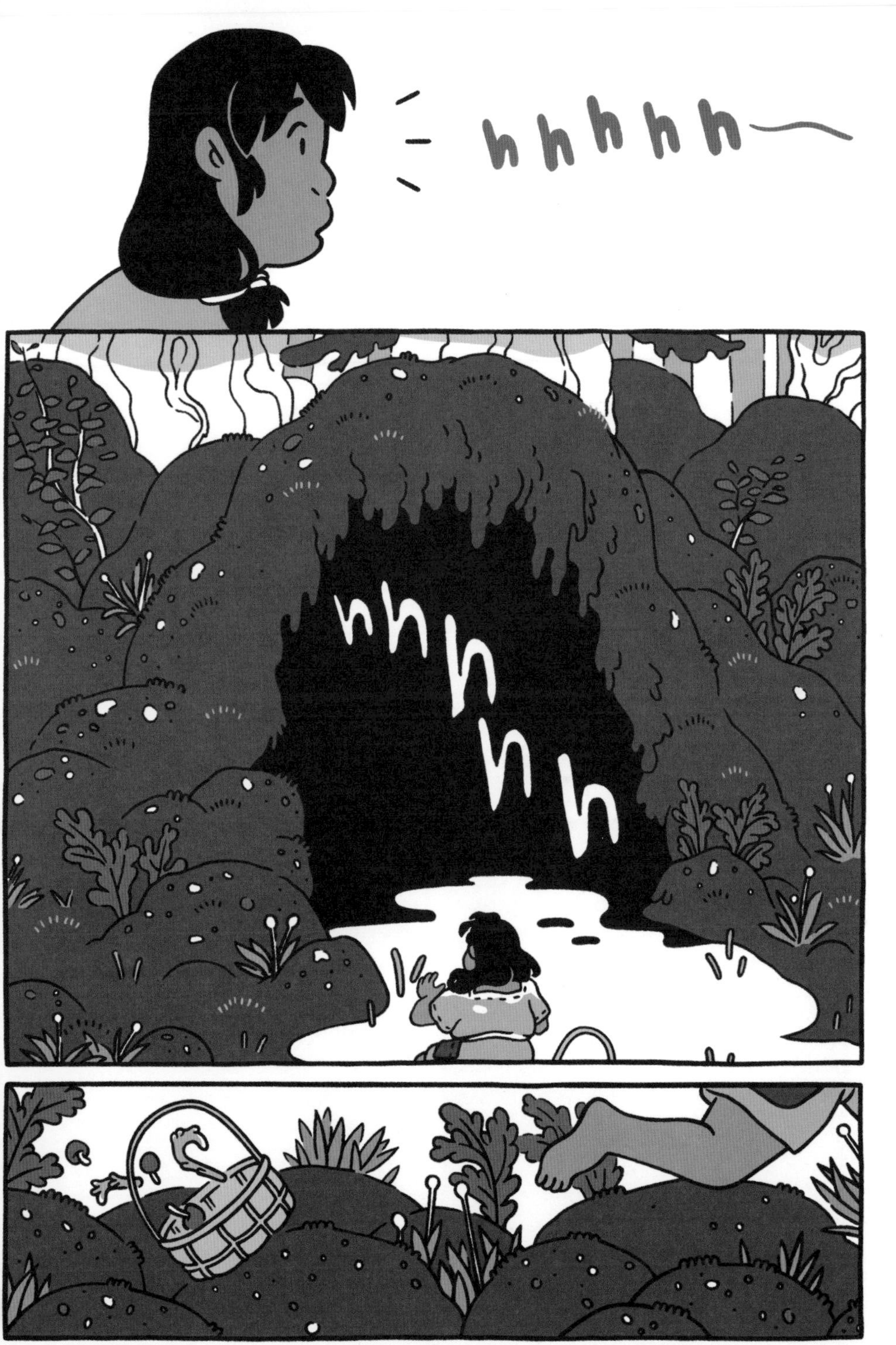
hhhhhh—
hhhhhh

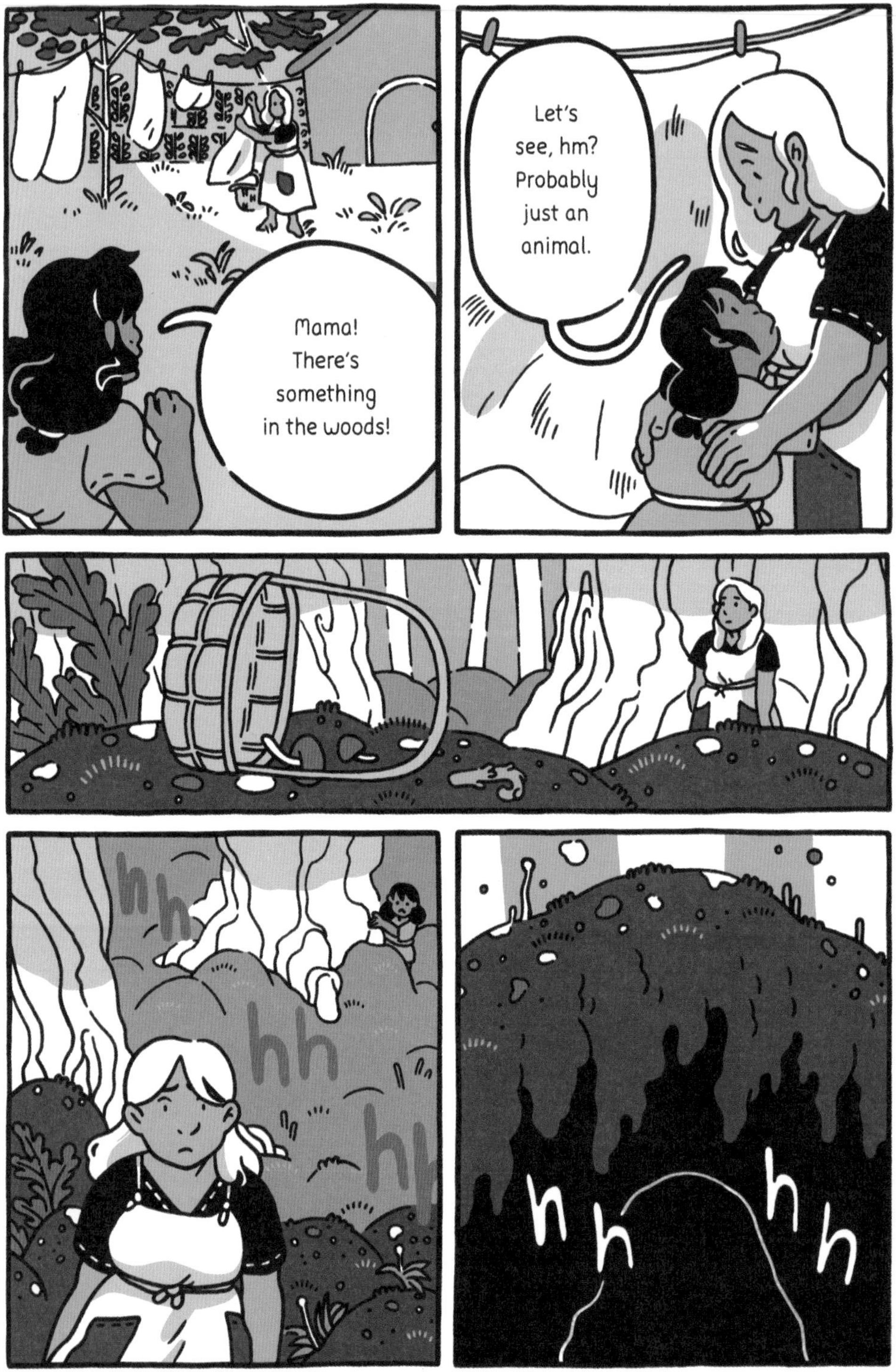
Mama! There's something in the woods!
Let's see, hm? Probably just an animal.
hh
hh
hh
h h h h

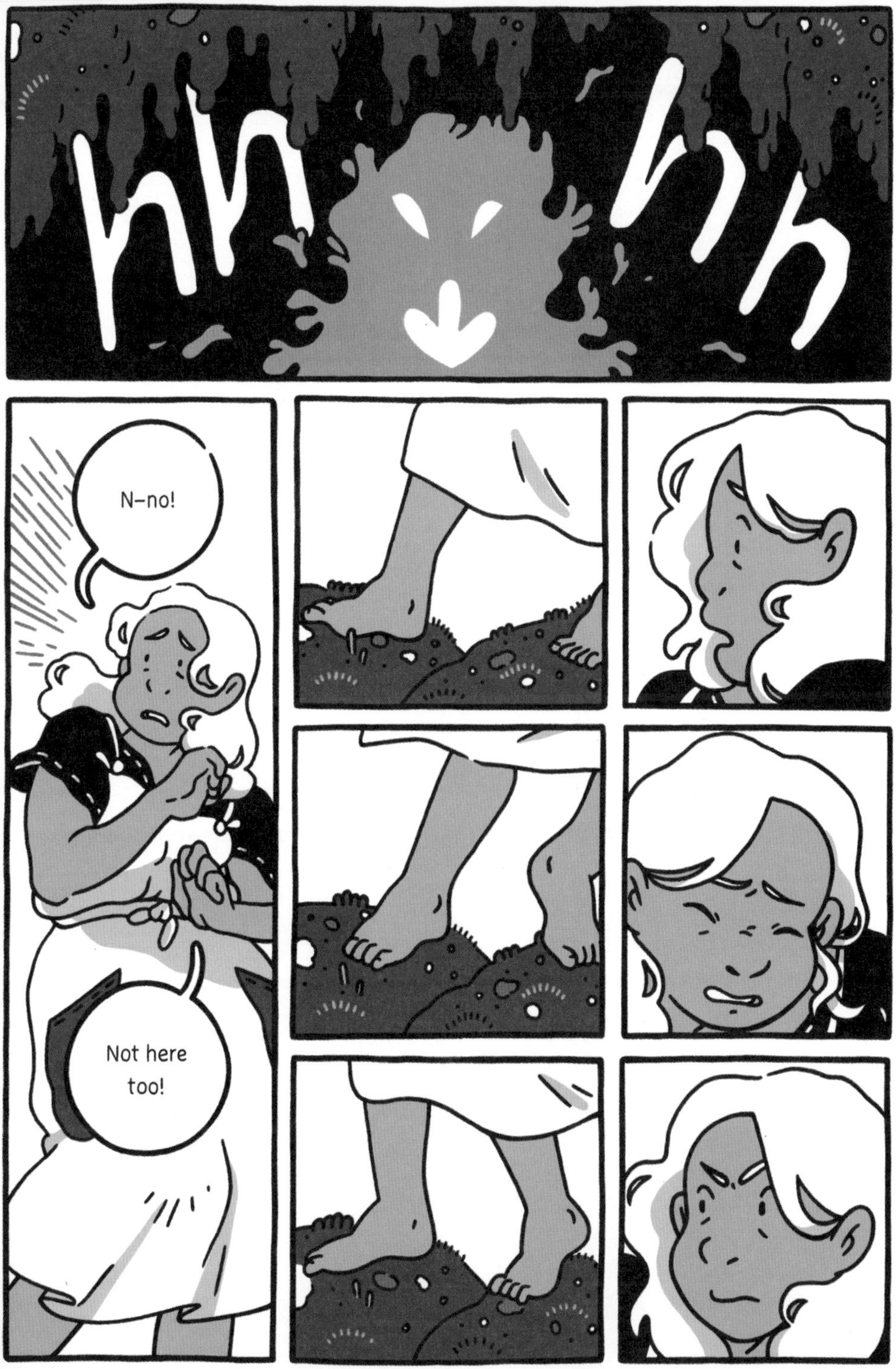
hh hhh
N-no!
Not here too!

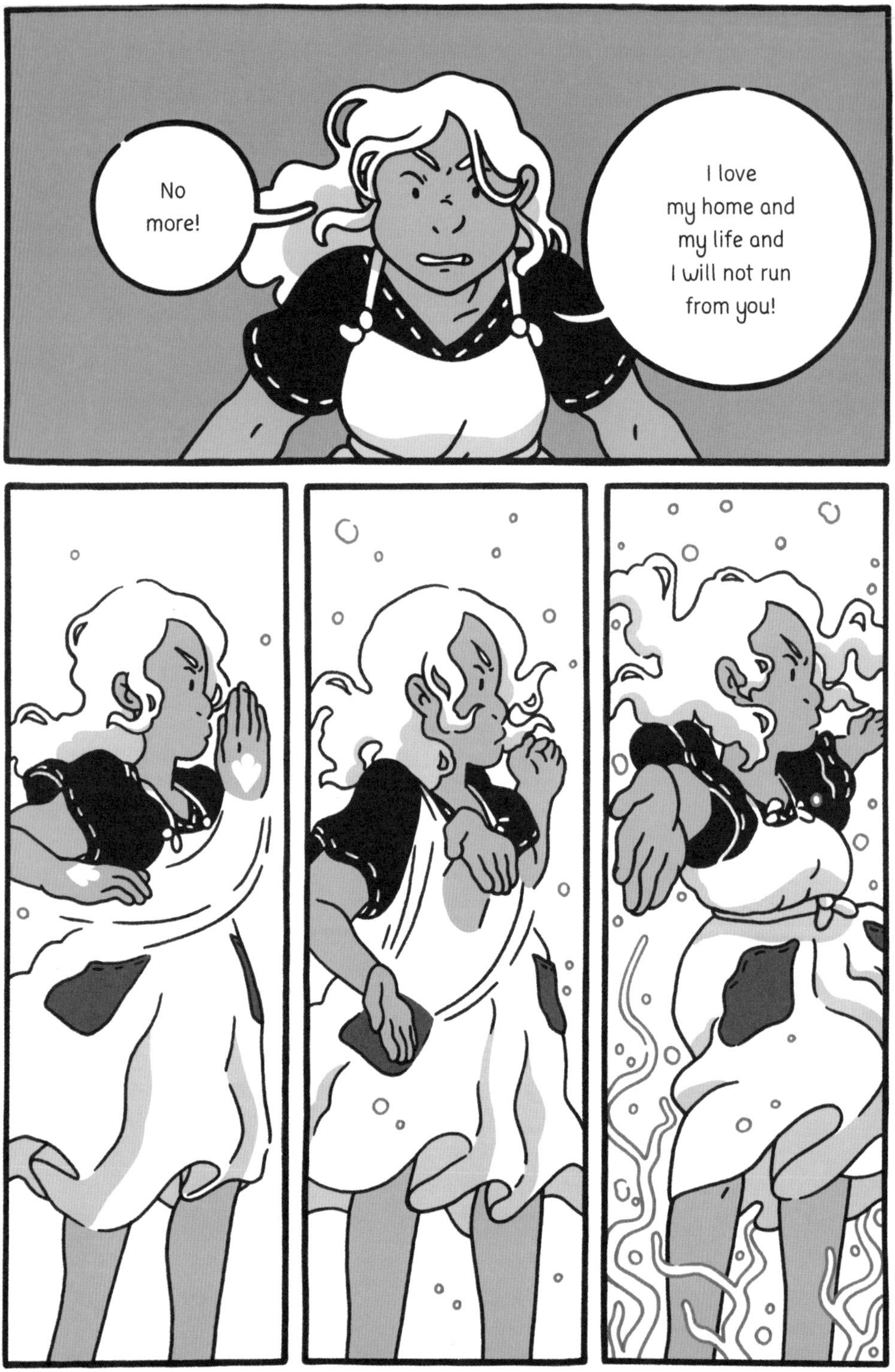
No more!
I love my home and my life and I will not run from you!

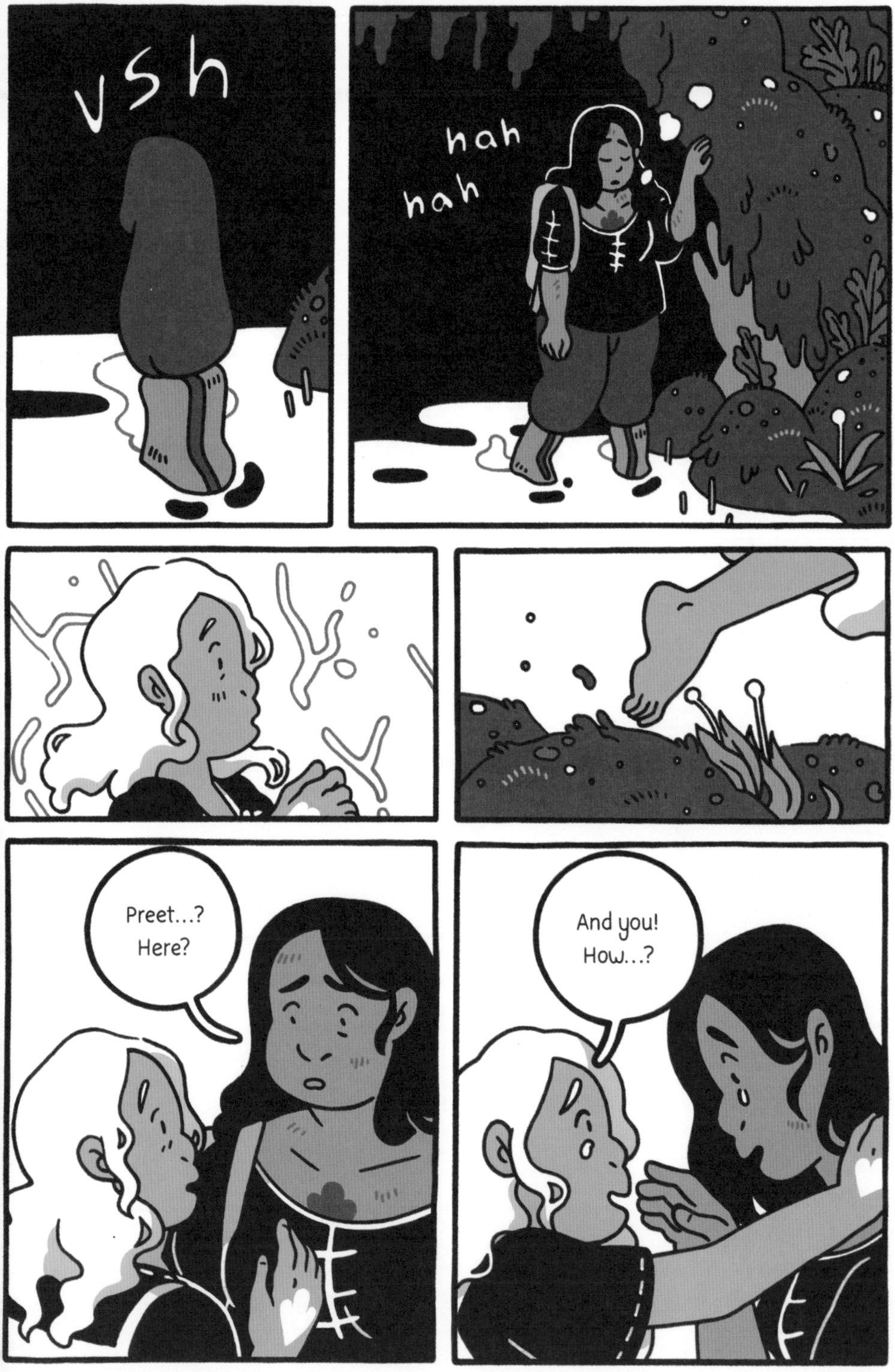
vsh
hah
hah
Preet...?
Here?
And you!
How...?

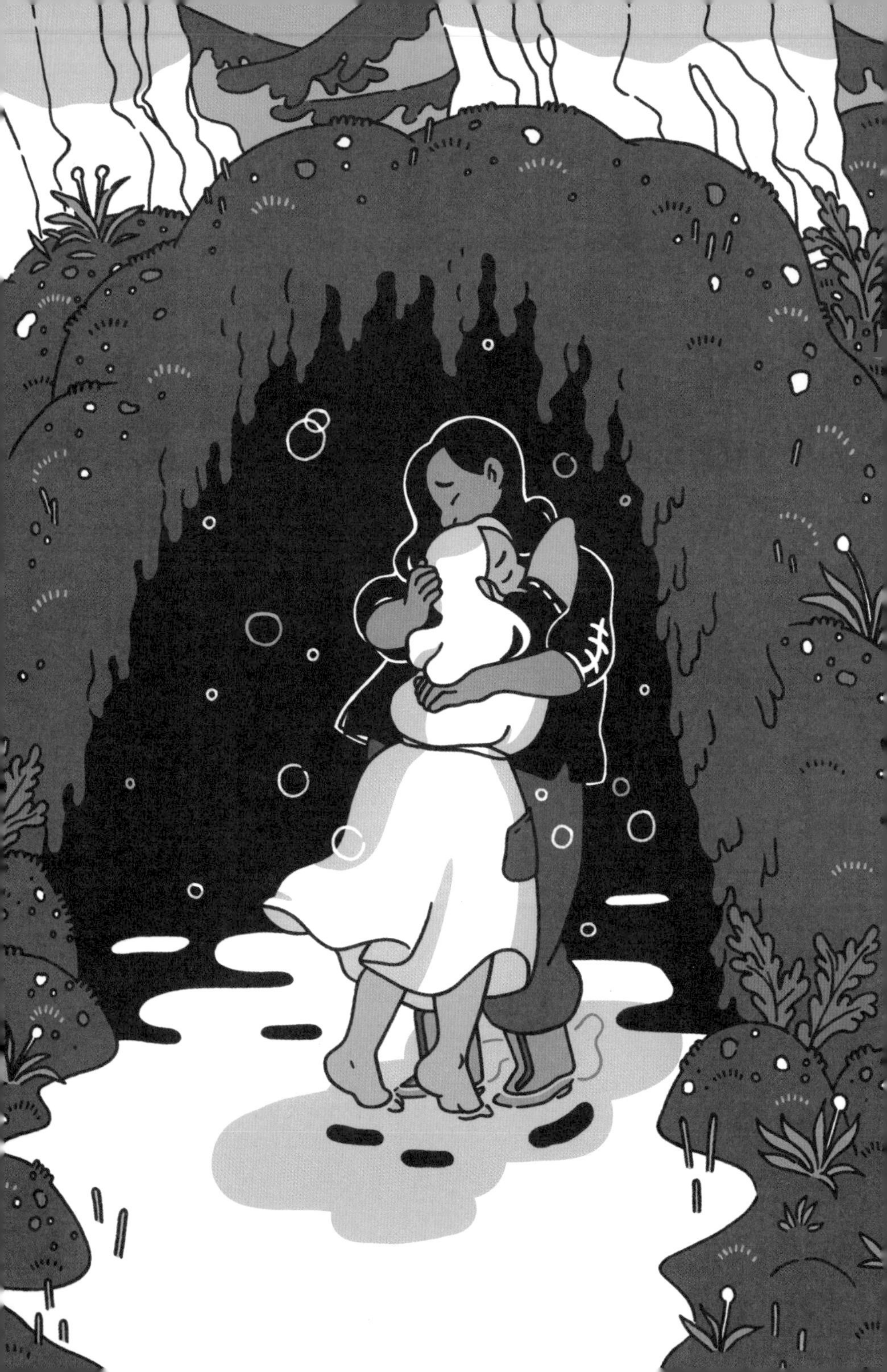

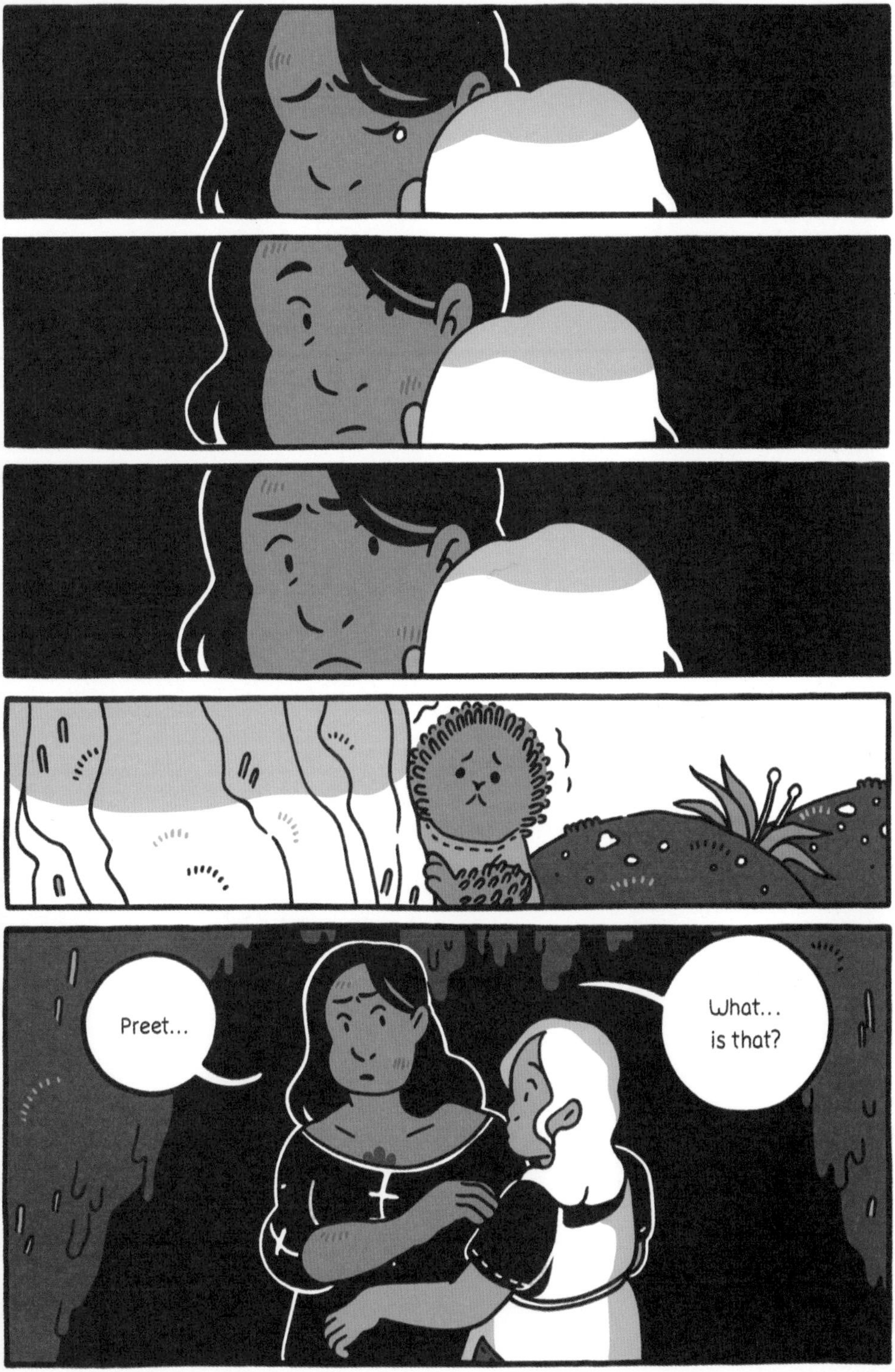
Preet...
What...
is that?

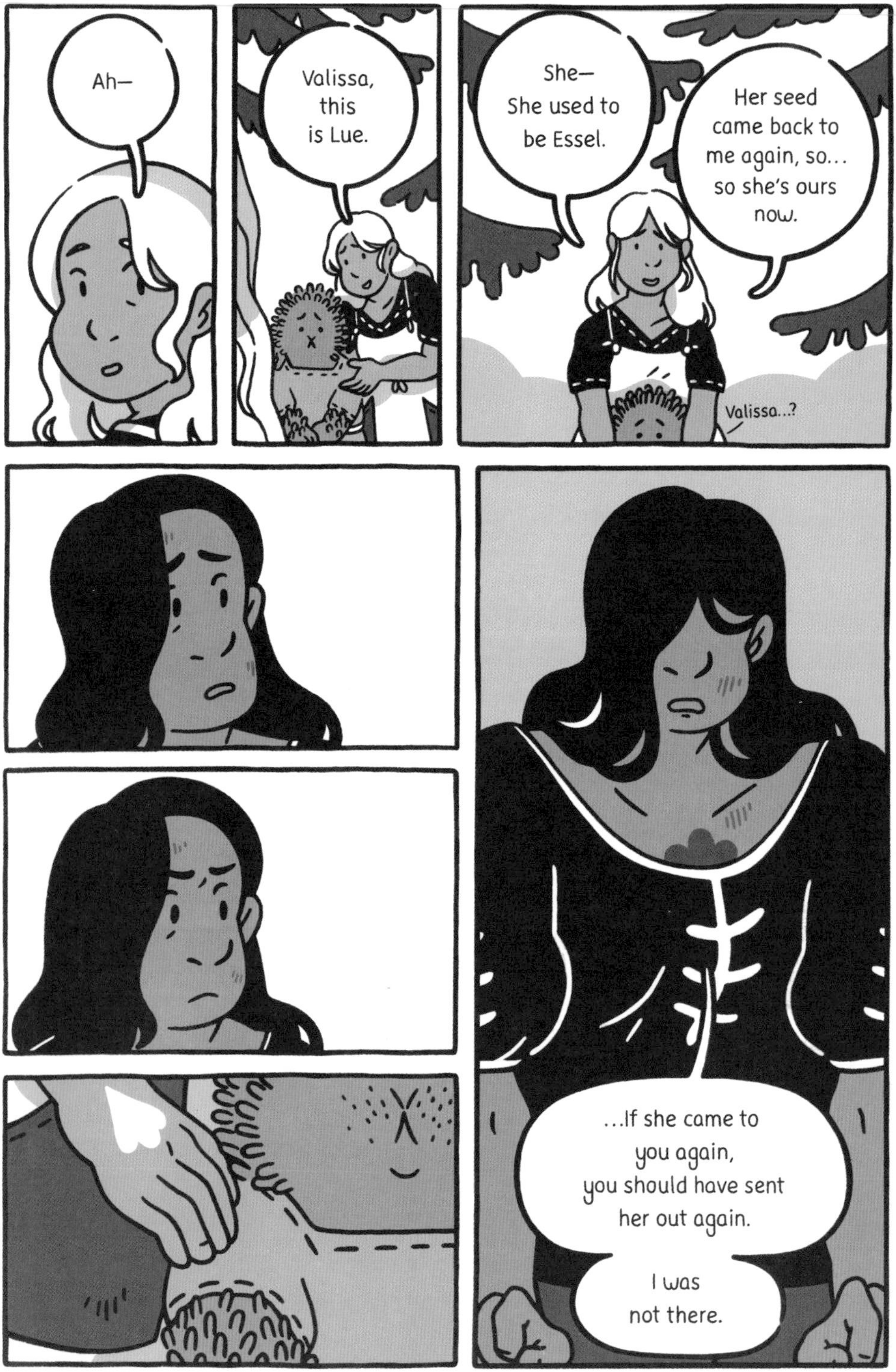
Ah—
Valissa, this is Lue.
She— She used to be Essel.
Her seed came back to me again, so... so she's ours now.
Valissa...?
...If she came to you again, you should have sent her out again.
I was not there.

But—

It's our way, Preet!

I can guess now why you're here, so far from home!

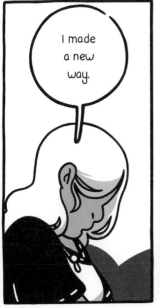

I made a new way.

I feel guilty and ashamed, and I have suffered for it, but I don't regret what I chose to do.

I will never regret Lue.

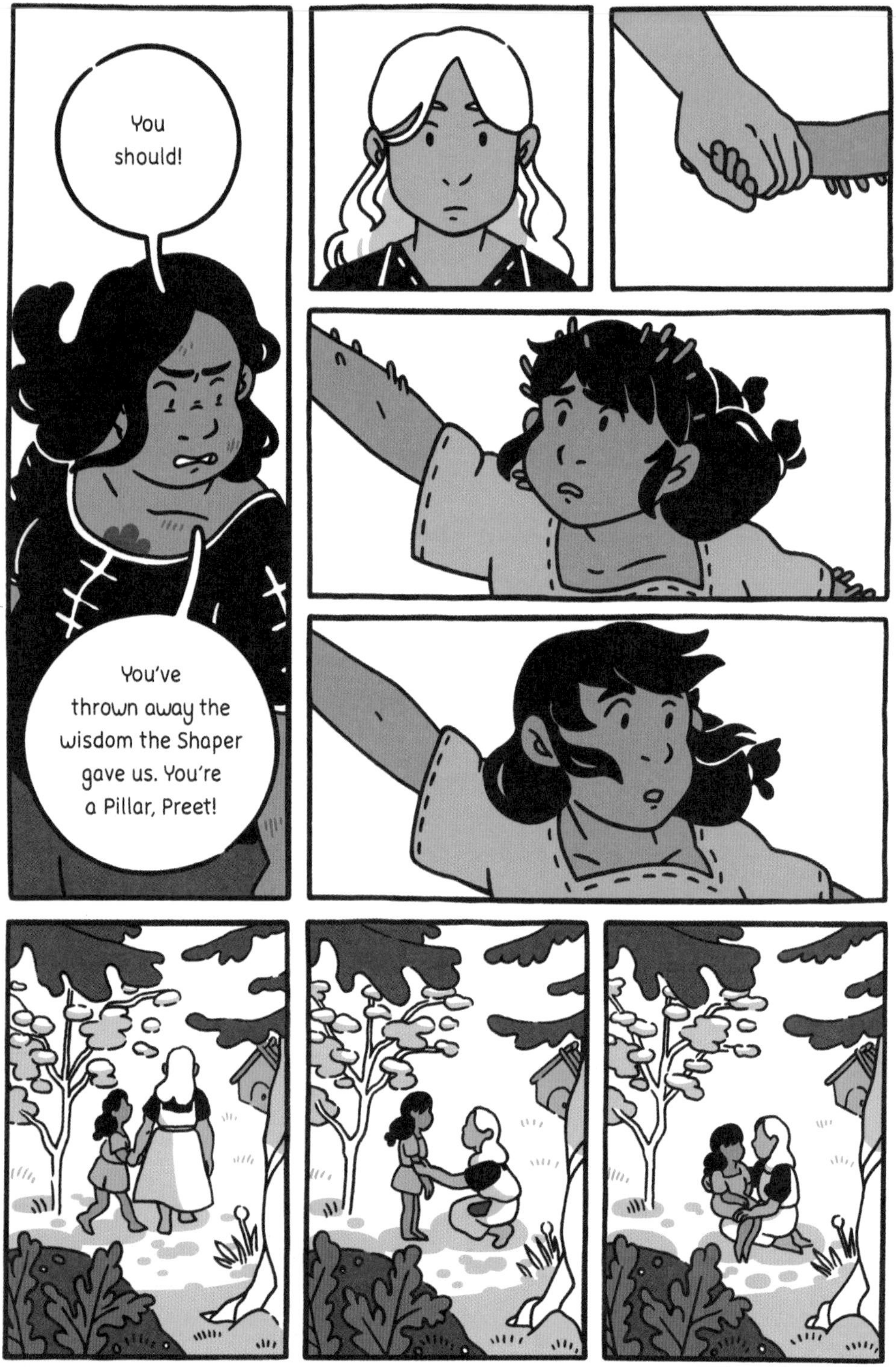
You should!
You've thrown away the wisdom the Shaper gave us. You're a Pillar, Preet!

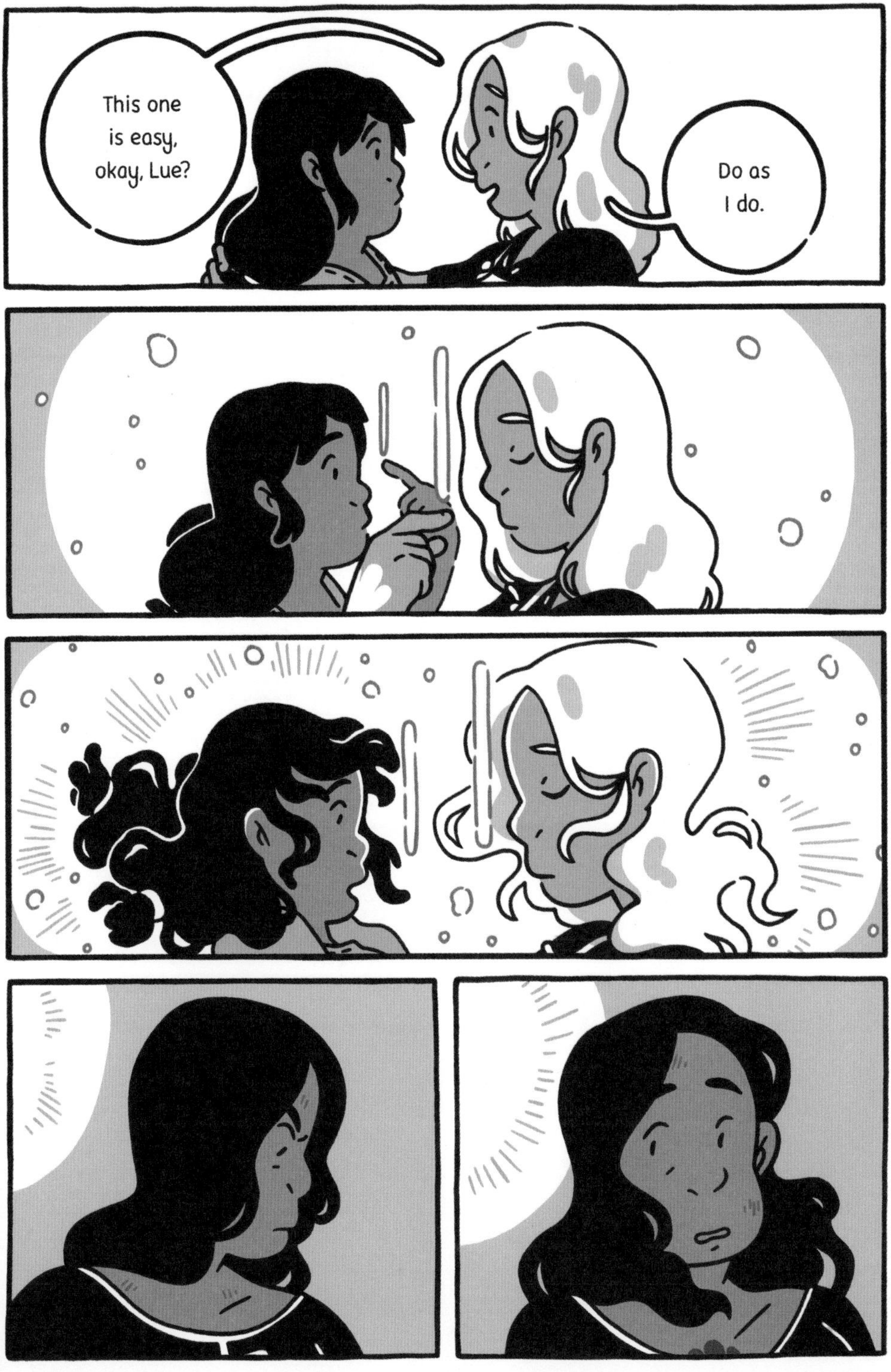
This one is easy, okay, Lue?
Do as I do.

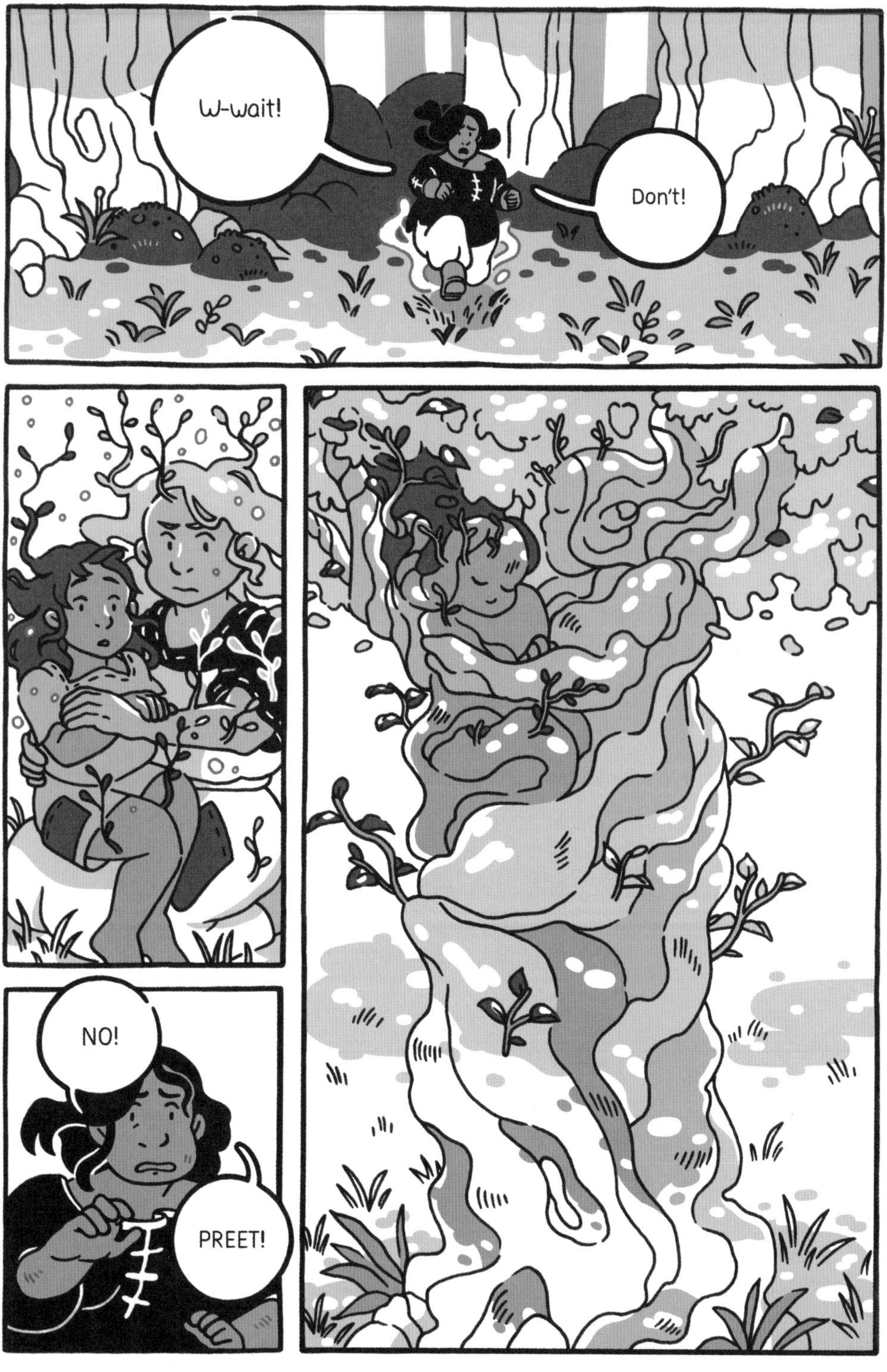
W-wait!
Don't!
NO!
PREET!

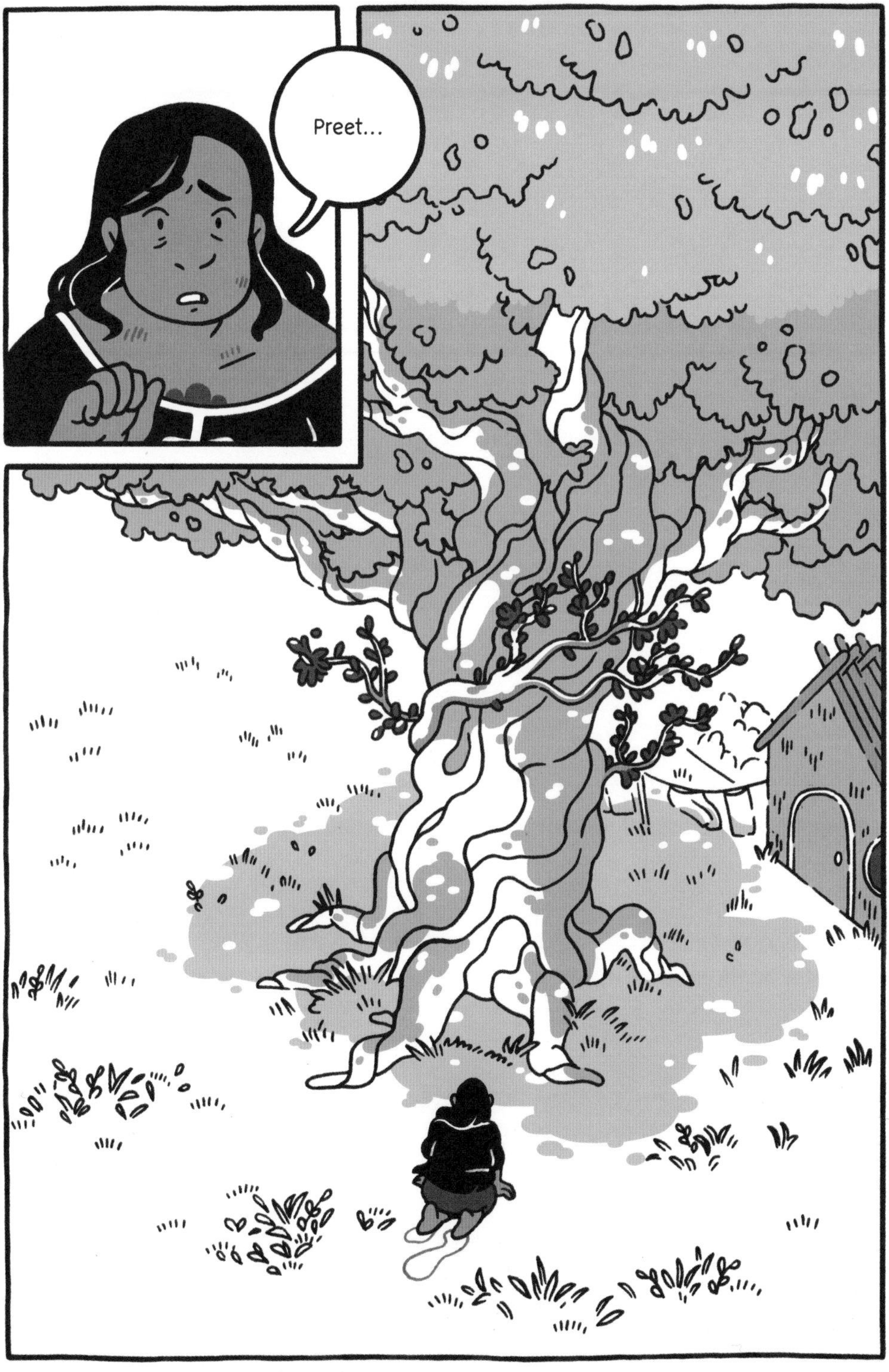
Preet...

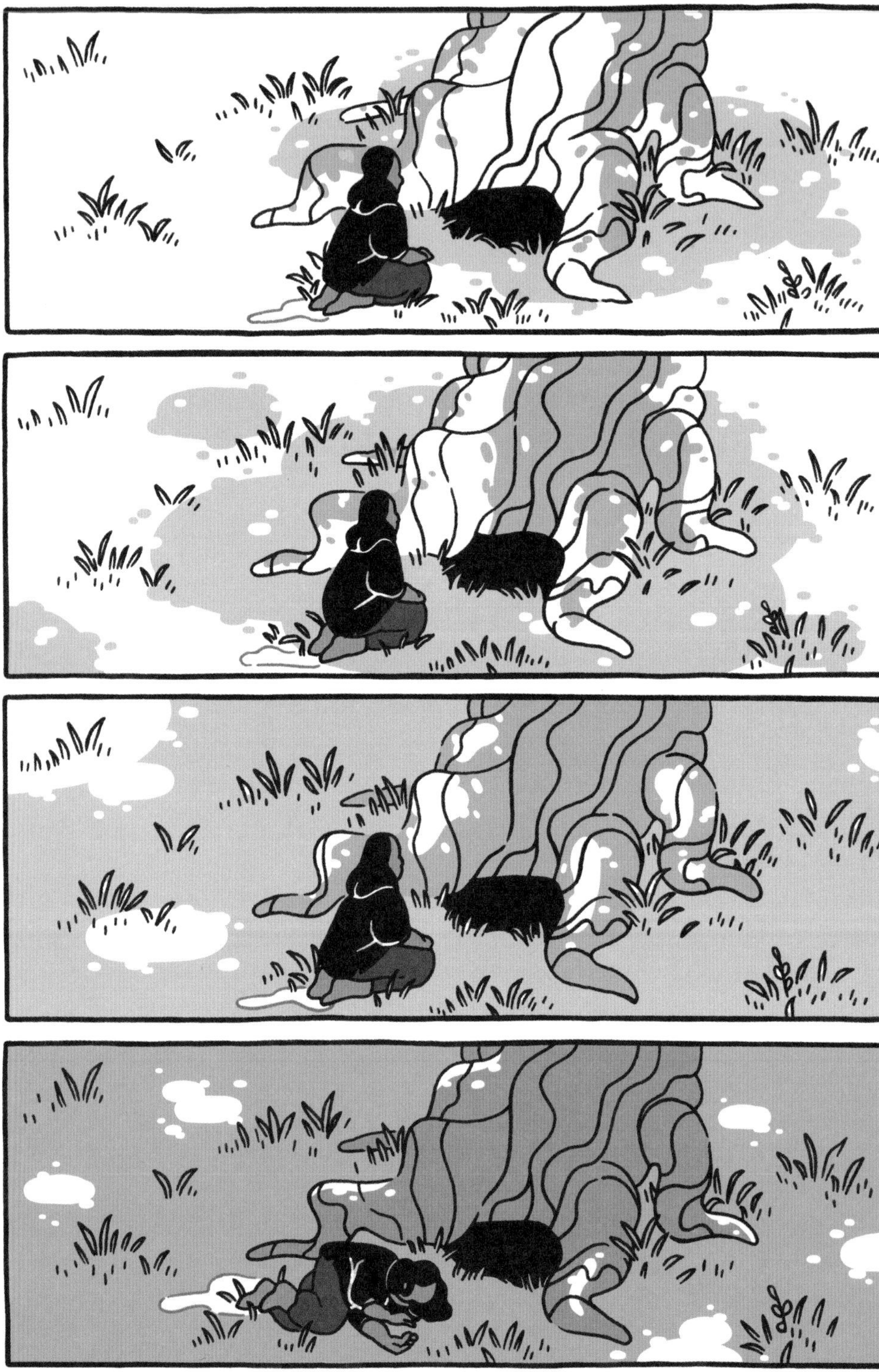

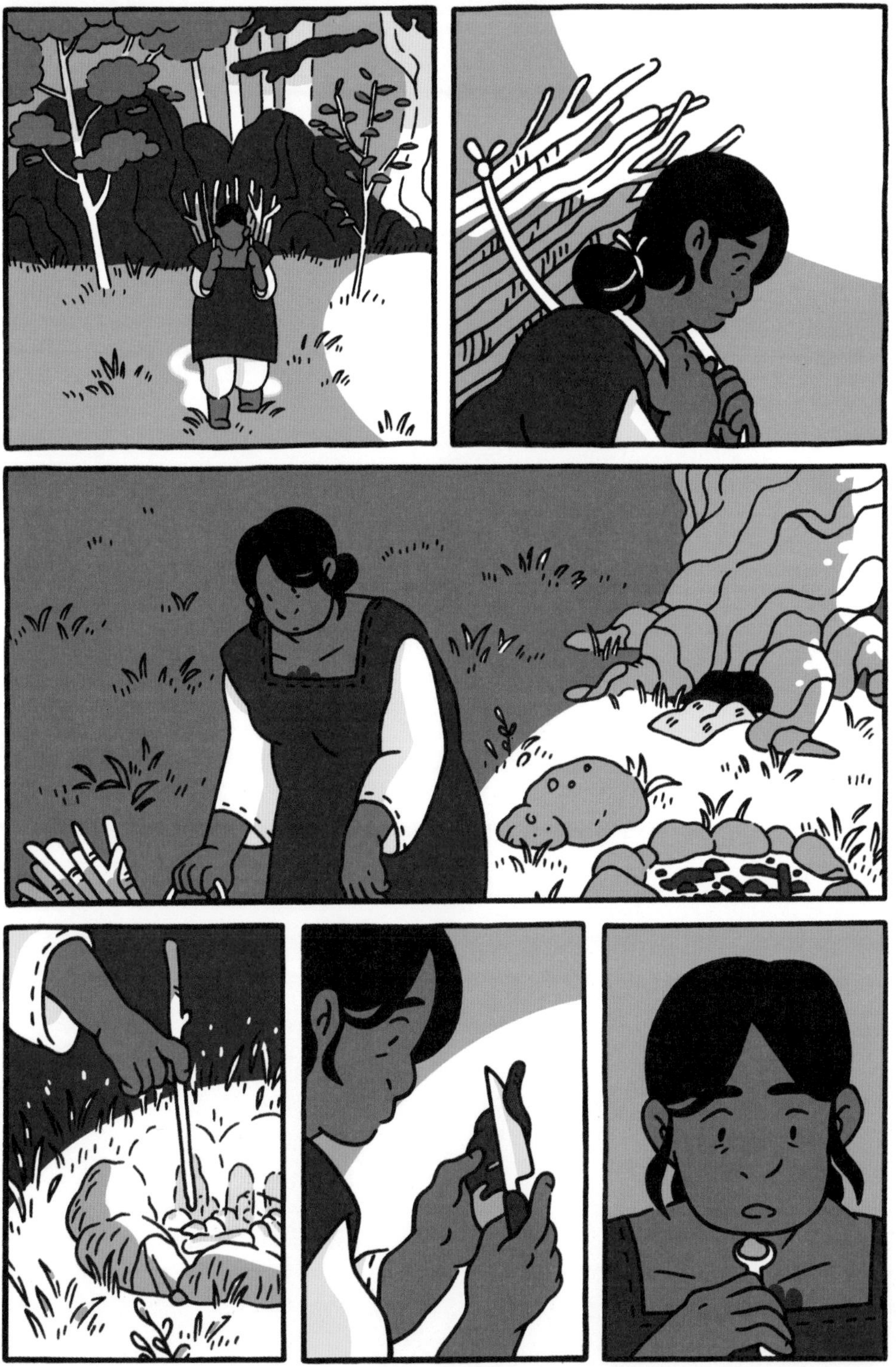

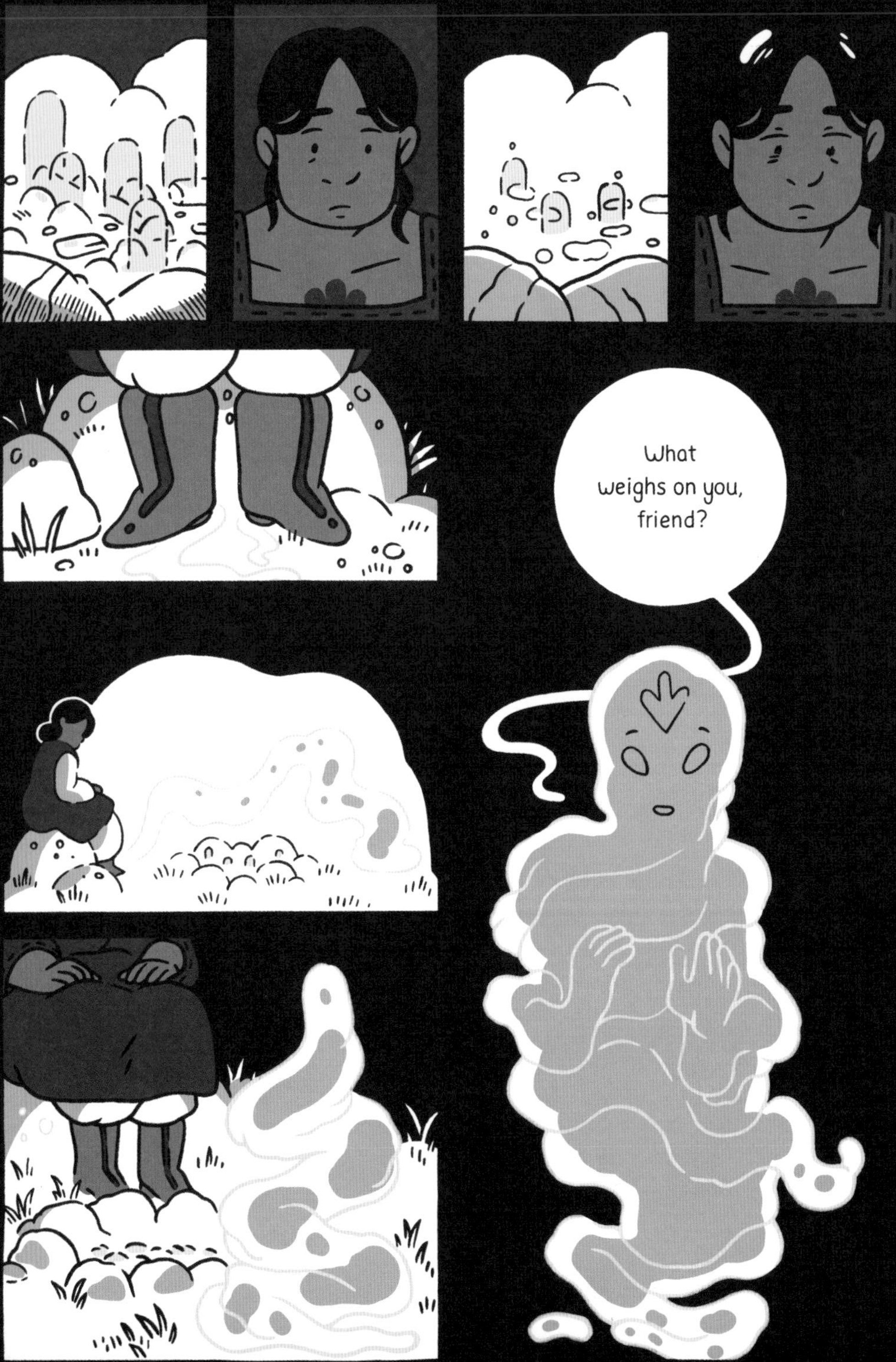
What weighs on you, friend?

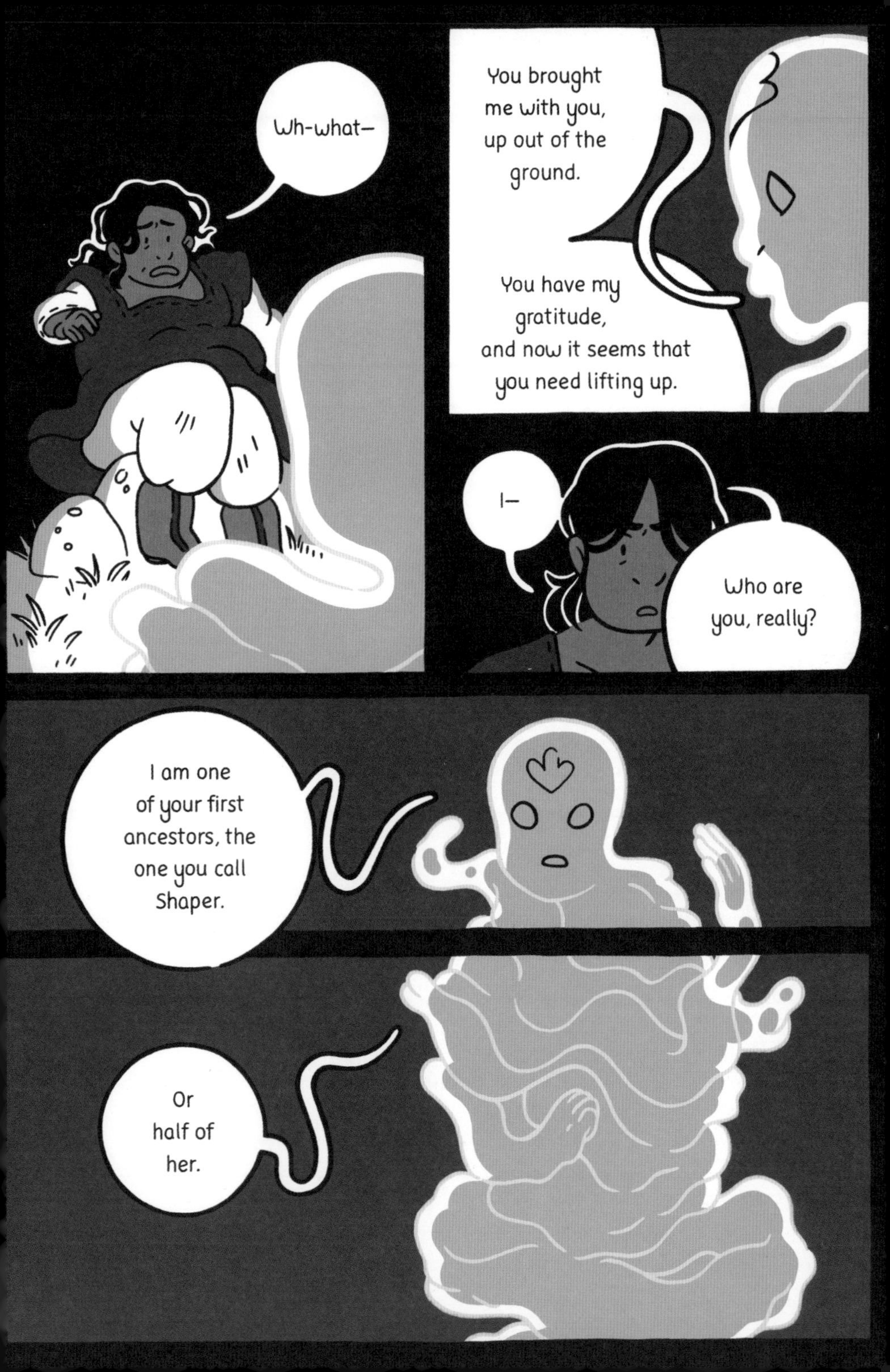
Wh-what—
You brought me with you, up out of the ground.
You have my gratitude, and now it seems that you need lifting up.
I—
Who are you, really?
I am one of your first ancestors, the one you call Shaper.
Or half of her.

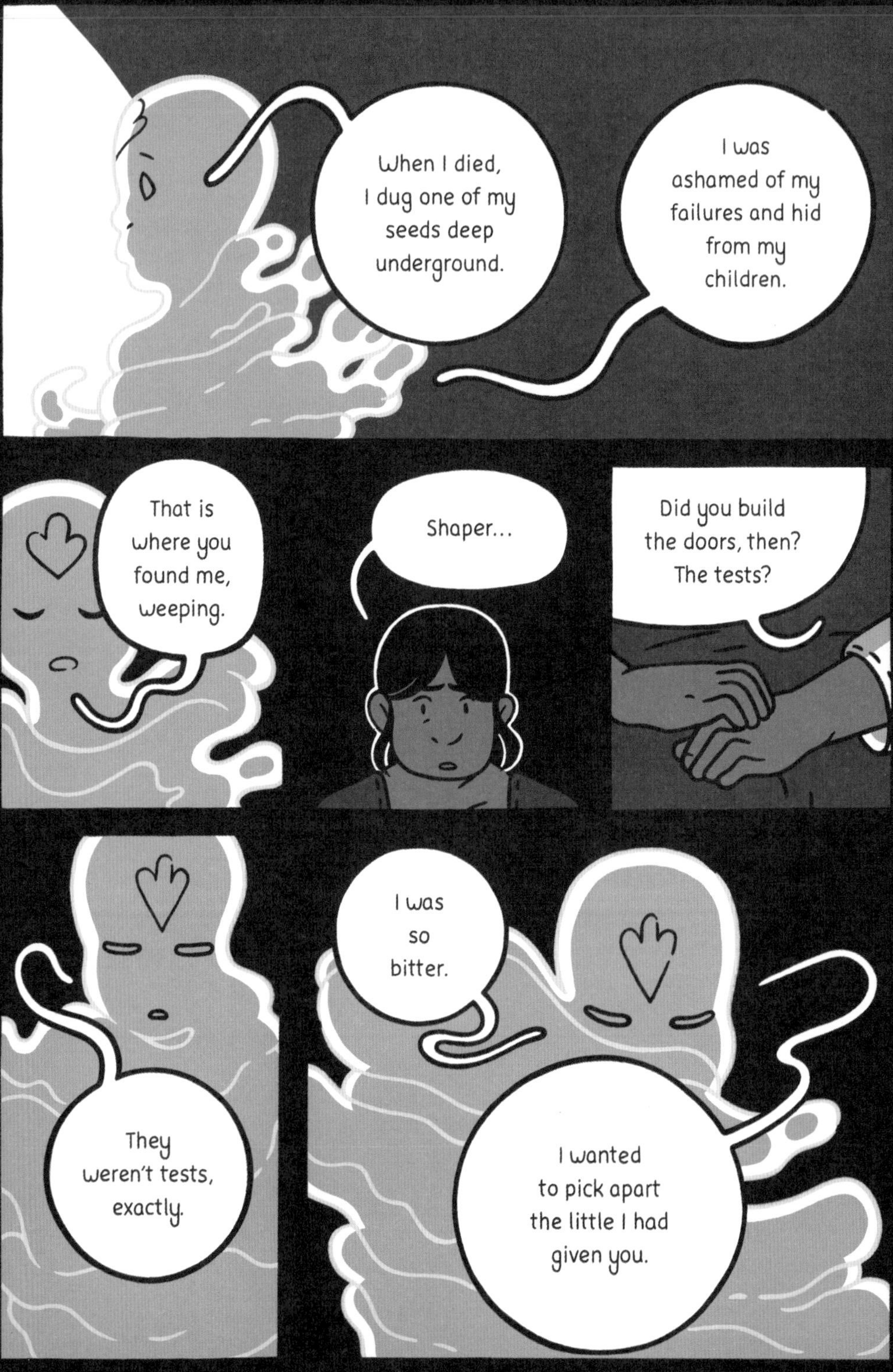
When I died, I dug one of my seeds deep underground.
I was ashamed of my failures and hid from my children.
That is where you found me, weeping.
Shaper...
Did you build the doors, then? The tests?
They weren't tests, exactly.
I was so bitter.
I wanted to pick apart the little I had given you.

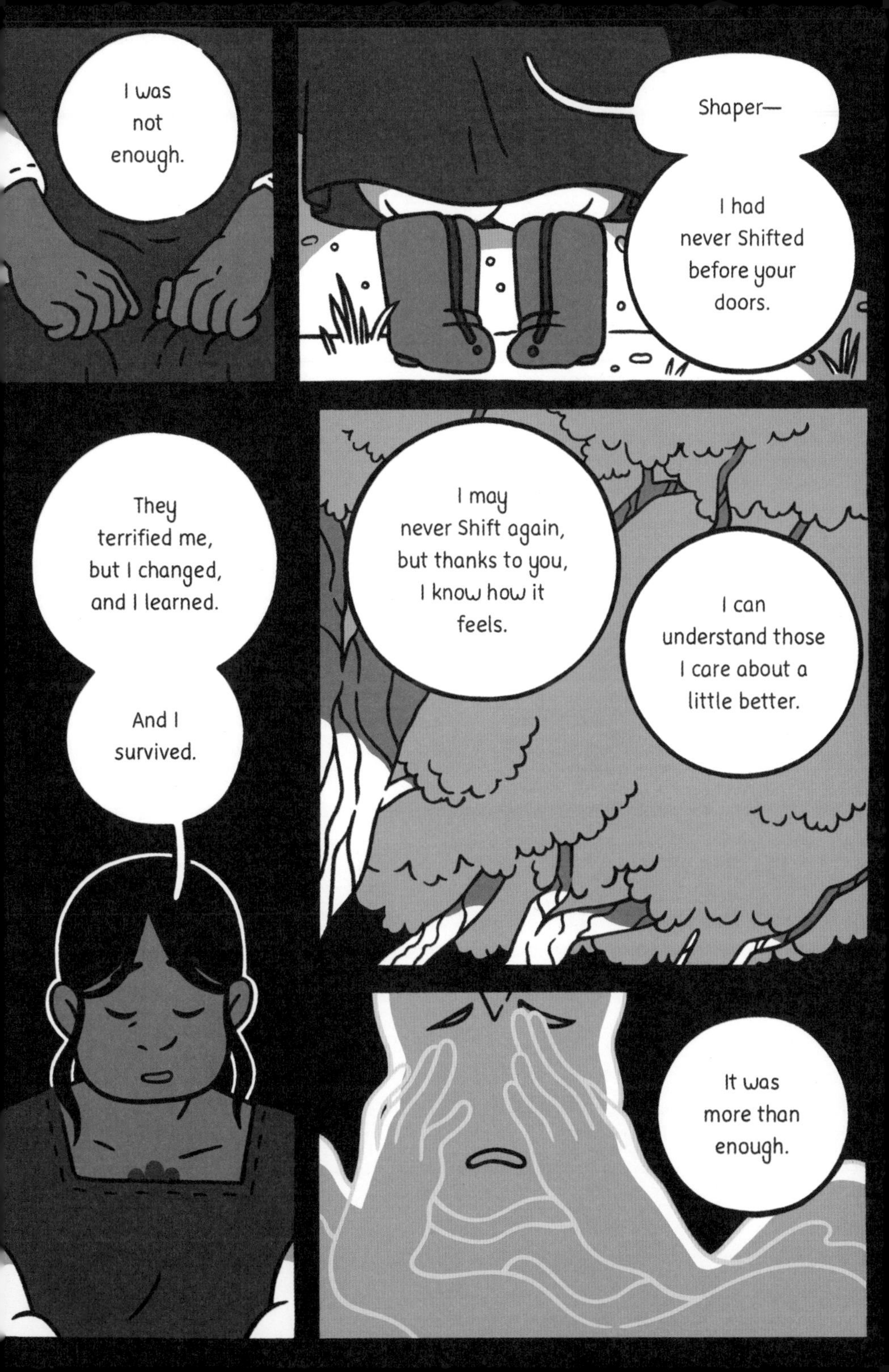
I was not enough.
Shaper—
I had never Shifted before your doors.
They terrified me, but I changed, and I learned.
And I survived.
I may never Shift again, but thanks to you, I know how it feels.
I can understand those I care about a little better.
It was more than enough.

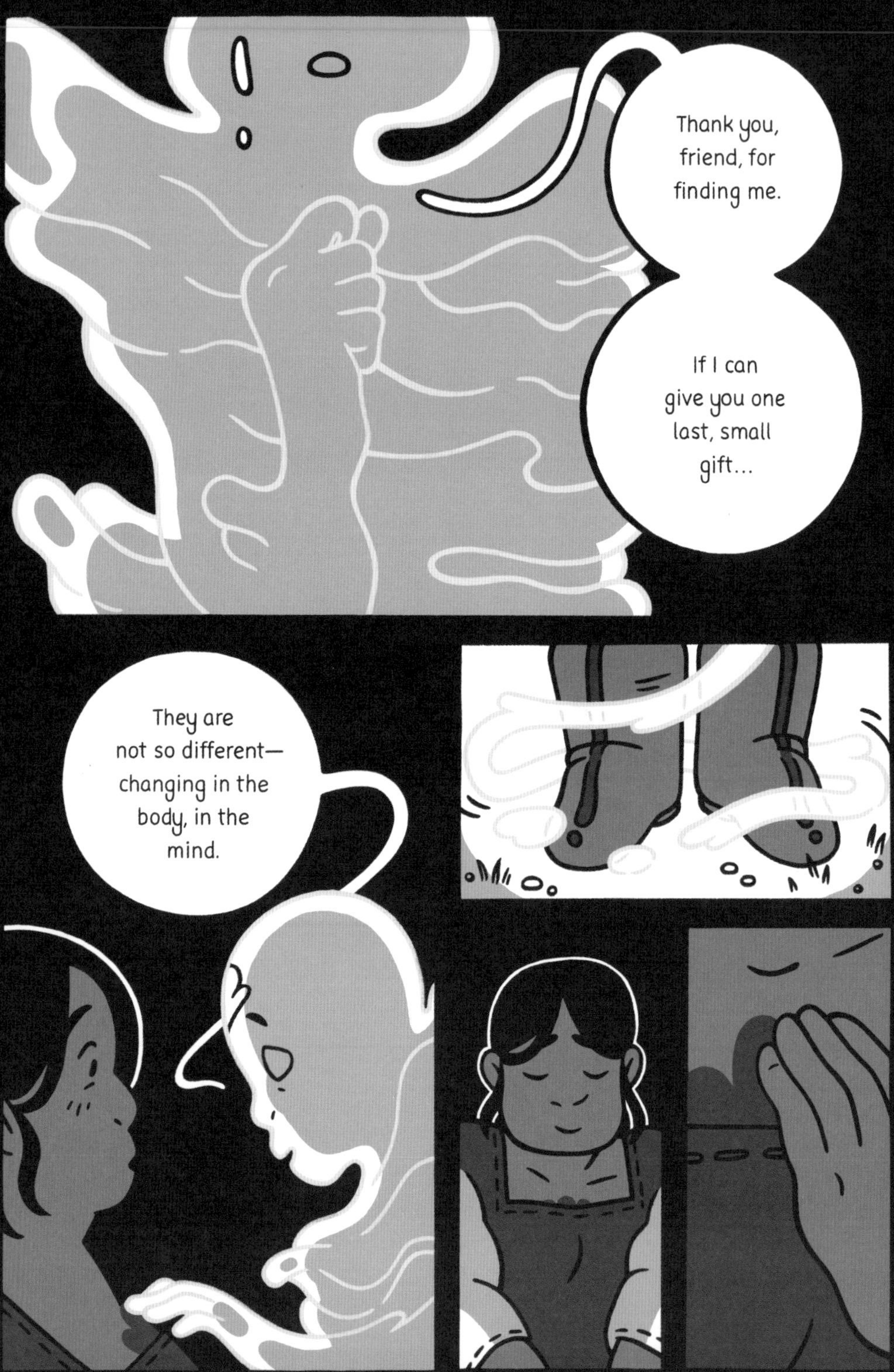
Thank you, friend, for finding me.
If I can give you one last, small gift...
They are not so different— changing in the body, in the mind.

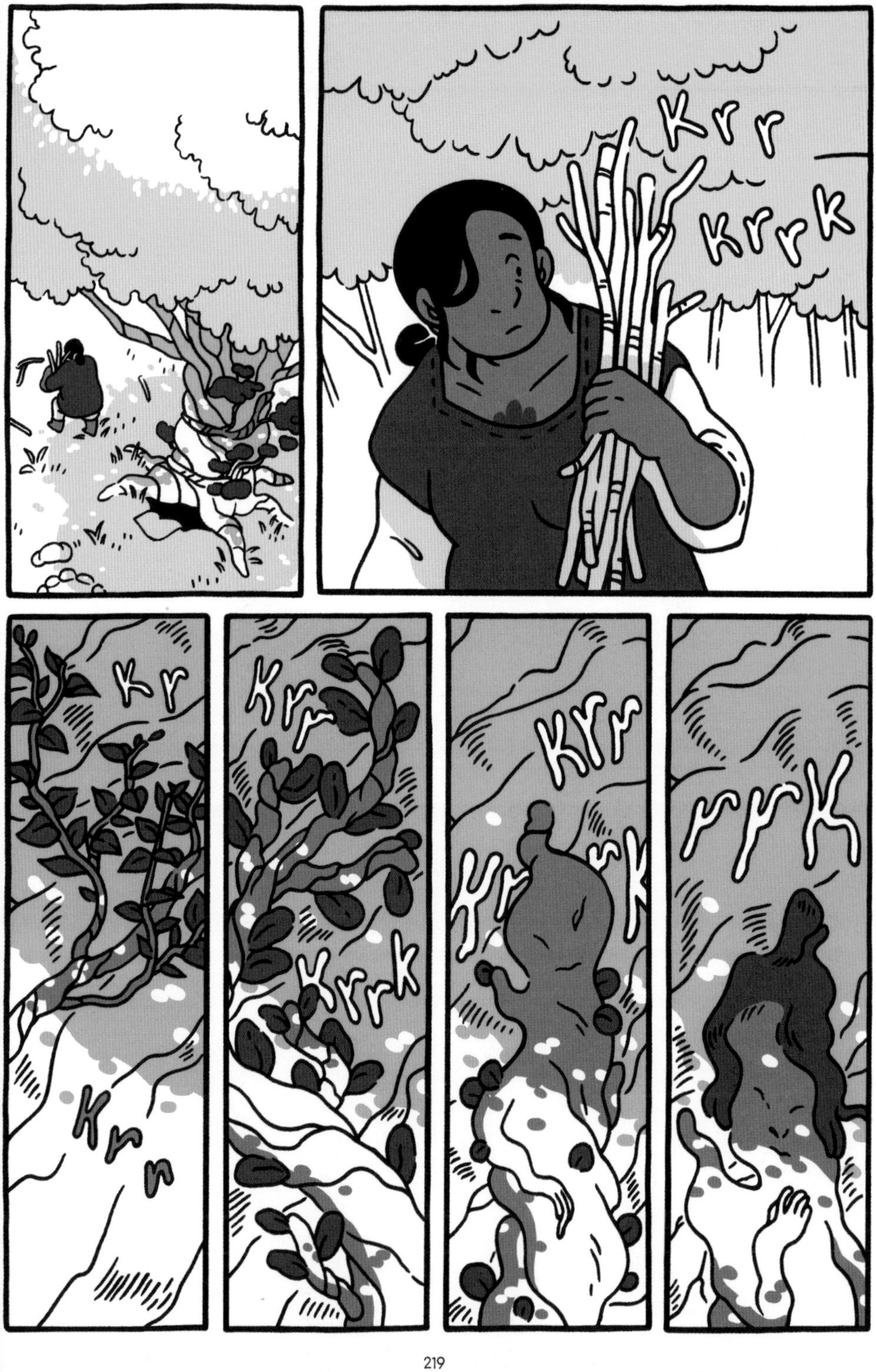
Krr
krrk
Kr
Krn
Krr
Krrk
Krr
rrk

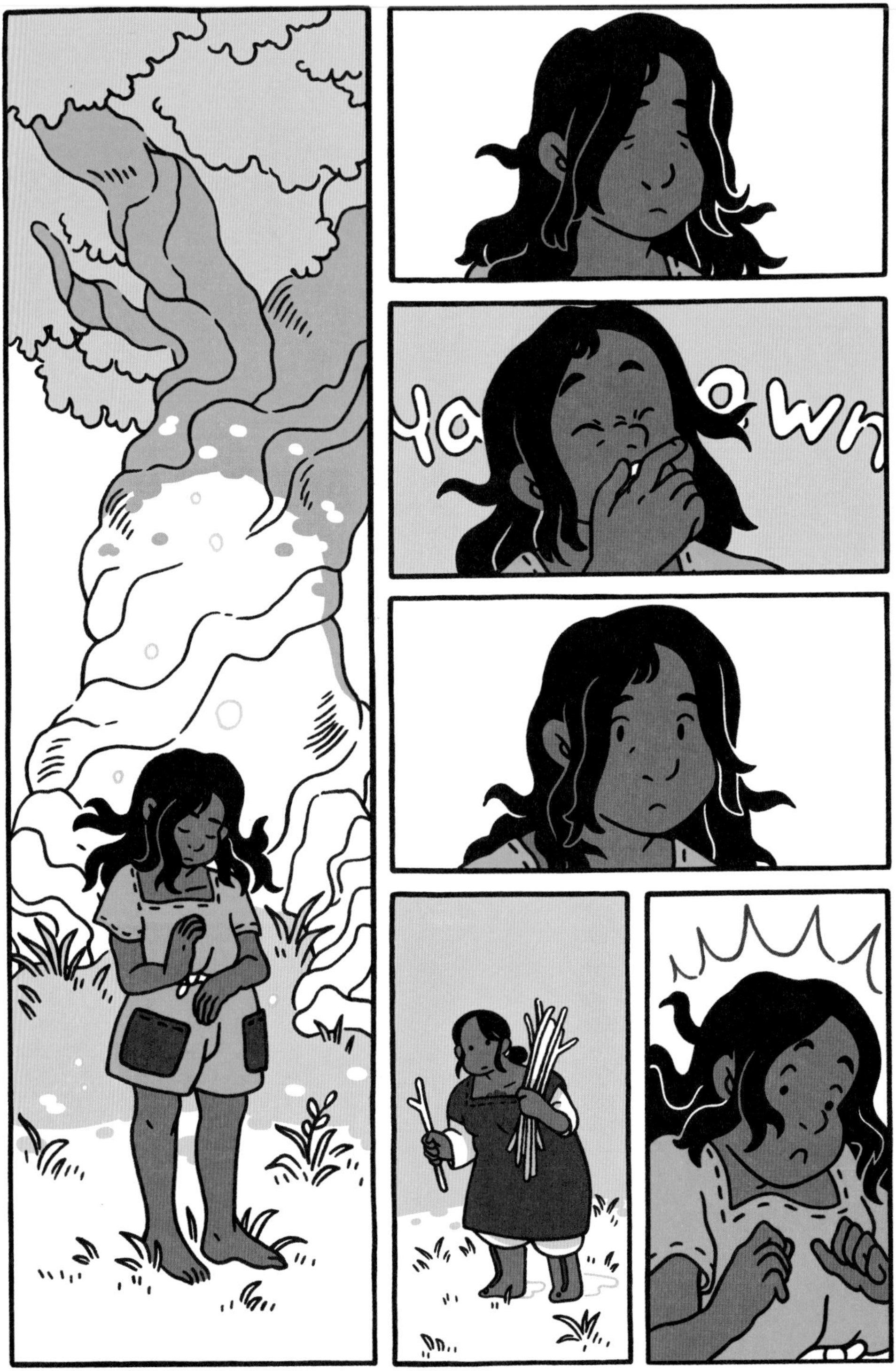
yawn

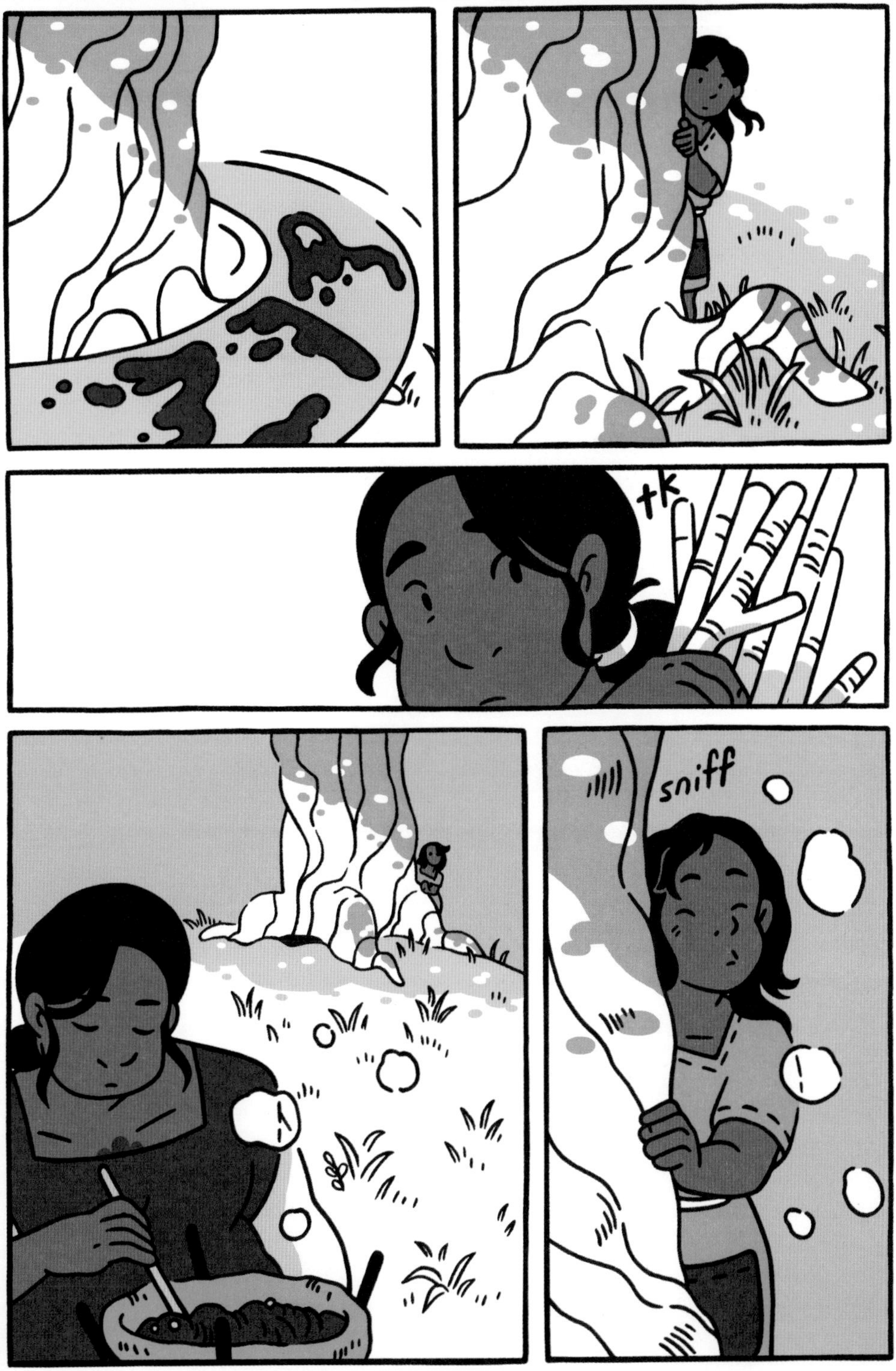
tk
sniff

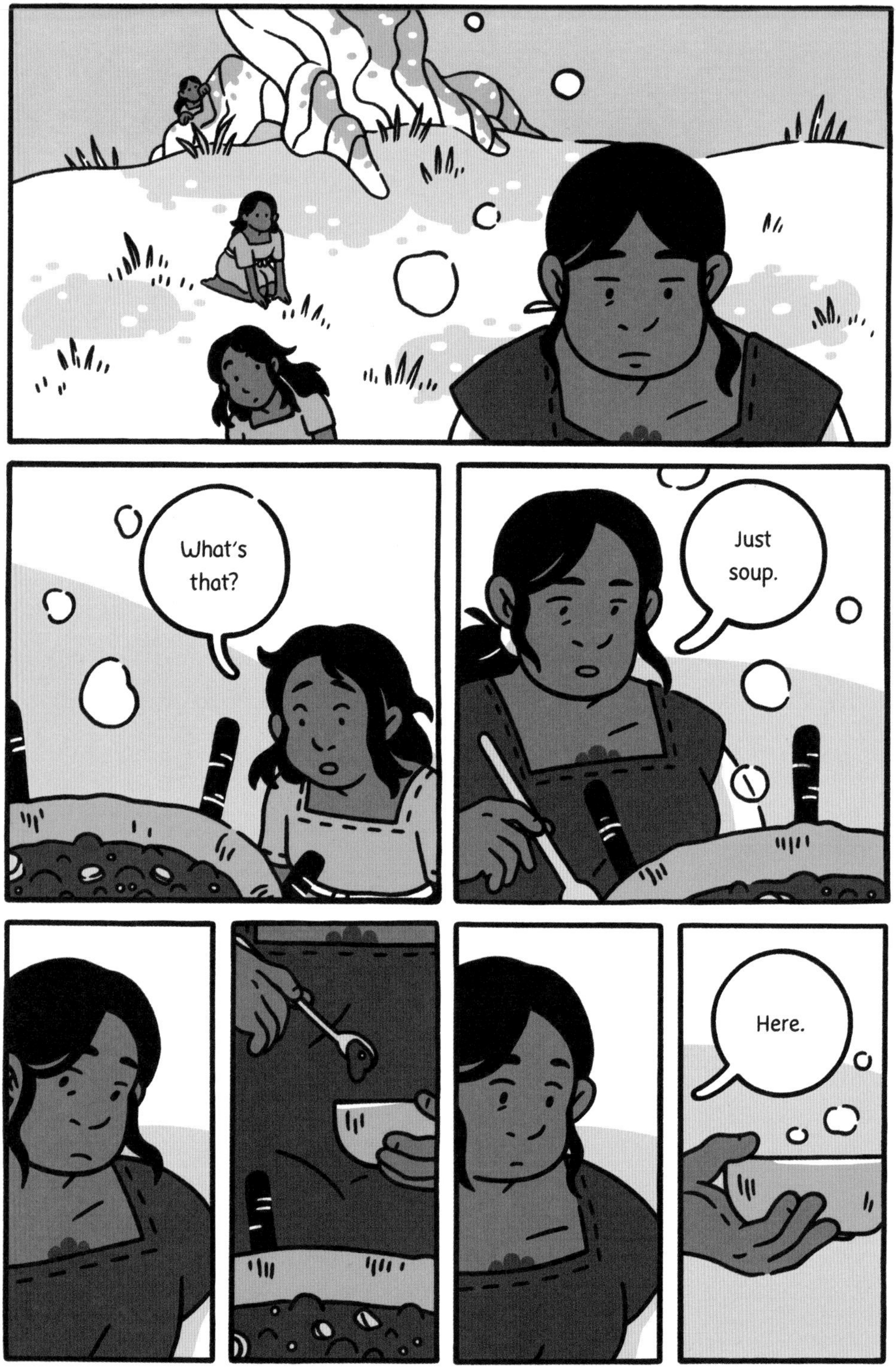
What's that?
Just soup.
Here.

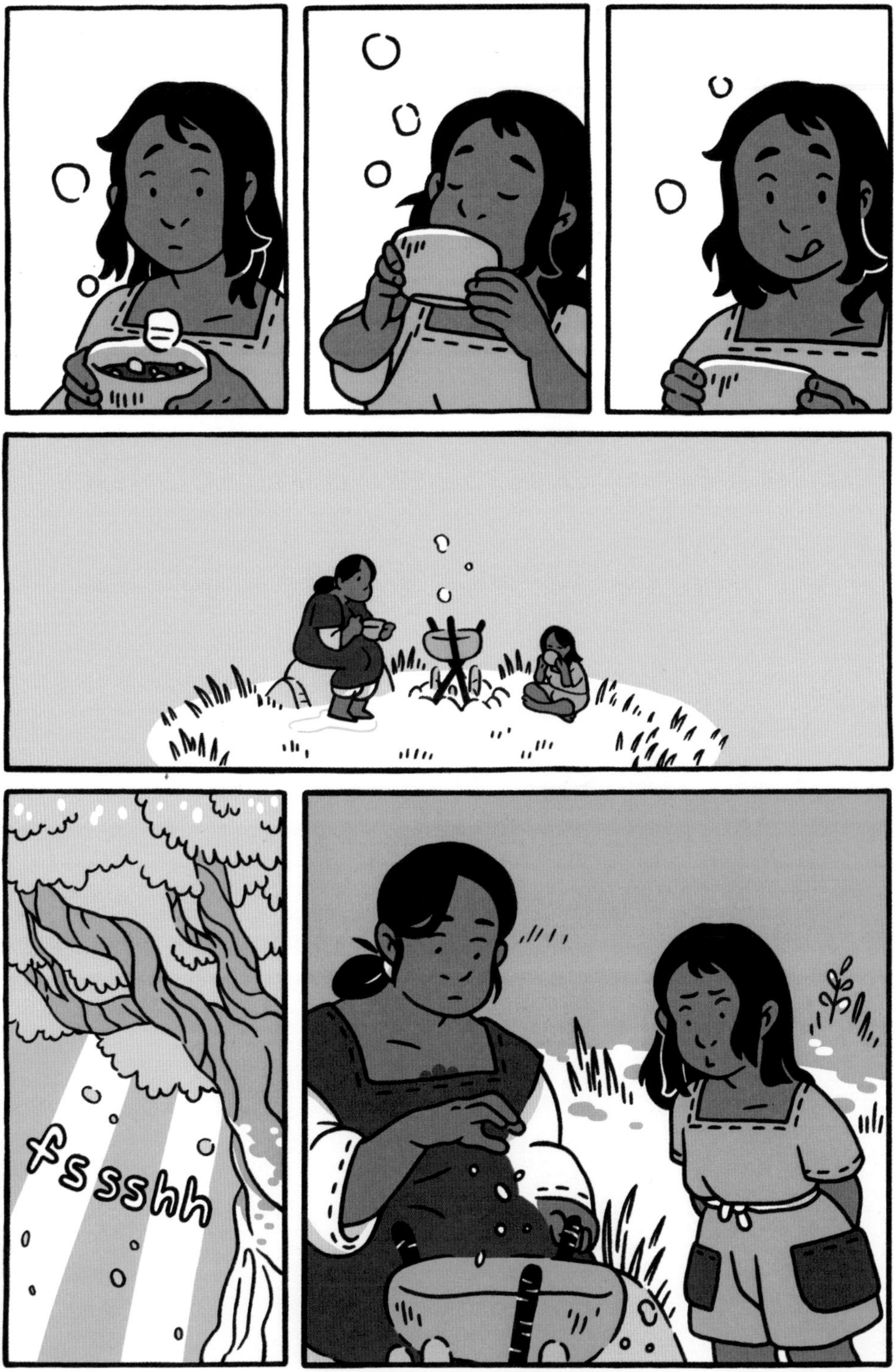
fssshh

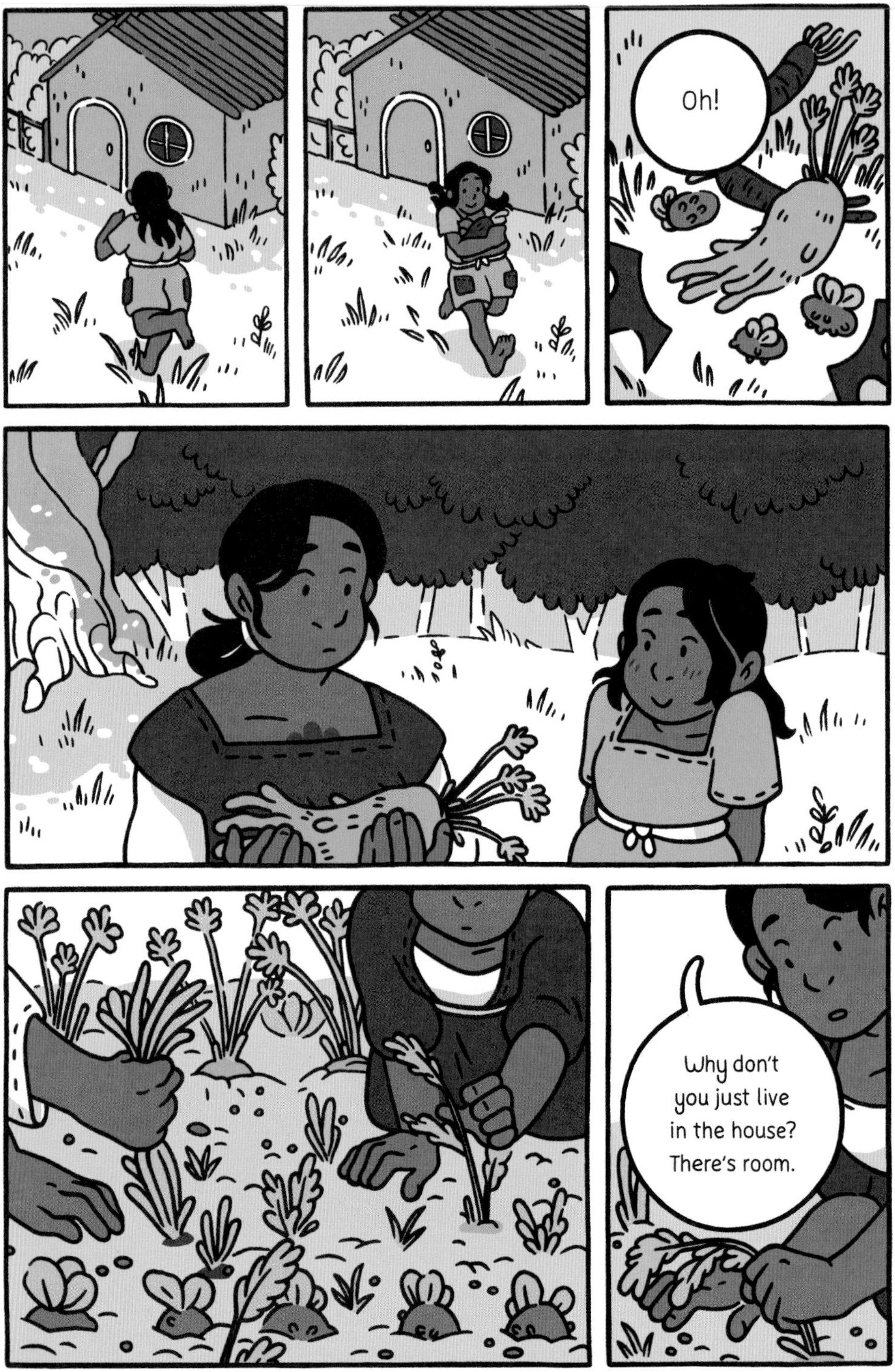
Oh!
Why don't you just live in the house? There's room.

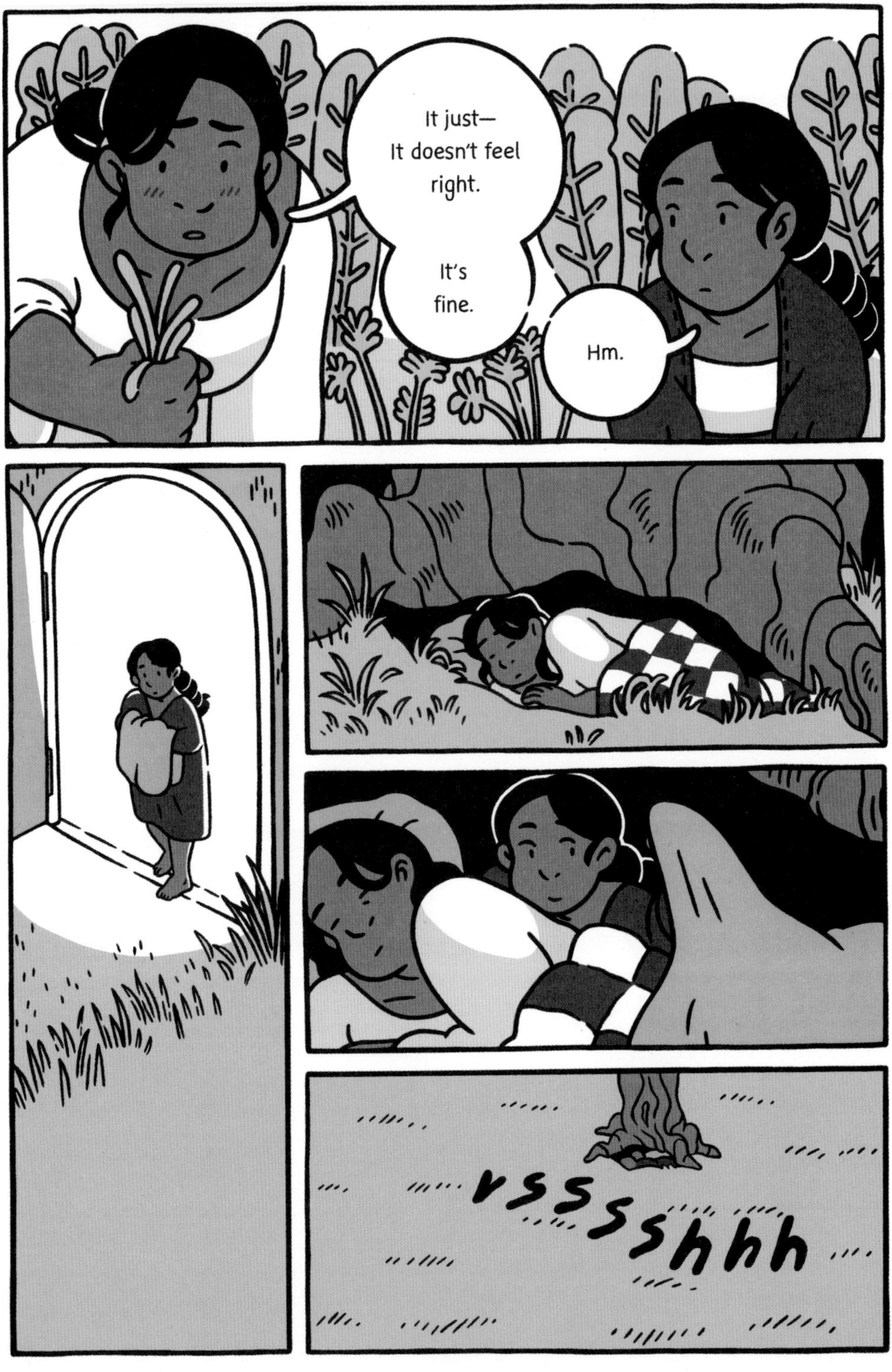
It just—
It doesn't feel right.
It's fine.
Hm.
vsssshhh

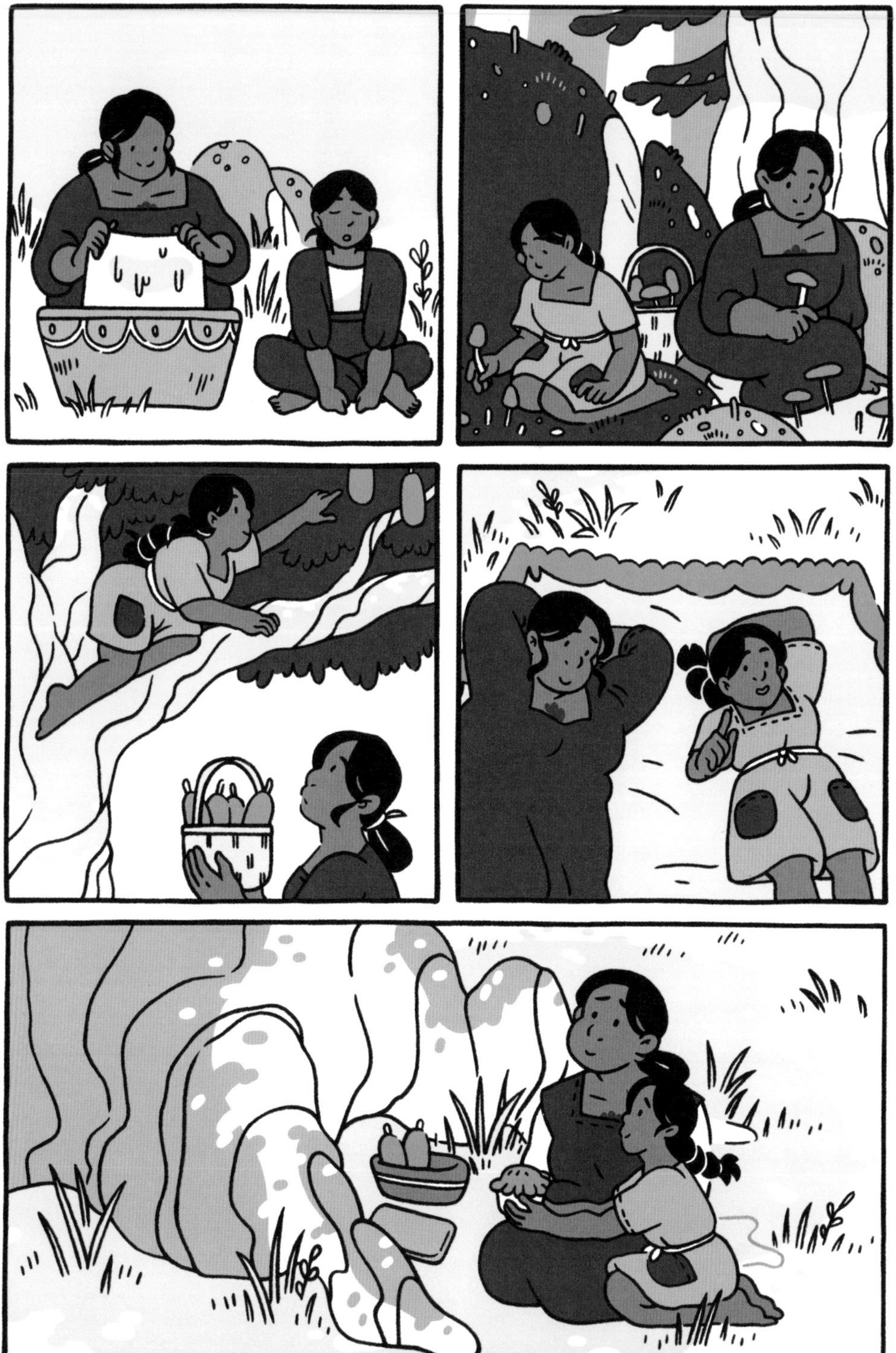

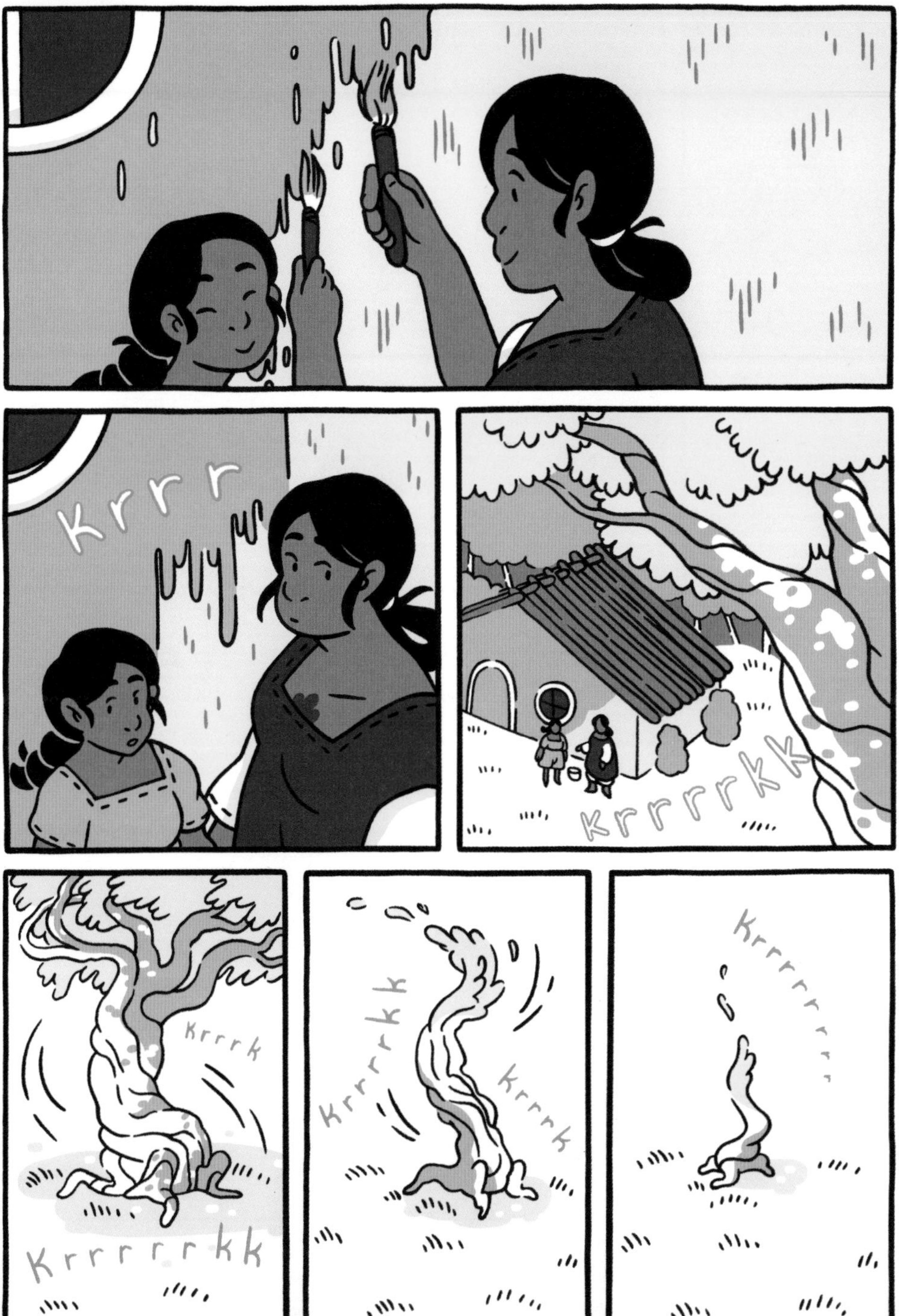
Krrr
Krrrrrkk
Krrrk
Krrrrrkk
Krrrrkk
Krrrk
Krrrrrrrrr

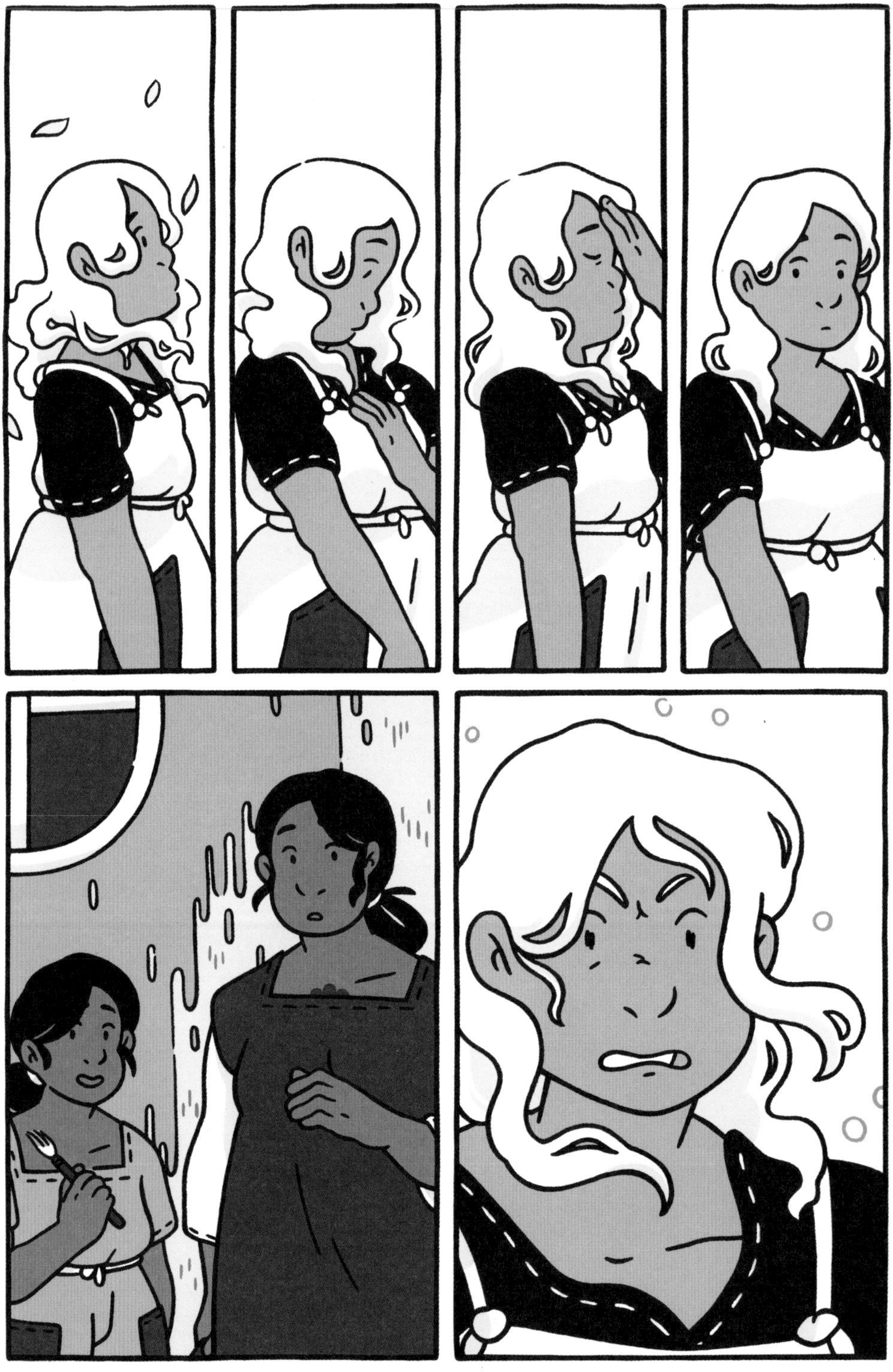

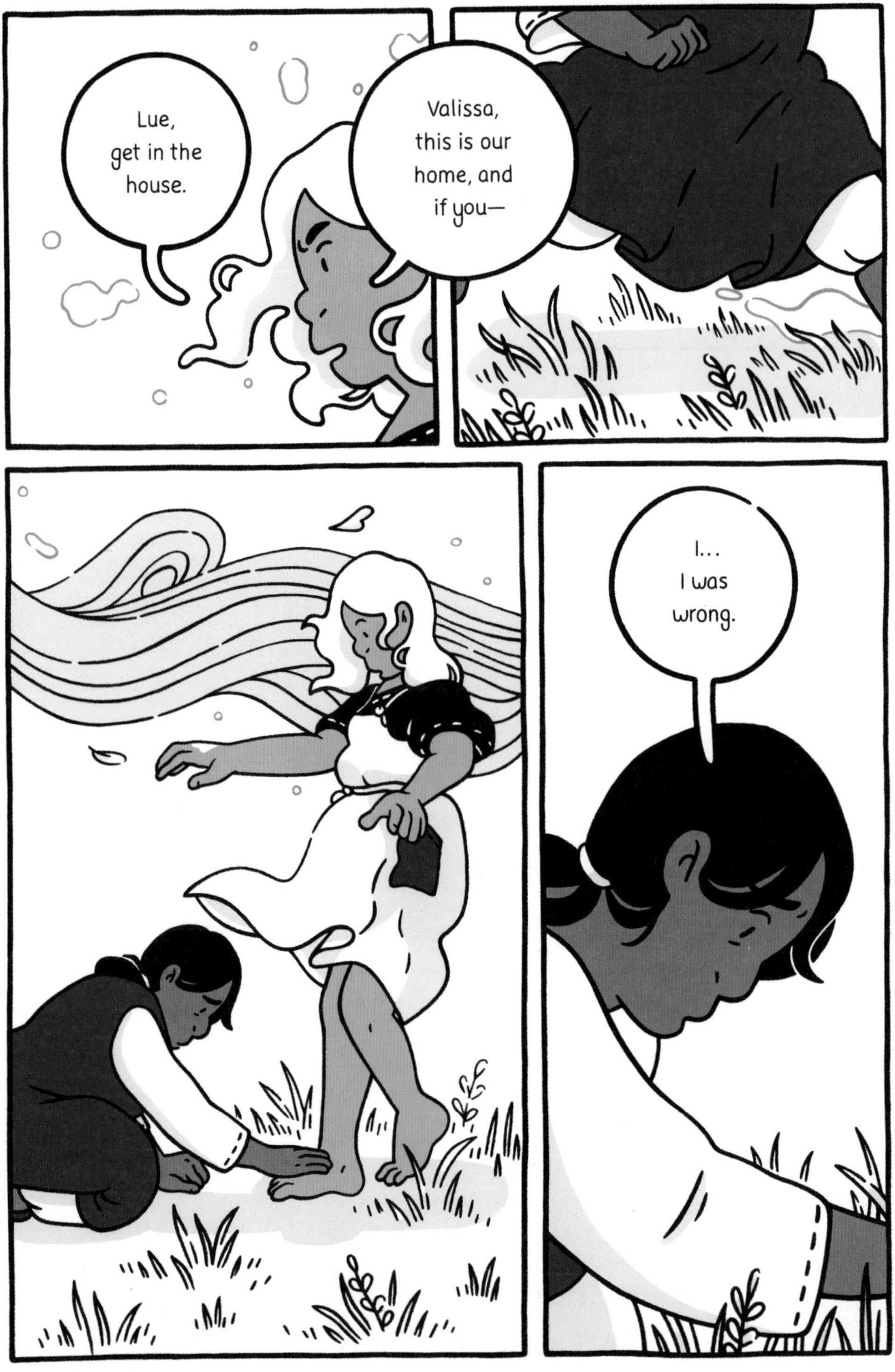
Lue, get in the house.
Valissa, this is our home, and if you—
I... I was wrong.

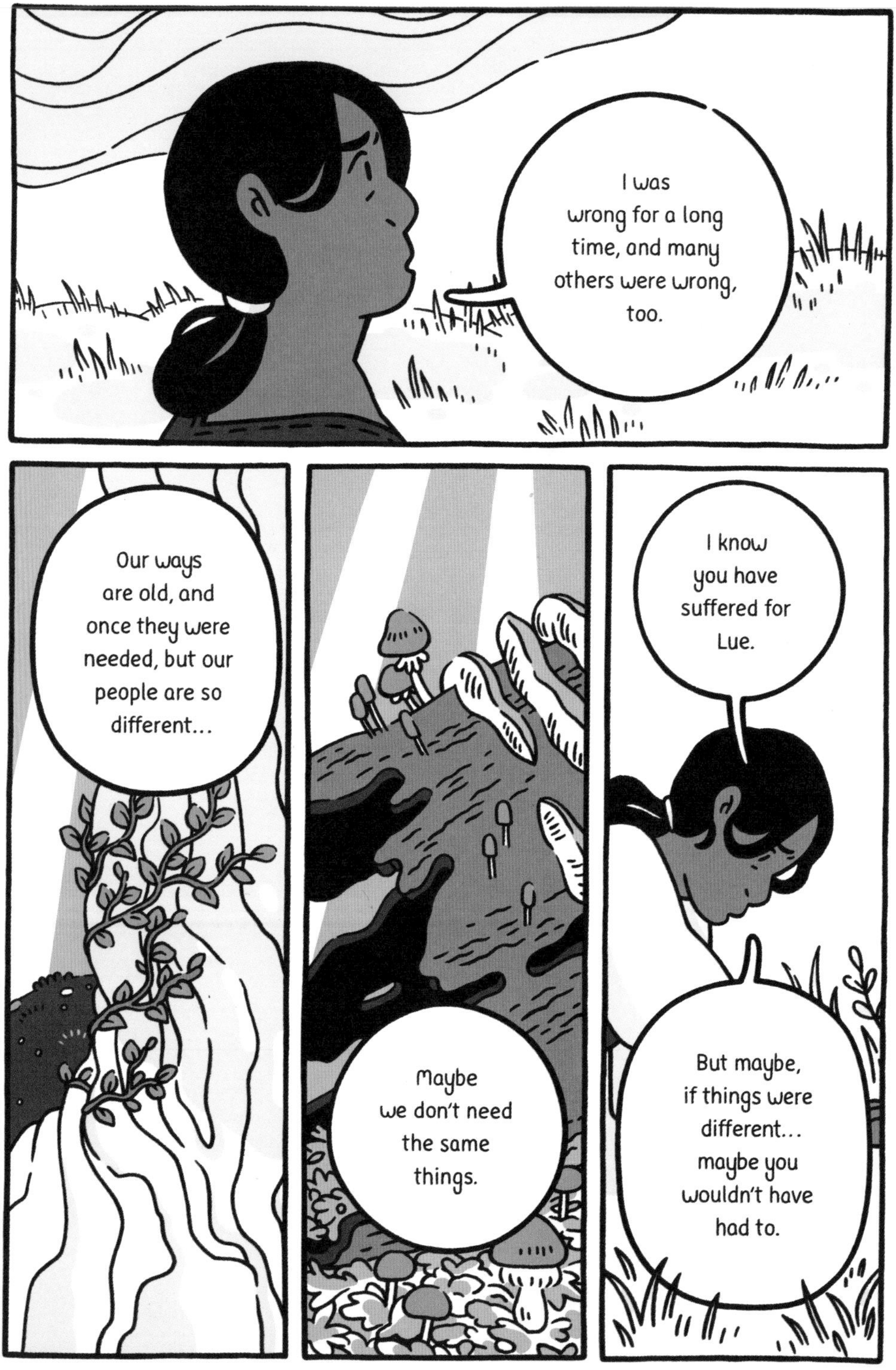
I was wrong for a long time, and many others were wrong, too.
Our ways are old, and once they were needed, but our people are so different…
Maybe we don't need the same things.
I know you have suffered for Lue.
But maybe, if things were different… maybe you wouldn't have had to.

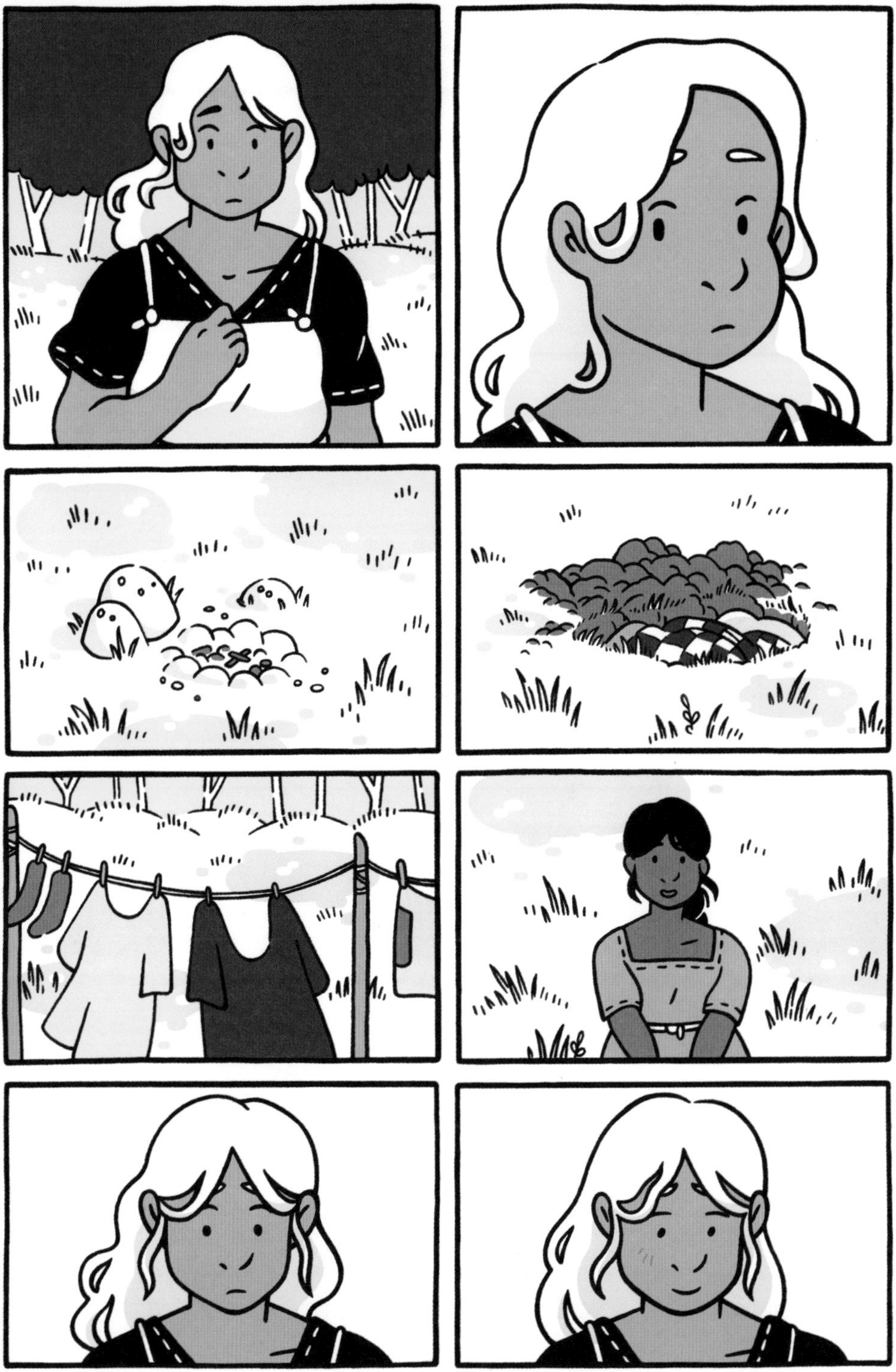

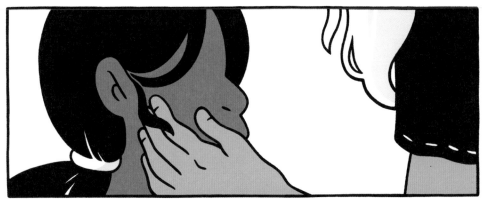

Thank you for coming back to me.

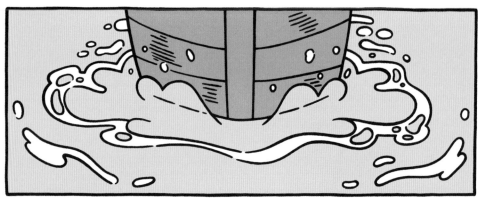

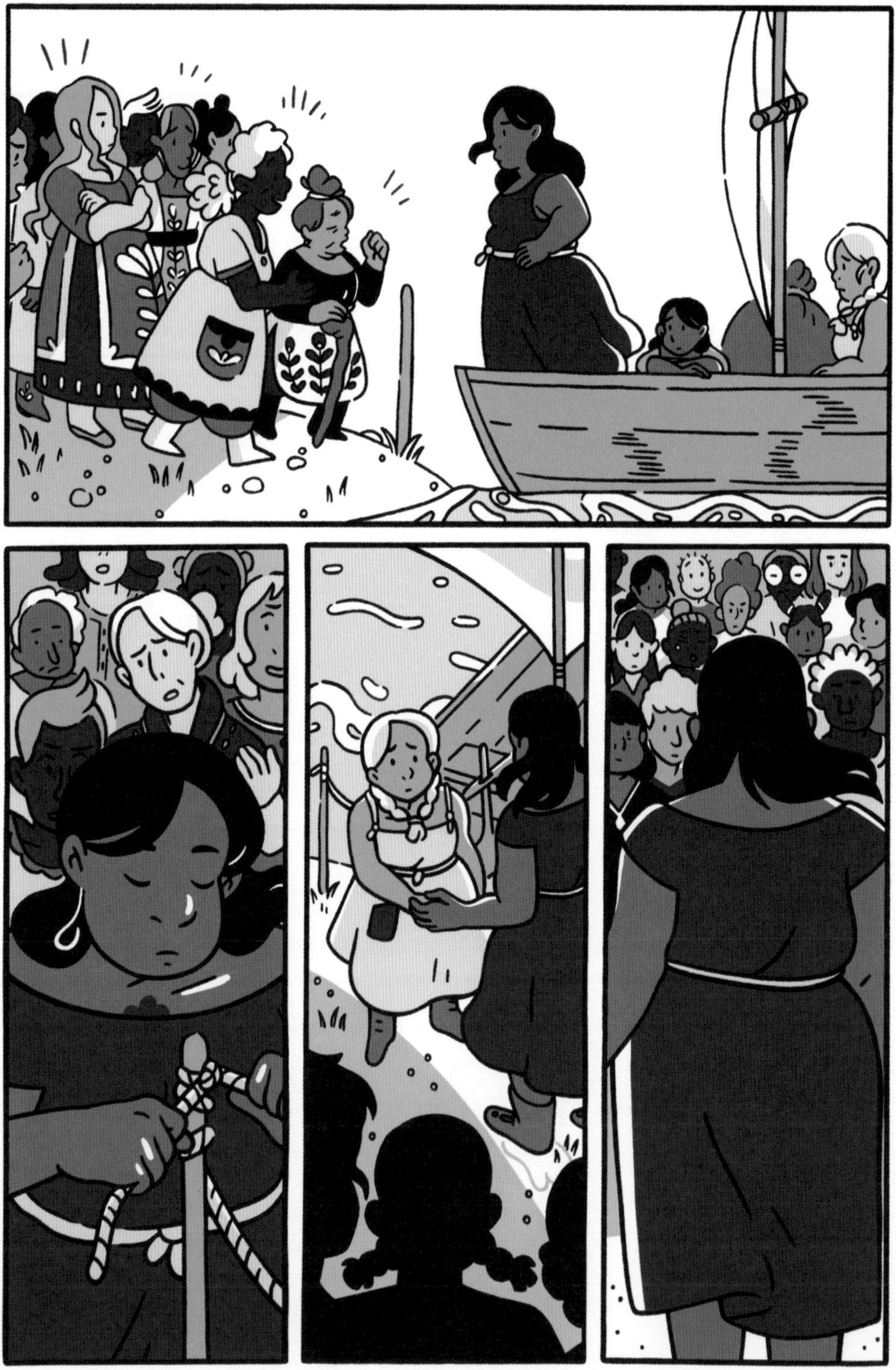

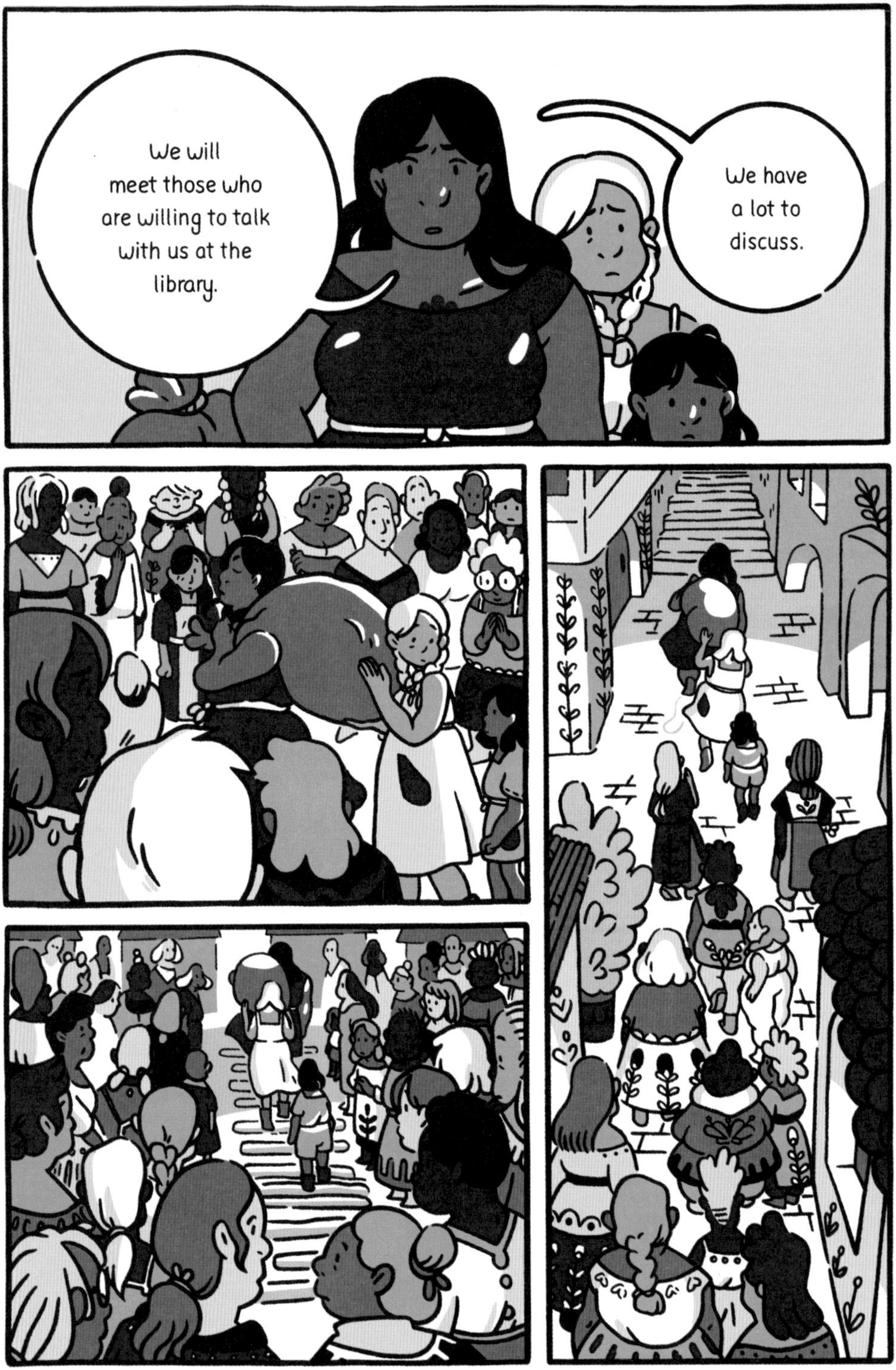
We will meet those who are willing to talk with us at the library.
We have a lot to discuss.

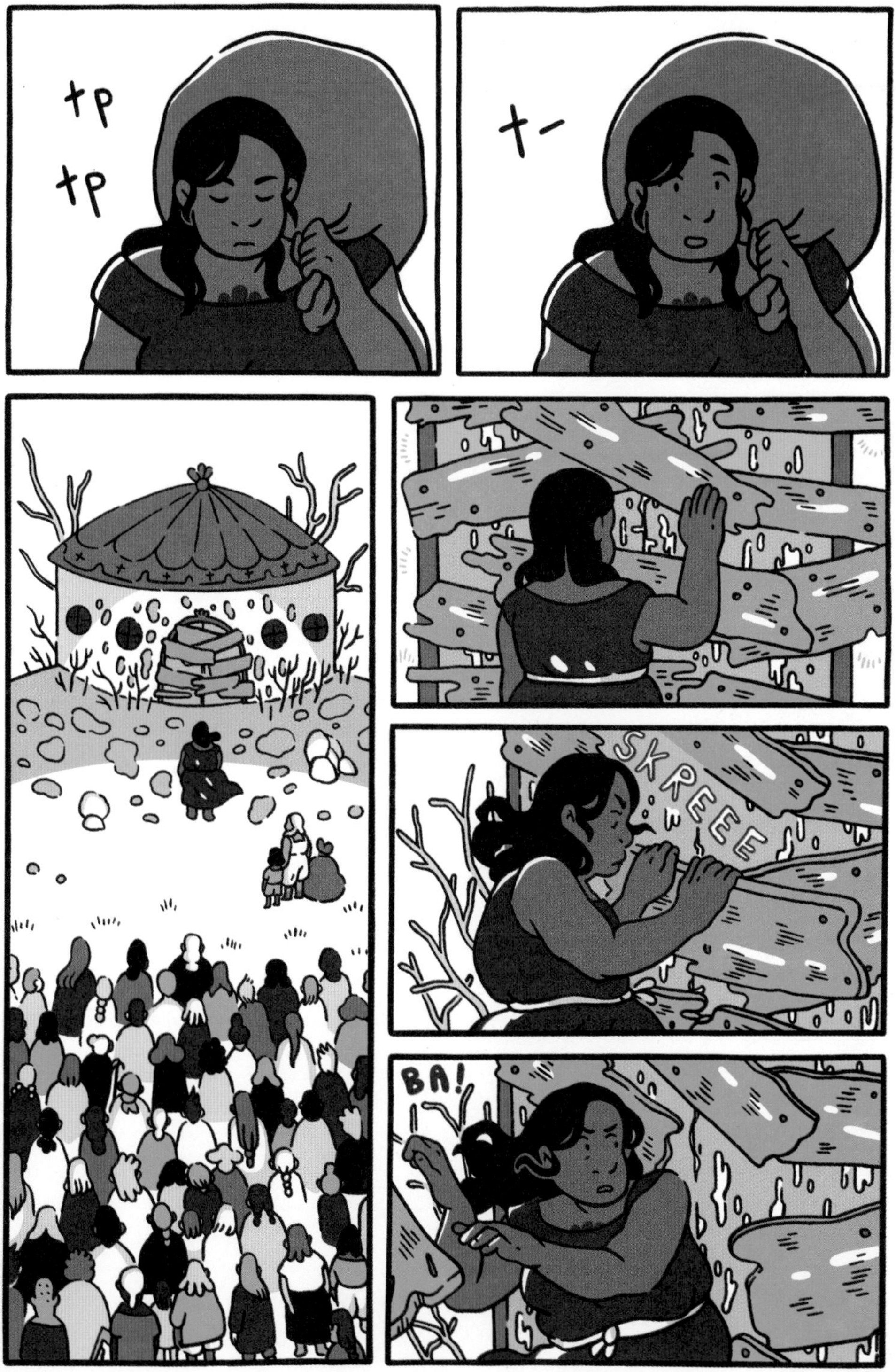
tp
tp
t-
SKREEE
BA!

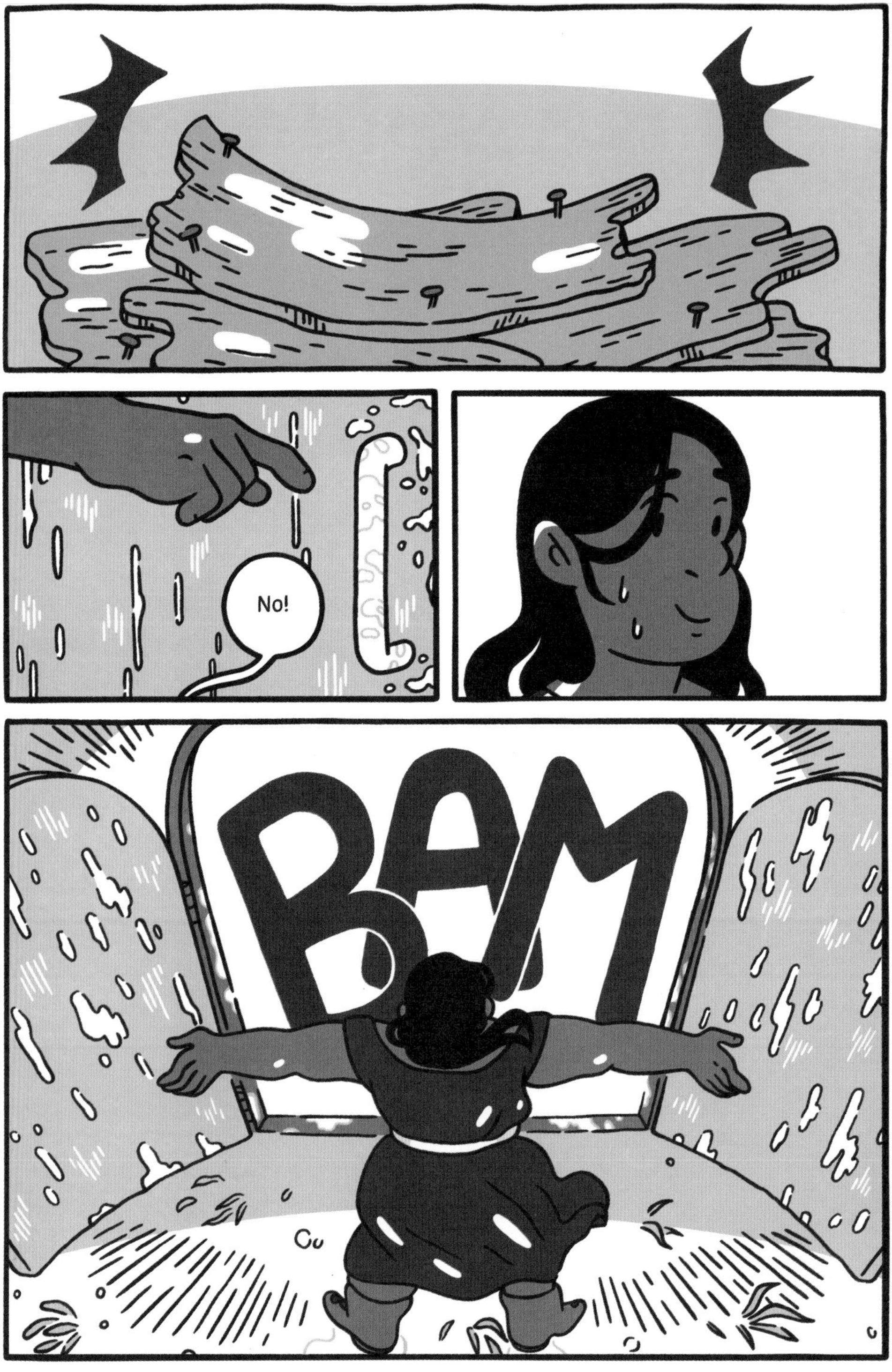
No!
BAM

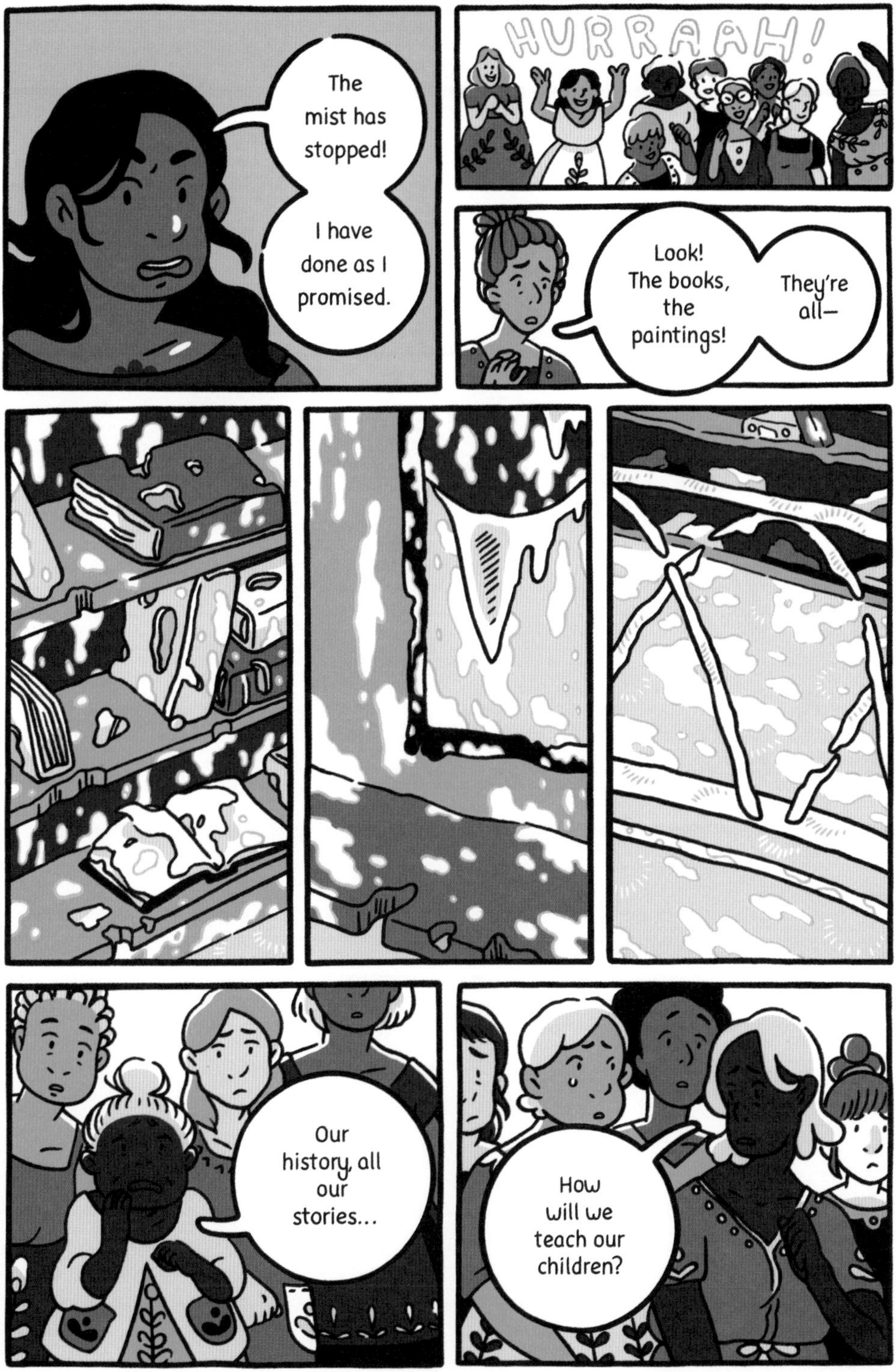
The mist has stopped!
I have done as I promised.
HURRAAH!
Look! The books, the paintings!
They're all—
Our history, all our stories...
How will we teach our children?

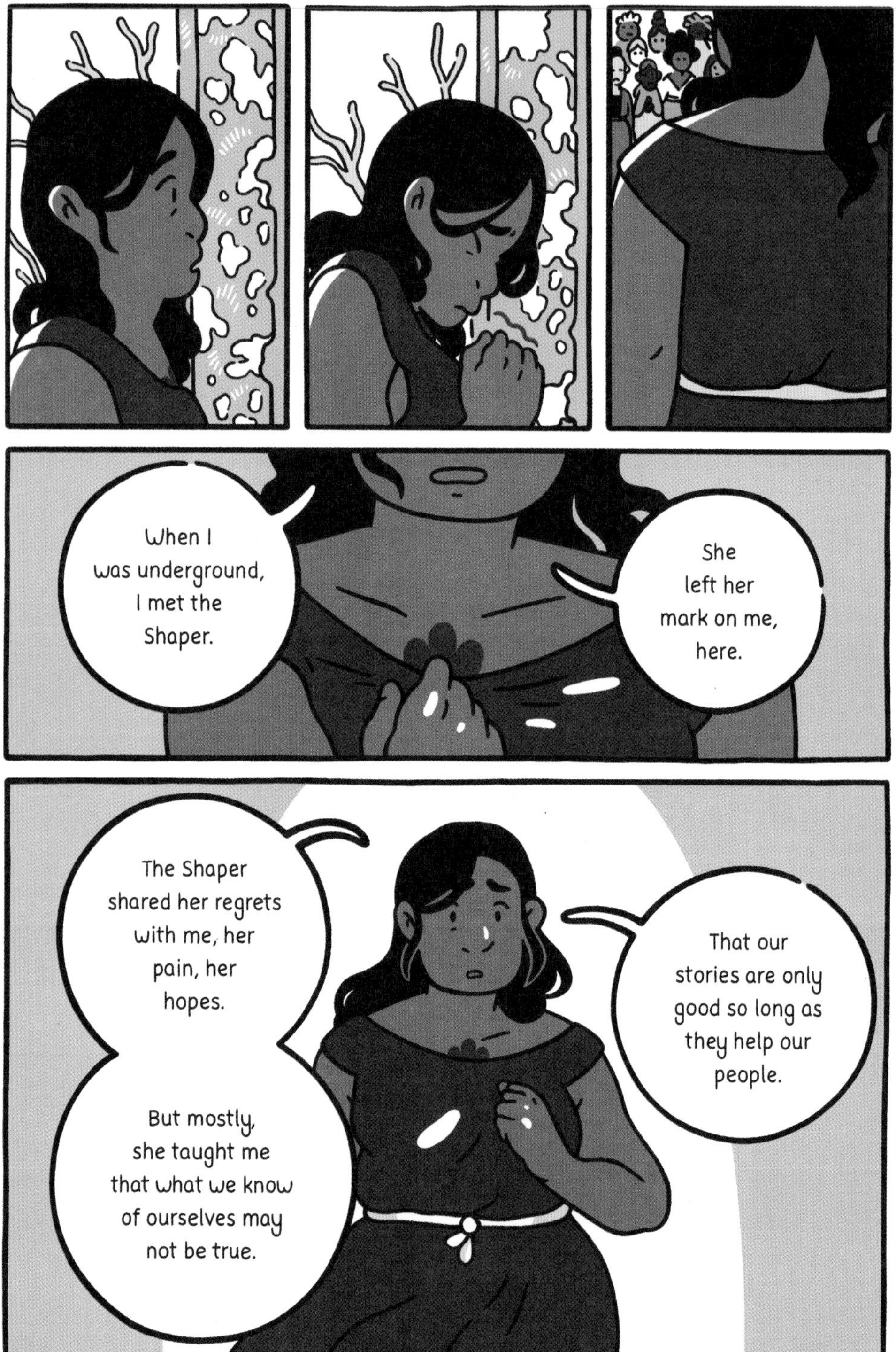
When I was underground, I met the Shaper.
She left her mark on me, here.
The Shaper shared her regrets with me, her pain, her hopes.
But mostly, she taught me that what we know of ourselves may not be true.
That our stories are only good so long as they help our people.

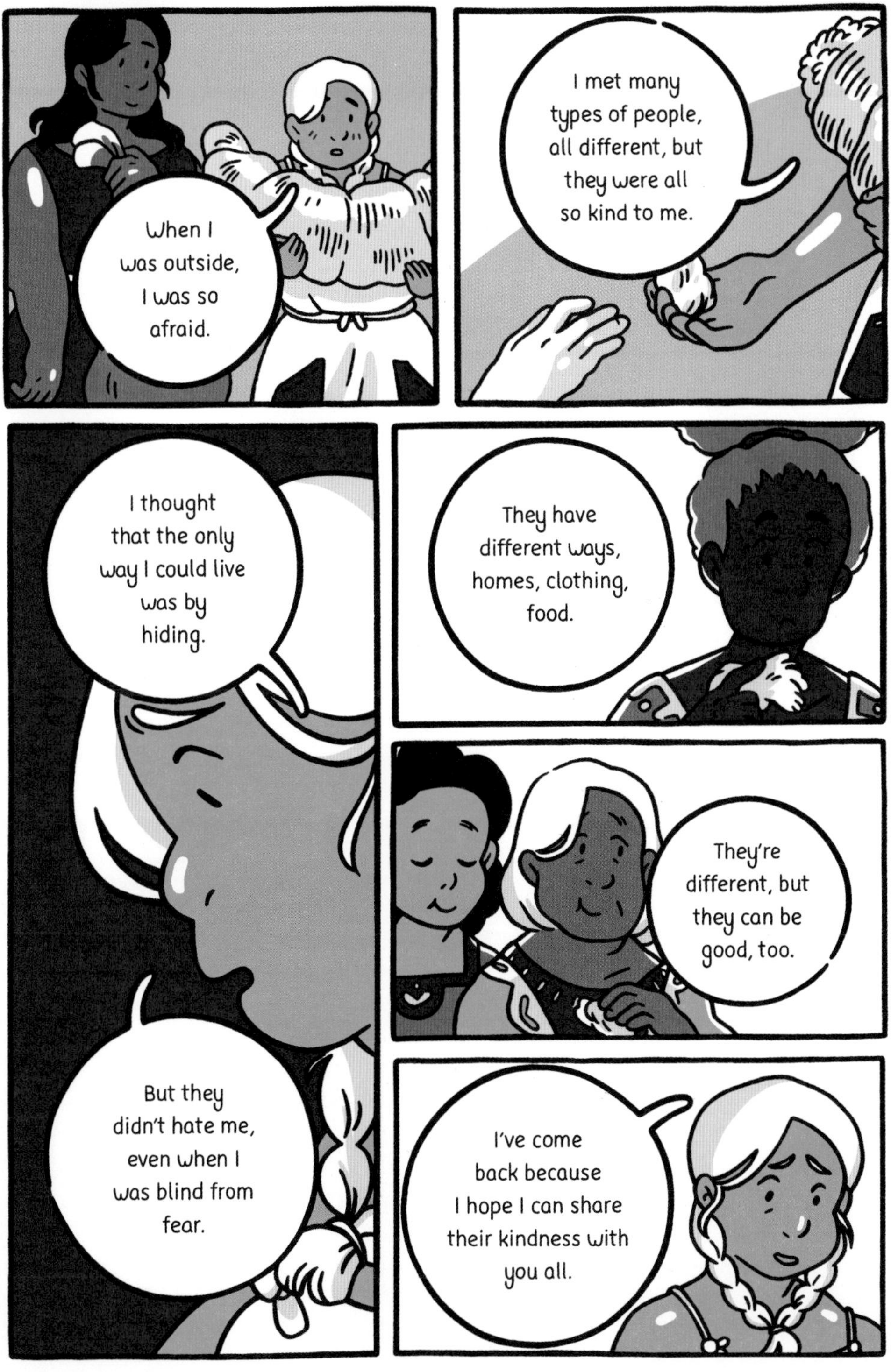
When I was outside, I was so afraid.
I met many types of people, all different, but they were all so kind to me.
I thought that the only way I could live was by hiding.
But they didn't hate me, even when I was blind from fear.
They have different ways, homes, clothing, food.
They're different, but they can be good, too.
I've come back because I hope I can share their kindness with you all.

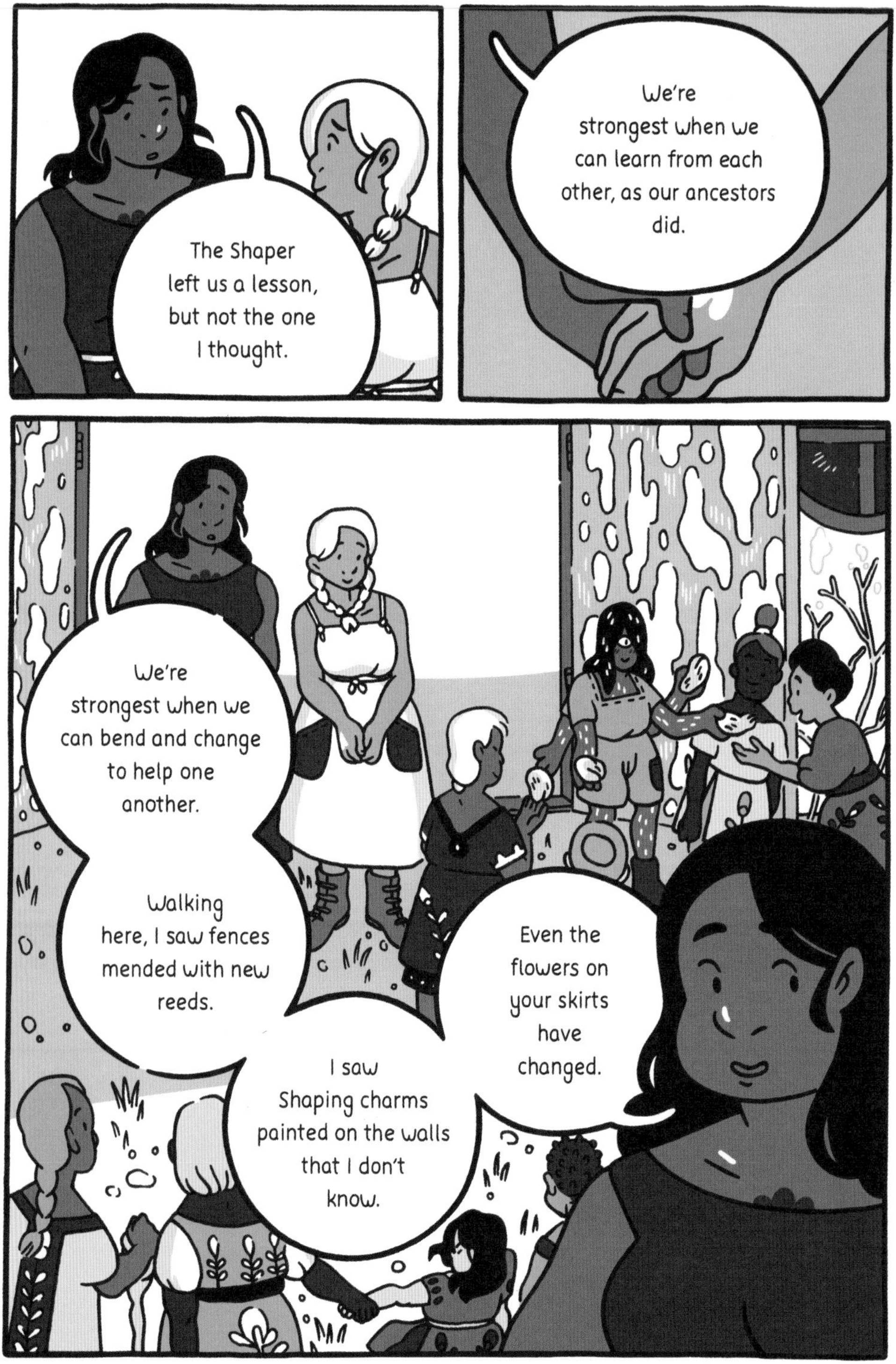
The Shaper left us a lesson, but not the one I thought.
We're strongest when we can learn from each other, as our ancestors did.
We're strongest when we can bend and change to help one another.
Walking here, I saw fences mended with new reeds.
Even the flowers on your skirts have changed.
I saw Shaping charms painted on the walls that I don't know.

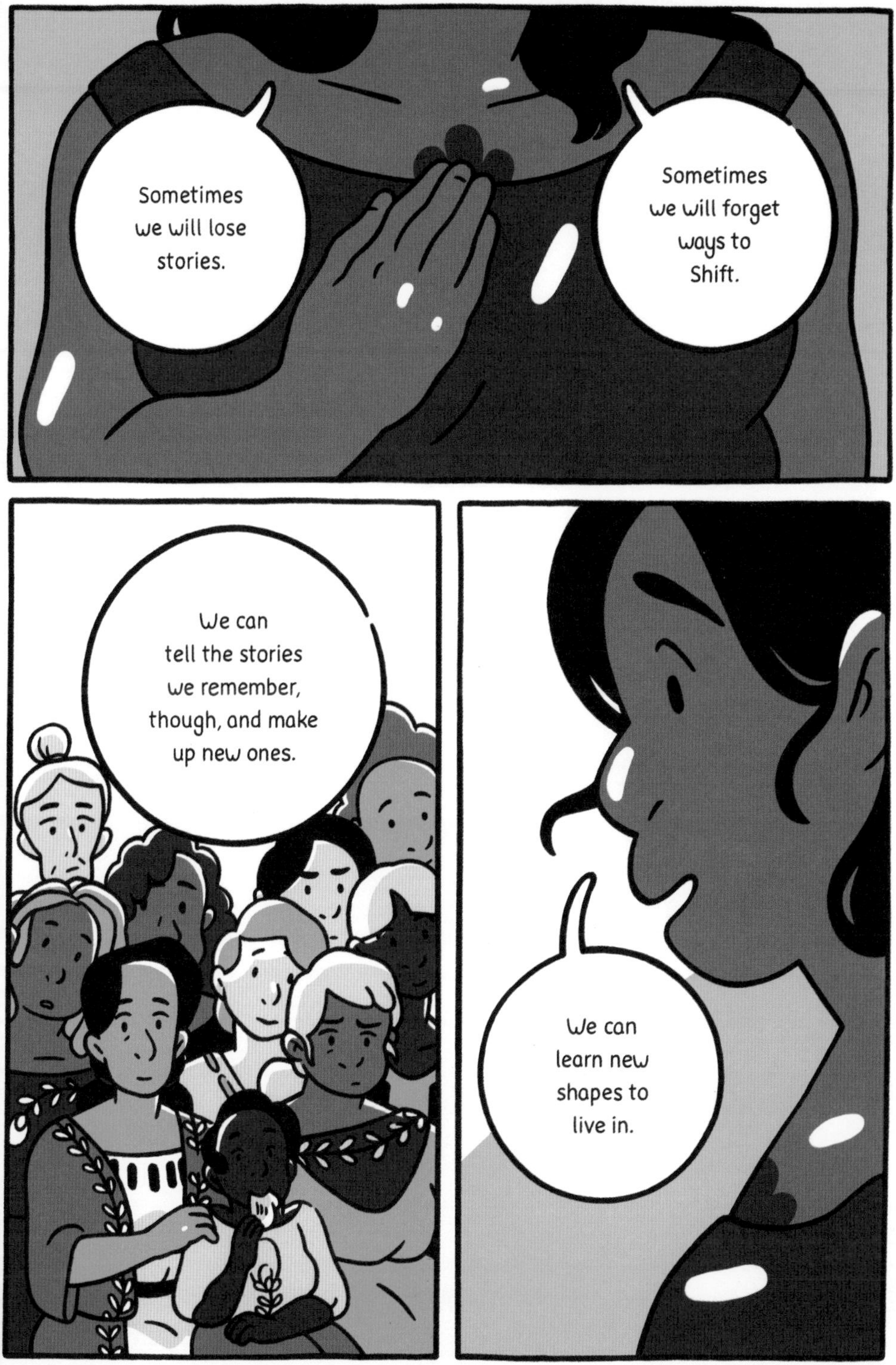
Sometimes we will lose stories.
Sometimes we will forget ways to Shift.
We can tell the stories we remember, though, and make up new ones.
We can learn new shapes to live in.

I want to hear a story about the outside.

Preet, what was it like?

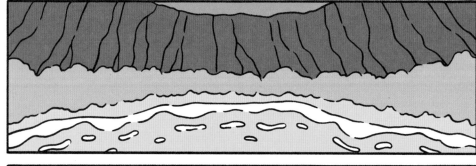

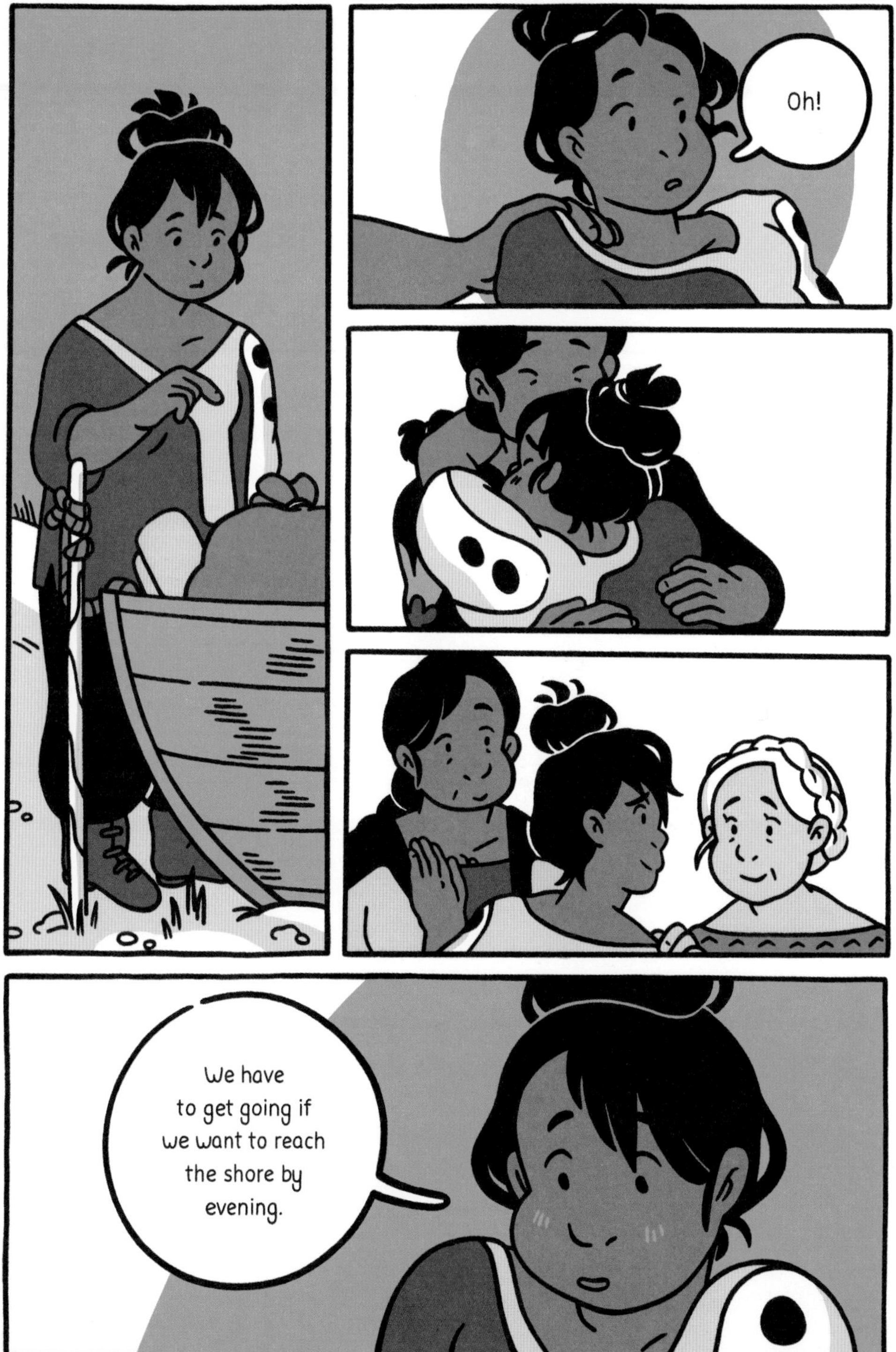
Oh!
We have to get going if we want to reach the shore by evening.

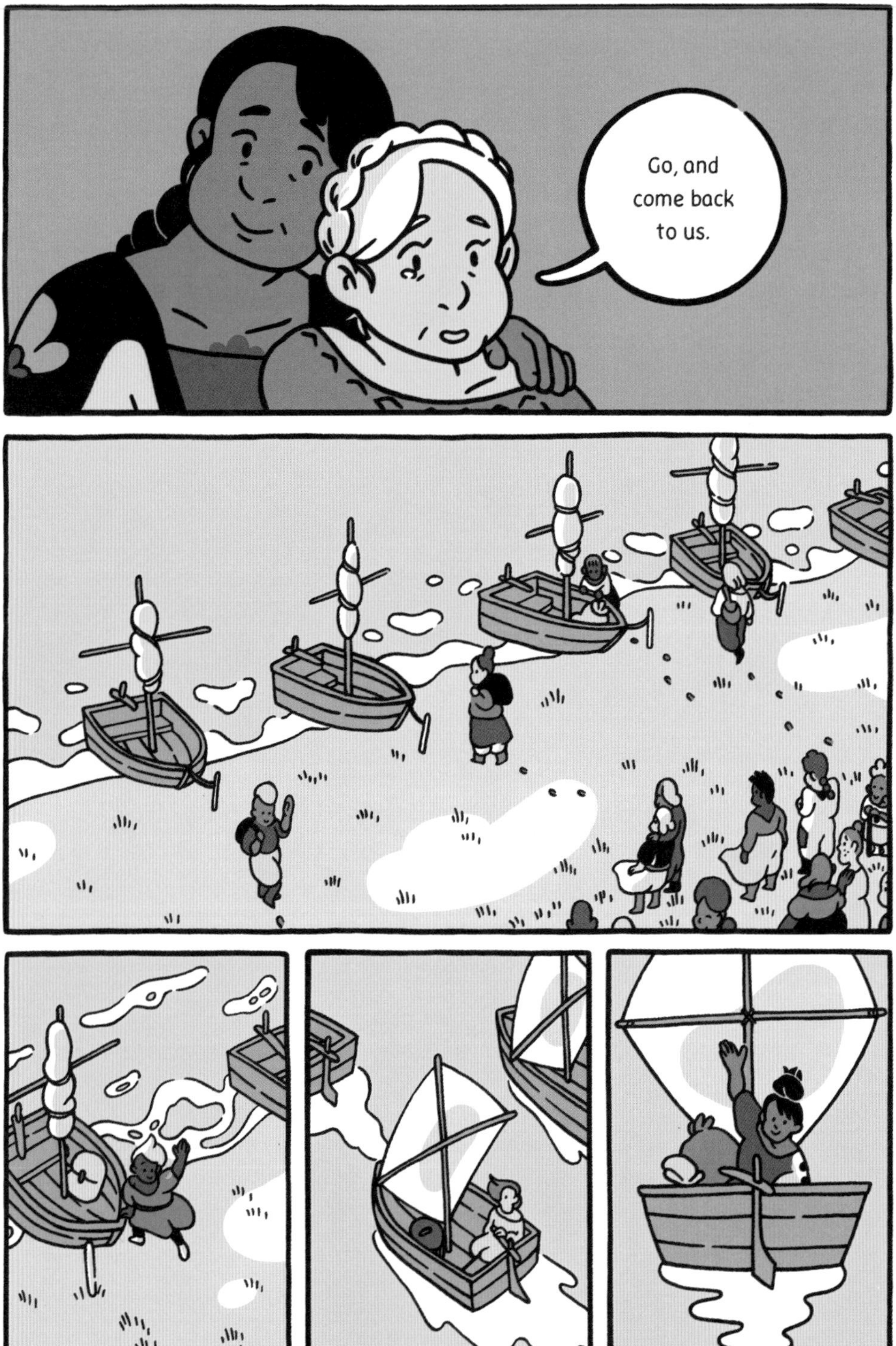
Go, and come back to us.

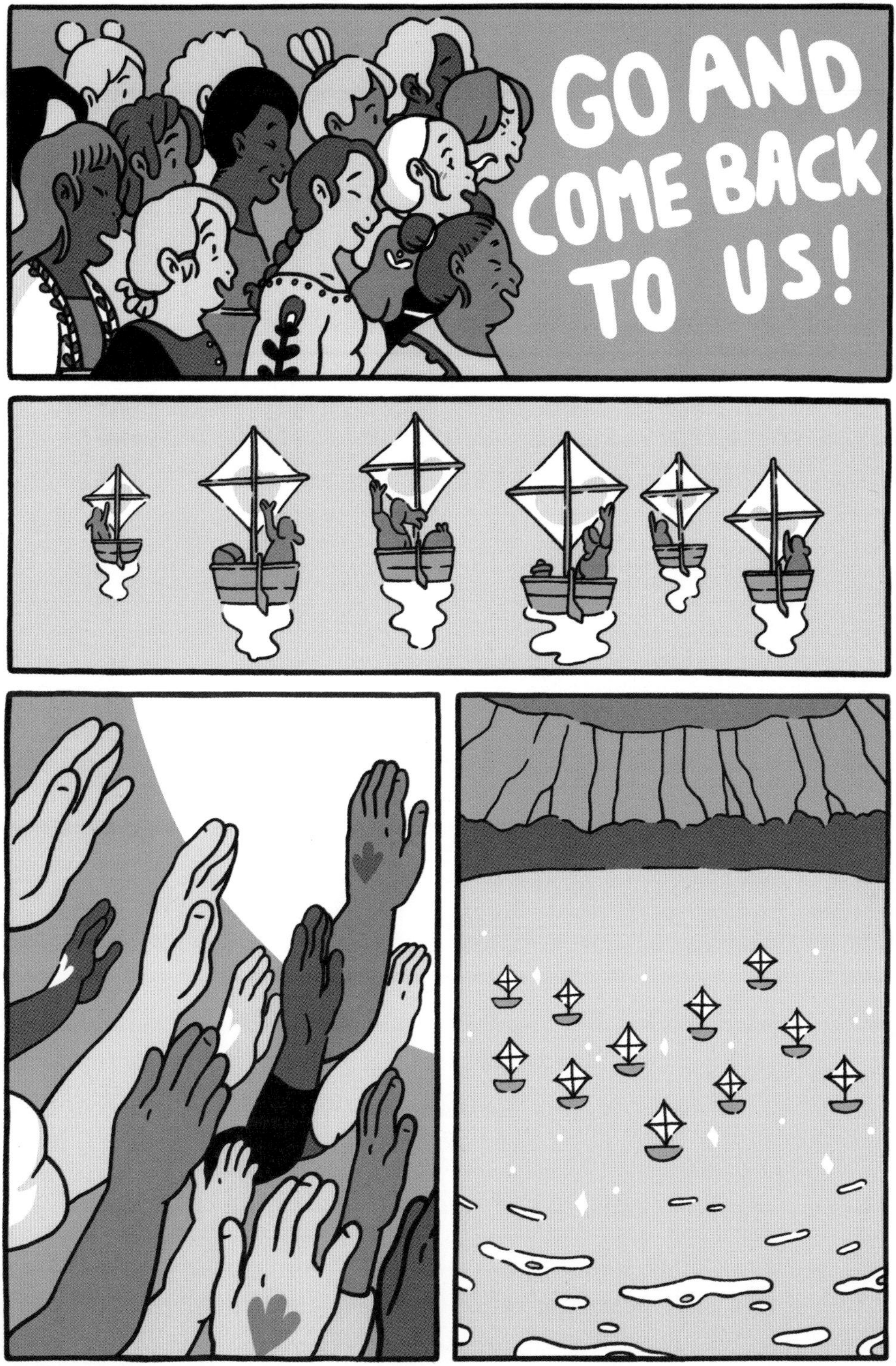
GO AND COME BACK TO US!

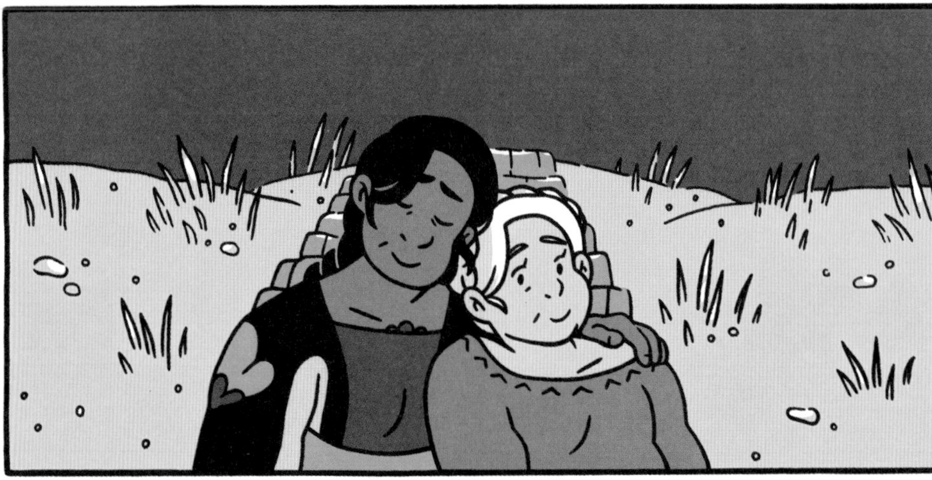

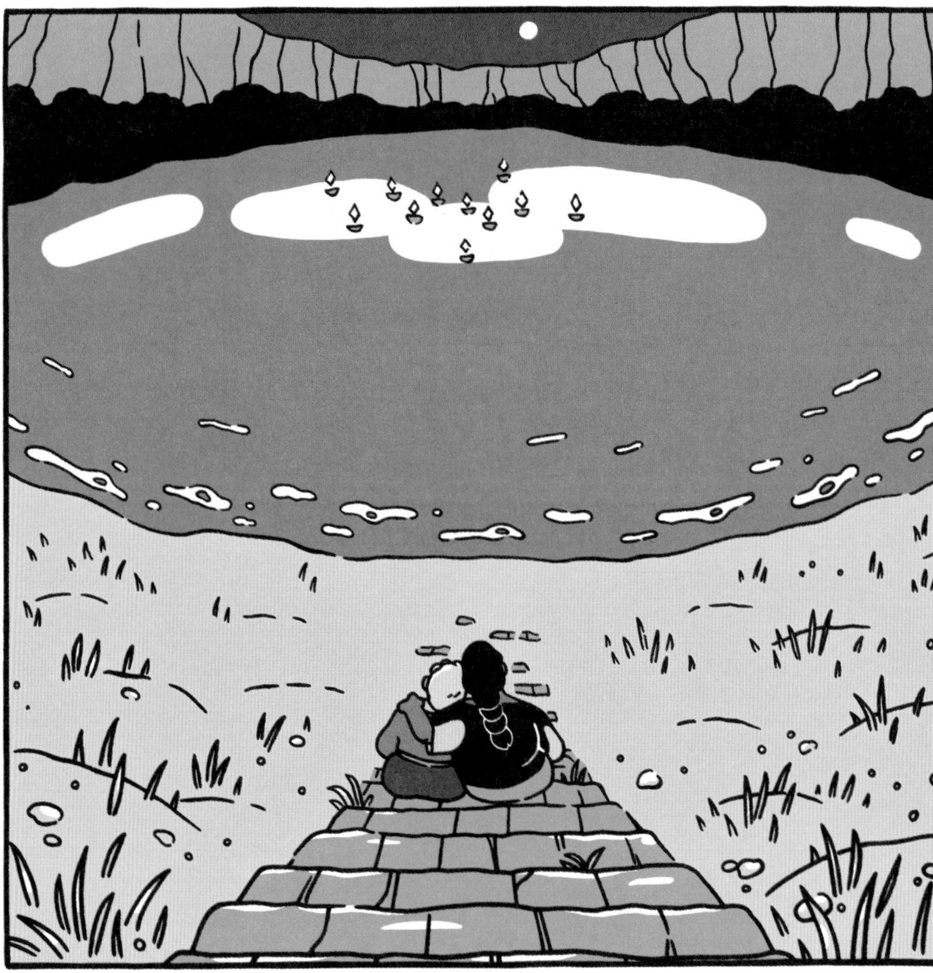

Author's Note

Hello and thank you for reading my book! I have only become more selfish as an author, and yet no one has told me to knock off making my weird stories.

Coming Back was made over two and a half enormously difficult years, both personally and for the world. As usually happens with my comics, having made it revealed to me what it's about—so much of my worry and anxiety from the time is clear on the pages, my longing to do better for myself and those I love. Sometimes these things are only visible if you look over your shoulder at them.

I'm writing this in April of 2021, and a lot is looking better, but so much is still uncertain. I hope that when this comes out in December, I can go to shows and bookstores to see you in person! Regardless, one way or another, I promise that I will still be making stories full of soft and difficult feelings.

Acknowledgments

Making comics is always a lonesome way to spend your time, but this book has been a particularly isolated process. Thank you to everyone and everything who has reminded me of the joy in the world and the worth in my heart, who helps my thoughts course-correct and keeps me stepping steadily toward who I want to be.

To Lauren, Kevin, Cathy, Jess, Jing, Em, Victoria, Jella, Kara, Tash, my tabletop group, my community garden, Judy, Whitney, Henry, paroxetine, all the podcasts and audiobooks I've devoured, to every seed which has sprouted and to every cutting which has grown roots.

Jessi Zabarsky is a cartoonist and illustrator living in Chicago.
She was born in 1988 in northern Ohio.
Her first graphic novel, *Witchlight*,
is also about girls and magic.
She keeps growing more plants, and if it's summer,
she probably has a fresh-picked zucchini to share.